Strange Capers

Tales of Love and Longing

Alan Keeping

To Rosemary

with love and gratitude

for your superb proof reading.

11. 06. 17

Alan

ISBN 978-0-9955317-8-9

A CIP record for this book is available from the British Library

Published in 2017 by
Llyfrau Cambria Books, Wales, United Kingdom.
Cambria Books is a division of
The Cambria Publishing Co-operative Ltd

Discover our other books at: www.cambriabooks.co.uk

Cover design by Carolyn Michel

To the memory of Neil Rhodes 1950 – 2016

Contents

The Vicar's Wife

She walks to the far end of the vicarage garden, opens the narrow wooden gate and enters the wood beyond. Only an hour before darkness, but she has to escape the house. It has just stopped raining. Tiny spheres of water weigh down the thin bare twigs of beech and, one by one, detach and fall onto the bed of leaves beneath. Over the soft, soothing songs of gentler birds comes the harsh, jarring rasp of the crow.

Striding along the path, she kicks her way through the dead, russet leaves strewn with empty cases of chestnut. She's dressed for protection against the cold and the damp air that smells of decay: a long, heavy overcoat, belted at the waist; a round, red woollen hat; black leather gloves and boots.

She chooses her favourite path that threads the woodland to a stream. She loves this place for its solitude, the assurance of not meeting someone she knows and then having to stop and exchange pleasantries.

As she approaches the stream, she sees there's a light in the wooden hut. This is strange. The hut, which normally she passes without heed, is always locked and unused. Moss covers its roof and window ledges and it has the air of hunching down into the ground.

This is not their woodland. It lays within a private estate owned by a millionaire who lives in London. The estate manager has raised no objection to the vicar's wife walking the wood. It's not her business if someone is using the hut. But what if it were kids or a tramp? She steps quietly up to a window and peers in. The light comes from a lantern placed on a rough wooden table. She sees a man sitting at the table, eating. He's about thirty with short, curly black hair and a dark-skinned face. He seems to be alone. He doesn't look like a tramp. Silently, she moves away and returns to the vicarage.

In the functional, rather spartan, kitchen she prepares their meal. The vicarage is a modern bungalow at one end of the village, much more practical than the rambling, cold, impossible-to-maintain residence of past years that, with relief, the Church sold to a property developer.

Edward, the vicar, is a tall, imposing man in his mid-forties. They met when she was studying theology at university and he was then a visiting part-time lecturer. He was attracted to her for the qualities that made her an excellent vicar's wife: neat in appearance without flamboyance, quietly efficient, impeccably polite to everybody and with a soft attractive voice. She passionately believed the only life worth living was one of dedication and, soon after she graduated, when he asked her to marry him, she accepted.

In the early years of their marriage, discussing the intricacies of Christian doctrine was a shared pleasure. She was much influenced by Edward's views, but, unlike him, she kept up with the works of contemporary theologians. Reading widely, she held a finger on the pulse of debate within the Church that emboldened her, on occasion, to challenge his more orthodox opinions.

She did everything in her ability to support his work as a priest: the housework, keeping his diary, making appointments, fulfilling the various social roles of a vicar's wife. It wasn't in itself fulfilling, she ruefully called it a life of chit-chat and chores, but it gained meaning from the importance of Edward's work. Finding it a struggle to live on his stipend, she also took on some part-time teaching.

Their sex life was not a success. Early on in their marriage, he did it more from a sense of obligation than pleasure and, as their sleep routines diverged, so as not to disturb her, he took to sleeping in the other bedroom.

When necessity demanded, she sought relief in touching herself.

Trained from childhood to abnegation, she is philosophic. What does it matter to be without physical pleasures, the important thing is the good they are able to achieve in the community. She's dismissive of the comforts of the body. It's not that she cannot enjoy good food, fine wine, beautiful clothes, sexual release; she just gives them no importance.

Yet deep within her there's a dissatisfaction. She has powers and capabilities that have no outlet. She feels she's a racehorse hitched to a plough. Her response is to seek escape. Books are her exit, mostly biographies and modern fiction. Every year she reads all the books on the Booker Prize short list, making her own choice of who she believes should win. But her single most joyous pleasure is to walk, in all seasons, on her own, in the woodland.

Over dinner, she tells Edward of the man in the hut.

'Did it look as if it were broken into?'

'No.'

'And he didn't need help?'

'I don't think so.'

'It's not our wood. This is their concern, not ours.'

'But I don't care to walk down there if there's a strange man about the place.'

'Walk somewhere else then.'

'I think I'll phone Martin.'

Now and again, Martin, the estate manager, delivers to the vicarage a brace of partridge gained from a weekend shoot. He and Edward don't mix socially; he never attends church and Edward doesn't go to the pub. However, she, without Edward, enjoys the parties that Martin provides every Christmas-time. Martin tells her not to worry, he knows that a man is staying in the hut and that's fine. He thanks her for the call. There's a pause, then he says, 'Have you told Edward? Would you mind keeping this to yourselves.'

Two weeks pass before she ventures that way again. Why, she asks herself, should she be deterred from taking her favourite walk? It's fresh but bright in the morning sunshine. The early primroses shiver with the cold. Her strong shadow follows her along the earth bank at the side of the path. Lime green moss shows vivid on the silver birch. Wrens, with little darting movements, seek out grubs and beetles.

She hopes the visitor has departed and slows her walk as she approaches the hut. It looks empty. Relieved, she walks on. Before reaching the stream, the path makes a sharp turn to the left and, as she rounds the corner, she sees him. He's standing in a shallow pool in the stream. He's washing himself. He's naked.

As he splashes himself, he emits repeated little groans at the sting of the cold. His body has the colour of chestnut and he's strong. In the bright sunlight, as he twists, she sees the muscles and sinews of his back flow beneath his smooth skin. Transfixed, wide-eyed, she stares at him. Her breathing quickens. The strong, healthy body excites her. Powerful emotions frighten her. He turns to reach for the towel that hangs from a twig and her gaze is drawn irresistibly to his groin, his penis hanging flaccid beneath a triangle of jet black hair. And then she runs.

Breathing hard, she reaches a height and turns to look back. She sits on a moss-covered stone to recover. Why, she asks herself, why is she so disturbed, just a naked man, just a naked man? But there's no denying she's aroused and she couldn't bear to have had him catch her watching him.

For a while, she takes her walks elsewhere. She observes the subtle precursors of spring: the earth and the trees and the animals newly animated. Spring saddens her. It's always so fleeting and, like a striking clock, it chimes the passing of the year. She feels as if she were merely a bystander at an event miraculous and of great importance, like a tourist at a foreign religious festival. She observes the wild ecstasy around her but cannot be part of it. Spring will erupt with exuberant joy. She will see it all, and rejoice in its arrival, but she cannot participate.

Beyond the hut, the far side of the stream, is an open area that, she knows, hosts a profusion of cowslip and primrose and daffodil. She has to see them. It's warmer today. She goes without a coat, just a red tartan skirt, a pleated cream blouse and a light grey cashmere cardigan. She's determined this time, naked man or not, to reach her destination.

Ferns are beginning to unwind. She waits to watch a squirrel jump from a tree onto the fallen leaves and then hop, hop, hop to reach a new tree. She runs over. Putting her hands on its rough, striated bark, she peers up as the squirrel scurries into the high branches.

She sees him well before she arrives at the hut. He's sitting in a patch of sunlight, reading a book. She stops on the spot, hesitating as to whether to continue or abandon the walk. 'Damn it,' she says to herself. As soon as he hears the shushing of leaves, he jumps up, startled as an animal ready to flee or to fight.

'Good morning,' she says, in a flat voice.

His look is hostile as if to say, 'Who the hell are you?'

To justify her trespass, she says, 'I live back there, in the bungalow.'

He looks into her face and sees large dark eyes, a straight nose, full lips, the lower one with a slight pout, black eyebrows, and high cheek bones. A beautiful face, he thinks, and so vulnerable. His shoulders relax.

'Martin told me about you. You are the wife of the vicar.'

His accent is peculiarly dated, as if from old English movies. He's wearing a white shirt with sleeves rolled up. He's clean-shaven and has deep brown eyes that remind her of a Lebanese friend from her university days.

'I hope you don't mind if I walk this way.'

He's trying to make up his mind whether it's better to befriend her or to keep her at a distance.

'Are you always alone?' he says.

'Yes. Will you be staying here long?'

'I do not know how many days I will be here.'

He thinks it could be to his advantage to get to know her. 'Look, I am about to make myself a coffee, would you like to take one?'

She hesitates, then her curiosity overcomes her reticence.

'Thank you, that would be nice.'

He gestures for her to enter the hut. It's more than a workshop. It might once have been a woodsman's habitation. There's an old fireplace. There are tools on shelves and a spade and pitchfork hang from nails on the wooden wall. In one corner is a small bed. There's a simple wooden cupboard with, on its top, camping gas stove, red tin kettle, coffee percolator and a saucepan; food items are stored inside. Two chairs are either side of the rough-planked wooden table that occupies the middle of the room. There's a smell of garlic.

'Please sit down.'

From an old, ochre earthenware jug he pours water into the kettle and lights the gas.

'Do you take the water from the stream?'

'Yes, it is excellent water.'

He puts two mugs on the table and a bottle of milk.

'Where do you shop?'

'I don't, Martin brings me everything I need.'

'What are you reading?'

He hands her the book; it's *Hamlet*. 'I now have a lot of time for reading.'

They drink their coffee. Then he says, 'I want to read the very best English novel. What do you suggest?'

Without hesitation, she says, '*Middlemarch* or *Emma*.

They're both masterpieces. *Middlemarch* is the greater achievement, but *Emma*'s easier to read. Why don't you start with that? I have a copy at home. Would you like to borrow it?'

'Why yes, thank you.'

Then she says, 'I'm on my way to a clearing in the woodland, beyond the stream, where, by now, there should be a mass of wild flowers.'

'I would like to see that. Do you mind if I walk there with you?'

He slips on an old jacket. They cross the log bridge over the stream. He asks her about the bird calls and she names them. He stops to listen to a rat-a-tat drum roll. She tells him it's a woodpecker.

The clearing is delightful, a profusion of yellows from the pastel of the primrose, to the vibrant daffodil, to the deep jaune of the cowslip. She picks a small handful of primroses to take back to the vicarage. And, in imitation, he too picks some for the hut.

'Do you have a vase?' she says.

'I've some empty tin cans. They will do.'

She wants to ask him so many questions but is nervous of prying. Eventually, she asks him the country of his birth.

'Iraq,' he says.

When they return to the hut, just before parting, she says, 'If you prefer me not to come this way, I could walk elsewhere.'

He notices how, as she speaks, she closes her eyes.

'I am appreciating your company. It gets lonely here on my own. It would be best though if you did not tell anybody of my being here.'

'Are you in hiding?'

He turns to look at her intently; can he trust her?

'Sort of.'

'Are you in Britain illegally?'

'No.'

He could be lying, but his manner is calm and passive.

'My name's Ruth.'

'I am Nadim.'

'Is that your real name?'

He smiles. 'In a way. It is what my mother called me.'

The next day, she carries *Emma*, a thick wedge of home-made cake and a glass vase to the hut. He isn't there, so she leaves them on the step. She walks on towards the clearing but is distracted by the noise of a chainsaw. She finds him cutting up a half-fallen tree. Logs, cut to size, are strewn around. She waits, not wanting to distract him. She enjoys watching him, the careful, methodical way he works. He sees her and switches off the machine.

'I have to be working. I was getting so bored that I asked Martin if there was anything useful I could do here in the wood. He taught me how to use this thing. I am very nervous of it.'

He puts the saw down and starts placing the logs into a wicker basket. She helps him and when it's full, takes a handle to carry it to the hut.

'I bought you this,' she says, handing him the cake.

'Thank you. Perfect with our coffee.'

She takes the flowers from out of the tin can and re-arranges them in the vase, then places it on the table.

'Did you make this cake? It is delicious.'

She hands him the book, and he reads the first paragraph.

'I will read it,' he says.

She notices a couple of cans of lager on a shelf and thinks, even Muslims transgress. 'May I ask, are you Shia or Sunni?'

'Is that my choice? As it happens, I am neither of those.'

'You're Christian!' She says this with an eagerness at discovered shared identity.

'I am sorry to disappoint you, I am an atheist.'

'Can you be an atheist in Iraq?'

'Not openly, but there are more secular Iraqis than you think. How is it possible to believe in God when His followers commit such appalling acts in His name?'

'Is that why you're in hiding?'

'No, not that.'

She waits to see if he will tell her more, but he's silent. Where he prepares food, she notices, there are tin cans and bread and cheese.

'If you would like, I could bring you some food. Do you eat meat?'

He smiles, 'Home cooking, that would be a treat.'

'I have to go. I'm hosting the Women's Fellowship this afternoon. That's why I cooked the cakes.'

'The Women's Fellowship?'

'A small group of women from the parish. We read the Bible and pray together and discuss subjects that concern us.'

'I think tea and cake must be very important at such an event,' he says in a serious voice, teasing her.

'Absolutely vital.'

He thinks, how beautiful she is when her face lights up with a smile.

That evening, pointing to the flowers in the vase, she says to Edward, 'Aren't they lovely. There's a profusion of them in the wood. I think I will take my watercolours down there.'

'Good idea,' he says, only half listening to her as he attempts The Times crossword. 'Your pictures make excellent raffle prizes. Have you seen any more of the chap.'

'He's doing some work for Martin. He won't bother me.'

The next morning, she puts a pad of artists' watercolour paper into a satchel and, alongside it, paints, brushes, rags, little dishes and a bottle of water. Above these, she carefully places a small dish of shepherds pie and a packet of chocolate biscuits. She puts the strap of the satchel over her head and across her shoulder. In her left hand, she carries a collapsible stool and in the other a light portable easel.

At the hut, she taps on the door, waits, then, finding it unlocked, opens it a fraction. She calls out, 'Hello.' The room is tidy, the bed made and the table clear except, at its centre, the vase of flowers. There's no fridge so she places the pie with the biscuits on top of the cupboard.

As she crosses the stream, she sees him. He's a little way off the path, amongst the trees, swinging a billhook, giving battle to a burgeoning patch of bramble. As soon as he sees her, he stops and comes over to where she's standing. He's sweating and breathing heavily.

'Good morning,' she says. 'I thought I might paint the flowers in the clearing.'

'Let me carry that,' he says, taking the easel.

At the clearing, she walks about, looking at the interplay of sunlight and shadow, selecting the position that pleases her most. He helps her set up then says he's going to carry on working but to interrupt him when she's ready for a coffee.

She paints quickly, trying to capture on paper the fragility of the flowers and their resilience. She isn't aiming for a likeness but for the painting to evoke the same mood that the scene engenders within her. She works for two hours then packs up and goes to look for him. They stand side by side looking at the results of his labours.

'We need to clear this undergrowth so new trees have the chance to establish themselves and eventually replace the old ones that are dying.'

They walk to the hut. He thanks her for the pie and biscuits. From the stream, she fills the earthenware pot with water. He makes coffee. There's a calm deliberation to his movements and a gentle self-assurance in the way he looks at her that she finds comforting, putting her at ease in his company.

He asks to see her paintings. 'Oh, they're nothing.' She shows him the five she has completed. He studies each one carefully.

'They are good. I particularly like this one.'

She takes it from him, looks at it, then hands it back to him.

'Please, if you really *do* like it, keep it.'

'Are you sure?'

'I want you to have it.'

When he looks at her, he takes in everything: her vulnerability, and a sadness. He's drawn towards her but knows, while he's in concealed sanctuary, it would be a stupidity to become involved with a woman.

'Do you like being a vicar's wife?'

'We do our bit and what we do is important, but...'

'But?'

'There's so much awfulness in the world. I admire those doctors and nurses who volunteered to help with the Ebola crisis. Anyway, it's better than being a nun.'

He looks at her quizzically. 'A nun?'

'My mother is a devout Anglican. I'm her only child. She told me that the highest calling in life was to devote oneself to Jesus. When I was young, the idea was attractive but I don't think I would have made a very good nun. To my mother, Edward was the next best thing.'

'What about your father?'

'He's away for long periods. He's a captain in the merchant navy.'

'I learned English while working on British cargo boats. There was an officer on board, Colin Chapman was his name, who took it upon himself to teach me. He would lend me books, mostly thrillers, and get me to read aloud so as to correct my pronunciation. And we watched British films, Hitchcock and *Doctor Zhivago* and *Far From the Maddening Crowd*.'

She smiles, 'It's Madding not Maddening. He taught you well; your English is amazing. How are you getting on with *Emma*?'

Whenever she's free and the weather allows, she goes to the wood to paint. She enlarges her subject to include the trees, the hut, and Nadim working. She now leaves her paints and easel in his hut. He has knocked together a simple bird-table and puts out bread. Having seen this, she brings him bird seed. From the hut, they watch a blue tit, or a nut hatch or a chaffinch snatch a seed and dart away.

Whenever they have coffee or, on occasion, lunch together, they talk. They discuss literature and films and his life at sea. She asks him about life in Iraq. Aware of her own doubts, she probes his religion or rather lack of it. Reluctantly, he's drawn into defending his atheism. She says, 'Without the moral anchorage that religion provides, isn't humanity cast adrift on an ocean of uncertainty? God provides us with firm ground for a moral life, otherwise, we're at the mercy of moral relativism.'

He replies bitterly, 'Religious adherence doesn't seem to restrain those committing acts of appalling barbarity.'

'That's obviously true for those individuals, but surely enormous numbers of people around the world live more happily because of the moral guidance provided by the great religions.'

'I see myself as a moral person. I don't need religion to tell me how to behave morally.'

She changes the subject of her questions. 'Why is it that women are treated so badly in Muslim countries?'

He sighs. 'You band together Muslim countries as if they are all the same. Do you do that with the Christian countries: Europe, the U.S., Africa, the Philippines? How different are the lives of women in those countries? Muslim societies are equally varied in their attitudes and ways of life.'

'But do *you* believe women should have equality with men?'

'Yes, I do. But it is obvious that men and women have differing strengths. Make the best of those differences. Let men do what they are good at and women do those things they do better than men. What they both can do, although different, has equal value.'

'But that's the age-old slogan that confines women to housework and childcare and leaves men to dominate religion and politics.'

Very gently, he says, 'And is your life so very different?'

He thinks, how unbridgeable is the chasm between them of ideology, of experience, of expectation.

She's both attracted by and nervous of his otherness. She finds him exotic but cannot intuit what he's thinking. Often, lapsing from conversation, they sit in a relaxed silence, listening to the bird calls and the wind in the trees. She feels the sexual pull, it's thrillingly disturbing, but she keeps that distant from her consciousness. What matters is his companionship. She has never felt so happy.

Rain keeps her away from the wood for some days but then the black clouds separate to give alternations of bright sunlight and heavy downpours. She can wait no longer and, late afternoon, wearing an old dark-green oilskin coat over her dress, she runs down to the hut. Everything is fresh and green from the recent rain. Wherever there's space between path and trees, newly washed celandines appear cheerily yellow against their dark-green leaves.

He puts down his book and welcomes her. She gives him a broad smile. Did she know what she's doing to him? Against the walls of his determination of abstinence, crash waves of longing and desire.

She asks him to pose for her, to sit on a log beside the stream, reading a book. The light is amazing. He's illuminated in the low, bright sunlight against a background of dark clouds. She starts to paint. Without warning, full, fat raindrops splash the paper. They quickly gather up her things and run to shelter in the hut.

Standing side by side, they watch the rain. He puts his arm around her waist. She doesn't move. Then, almost imperceptibly, she relaxes against him. He slips his arm further round, gently placing his hand over her breast. She puts her hand over his and pushes it more firmly onto her breast. She turns in his arms and brushes the side of her head against his cheek. With eyes closed, she releases herself into his embrace.

His desire quickens, but he pulls away from her, looking into her eyes, giving her time to withdraw. He wants reassurance that she's willing. He kisses her cheek and she arches her head back inviting him to kiss her neck. He holds her close, his left hand outside her coat, stroking her back and the other beneath the coat clutching her bottom.

'Do you want to do it?' he whispers.

'Yes,' she says softly.

She stands passively as he lifts the coat from her shoulders and places it on a chair. He takes her arm and leads her to sit on the bed. He kneels down in front of her to remove first one boot then the other. The bare boards creak as he shifts his weight. He helps her lift her legs onto the bed and she lays supine, waiting. She hears his deep sigh as his hands find the bare skin of her thigh. She closes her eyes and her mouth opens, her breathing more urgent. He slides her dress above her waist. Lifting her bottom, she helps him to remove her panties and he places kisses over her belly and then she feels the brush of his cheek. She finds it mysterious, the way he's enthralled by her body. Mysterious, yet how it pleases her to be uncovered, discovered, as being desirable.

He takes off his belt. He has an intense seriousness about what he's doing. He climbs onto the bed, kneeling between her raised legs. He gives out a little groan of pleasure as he enters her. She lays still as she feels him move within her. Her eyes are open. She's alive to everything that's happening. To him, the sex is urgent, demanding release; to her, it's enough to be giving herself. He has his climax, but she's out of it, distant.

He lays still. He feels a calmness like a homecoming, as if he has passed from turbulent seas into the tranquillity within the arms of harbour walls. His beautiful weight upon her, she thinks of the enormity of this irrevocable step. He sleeps on his front, his arm across her waist. She lays on her back, her eyes open, her hand, carrying her wedding ring, resting lightly on his shoulder.

She sees the light fading from the window. To wake him she whispers, 'I can't stay. I've got to get back.'

He picks up his belt and stands at the door looking out, tucking in his shirt, adjusting his trousers. He isn't smiling. He appears worried.

She retrieves her panties and puts them on, smoothing down her dress. She keeps looking at him wondering what he's thinking.

Without turning round, he says, 'Wherever I go I create trouble.'

She stands up, smiling at him. He puts his hand to her face, and tenderly strokes her cheek. 'Say something,' she says. She wants tender words.

He puts his arms around her and holds her close. 'It was good, wasn't it?'

'Yes,' she says, 'it was good.'

He accompanies her through the dark wood. As they walk, they are hardly able to see each other's features. There's a screech of pheasant. A soft drizzle infuses the air, settling on their hair, faces and clothing. They reach the gate. To their eyes accustomed to the darkness, the open garden lawn ahead is in a half-light, shining with the wet grass. She passes through the gate and, on impulse, swivels back to him. 'Kiss me.'

Her face is illuminated in black and white from the faintest of light. 'I'll come tomorrow if I can.' He hugs her one last time, unwilling to let her go. She pulls away softly, says, 'goodnight' and touches him on the lips.

Back at the vicarage, she's overcome with guilt. She has

sinned. She's now a woman taken in adultery. She has broken her sacred marriage vows. She feels her transgression is as evident upon her as if she were a creature of another colour, green of infidelity or red of passion. She cannot understand how Edward does not recoil at the alteration in her. The fact that he does not is proof to her that although he might look at her, he doesn't *see* her. This too, appals her. Everything has changed and yet everything continues as though it hadn't.

She prays to God for forgiveness, but she knows that *He* knows that she's not wholly contrite; she cannot repudiate the warmth of the intimacy which gave her such joy. She turns to Jesus and seeks, instead, compassion.

On one thing she is ruefully shamefaced. As a vicar's wife, she has on occasion preached to girls and young women about the dangers of unprotected sex. 'Sex,' she would say, 'is best enjoyed within a monogamous, long-term, loving relationship, but if you do have casual sex, at least protect yourself against infection and unwanted pregnancy.' Hmm! Oh well, not much she can do now about infection. As for contraception, having had until now no need, she arranges for the delivery by post of a morning-after pill.

She determines she must not go to the hut. She has always been the perfect vicar's wife: seeing to Edward's food and comfort; hosting innumerable meetings and gatherings; when he wished, listening to, and commenting on, the drafts of his sermons; carrying out those functions he assigns to her. To assuage her conscience, she continues with all those things with a renewed assiduity, yet there breeds within her a rising fractious resistance to Edward's manner of talking to her. He speaks down to her as if she were still a student. Formerly she accepted this unquestioningly, now it grates.

Nadim is constantly in her thoughts. After a week, she feels she owes him an explanation for her absence. She wants, while retaining his companionship, to tell him she's mortified to have strayed from the path of righteousness.

At lunch time, slipping on a cardigan over her thin green dress, she hurries to the hut. He's not there. She brings out the old wooden chair to sit in the doorway and wait. She watches the gentle breeze stir the graceful tresses of the willow. She becomes aware of the soft continuous shush of the distant brook. She hears the cuckoo and the rattle of the woodpecker.

A number of times, she looks around expectantly then relaxes as he fails to appear. After an hour, she sees him, striding along the path carrying a brush-cutter. On seeing her, he breaks his stride. He carefully puts the machine away. She studies his face trying to assess his mood. He's inscrutable. She says, 'Would you like to walk?'

They stroll eastward, over the stream, to that part of the estate, where, in season, game shooting takes place.

'Are you all right?' he asks.

'Yes, I'm fine. I'm sorry I've not seen you.'

She pauses and he waits for her to continue. When she doesn't, he says, 'I understand. You're with Edward.'

'I'm sorry.'

'Why are you sorry? I knew you were married. It serves me right.'

They walk in silence. Then she bursts out, 'It's not because I don't...' She hesitates for the right word, 'want you. I like you, very much.'

He shrugs, 'Anyway, I'll eventually be gone from here.'

She stops still and takes hold of his arm. 'Can't we go back to how we were?'

He shakes his head. 'I want you too much.' Wryly, he says, '*You've* got your husband to keep you warm in bed at night.'

'Oh no, that's...' She breaks off aware she's about to be indiscreet. Instead, she says, 'What we, I, did was wrong. Adultery is wrong.'

He smiles, 'You and your religious absolutes. Two

people coming together in a loving relationship is not necessarily wrong even if it involves adultery.'

She looks at him sharply – a loving relationship, is that what they had? They turn and, with hardly a further word, make their way back. What more is there to say? At the hut, he calmly, resignedly, says goodbye and she walks back with a heavy heart.

Reading the agony aunt column of a women's magazine, she comes across a reader's letter that speaks to her. It's from a woman who loves her husband, but he doesn't want sex and she's increasingly distressed by their lack of intimacy. What should she do? The reply advises her to talk to her husband, insisting he acknowledges they have a problem. If there's a difficulty with intercourse, there are other ways of expressing sexual love. They should seek counselling. At the end of the day, if they're unable to resolve their sexual incompatibility and this renders her miserable and depressed, she should look for a more satisfying relationship.

One evening, she says to Edward, 'Do you ever feel the need for sex, because I do?'

He frowns and says, 'Can we talk about this later? I really have a mountain of work to get on with.'

She feels a suppressed anger. Did not *he* promise, in *his* marriage vows, to love her, and did not that include the physical expression of love? But then she turns that anger upon herself. It's unfair to blame him. What sustained effort had she made to face Edward with her need, not just for sex but, more importantly, for intimacy? Knowing it would have brought turmoil in their lives to have done so, it had been easier to shrug and ignore the problem.

Over the next few days, she's in a state of disturbed uncertainty. Powerfully drawn to be with Nadim, yet fighting it. She finds herself filing papers and other mundane activities, anything to distract.

In line with a programme of church renewal, resources

are shifting away from struggling rural parishes to churches in deprived urban areas, so rural-based vicars find themselves serving increasing numbers of parishes. At the moment, Edward has five. The following morning, he has to visit an elderly parishioner in Newchurch who had just lost her husband from a heart attack. It's a journey of eight miles by road. He asks Ruth to accompany him, 'for the feminine touch'.

On arrival, from habit, mechanically, the widow offers them a cup of tea. She disappears to the kitchen and doesn't come back. Ruth finds her, teapot in hand, staring blankly out of the window. 'There was no warning. It's not right, is it. No chance to say goodbye.'

Ruth gently puts an arm on her shoulder. 'You go and talk to Edward. I'll make the tea.'

After an hour, it's time for them to leave, but Ruth whispers to Edward, 'We can't leave her like this. You go, I'll stay.' Edward offers to return and pick her up later, but she says she's happy to walk back, it's not so far on foot. She's only dressed in a blouse and skirt and light grey jacket, but the day is fair, no hint of rain. She encourages the widow to talk of her husband, so many happy memories. She reviews what needs to be done over the next few weeks and how to access support.

Mid-afternoon, she strides across the fields that lead, via the woodland, back to the vicarage. Her thoughts, gloomy from her time with the widow, brighten in the sunshine. It's good to be alive. Pale-mauve lady's smock, the cuckoo flower, stand tall above the grass, stirring in the gentle breeze. On entering the wood, she notices the flycatchers have returned from Africa and found their old homes in tiny holes in the trees. A few more weeks and the bluebells will be out.

She comes to a descent when she sees Nadim coming round a bend and up the track towards her. He's carrying the chainsaw. He doesn't see her at first then his eyes fix on her. Those liquid brown eyes of his.

'How are you?' she says.

'I'm missing you. Missing your company.'

Her feelings are too turbulent to make a response. 'I've walked from Newchurch. I'm on my way home.'

He nods, 'Well, I won't keep you.' He walks away from her, up the path. She stares at his retreating figure. She slowly resumes her walk. But then she's suddenly overwhelmed by the loss of him. She can't allow this to happen. She turns and runs up the slope after him.

Breathing heavily, she catches hold of his arm and pulls him to face her, then grasps his hand and thrusts it hard against her breast. Her look is supplication, don't abandon me. Whatever the outcome, she's throwing herself upon his mercy.

He studies her face. It's difficult to disregard a look so needful. She can see his indecision and looks up at him waiting for a resolution. Her gaze falters and she looks down, then up again, anxiety and vulnerability on her face.

He feels, in his belly, a soft, warm coursing of the drug of desire. He strives to ignore it but it grows in strength. In an instant, he gives way and releases the barrier of control. Desire floods through him.

She follows every minute alteration in his face and, as she reads his mood, she has the look of love.

'Come on then,' he says, and turns back down.

Docilely, she follows. He leads her away from the sunlit path, into the darker, dappled light of dense growth. Briers clutch at her skirt, and she has to bend her head under branches, now green, spring green, with new leaf. In a clearer area beneath a mature beech tree, he lays his jacket against its trunk, then lowers himself to sit on it.

She stands above him, waiting for him to do what he will. He undoes his belt then slides his hands beneath her skirt to pull down her panties. She steps out of them and puts them aside on some fallen leaves. She places her hands on his shoulders to support herself as she lowers herself to squat on his lap. Little shafts of sunlight, filtering through the shimmering leaves, illuminate their faces.

He nuzzles into her neck and smooths his hands over her bottom. How lovely that is. She bends her head low, totally hunched over him, her weight on her knees. He has this musk-like smell to his skin. He pulls up his shirt and lifts his penis. Her eyes tightly closed, she emits a little groan as she settles upon him.

She rides him. She strokes his cheek and kisses him. From out of these gentle movements, she feels a new sensation; a pleasurable itch ignited inside her that demands to be satisfied. As she rises, his hands on her bum, she lifts her head way back before sinking down again.

The feelings she has now are totally new to her as if something has awoken inside her that demands release. With a shudder, he climaxes and she feels his penis shrinking from her. She gives a little cry of loss. He kisses her passionately and then she feels a stirring, a swelling growth within her and she's awake to the wonder of it.

She gently moves her hips, stroking the bud into new life. Her arousal grows again until the pulses of sensations from her sex possess her totally, driving her on. Her exertions are even more extreme, rising as high as she dare, then down, down, pressing hard upon him. She cannot stop. She cannot rest. She has to reach the summit. Heart bursting, now at last she knows she will get there. With her head thrown right back, she cries out in exultation as she's convulsed by the orgasm.

In a faint, she collapses, rolling, with him, onto the brown dry leaves. The branches above them stir in the soft breeze, sprinkling sunlight over them as they sleep. She wakes first, lying very still, enjoying the strange feeling of bodily contentment. She turns her head to look at him. He opens his eyes, coming out of his sleep, remembering what has just happened.

She leans across him to collect her panties abandoned amongst the fallen leaves. She gives them a shake. She stands up, takes a handkerchief from her pocket and wipes herself before stepping into them. Behind her he adjusts his trousers, rethreading his belt. She pulls off thin fragments of leaf that have fastened themselves to her clothing. He helps, sweeping his hand over her back, lifting leaves away from her hair.

'Thank you,' she says, 'for letting me...you know, come like that.'

He frowns. He has seen, in his past, plenty of young men willing to give rich white women 'a good time'. 'You do not need to thank me, I was not offering you a service.'

'I didn't mean...'

He leads her back through the undergrowth to the path. She takes a few steps, stops, turns, smiles and says, 'goodbye then.' He nods and watches her walk away. She starts to run from exhilaration. Her body is alive and full of energy and promise.

She has this strange, new sensation resonant within her like the extended, deep vibrations of a large bell. Something that was dormant and is now roused and powerful. As she goes about her everyday tasks, she's disturbed by a recurrent desire for him, not simply a wish to see him, but an internal physical ache like hunger.

That evening, she's unsettled, unable to put her mind to anything. Thankfully, Edward is working. She turns to the television for distraction. She rarely watches it, maybe joining Edward for the Ten O'Clock News, especially now that she has a particular interest in the Middle East. She picks up an unopened gift. It's a box set of *Poldark*. Yes, that's it, a romance.

She immediately identifies with Elizabeth, married to the wrong man and yearning for Ross Poldark. The story is of repressed desires. Ross would not reject Elizabeth if she went to him but she does not, cannot. What stops her? The shackles of social convention? The obligations of her marriage vows – Elizabeth is, after all, devoutly Christian? Or is it her pride?

So, she thinks, I am not Elizabeth. In continuing my relationship with Nadim, I *am* jeopardising my social status; I *am* defying my Christian values; I *am* breaking my marriage vows. But all her hesitations are as withered leaves, scattered by a wind of desire. Not to see him now is unthinkable. She will not fight the current but embrace it, let it take her wherever it will.

Her thoughts are interrupted by Edward coming into the room. Would she mind, there's a programme he'd like to watch? Reluctantly, she ejects the DVD. It's an interview with an Anglican Bishop. As the programme continues, Edward is increasingly agitated until he can't contain himself, 'Why can't the man make up his mind? Agonising on one's doubts is of no use to anyone.'

'But aren't we all assailed by doubts?'

'Without faith, Christianity becomes just another "ism", just another prescription for the good life. "For whoever would draw near to God must believe that He exists and that He rewards those who..."'

'Yes, yes,' she interrupts irritably, 'but can you claim that all of the Church's attitudes and practices are derived from Christ? We seem forever to be grudgingly dragged along, hanging onto the coat-tails of social change. We claim our doctrine is grounded in divine revelation, but how much is simply the historic baggage we carry of the ancient Church. We fight over the role of women. We oppose compassionate euthanasia. We support the traditional family over alternative family structures...'

'None of those issues detract from the divine nature of Christ's teaching. We Christians have insight into important truths. If we didn't believe that, we couldn't be Christians. Through opening our hearts to Christ, we are certain we will be forgiven. People rightly require and demand the comfort and security that that can offer. Are we to refuse them?'

'But there's no comfort or security in holding to a belief that becomes untenable.'

'You have to come off the fence, believe or not believe. It's doubt that's corrosive.'

But for her, this injunction doesn't work. These are times, she thinks, when former Christian certainties seem no longer secure. Cannot, also, the injunction against adultery be offset by the demand for love?

Nadim, too, is disturbed. He can't concentrate on his reading. When she hadn't appeared, he reasoned that it was inevitable that she should shrink from a continuing relationship with him; she had so much to lose, but, reason notwithstanding, he had felt deeply wounded. Now, coming together again, he's amazed and thrilled at her sexual response. He knows he cannot remain forever sheltering in the hut. Someday he would be leaving. He hadn't meant it to be like this. In his feelings for her, he felt he was running down a slope, nervously trying to steady his speed. But now he thinks, what the hell, why not release the brake, sprint pell-mell and enjoy the thrill.

The following morning, she's drawn inexorably toward Nadim. Her mood is exhilarated anticipation but, indulging her excitement, she does not hurry. She stops to gaze in wonder at the ground beneath a large beech tree. It is clothed in a spread of green and white. Above the covering of broad green leaves, shoot star bursts of small white flower heads, a congregation of ramsoms, allium ursinum, pungent with the scent of garlic. And, she notices, the little young firs have at the very tip of their dark green fronds, new growth, fresh green, like brightly painted finger nails. She turns the corner towards the hut and stops dead in her tracks. There's someone with him, a man. They turn and see her. It's Martin.

Martin lives in a lodge on the north side of the estate.

This house guards a gated vehicular access into the park. The broad track curves eastward towards the game reserve. A small grass path forks off the track and leads to the hut. This is the route Martin has taken to get there.

She walks up to them and, with a nonchalance she doesn't feel, says, 'Hi Martin.'

He looks at her steadily, taking in her radiance, 'Good morning, Ruth.'

Flustered, she turns to Nadim, 'I've brought you some cake.'

Martin says, 'Why should he be so lucky? I never get cake.'

She laughs, 'That can be rectified.'

Martin says, 'Well, I'll be off. I've much to do.'

Martin being there has unsettled her. She doesn't feel as secluded, with the security of concealment, as she did before. When he has gone, she says, 'Does he know I visit you?'

'I told him you come here to paint.'

She longs for him to hold her but, wanting to get closer to him emotionally, she finds herself provoking him into revealing his secrets. 'You're married, aren't you?'

He frowns, 'I'm divorced.' Then, as she silently waits for more, 'It was an arranged marriage. Our parents organised it. Many arranged marriages work, ours didn't. We quarrelled over everything, most bitterly religion. She regularly attended the mosque and was embarrassed by my refusal to go. Fortunately, we never had children.'

'Where is she now?'

'In Iraq.'

'Do you trust me?'

He stares into her imploring eyes. Opening their bodies to each other, they have achieved a joyful communion. For that to grow into something else, he would have to open his mind. 'Yes,' he says, 'I do trust you.'

'Tell me why you're here. Why are you in hiding?'

'I don't want to involve you in my troubles.'

'But you must. I have to know.'

He thinks for a long time, then shrugs. 'I was an interpreter. I worked in various government ministries.'

'In Iraq.'

'Yes, in Iraq. I ended up in the Ministry of Defence. Having worked on British ships, I had an affection for the British. I liked their humour, their self-deprecation, their gift for understatement, even their reserve. Many take it as snobbishness, and in some it is, but in the best of fellows, it's attractive. Anyway, through my job I got to know a number of Brits. They were part of a small contingent left in Iraq mostly for training. One in particular, Major John Stevens, was more than an acquaintance, we became friends. I know what you're thinking. I wasn't a spy. I would never betray my country.

'On one particular day, I was required to attend a meeting regarding arms procurement. Nothing unusual about that. There were four others at the meeting: two English businessmen in smart suits and striped ties, a senior official in the ministry, Hussein Doraji, and a captain in the army introduced to me as Abbas Lami. Doraji was in charge; suave and intelligent, he had the connections and authority. Lami, a big muscular guy, was the fixer, there to ensure the transaction proceeded smoothly. They were negotiating a fifty million pound purchase of heavy arms. They wanted me there to ensure the fine details of the agreement were clearly understood and agreed. If successful, it was to be the first of a series of deals.

'From the outset, a number of things struck me as irregular. Everything was cloaked in more than the usual secrecy. The two English guys weren't the normal agents. The mode of transfer of payment was strange, as was the shipping arrangement. But it was not my place to comment. My job was to translate as accurately as I could, reflecting if possible the manner and tone of the speaker, but without any aside from me.

'I had a close colleague in the ministry, a fellow interpreter named Jahmir. Absolutely unethically, for we were forbidden to speak of any of our work, I mentioned to him how I found the meeting strange. He said he too had been involved in a meeting that he considered odd relating to a shipment of oil to China.

'There was a follow-up meeting to finalise the mechanics of the deal. I paid close attention to everything and studied the paperwork. Later, conferring with Jahmir, we were forced to the conclusion that the two deals were connected and nefarious. The arms, ostensibly intended for the Iraqi army, were instead to be routed to Daesh. A tanker of oil from wells captured by Daesh was to head for China. The Chinese payment for the oil was to be forwarded to the Ministry of Defence to offset the cost of the arms. Hussein Doraji and his collaborators were obviously to receive a sizeable cut running into millions of pounds. How corrupt could you get, selling arms to the enemies of Iraq?

'We were sickened and frightened. We didn't know what to do. Who could we trust? Who was being paid off? But we had to do something. I'm a patriot, not a traitor. We had to stop this deal, so I went to see John Stevens. I thought the British would act immediately, but I was wrong. They wanted us to stay in post, and find out as much as we could, particularly where the ship with the arms was sailing from and the intended time and place of its arrival in Iraq.

'I lived those weeks in great fear. Eventually, with armed force, the British seized the boat in international waters and they tipped off the Chinese about the oil tanker. I was on my way home when I got a frantic call from Jahmir. He said they had come for him, they were at the door. He told me not to go home. They had obviously worked out where the leak of information might have originated.

'I saw a jeep screaming down the road. I immediately turned off my route, ducking into narrow side streets. I was on the run. There was only one place I felt I could gain sanctuary. I dashed through many little alleyways but I had to cross a major street to get to the British compound. Another jeep spotted me. There was a gunshot. I swerved down a side street straight into an oncoming armoured patrol vehicle. It was British. I stood in front of it waving my arms. Nearly running me down, they screeched to a halt. Thinking it was a hold-up, they had guns at the ready. I cried out, "Don't shoot. I'm a friend of Major John Stevens. They're going to kill me."

Keeping a gun trained on me in case it was a trick, they hauled me into the back of the truck. I hid on the floor. I heard the slam of car doors and men running. They spoke to the driver of the truck. I heard him say, "Haven't seen him, mate." Then they ran off.

'The British soldiers interrogated me. I gave them the whole story. They radioed and received assurance I was legitimate. Then they took me into the base. You can imagine my relief at gaining safety.

'It was too dangerous for me to stay in Iraq. They gave me a British passport in a new name and flew me to London. Quietly, feelers were put out to find me a safe place, hiding away at least until the immediate fury died down. I was introduced to Melvyn Hathaway. Do you know him, he owns this estate? And so I find myself here.'

'Are you still in danger?'

'They lost millions of pounds from the deal. They're bound to have circulated my photograph. Until things cool, I'd best keep my head down, stay away from cities with large Muslim populations.'

'What happened to Jahmir?'

'They killed him.'

The brutal finality of those three words makes her shudder. She puts her arms around him to hold him tight. Now, more than ever, she wants to protect him. He kisses her.

'I have to go,' she says.

'Can you come tonight?'

'I'll try.'

Making sure Edward is asleep, she pulls a coat over her nightdress and slips quietly out the house, only turning on her torch when she reaches the cover of the woodland. Even at night, the wood is alive, a rustle of leaves, an owl hooting. She senses the night animals are awake – bats, mice, badgers, foxes, going about their night-time business.

The hut is in darkness. She doesn't want to frighten him. She turns off the torch, opens the door and gently calls, 'Nadim.'

He rouses from sleep and says, 'You've come then.'

There's a faint redness from the embers in the fire. She lights the lamp. He gets up, he's wearing tartan pyjamas, and throws some kindling onto the fire. He intertwines his fingers and stretches his arms above his head.

'Would you like a drink?'

'I'd like some tea. I'll make it.'

Sipping their mugs of tea, she says, 'Have you made love to many women?'

'I don't know. About twenty, I suppose.'

'Twenty!'

'What about you?'

'Just Edward, and now you. How many of those twenty were important to you?'

He considered her question. 'Including you, three.'

'Why?'

'What do you mean, why?'

'Why am I important to you?'

'Because I know parting from you will be painful.'

'Do you regret being with me?'

'Of course not. Do you regret being with me?'

Even though she had presented the question, it surprises her when it's returned. 'I think my life would have been simpler had I not met you.'

'Yes, I knew I would create trouble for you.'

She rises from her chair, goes round behind his and puts her arms around his neck and whispers in his ear, 'I want you to make love to me.'

He leads her towards the bed, for her to lay down, but she resists.

'I want to see you,' she says. 'I want to see you and touch you.'

Self-consciously bashful, he removes his pyjamas and lays on the bed. She touches his cheek and runs her fingertips over his lips, strokes his neck and smooths her hands over his chest and belly. She parts his legs and feels the inside of his thighs. She cups his balls in her hand and gently squeezes, measuring the soft oval fruit inside. She slides a finger along his circumcised penis, scrutinizing the intricacies of its structure. What gives it its power to so excite her? It's not her intention to arouse him, which of course she does, but simply indulge the pleasure of looking at him.

She climbs on top of him, her legs between his parted thighs, and he enters her. Her body undulates in rhythm with her deep breathing. It's every bit as lovely as before, but too soon he has his orgasm and wilts away from her. Bereft, she curls up on the bed. He knows her grief. Kneeling above her, he massages his penis, willing it back to life. He gets her to crouch into a ball and encloses her within his arms and thighs. Rabbit-like, he mounts her. He takes his hand to her clitoris and is eventually rewarded with a cry of achievement. He doesn't stop moving but accedes to the urge to come a second time. But it won't arrive. He thrusts vigorously trying, and failing, to climax, and in the process, brings her to a new arousal. Panting, they slump onto the bed. She covers his body with kisses and discovers that, although not fully erect, his penis has not returned to repose. She kisses it back to life, then lays back, pulling him on top of her. It's as if they've passed beyond a barrier of satiation and their desire is now inextinguishable. They become shameless. They lose themselves in time, their reckless sensuality overpowering them. Only after untold hours, both so sore that the pain overrides the pleasure, do they desist, and fall into a deep sleep, still enwrapped in each other's arms.

They stir sometime after four o'clock. There's the faintest hint of the new day at the window. Locked warm in his arms, his hand beneath her, cradling her breast, she is loath to rise. For her, the night has been revelatory, a sudden realisation that her beliefs about the body are completely wrong. She had conceived humans as like onocentaurs, their heads and torsos human, and their lower parts as donkeys, liminal beings, halfway between their animal origins and a transformation into a likeness of God. The body, in this view, is merely a repository, unimportantly necessary to carry the intellect. Now she sees her mother is pervertedly, blightingly wrong. That our animality makes us as one with nature. That sensuality, heart and mind are an indivisible unity. That the evolution of sensuality is every bit a gift of God as is intelligence. That a life without sensuality is but a half of a life. Devotion to God is not, as her mother would have her believe, about denial, but, to the contrary, embracing all of His wonders. One of such wonders is Nadim. She thanks God for sending her a man who has been gentle enough, yet persistent enough, to pull apart her curtain of denial and reveal to her the other half of her life.

He lights the lamp. She stares at his penis, 'How curious it is, tiny now.'

Outside, he places a bowl on a chair, fills it with water from a white enamel jug and, stripped to the waist, washes his upper body, throwing water onto his face and spreading wet fingers through his hair.

Close together, side by side, they walk the path through the wood, the hem of her long white nightgown glowing bright beneath her dark green coat. The very earliest of the birds, the blackbirds and robins, commence the springtime concert. He leaves her, as before, at the gate into the garden. She holds onto him, unwilling to surrender the tender closeness of their night.

She shops for food in the nearest town, a thirty-minute drive. In the car, she thinks about her mother and starts to question everything she has been brought up to believe.

In the town, there's a Moslem community. In the spirit of ecumenical solidarity, she has, on a number of important religious festivals, been invited, with Edward, to the mosque. She knows from her own experience that in this community, in spite of some hostility they've experienced, the overwhelming majority are well-integrated, amiable and tolerant. But could there be, amongst them, some young hot-heads who would respond to injunctions to root out enemies of Islam? Was there a hit list and was Nadim on it? Now, driving in the busy streets and shopping in the supermarket, she's vigilantly aware of the dark-skinned men she sees, especially those with beards.

On her return, coming out of town, the street is half blocked by a skip parked in the road. She has to wait until there's a gap in the flow of the oncoming traffic. She watches the workmen shifting scrap from the house being renovated.

When she gets back to the village, she drives not to the house but to the gated driveway into the estate, next to Martin's lodge. The gate is locked so she leaves her car there, goes through the pedestrian gate and runs down to the hut to find Nadim. 'Come and help me,' she says. 'I've got a present for you.'

When they arrive back at the car, he says, 'What have you got there?' With the tailgate up, jammed into the boot, intact except for a few chips, is an old enamel bath. They carry it down to a secluded flat area alongside the stream and give it a wash. She jams a screwed up polythene bag into the empty plug hole. They construct four stone pillars for it to sit on. He climbs into the bath to ensure it's secure, then, while she buckets water from the stream, he lights a fire beneath it.

When the water is hot, he douses the fire. While she watches him, he undresses. He hesitates to remove his underpants. Laughing, she tugs at them. 'Come on Mr. Modesty.' Making little cooing sounds, he slips into the bath, then draws his head beneath the hot water. When he re-emerges, he says, 'This is wonderful.' She runs up to the hut and returns with shampoo, soap, and towel. She throws off her clothes and climbs in with him. She shampoos his hair. 'Stand up,' she instructs, 'I'll wash you.' She soaps his body, enjoying smoothing the muscles of his back and his buttocks. She playfully teases his penis, making him groan as it grows erect. 'There you are, you'll do,' she says laughing, and they sink back down into warmth.

'I must go,' she says. 'I don't know when I can next get away. Easter week is coming up and it's a busy time for us.'

'Can you come to me again one night?'

'I'll try.'

In the churches, Edward has pinned up posters drawing attention to the plight of Christians in the Middle East. In his sermons, he asks the congregations, swollen in number because of Easter, to pray for all refugees, and especially those Christians persecuted as the result of religious intolerance.

Somehow he has got to know that the man in the hut on the estate is Arabic. Ruth is alarmed when he asks her about him. She's vague in her reply. 'He keeps himself to himself. I understand from Martin that he's there at the wish of Melvyn Hathaway who offered him a safe place to hide away. You remember Martin asked us to keep it to ourselves.'

'Do you know why he's hiding?'

'No,' she lies. 'Whenever I go to walk or paint there, he's doing forestry work.'

'Maybe I ought to meet him.'

She enthusiastically enters into the activities of Easter: the greetings and meetings, the singing and praying, the talking and reflecting, the hosting and the cooking and the waiting. Waiting at table...and waiting to see Nadim again. Through all the animation, she carries upon her, like an imprint, as sharp as teeth marks from a love bite, the bodily memory of making love. When she stands before the Women's Fellowship, she thinks, what if they were to know? It's as if she were peering over the edge of a sheer cliff, seeing the waves crash on the rocks far below, feeling that urge to jump, terrifying and yet tinglingly exciting. What if she were to say to the women in the Fellowship, 'I'm a woman given over to fornication, fucking a man of dark skin and alien culture?'

She has always delighted in the progression of festivals and seasons in the liturgical year. Now it is Easter, then Pentecost, Harvest, All Saints, Advent, Christmas, Lent; the year proceeding in its steady annual cycle as the Earth circles the Sun. But now she feels moved by other forces. The demands of her body have been roused and set free and are as impossible to deny as the free ocean could refuse the attraction of the Moon.

Nightly, withdrawing unto herself, she feels the pull of the Man. She resists. Part of her hates this power he has over her. It's as if she has lost autonomy. But there's no stuffing the craving back in the box of repressed desires. Her mother would starkly personify such longings as the work of the devil. If it were a devil, what joy he creates. But she doesn't believe in devils.

Defining her affair with Nadim is its impermanence. One day for sure, maybe soon, he will be gone. That makes it the more precious and also means she hasn't had to ponder the future. For them, there is no future.

The only way she has been able to give herself licence to be adulterous is to blot out any thought of Edward. But now she does think of the future. If she were discovered, how would he react? He would be hurt, horribly hurt. Would he forgive her? Did she want forgiveness? She knows there's no turning back.

Although frustrated by its limitations, she believes it's a good life, the wife of a rural cleric, but to continue that life without love, visceral, sexual love, is unthinkable. Oh, why can't one have the Sun *and* the Moon!

For the first time, she contemplates having to make a choice. Leaving Edward? The thought is terrible. The anguish for both of them. And for what? To make a new life with Nadim? Undeniably, she's drawn to Nadim, not just the urgent sexual pull, but by a joy she finds in his company. Does she love him? Does he love her? Would he want to be with her? Wouldn't it be doomed by their disparities of outlook, ethnicity, and religion? Had he not said that men and women each have their roles? No doubt, for him, the woman's was in the home, caring for her man and her babies. So many questions and no answers.

She has to see him. During the morning, she has one hour free. She runs to the hut and finds him with his hands clamped to his jaw.

'What's the matter?'

'Toothache.'

'How long have you had it?'

'Since yesterday.'

The poor man is obviously in great pain. Fortunately, she has her mobile. She phones her dentist who says to bring him to the surgery and he'll try and fit him in sometime in the morning.

She phones through her excuses for the appointments she has later that day. As she drives into town, although he dismisses the risk, she's paranoid that Nadim will be seen. Walking to the surgery, they pass Muslim families. They sit for a long time in the waiting room. People come and go. An Arabic-looking man arrives and sits opposite. He observes them both, then makes a remark in Arabic to Nadim. Nadim, holding his jaw, doesn't say a word.

At last, Nadim is invited into the surgery. When he comes out, he's a whole lot happier. She pays the bill in cash. On the route back they stop at a pedestrian crossing. A crowd of lads of Asian ethnicity are waiting to cross. 'Get down,' she says.

He says, 'Don't be silly, you're being paranoid.' The lads stroll across. Some turn to look at them. 'They're going to move me in a week or so.'

'Where?'

'Swindon. There's a bed-sitting room I can use. I'd rather stay here, but they're unhappy about it. At least I'll be able to look for work. Swindon has lots of factories.'

She always knew this was going to happen, but it's all too soon. She drops him off at the estate gate. 'Do you love me?' she says.

He doesn't know how to respond. How can love flourish between them? His position is so impermanent, their lives so very different. He doesn't want her to act recklessly, destroying her marriage and then regretting it. 'Yes, I love you, but it's impossible, isn't it?'

Kissing him, she says, 'I'll come to the hut as soon as I can.'

Two days later, Edward is out and she has the evening free. Even though it's sheeting with rain, she has to go to him. She wears a fawn fleece and jeans. She pulls on boots and a long shower-proof mac with a hood. The rain hammering on leaves has the noise of a rushing stream. She hurries to gain the shelter of the hut. It's in darkness. She calls, there's no reply. As soon as she lights the lamp, it's obvious something has happened. A chair is overturned. There's a trail of blood from the door to the table and then to the bed which is in disarray with the sheet missing.

'Oh, my God!' she cries. Holding her torch, she returns to the rain, calling his name and searching the ground around the hut, praying she won't find a body. She has to seek help. She runs, the stupid rain-hood won't stay up so she leaves it off. Martin's eyes widen when he opens the door to her. Her hair, in thick strands, clings to her face. Her features are as distraught as a mother who has lost a child.

'Ruth, whatever is the matter? Come in out of the rain.'

She stands, dripping, on the hall doormat.

'They've taken him.'

'Taken who? Is Edward all right?'

'Nadim, they've got him.'

At no time during these many weeks have they had a conversation about his hidden guest. Suddenly, he understands all. He's sympathetic. He always thought Edward a dry old stick, not the ideal husband for a pretty young woman. His concern is to avoid fuss. His employer's instructions are to quietly harbour a man until an alternative place is found for him. Now he has to deal with a half-demented vicar's wife.

'He's safe.'

'Thank God!' Crying with relief, she collapses onto the chair that Martin proffers her. 'But there's blood.'

'He's had an accident. I took him to the hospital. They're keeping him in.'

Her face turns white. 'Is he all right.'

'Yes, don't worry, he's ...'

'I must go to him.'

He sees her distress. 'I'll take you.' On the way to the hospital, he says, 'They may not let you see him, it's after visiting hours.'

'What name shall I say?'

'Khalil. Nadim Khalil.'

When he drops her off, he says, 'I'll wait for you.'

With the nurse on duty, she's at her most charmingly authoritative. 'I know it's past visiting hours, but I'm the wife of the Vicar of Broughton and Mr. Khalil is in our care. I'd be most grateful if you could let me have a brief moment with him.'

His head is wreathed in bandages. He's sedated but awake and smiles on seeing her. She takes his hand. 'I thought they'd killed you.'

'By my own hand, I'm afraid.'

'What happened?'

'The chainsaw. I was making a cut when it kicked back striking my head.'

She touches his lips. 'How do you feel.'

'Sleepy and sore.'

They hold hands, silently gazing at each other.

'I must go, Martin's waiting for me, but I'll come back tomorrow.'

She leans forward to kiss his lips. Tears start in her eyes, 'I love you.'

Martin takes her to the vicarage. She finds Edward is waiting for her. 'I was worried. I didn't know where you were.'

'I'm sorry. The man in the hut had an accident. I went with Martin to take him to the hospital.'

She abhors lying and can see the quagmire of deceit opening up before her.

'Is he all right?'

'Yes. He had to have stitches to his head. It was the chainsaw.'

'They're deadly things.'

'I'm sorry you were worried. I'm tired. I'm going to bed.'

The following morning, she prepares their boiled eggs for breakfast. Edward's head is hidden within the folds of The Times.

She says, 'I've been having an affair.'

Slowly, the pages of the newspaper descend. He frowns. 'What sort of affair.'

'*Une affaire de coeur*. A love affair. What other affairs does one have?'

He looks at her as if she'd just admitted stealing from

Marks and Spencer. She sees in his face astonishment that she could be capable of such an action, incomprehension as to why she should do it, and disgust. He swallows hard. 'Why?'

It's the question she finds impossible to answer. She was ready with the who, what, where and when, but why... How could she explain to him an imperative that overrode even her marriage vows? At her silence and needing to elaborate his question, he says, 'What we have here is good.'

She immediately understands both his meanings: that the work they do is worthwhile, and their everyday working relationship functions well. She cannot refute either. And yet...and yet... She says, 'You're a good man Edward, and I admire the work you do...'

He interrupts her. 'You said, "You've been having an affair." Does that mean no longer?'

'I don't know.'

'Who is it?'

'Nadim, the man in the hut in the wood.'

'But he's a Muslim!'

'Muslims, as well as Christians, are capable of love. But no, as it happens, he's an atheist.'

'An apostate Muslim! Now I understand your renewed interest in painting. It's disgusting.' His lips are pressed tight in controlled fury. 'After everything I've given you, everything I've done for you, you betray me. For what?'

'For love.'

'Carnal desire! You call that love?'

They're silent, both shaken. Up to now, her simple wish was to own up to the truth. She had made no decision as to what she was going to do. Had he said he loved her, had he in anyway indicated an understanding of how she felt, she might have reacted differently.

'I'm sorry Edward, I can't continue living with you.'

'All our people here will reject you. You'll never be able to come back. And what about your mother? She'll disown you. This is madness. Your life will be ruined.'

She wants to say something to soothe him but can find no words to serve. 'I understand your bitterness and I'm sorry for it. I'm leaving today. The sooner I'm gone the better.'

Her composure infuriates him. 'You're going to him, aren't you? Your lover. Driven by lust to an adulterous bed. Have you no pride, no honour, no self-respect?'

'I...' She's about to be drawn into a defence but sees this means attacking him and this she will not do. She turns and leaves the room, the eggs and toast left forlornly cold on the breakfast table. She goes to her bedroom and packs essentials in a rucksack. She collects her bicycle and walks it along the path to the hut. She deposits the contents of the rucksack there and walks on to Martin's. He's not in. She's about to cycle away when he returns. She gets off her bike.

'You know that Nadim and I...' She shrugs, 'You know.'

He nods.

'I'm leaving Edward.'

'To be with Nadim?'

'I don't know. We've not discussed it. Nadim's always assumed I'll remain with Edward.'

'What are you going to do now?'

'Until I'm able to sort myself out, I wondered if you'd allow me to stay in the hut. At least until Nadim gets out of hospital.'

'If it's for a short time, I don't think that's a problem. But are you sure? You could stay in the lodge.'

'Bless you, but I'd rather be in the hut. With Nadim going to Swindon, you'll soon be free of responsibility for him.'

'He's a nice bloke. I was never told the details, but I understand he did this country a good turn.'

'I'm going now to cycle into town to see him.'

'Would you like me to run you in?'

'If I can put the bike in your boot, I could cycle back

and you wouldn't have to wait around.'

As he drops her off, he says, 'Do you need money?'

'I'm all right for the moment, thank you.'

'Well, don't be too proud to ask. You can always pay me back when you're set up.'

She finds Nadim still bandaged up but much recovered. She leans forward and kisses him on the lips. She puts the bunch of flowers she's bought into a vase and fruit into a bowl. She hands him a copy of Graeme Green's *Brighton Rock*. 'It's a thriller. Have you seen the film?'

'Thanks, I'm very bored and they wake you up so early.' She sits by the bedside stroking his hand, and this is how, on his rounds, the doctor finds them.

He examines the wound which appears so horrendous it makes her wince. The doctor says to her, 'It's not as bad as it looks. It's healing well. He's a very lucky man; a fraction deeper and it would have been very serious. All being well, we'll release him tomorrow. Will you be caring for Mr. Khalil?' She nods. 'You need to dress the wound twice a day. The main concern is to avoid infection. We'll try as much as we can to minimise the scar.'

When the doctor has moved on, she's tempted to speak of her break with Edward but decides that this would only worry him. Instead, she tells him how the bluebells are coming out. They talk of yet another bomb outrage in Iraq that he has seen on television. He asks her to read to him from the book. Eventually, he stops her saying he's tired and will go to sleep. She kisses him goodbye and says she'll see him the following morning.

She does a bit of shopping, putting the items in her rucksack. While cycling through the town, she's hailed by a woman, it's Sally, a church warden. 'Good heavens Ruth, whatever are you doing here on a bicycle?'

'Visiting a friend in hospital.'

'And you've cycled all the way! Couldn't Edward have let you have the car?'

'He's busy.'

'I'm glad I've bumped into you. I can't do the flowers for Sunday.'

'Would you mind, Sally, not just now, I need to get going.' Precipitately, she cycles away.

Being in the hut on her own is eerie, it being so tied up with Nadim's presence. It's the stage on which they played out their love affair and she vividly recalls all those moments over the past weeks when she was there with him. It's also a relief to be alone. Alone in the wood with the birdsong. She phones the school where she teaches and tells them she's unwell. She gets on with domestic tasks. Cleans up the blood. Sweeps the wooden floorboards. Remakes the bed with a sheet Martin has given her. Splits logs for the fire. Brings in bunches of flowers for decoration. Makes herself soup.

The following morning, remembering her first vision of him, she strips off and, like him, splashes in the stream to wash. The water's still biting cold but invigorating. She goes with Martin to collect Nadim. Inevitably, they're seen returning through the village. Gossip has wings. The vicar's wife suddenly abandoning her wifely duties and then together with a man with a head wound. Conjectures will circulate and in the process crystallise into fact. Martin says to Nadim, 'The sooner we can get you to Swindon, the better.'

Alone, at last, together in the hut, aware that his reaction will determine her future, she tells him she has left Edward. She scrutinises his face. There had been no discussion, no understanding between them. On leaving Edward, she hadn't assumed she would have a life with him. He had said he loved her, but she recognised she had prompted him into declaring that. Any questioning from him as to the wisdom of her decision would mean he didn't want to be with her, and although that, she knew, would make her wretched, it was an outcome that had to be accepted.

He's very quiet and serious, then says, 'I'm an immigrant in a land where I know nobody. I cannot join a community. I have no money, even my clothes are not my own. I have no job. For my welfare, I'm dependent on the generosity of others. I don't even have the self-determination to be able to choose where I want to live. And now I'll have an ugly scar on my forehead. I understand why you should want to leave Edward but to swap Edward for me...'

'But do you love me?'

'You're the best thing that ever happened to me. Of course, I love you, but...'

She stops his speech with a kiss.

She feels liberated. Wonderful to be together with Nadim now without the imperative of watching the clock. How love imbues all the mundane tasks of living with joy. Fetching water, lighting the fire, preparing food, all she does with a gladness of heart. Heedful of his wound, they make love gently, lingeringly. Afterwards, she enfolds his penis in her hands, as if it were a delicate wren. 'I love your penis. Your prodding, probing, persistent penis, pursuing its purpose to fulfilment.'

He laughs. 'No penis can stand all that alliteration.'

During the following day, Edward arrives at the hut. Of Nadim's presence, he makes no acknowledgement. Addressing Ruth, he says, 'Can we talk?' They go outside. Nadim watches them through the window; Ruth, slight in figure, Edward, towering above her. He thinks that, in spite of her words, it's more than likely she will return to Edward.

'I want you to come back. I can't live without you. I admit I've been less than attentive of you, but that can change. It's natural for couples to lose their early pleasure in being together, but we can use this upset to renew the relationship we once had. Don't throw away what we have. Surely it's worth far more than where you're going now. It's not just me, our community needs what you give.'

'What status would I have now? People would just laugh

at me. But that's besides the point. I've changed. I can't live as we were. You don't need a wife. You need a housekeeper and a secretary. You could find both very cheaply from within our parishes.'

'What sort of Christian are you? You made vows before God. There's purpose in our Christian teaching; we cannot sin without consequence. There's still time for you to repent. You were foolish and we all make mistakes...'

'I'm sorry, I'm sorry, but I can no longer live with you.'

'So you're going to persist with this madness. You'll come to regret it. You've no money, no home. Is that man going to look after you? You've turned bad. And, now I realise, you were trying to undermine my faith. God have pity on you. I hope you find your way back to the path of our Lord.' Then as he walks away, 'I'll pray for you.'

Martin comes down and says to Nadim, 'We're moving you. As things stand, there's too much attention now drawn to you. We want to get you out. I'm instructed to take you to Swindon. Is that OK?'

He turns to Ruth. 'Are you going to stay on in the hut?'

'No,' she says, 'I'm coming with you to Swindon.' They pack their few things, then wistfully take their leave of the hut, the scene of their happy times together. Martin locks up and takes the key. In Swindon, Martin finds the accommodation allocated to Nadim. It's a dark room on the first floor at the back of a large Victorian house converted into flats. It's not much bigger than the hut, but it does have a tiny loo and shower. There's one window looking over a dismal concrete yard with accumulated rubbish. There's a microwave and an electric hob with two rings, and a four-foot-wide double bed.

Martin looks around the flat, then at them, but doesn't say what he's thinking. Telling Nadim he needs to set up a bank account, he gives him a cheque for a thousand pounds, and in an envelope, two hundred pounds in cash. 'This is from Mr. Hathaway to get you going. I think you can expect to be on your own from now on. The first month's rent has been paid.'

They shake hands, Nadim saying how grateful he is. Ruth kisses him on the cheek and thanks him for all his kindness. And then he's gone. They stand looking at each other. They feel like young lovers beginning the adventure of a new life together.

Their first task is to seek work. Ruth has a joint bank account with Edward, but will not draw on it; Edward will close it anyway. She does have her own personal account which received her pay from teaching, but there's not much in it and she's had to phone the school to say due to circumstances beyond her control, she's not able to continue working there. The money they have won't last long.

Swindon has a mosque. She's more worried about it than he is. 'I'll avoid the big cities, but I won't spend my life in fear and hiding.' They tour Swindon's charity shops and fit themselves out with clothes. For Nadim, she finds a smart pair of trousers, a dark jacket, black shoes and a neat tie. 'Your looking-for-work outfit,' she says. She walks into a primary school, sees the headteacher, explains that although she doesn't have qualified teacher status, she does have a degree and is immediately available for supply work. The head says they're short staffed, that she can offer her a half day a week with the possibility of more on a day-to-day basis.

In his new outfit, Nadim goes off for an interview. The plaster on his forehead gives him the look of a desperado. He comes back to the flat triumphant. 'I've got a job,' he announces proudly, 'cleaning in a factory. They laughed at my English, said it reminded them of Ealing comedies.'

To get to work, they buy another second-hand bicycle. They live mostly on rice and vegetables. She's used to being hard-up and he's abstemious so they eke out their pennies. Their biggest expense is the rent. Their only luxury is because she decides that in spite of their meagre income, being in town they must enjoy the arts scene. She takes him regularly to concerts, the theatre, cinema and picture gallery. He laps this up, even though he has to work two hours to earn the price of a theatre ticket. But the library is free. Like young lovers, they make love every night and Sunday morning and that too is free.

She seeks a space to pray and goes to a small church. Cathedrals and great churches are, for her, temples to the love of God, but not conducive to an intimate discussion with Him. She eschews joining the congregation. She doesn't want to be preached at. She prays for understanding. Her faith has shifted. She now no longer believes the Bible is divinely inspired, but that it is no less profound for being a human construct, the visionaries who created it attempting to make sense of a mysterious world. The importance of this change in faith is fundamental. It means that since the words are not God's, one must understand them within the context of the lives of the men who wrote them. One must re-evaluate their significance and discover what truths they have for one today. For her, now, being a Christian is not a matter of faith but of leading a life of which Jesus would approve.

One evening, Nadim finds her with the Qur'an. 'Good heavens, why are you reading that?'

'I studied it at university. I'm re-reading it now because I want better to understand your ideological roots.'

He recites a passage in Arabic by heart.

She says, 'I appreciate your revulsion at those who commit evil deeds in the name of religion, but is that all that makes you an atheist?'

'To have faith in organised religion is to put yourself within the power of men who claim they speak with the authority of God. They say, for your own well-being, you have to obey us because we have the truth. But unshackle yourself from their faith and you become free. Free to create your own understanding of the mysteries of our existence.'

'But to spurn the beauty within religion is to reject the music of Bach because it's religiously inspired. The religious portrayal of heaven, up there above us, is, of course, nonsense. But even if there were no afterlife, the concept of a place where there is no war, conflict, terror, where there is universal justice, where there is no suffering, where people love one another and live in harmony with nature, that concept is beautiful. It provides us with a powerful vision of what we should strive towards in our chaotic world.'

He says, gently, 'Our beliefs, yours and mine, are not so very different.'

She's happy but pricked by conscience to make more of her life. Had she been on her own, she would have volunteered for work in Africa. She keeps her eye on advertisements for charity jobs. She sees one that attracts – a resettlement support worker to work with Syrian refugees arriving in Gloucestershire.

She says to Nadim, 'Do you think this would be too dangerously exposed for you? There would only be one salary, but maybe we could offer ourselves as a team. Your language skills would be invaluable.'

'It's a dangerous world. We take our chances. I can't think of a more worthwhile job.'

She downloads the job application. She reads, 'List your employment history commencing with your most recent employment.' She makes only one entry, 'Vicar's wife'.

Awakening Desire

They were sitting in the café window, watching the flow of people outside in the street when he saw her. He knew it was her, clearly older, but the same unforgettable features. There could be no mistake. He dashed up from his chair, told Sheena he'd be back and sped up the street.

He soon caught up and, not giving himself time to think, said, 'Excuse me.' She was with a man and a young woman who he guessed to be her daughter. They stopped and turned to look at him. She had aged, crows feet at the eyes, lines etched around the mouth, but she was still beautiful, and there was that dancing look in her eyes.

'I think we met,' he blurted out, 'many years ago, in Greece.'

Vishal was listless. He was in a humour where everything seemed stale. He couldn't settle on a book to read. Television was dull. Even music failed to provide its usual magic. He thought of going out to meet friends, but they always did the same old things, repeated the same old conversations.

His mum phoned. 'How are you?' she said. She was worried about him. After five years together, he had taken the split from Ellie badly.

'I'm all right.'

After further probing his feelings and receiving reluctant answers, she said, 'You know we're going to Alonissos for a week. Why don't you come with us?'

'No thanks, I don't feel in the mood for holidays.'

His parents were young children when their parents, his grandparents, were expelled by President Idi Amin from

Uganda. There had been a ruckus in the family when at university he paired up with Ellie, who was white, English and Church of England. He and his parents had always been close, but when he had to choose between his love for them and his love for Ellie, he broke from his parents. It hurt him how upset he had made them. Now Ellie, recruited to management in an international company, had gone. She wanted the freedom to explore new countries and new relationships. Missing her and feeling wretched, he plodded on with his work in a company offering website design. With Ellie's departure, his mother was now making efforts to build bridges.

He suddenly changed his mind. On Alonissos, he would spend time with his parents in the evenings, but, during the day, go for vigorous walks on his own. In physical activity, he would find distraction from his misery.

They stayed in a small hotel in Patitíri. He spent the first day with his parents exploring the town. The June weather was hot but there were cooling sea breezes. The following days, he packed a picnic and took himself off to the wilder, more remote areas of the island.

Every evening, after dinner, they sought a bar for music and Metaxa. The days slipped by. Walking eased his discontent. He took pleasure in the unfolding panoramas, the wild flowers, the scent of pine woods.

On the evening before their departure, they were relaxing in a bar. He couldn't help but stare at a young woman. With her long black hair, tied with a red hairband, she looked Greek. She was beautiful, but what held his gaze was her look of lively playfulness. She was with an elderly woman, also Greek, who he took to be her grandmother.

He watched them for a while then, leaving his parents, stepped out onto the balcony with its view overlooking the bay. He leaned on the wooden rail, admiring the half-circle of lights that fringed the harbour and enjoying the cool evening air on his face.

He sensed someone approach alongside him. He turned his head. It was the young woman.

'It's great though, isn't it?' she said.

Vishal grinned. 'You're from Newcastle. I thought you were Greek.'

'Sunderland, actually. And I thought you were Asian.'

'London. Complicated ancestry. Is that your grandmother with you?'

'Yes. She lived here until she married Grandad and came to England. And you're with your parents?'

Vishal nodded.

'Have you just arrived?' she said.

'No. We're going back tomorrow.'

'I haven't seen you on the beach.'

'I've been walking, exploring the island.'

'With your mum and dad?'

'No. I prefer to be on my own. Where are you staying?'

Before she could reply, her Grandma came up, nodded to Vishal, then said, 'Shall we go now, Claudia.'

'I've got to go,' she said and touched his arm before turning to follow her grandmother.

Vishal shrugged, pity it wasn't the beginning of the holiday.

Return to the UK involved catching the 6pm ferry to Skiáthos, then a late flight to Gatwick. Time for one last walk.

He rose at dawn and set off carrying a rucksack with his picnic, water and a slim paperback, *A Month in the Country*. He took the twisting road to the west of the town. As he gained height, he kept stopping to look back, his view of the sea widening. The sun was low but growing in strength. The air was still cool and everything felt to him as if the Earth was reborn, fresh and vibrant.

He left the road to follow a broad stony track to the right, still rising. It curved steadily seawards, leading him to the top of an escarpment, where it abruptly came to an end.

Three little paths lead onwards. He dithered as to which of them he should choose, then settled on the one on the left. It descended, gently at first, then more steeply through dense shrub woodland.

He walked for something like two hours, becoming disorientated. There were only occasional views of the sea through the trees. He was hot and sweaty and fearful the path wouldn't lead him to a satisfactory end. It was going to be a long slog back.

At last, he broke cover to find himself standing above a small cove, the fingernail of bleached sand framing the blue water. The place was totally isolated. At the far end, the beach was unshaded except for a single tree. He climbed down, kicked off his trainers and made his way there. The sand was already hot. As far as he could see, his path was the only landward access to the bay.

He undressed, placing his clothes in a neat pile by the tree. The sea was wonderful. How delicious to swim without the encumbrance of swimwear. Eventually, he returned to the tree, lay naked in the dappled light and picked up his book.

He must have fallen asleep because the next thing he became aware of was a trickle of sand on his foot. He looked up and saw, kneeling by his feet, the young woman, Claudia. She too was completely naked. She was letting the sand stream out of her raised hand whilst looking directly into his eyes.

She said, 'I'll go away if you want me to.'

He shook his head. She moved nearer and very slowly brought her face down towards his. There was no mistaking, she was going to kiss him, but she was also giving him the option to turn away. He lay still and accepted the touch of her lips. She rocked back on her heels and, seeing the rising of his desire, again slowly and with obvious intent, reached her hand forward and fingered him, very gently, with her slender fingertips.

He became intensely aware of every sensation: the sun on his body, the sand beneath him, the swoosh of the sea on the beach, his blood pulsing and her caressing fingers. It was like a vivid erotic dream. He dared not speak. He sighed with the pleasure of it. She moved so as to straddle him, all the while looking intensely into his eyes. With a slow rhythmic motion, she lifted and lowered herself. He knew this moment would be with him forever. He quivered and groaned as he came and she thrust down upon him with all her weight. Then, passion subsiding, she leaned forward and kissed him before laying herself alongside him and nestling in his arms.

There were so many questions he wanted to ask, but he remained silent, enjoying their relaxed togetherness. He had no idea how long they lay, holding each other, on the sand, in the shimmering, dappled light of the tree. Suddenly, she sat up. 'I must go.' And she ran up the beach and into the cover of the trees. He guessed she must have left her clothes in the wood. He walked up, hesitating to follow her while she dressed. He shouted her name, but there was no reply. He entered the wood to look for her, but she had gone.

Should he run after her? Try to catch her? She obviously didn't want that. He went into the sea. Then lay on the beach, thrilled and puzzled, reliving what had just happened. What made her do it? Why did she run away? A mystery.

During his life, the incident on the beach would, now and again, come to mind. He wished he had a photograph of her, but the memory of the seduction, burnished by recall, remained vivid. There was a joy in how it came out of the blue, and the mystery too was part of its magic. In one sense he was glad he knew nothing about her. He enjoyed the enigma.

He married Sheena. She was confident, good fun to be with and gregarious. She also enjoyed the delighted approval of his mother who was 'over the moon' to see him happily married to a person with whom she could bond. They had two sons, a dozen close friends and a cat.

As the years passed, Sheena inclined to put on weight. She was an unusual woman in being entirely comfortable with being fat. If the choice was misery on a diet or happily plump, there was no contest. This made her a very pleasant person to live with, but, for Vishal, sexually unattractive. However, Sheena's increased girth was not balanced by a reduction in her libido. She made demands upon Vishal that he found hard to rise to. His solution, one that had she known it would have made her livid, was to close his eyes and revisit, in every detail, Claudia on the beach.

He had but to wish himself back on the beach to see it all, experience it once again: the rhythmic wash of the waves, the soft sand, the warmth, the drift of breeze on his skin, and Claudia, her long black tresses, her slim naked body, the dappled light on her breasts, the impish, playful look on her face, unembarrassed, uninhibited. Most of all, it was her beautiful face that aroused him. Over the years, he found himself looking for that face.

He and Sheena were in Charing Cross Road having tea and cake. They were sitting in the café window, watching the flow of people outside in the street when he saw her. He knew it was her, clearly older, but the same unforgettable features. There could be no mistake. He dashed up from his chair, told Sheena he'd be back and sped up the street.

He soon caught up and, not giving himself time to think, said, 'Excuse me.' She was with a man and a young woman who he guessed to be her daughter. They stopped and turned to look at him. She had aged, crows feet at the eyes, lines etched around the mouth, but she was still beautiful, and there was that dancing look in her eyes.

'I think we met,' he blurted out, 'many years ago, in Greece.'

They stood there for a moment, then she said, turning

to the man, 'Go on, I'll catch you up.'

She looked back at him. 'I'm glad to see you. How strange it is that we should meet at this time. I'm amazed that you should remember me. But look, I've got to go.'

He hurriedly said, 'Perhaps we could meet,' and knew, as soon as he said it, that this was a proposal fraught with potential problems.

She was about to reply when Sheena arrived. 'I must go,' she repeated. 'But give me your address, I have something I should send you.' He scribbled his address on the back of a till receipt, and she hurried away.

A week later he received a letter, handwritten, no address.

By a remarkable coincidence, at this time I have reason to remember you, but I remain amazed that you recognised me.

That morning was so beautiful. I was up on the escarpment before you arrived. I was enjoying being there alone. Didn't you say you preferred to walk on your own? So I hid myself. But I was also intrigued by where you were intent on going, so I followed you down the path. I watched you for sometime and, I admit it, enjoyed looking at your naked body. I was tempted to join you in the water but hesitated for too long. By the time I had found a spot in the wood and undressed, you were lying under the tree.

I had some sense of what you were like from our brief conversation and the sight of you, naked, asleep, aroused me deeply. I gave way to impulse, I saw no harm in it. I guessed you wouldn't refuse me. For me, it was a lovely, treasured, experience, so I've no regrets. I hope that's also true of you.

This is rightly yours. Think of me as having borrowed rather than stolen it. Claudia.

Folded within the pages of the letter was an envelope

and within that, a photograph. It was of himself when young, lying naked, asleep on a beach. He was astonished. She must have left her camera with her clothes.

Also enclosed with the letter was a card: 'The Beaumont Galleries. An exhibition of the works of Claudia Arguelles. 10th to 24th April. Free admission.'

He went on the 15th. A young woman in a black stylish business suit and high-heeled shoes was in charge. She invited him to sign the visitors' book and offered him a glass of wine. The exhibition was in two rooms. The first contained a mix of abstracts in various mediums, swirling blues and greens, suggestive of landscape. They were offered at a surprisingly high price and many had the little red dot of sale achieved.

In the far room, the paintings were still-life and portraits. Then he saw it, on its own, in a corner on the right. It was the photograph translated into oils, a male nude reclining on a beach. The note on the wall gave its title as 'Awakening Desire' and the words, 'Not for sale'.

Maureen McCullough

Maureen McCullough cuddled close her three-year-old son as the ancient bus juddered along on its way to Dublin. She was agonising over the most momentous decision of her life: to stick with the steady but dull father of her son, or take off to a new life with the man she was destined to love.

It was the same choice, she recognised, as Kitty Foyle had to make. Back then, when she saw the film, she unhesitatingly said that Kitty should have eloped to South America with the man she loved, but now...now, she was hesitant. 'Oh, if only we could split in half and have two lives,' she said to herself.

The bus was the very one, eight years previous, to have carried her away from her Ma and Pa. Carried her away from their isolated farm on the edge of Kilbrittain Forest in County Cork, her home until that very morning, the day after her eighteenth birthday.

She was different from her sisters. They had hair the colour of polished cedar, hers was fair. They were strapping, she was delicate. They wished for no other life than the farm, she yearned for the adventure and romance of the city. When they were out courting the local lads, she escaped into a world of dreamy heroines and dangerous lovers.

Her Pa said, 'When I look at our Maureen, I wonder where, for the love of Jesus, from whence she came. 'Tis a wonder she's a child of mine.'

Her Ma retorted, 'Stop your nonsense. What good ever came from wondering?'

For years she kept badgering them to release her. Putting her off, they said they'd consider it when she was older.

'How old?' she persisted.

'Oh...maybe when you're the broader side of eighteen.'

So it was, her eighteenth birthday, and the following morning she was away.

There was an aunt, her mother's sister, in Dublin, and that's where she lodged. She gained employment as a waitress in a restaurant close by the hospital. Life was harsh. Although the Republic held to neutrality during the Second World War, Irish shipping suffered and the country was effectively blockaded.

She worked long hours, six days a week and her feet ached. Mondays were her free day. Magnificent Mondays, hers to sleep in late, to shop, to savour the city. But she had ambitions and so, in spite of her reluctance to lose the luxury of relaxation, she enrolled for a course of training in secretarial skills. She learned to type and acquired proficiency in the Pitman's shorthand.

Of all the tedious, unremarkable, waitressing days, one was ever remembered: the day she served a table at which sat a fine young man with a happy, open face and a sweep of curls. He was talking earnestly to an older man and so didn't acknowledge her at first. But when he looked up, he examined her face intently, almost rudely, then gave her the most engaging smile. When they had gone and she was clearing the plates, she found he had left there a tip of memorable generosity.

Two days later, the young man came again, this time alone. He said his name was Anthony and asked her if he could take her to the pictures. She said, 'I'll think about it. Ask me again tomorrow.'

And back he came the following day. 'Well,' he said, 'do say you'll come.'

'Monday's my day off,' she said.

They went to the Strand Cinema where they were showing *Kitty Foyle* with Ginger Rogers in the starring role.

She loved the film. Kitty faced a life-changing decision: marry the doctor who had proposed to her or run away to South America with the married man she had loved for many years.

Maureen said, 'She should have trusted her heart and hopped it with the man she loved.'

Anthony said, 'That's crazy. The medic has to be the right choice.' Then, laughing, he told her he was soon to qualify as a doctor.

Maureen took an old navy-blue shirtwaist dress and sewed on a new white collar and white cuffs, an exact imitation of Kitty Foyle's dress. Twirling round, she showed it off to Anthony.

'Well, there's a thing,' he said. 'Just like Ginger Rogers, except you're more beautiful.'

They went out together in a regular way. They never spoke of how they felt, just a tacit understanding that they enjoyed each other's company. They went dancing and, like every other couple on the dance floor, took advantage of the slow numbers to smooch earnestly.

Delirious with desire, they sought the ill-lit byways of the Liffey, where she let him kiss her and fondle her breasts. She gently repelled his urgent cajolement for more. Whatever *other* girls did, to be, on her wedding day, as pure white as her bridal gown was too fixed a precept for *her* to give way to his urgings.

Anthony qualified and soon found a placement in a hospital in County Mayo. He said he would miss her and visit her whenever he could. It now seemed to her that she was spending her life waiting. In a mood of indulgent melancholy, she read poetry, Shakespeare's Sonnets and Yeats, especially Yeats: '*A woman's beauty is like a white frail bird, like a white sea-bird alone at daybreak after stormy night.*'

She took to sending him long passionate letters. She was surprised by how much she enjoyed the process of writing, the placing of words to capture her dreams. Her letters became increasingly lyrical and, with his absence, she could now let loose all constraint on expressing her sexual longings. Writing late at night, her letters explored many moods of love.

She counted the days waiting for his replies, and when they arrived, stored them up to read in the privacy of her bed. His letters were tender but more matter of fact: his life in Mayo, work in the hospital, his colleagues, new friendships. They left her with an ill-defined feeling of disappointment. She was exposing her heart to him and there was no reciprocation.

At first, he wrote frequently, then his letters became more intermittent. He apologised and complained of overwork. Then, one day, following a long wait, a letter arrived; he had become engaged to a nurse. He hoped they could remain friends.

She felt bereft and fell ill with glandular fever. Her aunt took her back to Kilbrittain Forest to recuperate under her mother's care. She came to realise that his lack of response to her letters meant that she had made of him a person other than he was. She had imagined him as much a romantic as she was, but he had remained unmoved by her declarations of love. No doubt he enjoyed reading them, who wouldn't feel pleased to be the object of a person's dreams? She felt more stupid than bitter. She wrote to congratulate him and wish him well.

A package arrived – all her letters replaced in their original envelopes. Now she was angry, even her love had been rejected.

Her aunt wrote that she had obtained for her a promise of a job at O'Neil Hennessy Chartered Accountants. While packing to return to Dublin, she came across the letters. She read one, but couldn't bear to look at the others. She decided to burn them but, at the last moment, wondered if she might come to regret it. She didn't want to take them with her and certainly didn't want them found. She wrapped the package of letters in oilcloth and pushed the bundle into a tin box. Across the yard from the house was an old hay barn with a high slate roof supported by mighty wooden cross-beams. She placed a long ladder against one of the beams, climbed up and slid the box to rest on top of the beam.

At O'Neil Hennessy, the accountants, all men, and the typists, all women, never mixed. They would meet only if a letter needed dictating, even then, many of the accountants wouldn't be able to say which one out of the pool of women had provided the service. But one of the younger accountants did notice Maureen. His name was Lorcan O'Brien. He was a little overweight and already losing his light brown hair, but he had an infectious laugh especially when, in contrast to the pompous arrogance of many of the other accountants, he would make self-deprecating jokes. He was considerate to Maureen and, she noticed, not just to her but to all his colleagues, including the typists.

He courted her with flowers, sweetly perfumed soap and other luxuries not easily found. After they had gone out together a few times, teasingly, she asked him why *her* rather than any of the other typists. He answered her seriously, 'You bring into my life the imagination that I lack.'

He asked her to marry him. The other girls were envious, but she was hesitant. Her dreams were of a man who would lead her into wild ways. She tried him out on her parents. His polite manner charmed them, and they purred when he revealed a knowledge of the finance of farming. What a man to have as son-in-law! However, it was not her father who propelled her decision, but *his* mother.

He took her on a visit to introduce her to his parents. Mrs O'Brien always had ambitions for her son; marriage to the third daughter of an ignorant farmer with five cows and a field of oats was not one of them. As soon as she perceived that Lorcan's attentions were more than casual, she showered Maureen with all the icy disdain of which she was capable. Maureen was incensed, and it was only her regard for Lorcan that bridled retaliation.

He tried to avoid an open break. When they left, earlier than planned, he gave vent to his pent-up vexation at his mother's behaviour. He pleaded with Maureen not to reject him because of his mother. He again asked her to marry him. Among the many complex emotions that led her to say, 'yes', was an itch to spite his mother.

Their marriage was exuberantly celebrated by her family and formally acknowledged by his. She anticipated her loss of virginity with excitement and trepidation. Afterwards, she didn't feel as different as she thought she would. She was puzzled by how much fuss was made of it. She couldn't now think she would have felt besmirched had she not been a virgin on her wedding day.

She continued to work at O'Neil Hennessy discovering, to her surprise, she was now awarded a more respected status. In two years a baby arrived, a boy. She gave up her job and, in caring for Paddy, enjoyed a great happiness.

Her mother-in-law remained hostile but, wanting to see her baby grandson, grudgingly accepted Maureen's visits. While there, Maureen asked about Lorcan's childhood. His father took her into his study and opened a cabinet. There, meticulously catalogued in chronological order, were all the documents and photographs of Lorcan's life: details of his birth, medical records, holiday photographs, birthday cards, letters he had written, school reports. She pulled one out, Mathematics – A plus, Art – D minus. She laughed that his strength and weaknesses should be evident so early. His father left her to browse at her leisure. Working her way from front to back, she picked items out at random. Towards the rear of the drawer was a letter in its original envelope. She took it out and read it. It was dated one month before their wedding.

Dear Ma, I'm sorry I hung up on you, but what <u>do</u> you

expect? These last few months of enforced separation have made me very unhappy. I do feel an attachment to you both, but now I also feel a strong attachment to Maureen – far too strong to allow you to break it. How can you imagine you can say such terrible things about her without hurting me? I don't know what you hope to gain from this, you won't change my mind about marrying Maureen.

Surely you want my happiness? For the last time, because I find it degrading, I will speak of Maureen's virtues, to which you seem blind. She cares about people, talks to everybody, shows an interest in them. If you weren't so prejudiced against her, you would see that. Everybody likes and admires her. She's intelligent and perceptive and has a great sense of humour. She's passionate about those things she believes in and she has a wit and imagination that I wish I had myself.

Don't believe love makes my eyes blind. Your attitude has brought me up to be very critical towards women. Now I've realised you're wrong. You respect all the wrong things.

Maureen thinks everything is going fine. She's busy making a palaver of preparations, so I'm not going to tell her anything. I want her to be happy and untroubled. I don't know how you will act, but if you care a jot about my happiness, you will show Maureen all the kindness and consideration that is due to the loveliest person soon to be my wife.

Hoping to hear from you, Lorcan.

Her eyes so filled with tears, she had trouble reading to the end. She carefully refolded the letter, replaced it in its envelope and returned it to the drawer. She had to wait to allow her trembling emotions to ebb away to equanimity. Then she returned to the others, saying nothing of her find.

***

It was summer, the child three years old when she badgered Lorcan to take a week of holiday to stay on the farm with her parents. He said he was too tied up with work. 'You go. It'll do you both good to get away.'

'I'll go Monday, come back Saturday,' she said.

The old barn had a new roof. Remembering her letters, she took the long ladder and climbed to the cross beam. The tin box was not there.

'You've repaired the barn roof,' she said to her father.

'Aye, and have we not made an excellent job of it?'

'You didn't do it on your own?'

'Me and Fergal together.'

She knew if her father had found the box, he would have discreetly left it in place.

'Who's Fergal?'

'Well now, you haven't met Fergal. He's a young fella, a poet he says, comes to the door, asking for work. "I've little use for a poet," I says, "but if you've strength enough in your arm to hold a hammer rather than a pen, I could do with a hand on the barn roof." He soon got the manner of it.'

'Where is he now? Has he moved on?'

'He does bits and pieces for all the folks hereabouts. He's taken the little herdsman's cottage in Beckett's Wood.'

The following morning, Tuesday, taking Paddy with her, Maureen walked to the cottage. Going was slow, Paddy wanting to kick a football and play hide-and-seek along the broad forest track. The cottage lay behind a screen of trees, a small tumble of a house beside a vivacious brook. As she expected, Fergal was not at home. She slipped a note under the door, '*My name is Maureen. I'm daughter to the McCulloughs. I would be most grateful if you could spare a few moments to call upon me at the farm.*'

Halfway back, on hearing a noise behind her, she turned to see a rider on a pony cantering through the wood. When he got to her, he stopped abruptly and slid, agilely, from the horse's back. He was tall and slim with black hair and dark eyes. She judged he was about her age.

'I'm Fergal. I read your note.'

Paddy was fussing with the pony.

'Would you like a little ride, young fella?'

He sat Paddy on the pony's back and walked forward alongside Maureen. He kept looking at her intently.

'I know why you want to see me. I've a weight of work this afternoon, but I could come tonight.'

'So you have the box?'

'Yes.'

'If you don't mind, in spite of what I put in my note, it would be better if you didn't come to the farm. I'd rather not have to explain to my parents. Could we meet somewhere else?'

'Why don't you come to the cottage, if it's not too far for you.'

He returned Paddy to the ground. He seemed to be about to say something more then changed his mind. 'Until tonight then.'

Later that day, she said she would like to walk over to her oldest friend Deidra. Would Ma entertain Paddy and put him to bed?

It was dusk before she kissed Deidra goodbye. The gathering darkness unnerved her. An assignation made innocent by broad daylight now appeared furtive. She was in half a mind to return directly to the farm but, finding no rational cause for apprehension, dismissed her fears. At the cottage, the curtains were not yet drawn and yellow light boldly filled the square of window. She peered in and saw him seated at a table. He was writing, a Tilly lamp illuminating the page. She tapped twice on the door. He threw it open, holding up the lamp to see the face of his visitor.

'You've come then.'

There was just the one room. She could smell bacon.

He invited her to sit on the only chair. He sat on the narrow iron-framed bed.

'Da says you write poetry. Are you writing a poem this minute?'

'I am that. It's a poem to you.'

'To me? Why ever would you write a poem to me?'

'I read your letters.'

'You were wrong to do that.'

'I know, but I don't regret it. Don't worry, I've kept it to myself.'

'So you're an odd job man who writes poems.'

'No, I'm a poet who, to earn a living, does odd jobs.'

'Have you had any of your poems published?'

'Not yet, but I will when I get to America...'

'You're going to America?'

'There's not much to detain me here. I want to address new themes, write about city and race, about immigration and extremes of wealth. There's more of an audience for poets to read their work in America. I want to see New York. I want to descend into smoky dives where black jazzmen play saxophone and trumpet. I want to travel West, the prairies, the Rocky Mountains, California. I don't care how I travel, bus, train, hitching a ride; it's the journey just as much as the destination.'

'You're very confident.'

'I'm clever and resourceful. I'll make my way.'

She smiled, 'And not lacking in self-promotion. Can I hear your poem to me?'

'It's not finished, you'll have to come back tomorrow.'

'What about another poem then?'

He shifted through some miscellaneous sheets of paper and pulled one out. His voice took on a deeper, resonant intonation. The poem made comparison of the activity of an ant going about its business in a woodland being cut down by a forester, and the concerns of the forester, going about *his* business in a vast and indifferent universe. The language he employed was rich and too obscure to fully understand on one reading, but she was impressed.

'Even I can tell that's very good,' she said. She felt a dangerous attraction to this young man with his strong features and serious dark eyes. 'If you'd give me my letters, I think I ought to go.'

'Don't go, not yet. Stay and talk with me. Tell me about Anthony, the lucky man to whom you addressed your letters. He didn't deserve them, only a poet could reciprocate such letters.'

'Such as yourself.'

'Such as myself. He must have been exceeding dull not to have penned you a thousand love letters in return.'

'He was not dull at all. And how do you know he didn't write me such letters?'

'Oh, it's perfectly plain from your letters to him. They pierced my heart. They're the poetry of love made prose. They are the elixir of longing. So passionate, so wild. I read, and re-read and read them again. I wept at the beauty of them. I wept at the person revealed in them, your innocence, your romantic open heart, your overflowing love.'

She blushed. She was moved by his words but didn't know how to respond. He stood up and said, 'I believed I was in love with you before I met you. Now I see you, I know I am.'

She turned to look at him and laughed, 'My God, you're forward.'

'What time do I have?'

'I'd better go,' she said.

He handed her the cold tin box and, as she took it, he enclosed her hands in his.

'I must see you again. Come again tomorrow. I'll have finished the poem and I will read it to you.'

'I don't think so,' she said.

'Come again tomorrow,' he said.

All next day, Wednesday, she thought about him. He had produced in her a deep disquiet. She instinctively knew that had he been the one in the café, had he been the one to take her to see Kitty Foyle, had he been the one to whom she had sent the letters, she would have married him with all her heart.

He said he loved her. Was it possible to be in love with someone, not the image, fantasy, construct of a person, but the real, complex, unique being; was it possible to love them solely by reading their words? She knew it was dangerous to see him, but that very danger excited her.

She arrived at the cottage again at nightfall. He smiled and took both her hands. 'I didn't think you'd come.'

'I came to hear the poem. Have you finished it?'

She sat on the bed while he read at the table by the light of the lamp. It was a meditation on his response to her letters as if *he* had been the object of her love. She was amazed by its mastery and beauty and was deeply moved. They talked long into the night. He said, 'Come away with me to America.'

She laughed, not taking him seriously. 'I'll thank you to remember, I've a husband and child.'

'Yes, I know. And he's dull too.'

'He loves me.'

'Not as I love you. Stay the night,' he said, but she shook her head. He walked her back to the farm. She let him kiss her goodnight. Kissing him thrilled her.

'Come again, tomorrow.'

'I don't think so,' she said.

She didn't go the next day. On Friday, the eve of her return to Dublin, she thought, what am I saving myself for? She went to the cottage. He took her in his arms and kissed her. He offered her beer from a brown bottle. Under the table, she noticed he had a violin case. 'Will you play for me?' she said. He played a happy jig and then a slow air that melted her heart.

They made love, the thin bed creaking and groaning to their rhythm. She lay in his arms indulging the sensuous peace that follows the strenuous striving for climax.

He said, 'We are cut from one cloth, you and I. Come with me to America.'

The idea was exhilarating, like the thought of flying. A new exciting life, in a new country with this man who she would love like no other.

On the bus to Dublin, her son's head on her lap, she reflected on her life. She thought of Anthony, her first love. She thought of Lorcan and her happiness with her baby. She thought of these last few evenings and her romantic heart yearned to go with Fergal. Then she remembered Lorcan's letter to his mother and knew she could not desert him. The time with Fergal would stay with her as memories, stored like love letters in a safety box, locked away until the quiet moment when they could be secretly savoured.

She had a contented life in Dublin. There was a daughter and then two more boys. One day she received a package from America. It was a slim volume of poetry, *Innocence and Incidents.* And there, on page five, 'To M'.

Occasionally, she would gaze on her three fair-haired sons, and then the dark hair of her daughter and wonder. But then, as her Ma always said, 'What good ever came from wondering?'

Knowledge of Angels

How long had she been watching me? As soon as I noticed her, standing by the garden gate, I switched off the mower and walked across the lawn. She was a few years older than me, mid-thirties I guessed. Although she had a pretty face, she wasn't my type. I like women who look, well, womanly: narrow waist, wide hips, long legs, biggish boobs, long silky hair and wearing make-up. Women who look feminine. She was some inches shorter than me and slim. Straps of a rucksack pulled her turquoise tee-shirt tight over small breasts. Her denim shorts revealed a narrow waist and firm, stocky legs stuck into walking boots. Her hair was short, punky and blonde. She was sweaty. But then so was I. It was hot.

'Can I help you?' I said.

'Yes, I need a man.'

I pulled back my shoulders, pushing out my bare chest. 'Would I do?'

'Possibly, you do have a few muscles,' she said with a grin. 'There's a woman up the lane who has run her car into a ditch. We might get her out if we push.'

I slipped on a shirt, then found a length of rope and put it in the car. 'Hop in,' I said. She put the rucksack down by her legs.

'So,' I said, as I drove, 'we men do have our uses.'

'Putting up flat-pack furniture, I grant you. Anything else?'

'Reverse parking?'

'They've brought out a car that does that automatically.'

An elderly woman was standing by her car, which had two wheels well down in the ditch. She was obviously distressed. 'Don't worry,' I said, 'we'll have you out in a jiff.'

I tied the rope to my rear tow-hook. When I turned round to tie the other end to the woman's car, I saw the young woman on her knees already doing that. I inspected her knot. 'Not bad.'

'I'm not a complete idiot.'

She got into the driving seat of the elderly woman's car.

'Keep it light on the accelerator,' I said.

She gave me a withering look. The car came out easy as a cork from a bottle, but the strain had tightened the knots. As I struggled with untying the knot at my end, the young woman stood over me swinging her free end of rope.

'Do you not know, there are knots designed for easy release?'

She said to the elderly woman, 'Will you be all right now? There doesn't seem to be any damage.'

The woman offered me some money. I shook my head. We watched her drive away.

'I could do with a beer,' I said. 'Would you like to join me?'

I invited her to sit at the garden table under the shade of a parasol. I brought out two beers and a plate of crisps.

'Sorry, do you want a glass?'

'No, no, the bottle's fine, thanks.'

'It's too hot to be walking. Where are you heading?'

'Nowhere in particular. I took the train to Standhope and walked from there. I love the country around here, that contrast between downland and pasture. You're very lucky.'

'Where do *you* live?'

'Buckinghamshire. Your garden's beautiful. Would you mind if I looked round?'

She examined everything in detail, many times offering the Latin names for the plants. As she moved, I had this strong sense of the vitality of her body. Like a gymnast, she had tone. I felt myself strangely attracted by her.

She was different, athletic with a sassy directness of look and speech.

'What's your job?' I asked.

'I'm an archaeologist.'

'Fascinating work, I imagine.'

'Writing reports is a fag, but site visits are fun, even if having to deal with recalcitrant landowners and irritated builders. They see me as a bloody nuisance.'

She bent over to sniff a rose. 'This is lovely.'

I observed her shorts pulled tight over her buttocks. 'Yes, it is,' I said.

She must have caught something in the way I said it, for she quickly looked up at me. She waggled her bum and said, 'Cheeky.'

I led her through an arch covered in clematis into an area enclosed by tall hedges of hazel and beech, laced with honeysuckle and eglantine. I'd put there a long bench under an ancient apple tree.

'How fabulous,' she said. 'Peaceful, private, sensuous. And what a beautiful bench.'

'One of mine.'

'You made this? It's a work of art.' She smiled, 'I can see there's more to you than muscles. You're a romantic, this secret, scented sanctum designed for indulgent pleasures.'

We went back to the shade of the parasol and carried on chatting: music (she liked jazz), holidays (we'd both been walking in Nepal), politics (she voted Green) and lots of other stuff I don't remember. I ought to have been getting ready to go out, but kept putting it off, not wanting to end our conversation.

'Kiss me,' I said.

'Pardon?'

'Kisme,' I repeated, pointing to the tabby asleep, warmly comfortable in a bed of long grasses. 'It's the name of my cat.'

She laughed, 'I bet I'm not the first woman to have had that joke played on them.'

Kev arrived. He's my chubby-faced, overweight chum

who I employ on an occasional basis when I need an extra pair of hands installing kitchens and the like.

'Hello, hello, who's this?' Kev said.

I said, 'This is...' and stopped because I didn't know her name.

'Rachel.'

'I'm Kev.'

'And I'm Graeme.'

'Aren't you ready yet?' Kev said. 'We gotta go.'

'I'll come along later.'

'Ah, come on. My kids are planning to take some money off you.'

'It's the local school fete,' I explained to Rachel.

'You've got children there?'

'Oh no, I don't have children.'

'At least none that he knows about,' Kev said.

'Take no notice of him, I help out with sets for school plays and setting up stalls for the fete. Things like that.'

Rachel said, 'I think that's great. Even though I've no children, I too am involved with my local school. They invite me into classes to tell stories.'

Kev said, 'Look, I'm not going off without you.'

I said, in a measured emphatic voice, 'I will finish my conversation with Rachel and then I will see you there.'

'I'd better be going,' Rachel said.

Kev said to her, 'Why don't you come to the fete. It's in a good cause and you might enjoy it.'

I said, 'It's too hot to walk.'

She smiled at us both, then said, 'OK, I will. But I need to use your loo first.'

When she had gone, Kev said, 'You're a one. I don't know how you do it. She's gorgeous.'

'Not my type.'

'Bullshit.'

We went in Kev's car, then sauntered around the stalls. Throwing a ball to knock over tin cans, Rachel won a box of chocolates. We arrived at a table where Julia and her two young children were running a tombola. She was dressed in an elegant sun-hat, calf-length, bum-hugging, bright blue jeans, high heels, and a very low cut frilly blouse that showed her cleavage as she bent forward over her stall.

'Hello Graeme,' she said in her la-di-da voice. 'Have you seen Susan she's meant to be bringing round some cold drinks can't complain though can we so lucky to have a sunny day today not like last year with all that mud ruined a pair of my best shoes you'd have to take your shoes off though to attempt the assault course you've set up mind you not that you'd find me doing that wriggling along on the ground but the kids might mightn't you kids...'

I interrupted, 'Good to see you, Julia, we're on our way to the tea and cakes.'

Julia suddenly noticed Rachel, looked her up and down, assumed we were an item, observed no make-up, tee-shirt, shorts and walking boots, and said, 'Well, have fun.'

We moved away. 'A former girlfriend?' Rachel said.

'How did you guess? We went out together before she was married.'

We were distracted by the assault course. People had gathered to watch scratch teams compete.

Rachel said, 'OK muscle man, let's see you do it.'

I formed a team with Kev and three other chaps. We didn't win. However Kev provided the entertainment, puffing and squirming beneath the net, teetering along on top of a log, then swinging on a rope and falling into the paddling pool. Rachel captured the action on her mobile.

The announcer said that it was now the turn of women's teams. There seemed to be a reluctance to take part. Only one team of young women came forward. 'Come on,' said the announcer, 'we've got to have a contest.'

'Your turn,' I said to Rachel.

'Oh no.'

I nodded at Kev, we took an arm each and marched her

over to the enclosure. She joined four others to make a new team and we cheered her on madly. She managed it with élan. We went to the marquee for tea and cake, then I told Rachel I was ready to leave. She said she had left her rucksack back at my place. Kev was tied up with his kids. There was now, thankfully, a slight breeze.

'We could walk back,' I said. 'It's only a couple of miles.'

We set off. 'Do you prefer walking on your own?' I asked.

'There are times when I like to be alone with my thoughts.'

'Memorising stories to tell?'

'And making them up. I go to storytellers' conventions where we share our stories.'

'What sort of stories?'

'Could be anything, adult as well as children's. A wide repertoire so as to have an appropriate story for any and every gathering.'

She asked me a host of questions about myself. Who doesn't enjoy talking about themselves? I responded with enthusiasm, often making her laugh. She asked if I had siblings. I told her about my brother, Matthew, and my two nieces.

When we arrived at the house, I said, 'Are you in a hurry to get back? I'm cooking myself a meal, there's plenty for two.'

'That would be great, but I haven't booked accommodation for tonight. I thought I'd take a chance, find a B and B somewhere. I'd better not leave it late.'

'Well, you could stay if you liked. I've a spare room. It'd be no trouble.'

She thought about it, then said, 'If you really don't mind. I'd enjoy spending the evening with you.'

I showed her up to the room. The lower sun filled it with light. She was enthusiastic, saying how lovely it was. I left her there and went to the kitchen to prepare the meal.

Five minutes later, she joined me. She'd rinsed her face and changed boots for sandals.

'I hope you're not a vegetarian,' I said.

'Nope. What are we having?'

'Lamb with apricots.'

'You're joking. I was expecting beans on toast. You like cooking? Can I help?'

'I'm what you might call a "seat of the pants" chef. Make it up as I go along. If I've got an ingredient, it can go in: if not, it can't. Would you like to slice the runner beans?'

She laughed. 'I couldn't be more different. If I'm cooking for a dinner party, I plan well in advance, keeping exactly to the recipes.'

I asked her about her parents. She said they were school teachers living in Kent. Her mother was Irish and her stepfather, English. Her biological father was also Irish.

'What happened?'

'Mum fell for this good-looking lad. It was his tenor voice that made her swoon. They got married and then had my brother and me. There were tensions. My father didn't like Mum's independence. And he was fiery fond of the Guinness. He had some casual affairs. Eventually, Mum gave him one last ultimatum, "desist or divorce", except you couldn't get a divorce in Ireland in those days. So she left him. She took to leaving us with Grandma and Grandad and spending months at a time with my uncle in Kilburn, doing whatever work she could pick up. And that's how she met Dad, in the Hammersmith Palais, dancing.'

'How old were you when they got together?'

'Five. Dad's been a wonderful father for me. There you are, beans are done. Anything else?'

'No, thanks. It's all simple now. I'll just get this casserole in the oven.'

'Would you mind if I have a bath?'

'Go ahead, there's plenty of hot water.'

I put a Prosecco into the fridge and took out some

cheeses. I fetched a bottle of Gigondas from my "cellar". I was just going for a shower when I thought that I had failed to provide her with a bath towel and hairdryer. I knocked on her door and heard a muffled reply that I took to be an invitation to go in. She was in the bath. 'I've just brought you a bath towel,' I shouted through the closed door.

She'd settled in. It's surprising with what few items a person can make a room their own. Draped over the back of a chair was a dress in a beautiful deep shade of blue, and on top of that were a tiny pair of white knickers. On the seat of the chair were folded her shorts and tee shirt. I had a deliciously tangible vision of her removing her clothes. On the table, in a tumbler, was a little posy of flowers; she must have picked them from the garden.

Beside the flowers, neatly laid out, were a map, suncream, pen, purse and mobile. I put down the hair drier with these items. On the bedside table, along with a travel alarm clock she had a book, a paperback, light to carry. I went over to read the title, *Knowledge of Angels*. It looked brand new and unread. It still had the Waterstones "two for the price of three" sticker on the cover.

After taking a shower, I placed a table in the lounge by the french windows. I set out cutlery, wine glasses, salt and pepper, serviettes and a candle. Then I sat at the open doors enjoying the garden as it cooled and settled into the evening.

When she came into the room, I was impressed. She was wearing the long, slinky, blue dress that I'd seen in her room, with its thin straps over her bare shoulders. She had put on striking earrings, indigo gemstones strung together with delicate silver work. I caught the scent of some sensuous perfume.

'You look good,' I said. 'Would you like a drink? I've a bottle of Prosecco in the fridge.'

I poured two glasses and said, 'To us.'

'You and me,' she said, and we clinked glasses.

Rather boldly, I asked her if she was attached.

'I finished with a man three months ago. It wasn't going anywhere.'

'Three months? Do you like being on your own?'

'Most blokes who are half decent are already in a relationship. What about you?'

'Free at the moment. My relationships don't seem to last that long.'

'I think men are strange creatures.'

'And I suppose women aren't?'

'No we're not. We talk to each other. We nurture our young. We telephone our parents. We read books and join choirs and we dance. We keep ourselves clean and make ourselves look presentable. We don't form passionate relationships with inanimate objects: cars, computers, cameras and the like. Our interests are other people. We don't watch men chasing a ball. We *do* look at the men watching the men chasing the ball, and find them astonishing. They're emotionally incomplete as if they've not grown out of adolescence. We may have our bitches and bigots, but we're not baffling.'

'Oh, come on, that's rubbish. There's a spectrum of personality traits in men as there are in women.'

'Sure. It's the masculine end of the spectrum that's weird. It's men's feminine traits, if they have them, that make them liveable with.'

'And where do you put me on this spectrum?'

'You're interesting.'

'Thanks very much.'

'You think of yourself as an alpha male, competitive and attractive to women...'

'But.'

'But there's a gentler, more caring, more romantic side to you. I suspect you go for the wrong women.'

'What sort of woman would that be then?'

'A woman who looks gorgeous but...'

'Like Julia.'

'Yes,' she smiled, 'like Julia.'

I brought in a bowl of lettuce. Before returning to the kitchen, I invited her to put on a CD. I checked the casserole and put potatoes to boil.

When I got back to the lounge, she was dancing to a salsa band, using her arms to give impetus to the sinuous movements of her body.

'Come on,' she coaxed.

'I can't,' I said. 'I've had lessons and I still can't do it.'

I did my best but knew I looked ungainly. When the track ended, I changed the CD to French folk music that I knew I *could* dance. We waltzed around the room.

'You can waltz,' I said.

'I love dancing.'

'Do you know the French waltz? Lean back onto my hand and imagine we're spinning round on opposite sides of a roundabout.'

As our steps synchronised perfectly, we spun as if in a dream.

'I'm getting giddy.'

'Look straight into my eyes,' I said, 'it will help.'

She had amazing eyes, light blue around the pupil shading into gentian blue at the edge of the iris. The motion suddenly flipped. Instead of us whirling around in a stationary room, it was the world that now spun in a blur around us, whilst we, at the centre of the universe, held each other calm and still and exhilarated. The music came to an end. We ceased to make our steps, but the world continued to whirl in a giddying spin. To prevent herself falling, she clung to me. We were both breathing heavily from the exertion, then I gently kissed her on the lips.

She came to help me in the kitchen, to bring the meal to the table. I poured the Gigondas.

'Here's to new friendship,' I said.

'Hang on a minute,' and she rushed upstairs. She returned with her phone, put her arms around my neck and took a selfie of the two of us.

We got into a conversation about love. I said I'd never been truly in love, but plenty times infatuated. I said, 'People scorn infatuation saying, "They're only infatuated. They can't see things as they are. When the madness evaporates, they'll come back to their senses, back to reality." They view infatuation as the insubstantial froth, like the head on a Guinness, that you have to get through to reach the rich liquid of real love that lies beneath. I think people have got it all wrong. What else can match that state of euphoric well-being? Infatuation should be celebrated and thought of as a gift to relish as long as it lasts.'

She burst out laughing. 'Bravo, what a speech!'

'Am I not right?'

'You're all froth like the head on your Guinness.'

'What about you? Have you been in love, like really in love?'

'Yes. It ended badly. Men are just grief.'

She helped me clear plates away and I made us some coffee and found some chocolate. I lit the candle.

'Let me hear one of your stories.'

'What, now? Are you sure? They go on a bit.'

'Earn your supper, tell me one of your stories.'

'What sort of story would you like?'

'What's on the menu?'

'Birth, death, nature, sci-fi, endeavour, odyssey, love, betrayal, desire...I have a story called, *Awakening Desire*, but it's a bit risqué with someone I hardly know.'

'Excellent! I'm all up for risqué. Is the title in the passive tense: a desire that a person finds is being awoken within them, or active: someone is setting about stimulating desire?'

'Both.'

Illuminated by the soft light of the candle, she told me the story of a young man, Vital, on holiday in Greece, seduced on a deserted beach by a beautiful young woman,

Claudia. As she spoke, the fingers of her left hand played with the thin strap of her dress on her right shoulder. A simple unconscious mannerism but I found it pleasingly disturbing, a combination of her drawing my attention to her bare arm, the thought of the strap slipping off the shoulder and the suggestive motion of her fingers. At one point she said of the woman in the story, 'She stroked him, very gently, with her fingertips.' I wondered if she knew how she was arousing me. She looked as innocent as if she had been talking about insurance.

When she finished, I said, 'I like your story. And you narrate it beautifully. I bet you don't tell *that* story in school.'

She laughed. 'I once told it late at night, at a party, to mixed company. The guys said it wasn't credible, a male fantasy, no woman would behave like Claudia. The women said that on holiday and in the sun, anything could happen.'

The story set me thinking. I said, 'We experience millions of incidents, most fly away into nothingness, but not all. A number of episodes are saved, in sharpest clarity, in our memory. For the remainder of our lives, we can bring to mind that particular happening, or mood, as if we were there, the bad as well as the good. They define us, give shape and meaning to our lives, so we view them nostalgically. For both Vital and Claudia, it wasn't simply an ephemeral quick shag on a beach. It had lasting significance. They experienced that moment of magic, of transformation, like connecting to a piece of music, a joy to be ever remembered. The fact that it arrived from nowhere and vanished as suddenly, added to its mystery.'

'That's very sage coming from someone in their...late twenties?'

'Early thirties. If I may be equally impertinent, how old are you?'

'Thirty-eight.'

'Really! You can slice a few years off that.'

'Thank you.'

'And there are moments,' I continued, 'what if moments when paths diverge. We happen upon one path, but the other would have led to a completely different life. Claudia and Vital could have made a life together, had children, gone to Argentina...it's the butterfly effect. A word, a look, a gesture at a critical moment could propel you towards a completely different end.'

And surely, I thought, her choice of story was not without significance. Was *Awakening Desire* intended to awaken *my* desire? Was I, I asked myself, being invited to make a pass?

'Is the story in any way autobiographical,' I asked. A thin line of chocolate was smeared into the crease where her lips met; a flick of her tongue and it was gone. She laughed, then sat back, placing her hands behind her head, pushing her neat breasts forwards and upwards. 'No, it's all made up.'

I glanced towards the window, then took her hand and led her into the garden. It now was a place of enchantment, the unremarkable made mysterious by the fleeing light. Trees hushed in silhouette, the air cooling, the sustained song of a blackbird. We turned towards the west and gazed at the sky over Haybury Hill. The rounded outline of the down was just discernible, black, beneath the crimson blush, the final goodbye of the parting day. I put my arms around her, then she turned and kissed me.

This kiss was not the tentative, almost chaste, meeting of lips after our dance. This was deliciously erotic in which my whole being, mind and body was subsumed. I lost consciousness of all around me, overpowered by the pleasure of our twisting tongues. When we eventually, reluctantly, disengaged, I knew for certain she was as eager as I was to make love.

I whispered, 'Would you like to invite me to your bedroom?'

She said, 'Now why should I wish to do that?'

I laughed, 'Oh, come on, don't play the innocent. Admit

it, your choice of *Awakening Desire* was as ingenuous as Julia choosing to wear a low-cut blouse. You knew exactly what you were doing.'

'A woman should be free to wear whatever clothes she fancies without concern for randy men.'

'For sure, but with Julia, titillating randy men was precisely her concern. But enough of this, are you going to invite me to your bedroom?'

'Yes.'

I went to clean my teeth then, wearing just my underpants, went into her room. She was in the bathroom. I got into bed. She took forever with her ablutions. It's always a mystery to me what women have to do before going to bed. She came out wearing a thin nightdress and smelling delightful and got into bed with me. I always found that first contact of skin on skin utterly delicious. Soon relieved of pants and nightdress, we kissed and stroked each other to a delirious arousal.

'Damn it,' I said, 'd'you think I ought to go and look for a condom?'

'You don't have to have any worries concerning me. What about you?'

'Ditto.'

I pride myself on giving the women I sleep with a good time. I try to ensure they climax before I do. I stroked her clitoris but I wasn't doing it right and she pulled my hand away. I lay on top of her and came before I meant to. I was annoyed with myself that I'd fumbled it, literally. I thought I'd make amends by going down on her, but she said, 'It's OK,' and pulled me back up. I lay on my back, my arm around her neck, her body stretched out against mine.

I said, 'Are you sleepy?'

'No. I like being in your arms.'

'Tell me another story, a romantic story.'

She gave it thought. 'This story is all about the power of the written word. It's called *Maureen McCulloch*. She's a romantic, having to choose between romance and reality.'

The story was of a young woman in Ireland in the 1940s who gets married, sensibly, to an accountant, a good man, but unexciting. Some years later, she's tempted by a young poet. When the story was concluded, I burst out laughing.

'What?'

'It's the same story as you told me earlier: a brief sexual encounter having lasting significance, and the potential for a different path, a different life.'

'Didn't you like it?'

I kissed her, 'It was great and I love listening to you. If you had been Maureen, what would you have done, gone off with Fergal the poet or stayed with Lorcan the accountant?'

'I know that you, the romantic, would have chosen the poet and then discovered he's a frightful egoist and an alcoholic. Lorcan, although boring, is a decent father. You can always go to the cinema and find romance on the screen. What do you think is the answer to the question posed by the story, is it possible to fall in love with a person solely through what they write?'

'Absolutely.'

'What makes you so certain?'

'My Grandad as a young man was away fighting in the Second World War. A friend gave him the name of a nice girl to write to. He did and through their letters they fell in love and she became my Gran. Until Grandad died, they had a long and happy marriage. Nowadays, people become attracted to each other through writing online before meeting. I wonder how many of those work out.'

I awoke sometime of the night. She was asleep, breathing gently, lying against me, her arm draped across my chest. Rachel, I tested her name on my lips. I felt supremely happy, a bubbling contentment that I'd never had before. It was as if I had commenced upon an exciting journey. Kev had said she was gorgeous; he had seen it before I did. Strange how much my perception of her had altered. Why had I not been immediately struck by how beautiful she was? I thought through every detail of our meeting, of the car stuck in the ditch, of the time at school and then the walk back. I recalled coming into this room while she was in the bath, seeing the little posy of flowers she had picked, the blue dress and the airy white panties floating on top. My mind drifted on re-visualising our dancing, our first kiss, the meal, that daring story, *Awakening Desire*, it certainly did. And then, in the garden. It was all meant to be.

When I next awoke, in the curtained morning light, she was in the shower. I went off to my bedroom to shower and dress then I went down to prepare breakfast. I turned towards her as she came into the kitchen. She was wearing yesterday's turquoise tee-shirt and denim shorts and carrying the rucksack. I wanted to put my arms around her but felt inhibited. I couldn't yet gage her reaction to having had sex with me.

I said, 'What would you like for breakfast?'

'Muesli, if you have it, orange juice, tea.'

It was another fine, sunny day. I opened the doors to the garden.

I said, 'How are you fixed, could we spend the day together?'

'That would have been lovely, but sorry, I need to get back. There's a train from Standhope at five to twelve. It's a Sunday service, so not many trains.'

'I'll run you there in the car. Anyway, have breakfast.'

I could see her paperback sticking out of the front pocket of her rucksack.

I said, 'How's the book?'

'What book.'

'The one you brought with you.'

'I don't know yet. I've only just bought it. A friend recommended it. I always like to have something to read.'

About eleven-o'clock, I put a couple of frozen croissant in the oven.

I said, as I made coffee, 'You said that the story *Awakening Desire* was fictional, but that's not true of *Maureen McCulloch* is it?'

'What makes you think that?'

'It has the feel, at least in part, of being based on someone's real experience. And you said you had Irish connections.'

'Maureen was my grandmother. Her daughter was my mother.'

'So your grandfather was a poet?'

'We don't know if he *was* my grandfather. As far as I know, that volume of poetry was the only thing he published.'

'Have you no desire to go and find him?'

'Maybe one day.'

We arrived at the station with five minutes to spare. I stood holding her, not wanting to let her go. She took out her mobile, 'Let me have your number.'

One final quick kiss, 'Ring me,' I said, and she was gone.

In the following days, she was always on my mind. Past hook-ups had slid away without consequence, but with Rachel it was different. I was wanting to see her, hear her speak, enjoy her company. I waited for the phone call. It never came. I thought, she must be busy, or she didn't have my number correctly. But then she did have my address. I cursed not having her surname or phone number. I didn't even have, as she did, a photograph.

After three weeks with no contact from her, I decided I couldn't just let her disappear into a fading memory. I wasn't going to be like Vital in her story. I, at least, would go looking for my Claudia. I needed help. Kev's brother-in-law, Pete, was a policeman. 'Kev,' I said, 'you've got to persuade him to help me find her.'

'She has your phone number. She knows where you live.

She's not contacted you. Forget it, mate.'

'I've got to try. I've never met anybody like her.'

'Look, you had a great one-night stand, you lucky devil. Move on, enjoy the memory.'

'I'll always regret it if I don't attempt to see her. I need to understand how she feels. Things were great between us, and when we parted, I had every reason to believe we would see each other again. If she doesn't want to further a relationship with me, that's OK, but I need to hear that from her. Is that too unreasonable? Come on, be a pal.'

'What do you want him to do?'

'Her name's Rachel, she's an archaeologist and lives in Buckinghamshire. Could you ask him to try to find her telephone number?'

'Not much to go on.'

A few days later Kev told me, 'Pete says there's no Rachel registered with CIfA, the Chartered Institute for Archaeologists.'

'D'you think all archaeologists are registered?' I said to Kev. 'Or perhaps she's registered under her first name but Rachel's her second name, the one she prefers to use? People do that.'

Kev had a different explanation, 'She tells stories. Maybe she would like to be an archaeologist but actually works in Tesco.'

If I could narrow the search down to a single town it would help. Just one idea occurred to me. The chance of success I knew to be unlikely, but it was all I had. The internet informed me that in Buckinghamshire, Waterstones bookstores were to be found in Amersham, Aylesbury, Chesham, High Wycombe and Milton Keynes. I drove to High Wycombe and found the bookshop. There was a young woman, not the manager, on duty.

I gave her my nicest smile and said, sweetly, 'Good morning. I'm conducting research for an article on the extent to which book groups give support to their local book shop rather than buy their books online. I'm concentrating, initially, on one or two titles favoured by book groups, starting with *Knowledge of Angels* by Jill Paton Walsh.'

'What do you want to know?' said the young lady.

'Do you stock the book? How many were sold in the last year? When was your last sale?'

If I got a positive response, perhaps a sale of the book in May or June, then at least I'd have a clue as to where she might be living. She could have paid by cash, but if she'd used a credit card, her name would be recorded. I'd no idea how I could access this information. If it came to that, I'd have to blag it.

She typed the title into "search".

'We don't stock it. We've sold two copies in the year, the last was in December, probably a Christmas present. Is there anything else I can help you with?'

'Not for the moment, thanks. You've been a great help.'

I tried Amersham, they had two copies, but hadn't sold any in the year. Chesham didn't have it in stock. I then drove on to Aylesbury.

I walked into the store and asked to see the manager. She led me upstairs into a tiny cramped office and invited me to sit down. I started on my spiel.

'Graeme, what the hell are you doing here?'

I turned round. 'Sara!' I jumped up and gave her a hug. 'How good to see you. I could ask you the same question.'

'I work here.'

'Since when?'

'A year ago.'

'I'm doing research into sales of a book.'

The manager, looking at her computer screen, said, 'We do stock *Knowledge of Angels*, and the last copy sold was on the 2nd of June.'

Sara said, '*Knowledge of Angels*?' She paused, looking at me intently. 'I think we need to talk. I have lunch in quarter of an hour. Go to the salad bar on the right as you leave the shop. Wait for me there.'

I really liked Sara. We had a relationship on and off for two years. It was great fun while it lasted. We parted perfectly amicably when she replaced me with a woman friend. Since then, three years ago, we had remained in tenuous contact. Fantastic good fortune that she worked at the shop, she might be able to help me with my search.

As soon as she had brought her lunch salad to the table, she said, 'I sold that book on the 2nd of June.'

'To a woman, spiky blonde hair, thirty-eight?'

'Yes, Elaine.'

'Elaine?'

There was a pause. Then she said, 'I see. What name did she give you?'

'Rachel. Why did she not use her real name?'

'Look, I'm caught in the middle here between two good friends. I don't want to offend either of you. I will give you her number and address, and then it's up to her.'

'At least tell me her surname?'

'Driscoll.'

Sara refused to say any more then left to go back to work. I spent the afternoon climbing Coombe Hill with its fantastic view over the Vale of Aylesbury. I was full of questions. Why did Rachel, or rather Elaine, give me a false name? Was the fact that she was a friend of Sara's a coincidence? It was possible, Aylesbury wasn't so big a town. If it wasn't a coincidence, her arrival at my house was not serendipitous. What about the woman in the ditch? Was that a fortuitous excuse to talk to me? If she intended to see me, was she just lucky to find me at home? Sara had said, 'then it's up to her'. What was up to her? I decided to drive to Rachel's...no, not Rachel's, Elaine's house.

She lived in a small two-storey semi in a leafy suburb of Aylesbury. The front lawn and flower beds were neatly cared for. I rang the doorbell, there was no answer, she wasn't back yet from work. I sat in my car to wait. At six-thirty she parked in the street and carried bags into the house. She looked tired. My heart flipped when I saw her and I knew why I had gone to all this trouble. I gave her five minutes, then walked to the door and once more rang the doorbell.

I laughed at her amazement when she realised who I was. I said, 'Hello, Rachel.'

Immediately recovering her poise, she said, 'Come in.' She ushered me through a hallway into the kitchen at the back. It was all very tidy and modern with an expensive, oval, polished wooden table by the window with its view over a small rectangle of lawn. Blue tits were competing for nuts at the bird feeder. Pinned to a cupboard was a month by month calendar with numerous pencilled entries. An open bottle of Pinot Grigio was on the table with a glass already half empty. She saw me looking at the wine and said, 'Would you like a glass?'

We sat looking at each other without speaking. I was trying to fathom her reaction to my sudden appearance. She didn't appear pleased to see me, there was no embrace, she was very calm.

I said, 'You didn't phone me.'

'No.'

'Why not?'

'I thought it better not to.'

'Why?'

She sighed, 'It would only have invited complications.'

'But now I'm here.'

'So I see. How did you find me?'

'I found you wonderful.'

She laughed.

We sipped our wine, then she said, 'Why have you come?'

'The night we spent together, you can't tell me it wasn't good.'

She nodded. 'It was great.'

'You gave me to believe you'd be happy for us to meet again. I'd like to know what changed.'

'We had a good time, but you're making too much of it.'

I shrugged. 'Well, that's a pity.' There was a silence, then I said, 'Why did you give me a false name?'

As intended, this jab hit its mark. She looked up at me with a frown, perturbed that I should know of her deception. She didn't make any reply. Eventually, I said, 'Your arrival at my house wasn't by chance, was it? You intended to find me.'

'I think it best if we don't talk about it.'

'Oh, I'm going to sort this out. If you won't tell me, I know someone who will.'

'Who do you mean?'

'Sara.'

She looked at me intently, then made up her mind. 'I came to see you to seduce you so that I might become pregnant. I didn't want you to find out, so I hid my real name.'

I struggled to take this in. 'You want to become pregnant?'

'Yes.'

'And you set out to seduce me to do that?'

'Yes.'

'And that was the only reason you spent time with me?'

'Yes.'

'So all the affection you showed me was manufactured, a pretence.'

'It wasn't difficult; you're a very attractive man.'

'But that's obscene. I suppose you thought, since I'm having to fuck the poor dupe, I might as well enjoy it.'

'You weren't meant to find out.'

'I'm nothing to you, am I? How do you think that makes me feel? Like a bit of bog roll, to use then throw away. Well, I tell you what, I feel soiled.'

'You must acknowledge, you are, how shall I put it, easy with your favours. So you've had yet another one-night stand. If, as I intended, you hadn't found out, where was the harm?'

'Where was the harm? You still don't understand how cruel you've been. Just imagine if our roles were reversed. You say you want a baby. Supposing I had your child, your son or daughter, and kept that from you. I'd be robbing you of the opportunity to be its mother. Wouldn't you feel angry?'

'Not if I knew nothing about it.'

'But I have found out.'

'I suppose Sara gave me away.'

'Why weren't you honest, straightforwardly telling me what you wanted? I'd have been flattered.'

'Because I didn't want the father, whoever he was, having any control over my child. Men are shits. I wouldn't trust even the best of them.'

'Including me.'

'Even you. I wasn't going to take a chance over something so important.'

'Why didn't you use a sperm bank?'

'I looked into that. They give you some basic information about the donor, but what do you really know about his personality, his intelligence, humour and creative energy? In those twenty-four hours we were together, I got to know a lot about you.

'I wouldn't want a child by any of the men I know, including the married. I'm thirty-eight, time's not on my side. I dated loads of guys, none of them were right. I talked to my women friends. Sara said to me, "If I ever wanted to have a baby, I'd do it with Graeme." I asked her more about you. We spent an evening together talking about you. Then, when we had lunch, during her break from work, she showed me photos of you. That's when I decided to suss you out. Meeting you confirmed Sara's opinion.

You're clever, practical, imaginative, creative and fun to be with. You also look good. I'd be blessed if a child of mine had your qualities.'

'Am I expected to take that as some sort of compliment?'

'Look Graeme, unlike most men, you're a decent bloke. You've slept around, so a one-night-stand is neither here nor there for you. Whatever my motive, you were up for it and we had a great evening. After that, what the eye doesn't see and the mind doesn't know, doesn't exist. How would any of this have hurt you? There would have been no harm if you hadn't found out.'

'Do you know if you're pregnant?'

'My period arrived a week ago.'

'Optimistic to hope you might succeed on the first attempt. Or were you planning to pay me a second visit?'

'I was thinking of it.'

'Difficult to carry through your disappearing act again without losing anonymity. Tell me, are you and Sara lovers? Are you lesbian?'

'No, I wish I were.'

'Why do you hate men so much?'

'As a heterosexual woman, I'm attracted to men, but they always fail you. I've had four long-term relationships and in each case, the guy turned out to be a shit-hole. Oh, of course, great to begin, then they reveal their true nature. Aggressive, domineering, unreliable, arrogant, boring, self-centred, drug- and drink- dependent, I've suffered them all. I wouldn't let a child of mine near any of them.'

'It seems you're as misdirected in your choice of partner as I am. I think I'd better go.'

And so I quickly left. I'd been a very willing victim. To perpetrate her deception, she'd had to do nothing but respond positively to my advances. My cockiness ensured that I never questioned her readiness to go to bed with me. I had assumed she was enamoured by my charm. Hurt pride? Absolutely. I'd so readily accepted faked response for genuine affection. It left me feeling foolish.

Over the next few weeks, to put her out of my mind, I applied myself to my work with more than my everyday vigour. But, at odd moments, she would invade my thoughts. Snippets of conversation and snapshots of interaction from that Saturday in June would arrive unbidden. Her first words of greeting, surely not unconscious irony, and that blissful moment in the garden when she leaned back into my arms. I now knew that she had made herself do that, but this knowledge didn't efface the memory of the pleasure I felt at the time, like a kiss that lingers whatever the motive of the giver.

Kev was as helpful as ever, 'Tell her *I'll* help her out.'

Then, after five weeks, I received a letter. Not an email, not a text, not a phone call, but a letter, hand-written on textured paper, dated 7th August.

Dear Graeme,

You're angry with me, and most like you'll screw this letter into a ball and bin it. But, when you came to my house, you said if I'd told you straight-out what I wanted, you'd have been flattered, and this makes me think that, in spite of all, you might, you still just might, be willing to help me.

I'm determined to try everything to have a baby. If necessary, I will apply to a sperm bank and accept whatever that provides. Of course, even if one chooses one's mate, there's no predicting the nature of the child – siblings can be so different. But at least some of the qualities of the parents are passed on to their offspring. Of all the men I've met, you're the only one I would choose to father my child. Yes, that is a compliment to you. I'm not alone in my opinion; Sara, who knows you far better that I do, sings your praises.

You have no reason to think well of me, but you have compassion and you might find it in your heart to forgive my original deception. I'm asking if you would help me to have a child. If I don't receive a reply from you, I'll have your answer and you won't hear from me again. If you do decide to respond, it will be an act of great kindness.

Elaine.

Written with her typical directness. I noticed the letter didn't contain an apology, too proud to say sorry. With the words, 'damn the woman', I tossed the letter into the bin, only subsequently to retrieve it. The truth of it was that I wanted to see her again.

Not to appear over eager, I counted ten days, long enough for her to think I was not responding. I considered carefully the mode of my reply and chose, as she had done, a letter, more formal than email. I sent it by the morning post of Saturday 20th August.

Dear Elaine,

I cannot but admire your cheek. You worm your way, like a con-man, into seeking what you want by subterfuge, then, when you're exposed, ask for a hand-out. Even so, I would consider helping you, but I cannot give you what you want. You need a man who will tender his teaspoon of semen then tiptoe away. I can't do that. You say you want single-parent control over your child, but how could I not be involved with my own son or daughter? Having met you, spent time with you, made love to you, we can't now pretend that didn't happen. A sperm donor doesn't know his recipient, but I do know you and the child will always be mine as well as yours.

Graeme.

My bet was that she wouldn't let the matter rest there, and I was right. A week later, Sunday 28th August, I received an email.

Dear Graeme,

I admire your wish to be a true father. As with the saying, "I wouldn't join a club that admitted me as member," I now see that a man who would accept my conditions for being a father to my child is not one I would choose to be its father. How do I solve this dilemma? Would you be prepared to accept a compromise? The child is brought up by me as a single parent, but you have regular access plus, of course, birthdays and other important events...this all reads ridiculous, discussing terms before the child exists, like negotiating a marriage contract before an engagement.

Yours in hope,

Elaine

I phoned her on Tuesday. 'Hello,' she said in that distracted way of people who answer the phone when deeply engaged in some activity.

'Hi, it's Graeme.'

'Graeme!' She pronounced my name with warm delight. 'Are you the hero to rescue another wretched damsel stuck in a ditch?'

'Employing a quick-release knot?'

'Not so quick, more a slip knot, free-running most of the time, but taut when required.'

I was amazed by the change from the formal, cool, serious manner of her writing, to this easy-going banter that from our first meeting I found so attractive. 'You're busy at this moment?'

'Work, I'm afraid, I bring the damn stuff home. I'm pleased you interrupted. What have you got to tell me? Good news, I hope.'

'You may not like it. I want my name entered as the father on the birth certificate.'

'Hmm, I thought you might ask for that. OK, I accept. We have an agreement then. Thank you.'

'When do you want to see me?'

'Unless we wait a month, next Wednesday would be the best day.'

'I'm working during the day and I play football every Wednesday evening. I could miss the match, but I'd rather not, it's the first of the new season.'

'How about I drive over after work and watch the end of your match.'

'I thought you didn't watch men kicking a ball.'

'I won't be watching men, I'll be observing a man.'

'Don't look too closely, I'm not that good. I might fail your criteria.'

'Don't worry, you've already passed with colours.'

I noticed her join the half-dozen spectators soon after the second half. It was raining with a fine drizzle. She wore a red waterproof jacket with a hood. It wasn't our finest hour: we lost and I managed to miss an easy goal. On the final whistle, we players all shook hands then, conscious of eyes upon me, I went over to greet her.

'Well done the blues,' she said.

'We've had better games. I'll take a shower and see you in ten.'

I anticipated the ribbing in the shower. 'Who's your lady friend' and ruder ribaldry, especially when I declined the post-match pint.

We drove back to my house in convoy. The drizzle had now turned to serious rain. I was thinking about how she might want to effect the transfer. Of course I wished to have sex, not just because I'm a man, but to strengthen a relationship with her. Now that she didn't need to, she might choose a method less intimate.

We hurried from the rain into the house. She was carrying a small bag that didn't look big enough for an overnight stop. I hung up her wet jacket. She teased her hair. She was wearing a red dress that looked good on her and calf-length black leather boots.

'Well, here we are again,' she said, smiling.

There was an awkwardness, to be expected, I supposed.

'Are you hungry?' I said. 'I've got some vegetable soup and there's cheese.'

Over our meal, we caught up, like old friends, with our doings since last we met. She had been occupied with her mother recovering from a knee operation. I told her of my long weekend with my brother's family in Bristol, enjoying my two nieces, Mia and Kirsty. Our conversation was bizarrely humdrum given the evening's purpose. I wasn't going to say anything, leaving the initiative to her. As we talked, I felt again that pleasure in her company.

When we were drinking coffee, I said, 'Well, what now?'

She pulled from her bag a small white plastic cup and a transparent syringe. 'Do you think you could...?'

So, I had my answer – strictly business. She then burst out laughing. 'If only you could see your face. It was worth the cost of the purchase.' She got up, came and sat on my lap, put her arms around my neck and kissed me. 'In spite of everything, you want to be seduced. It'd be a pity to miss out on the side benefits of attempting reproduction. But you must promise not to jump to any conclusions.'

As before, we went to the spare room. With the heating on, it was clothes-sheddingly warm. I said, 'Would you let me undress you.' She waited while I stripped, then I undid the little zip at the back of her dress and slipped it off her shoulders. The dress fell about her and she stepped out of it. I unhooked the back of her bra and slid my hands round on to her breasts whilst kissing her neck. With the palms of my hands, I massaged her nipples, feeling them enlarge and becoming firmer. I knelt down, unzipped and removed her boots, then reached up and, inch by inch, eased down her knickers. She was stroking my hair.

I stood up. She gently touched my cock, then tested the weight of my balls in her fingers. We held each other close, our hands roaming over back and buttocks. We kissed again, then got into bed.

This time I was determined to get it right. Barely touching the flesh, I let my fingertips slide over the inside of her leg at the knee. I kept repeating the stroke, each time rising a little more towards her sex. Her breathing grew more laboured and she opened her legs wider. As I got nearer and nearer to her vulva, she began emitting little sighs. Finally, when I reached it, she gave out a deep groan.

I took a position above her, readying myself to come in her, when she said, 'I'd prefer it if you come from behind.'

I rocked back and she rolled over and rose to support her body on her arms and knees, her head resting on the pillow and her bum in the air. I entered her. Not wanting to come, I kept still, barely moving my hips. With the fingers of my right hand, I teased her clitoris.

Her arousal was slow, but her groans of pleasure encouraged me. It was very tiring, and I imagined it was for her too. At last, after what seemed an age, she kept repeating, 'I'm coming, I'm coming.' Eventually, pushing her hand hard against mine, she gave a cry as she climaxed. My timing was near perfect and I came seconds later. We collapsed in a sweaty heap.

I woke up the following morning at the noise of the toilet flushing. I felt very pleased with myself; surely the sex we had last night couldn't but draw her closer towards me. I lay back in the bed anticipating her naked return. She didn't disappoint, walking boldly into the room.

'What are you grinning at,' she said.

Then, to my surprise, she climbed back into bed.

I said, 'Are you not working today?'

'I've appointments this afternoon, but I've arranged to take the morning off. What about you?'

'I've this and that, but they can wait.'

She lay half on top of me and I stroked her back, and then her bum. Then she was above me and kissing me, and then we were again making love.

'What was that,' I said when we had finished, 'a free one on the house?'

'Just making sure I've harvested all you have to offer.'

'Any pleasure involved being an unintended side-effect.'

'Absolutely.'

We had a long lazy breakfast. I said, 'Don't you think it's best for a child to have a dad around?'

'I've worried about that, but I've been reassured by what I've read. It's not the structure of the family that's important for the well-being of the child, it's the loving relationship within it. Children of single parents, where there's been a choice to be a single parent rather than divorce or widowhood, those children are no less likely to be happy, balanced individuals that children from two-parent families.'

'You don't need a study to know that a kid benefits from having a loving dad.'

We continued the argument. All too soon, it was time for her to leave.

Taking hold of my arm, she said, 'Graeme, I want you to know how grateful I am.'

I grinned, 'It's been a pleasure.'

'If there's no result, may we try again in a month?'

She phoned me on 25th September. I had been counting the days, it had to be bad news.

She said, 'Not this time.'

'I'm sorry, truly sorry.'

'I just assumed it would happen straight away. Can we make another date, 6th October?'

And so we got into this pattern: monthly sex alternating with menstrual phone calls. November at her place, December back at mine, then, as luck would have it, her most fertile day fell on New Year's Day. Most years I indulged Christmas at my brother's, joined there by my parents, then New Year at a friend's party.

'Why don't we celebrate New Year's Eve together?' I suggested.

'I'm up for that. I prefer to come to you if that's all right. Let's eat out.'

The weather was putrid, rain on the point of becoming hail, swept by an ill wind. Fearing snow, I told her to set out early. She arrived at six. As soon as I saw her headlights, I ran out with a large umbrella. Laughing, she tumbled into the hallway, threw off her jacket and kissed me. She went upstairs to change and came down in a clinging black dress with bluestone earrings.

'You gladden a man's heart to look at you,' I said.

'I have two gifts for you, one now, one later.'

It was a beautiful dark-red shirt. I stripped to the waist and put it on. 'Good fit. I'll wear it tonight. And I have a present for you.'

I took her into the lounge where there was a large box in gold gift wrap. I had made for her a rocking chair. She was pleasingly appreciative.

'I can see you in it,' I said, 'soothing a baby to sleep.'

The Jolly Frog was jumping with noisy conviviality and the meal was excellent.

I said, 'We don't have to go, but Kev's having a party.'

Kev's eyes opened wide when he saw Elaine; I'd not said anything to him about seeing her. 'Nice shirt,' he said, and made a fuss of Elaine. 'Champion of the assault course,' he announced.

The party was as jolly as the frog, a crush in the kitchen, loud music in the lounge. At midnight we counted the seconds, held hands and sang *Auld Lang Syne*. I claimed the first kiss of the New Year from Elaine. We left soon after.

When we got back to the house, she handed me a cylindrical package wrapped in pink paper. 'This is a thank you for being so wonderful.' It was body chocolate. We undressed. Once again I was struck by the delicacy of her features: ears, lips, breasts, bottom, all exquisitely contoured. She spread a towel on the bed and bid me lay on it, anointed me with the chocolate and started licking it off.

After a while, I had to call a halt as I became over-excited. 'Let's swap places,' I said, 'before we have a disaster.'

Each time we had made love, she had chosen a new position. This time she straddled me, her arms extended, her hands on my chest, holding herself upright. I stroked her arms and her hips and her breasts. I tried to touch her clitoris but my hand twisted awkwardly, so she stroked herself. She came to orgasm before me, then we rolled over to put me on top and I came soon after. 'Don't come out yet,' she said. Cuddled together, we fell asleep.

New Year's Day was frosty but bright, and we went walking over the downland. When she left in the early evening, I said, 'New Years come and go, but this one will be ever remembered, ever treasured.'

In spite of the promise of the new year, 17th January provided its seemingly inevitable disappointment. A week later, Elaine phoned again. 'I've undertaken tests. They can't find anything wrong with my reproductive anatomy.'

There was a silence as I took in the implications of this. 'Are you suggesting there might be something wrong with mine?'

'I'm suggesting nothing. They just said, "Keep trying. Have lots of sex." Apparently, having sex sends a message to the immune system that it's time to reproduce. It helps reduce the foreignness of sperm or embryos, and the likelihood that the body will attack them. Maybe we're not doing it enough.'

'Do you know, I think you might be right.' But this conversation, like a mind worm, wouldn't leave me. Eventually, for my own reassurance, I laid out thirty quid for a sperm fertility test. In ten minutes it told me I had a low sperm count. I sought further investigation from my GP. He gave me the bad news: my sperm were like the losing army in a medieval battle – wounded, dying or dead.

I felt un-manned, the conception of myself as strong and virile, now challenged. I was to see Elaine in six days. I thought not to tell her, at least, not immediately. But my conscience pricked me on.

In a bitter mood, I phoned her Sunday afternoon. 'I'm of no use to you, defective, dysfunctional. You selected me for the potential qualities of my genes but they lack the essential means of delivery. No doubt the first check of a sperm bank is the vitality of the sperm. You've wasted seven months putting your money on a non-runner.'

She tried to console me ('You weren't to know. At least we've identified the problem.'), but I felt utterly miserable.

'Are you all right?' she said. 'What are you doing this evening?'

'I had thought to go for a drink with the lads, but I can't face that now.'

I opened a beer and sat in front of some stultifying stupidity on the television. It had been a strange time, this joint endeavour. The monthly assignments for sex. Never having to question the nature of our feelings towards each other. Now at an end. Would she look for some other man and try again? The thought was a dagger in my guts. So this was what love, real love, felt like. I had no illusions that my love was reciprocated. She had made it clear all along that she didn't want to be close to any man, and I accepted that was the condition. But I had retained the hope that a child, our child, would anchor us together in some form of relationship. Now at an end.

The doorbell rang. The last thing I wanted was company. It was Elaine. 'My God, it must be bad if you're watching Big Brother. I've come hoping I can cheer you up. And we must talk.'

I kissed her. 'Do you know what you're going to do?'

'No.'

'Find yourself another man with Olympic sperm?'

'I don't want to do that.'

'Really?'

She took hold of my hand. 'Let's go to bed.'

I looked into her eyes. 'Even though...'

'Oh come on, you must have noticed I've not been entirely lying passively on my back thinking of England. Let's fuck and forget our worries.'

When we were contentedly relaxed, I said, 'Elaine, you do know I love you.'

She sighed, 'I'm sorry. You can't give me what I want, and I can't give you what you want. If ever I were to live with a man, it would be you. We have good sex, can you settle for that?'

'You can't live with me, but could you love me?'

'Maybe you'd be better off finding someone else.'

'Is that what you want?'

'No, but I wouldn't blame you if you gave up on me.'

There was a silence as we both digested this conversation. Then I said, 'So, is it going to be the sperm bank?'

'I have no other options, no man in my sights to seduce.'

'I have one idea you might like to think about.'

'Go on.'

'What if I found you a man with many of my attributes but more intelligent, more stable, with proven fertility?'

'Who is this paragon?'

'My brother Matthew.'

She sat up. 'You're not suggesting I seduce your brother?'

'I wouldn't put it past you, but no, it'd be the cup and syringe job.'

The following Friday evening, we drove to Bristol.

On the way, I said, 'If you decide you want to proceed, we'll have to tell them we'll be living together. They're quite socially conservative. They'd not approve of a person choosing to become a single parent.'

'So we need to give every appearance of a loving couple anxious to start a family.'

'You got it.'

Mia opened the door and ran through the house shouting, 'It's Uncle Graeme! It's Uncle Graeme!' Kirsty jumped into my arms. I made the introductions. Matthew and Clare were fascinated; it had been a long time since Uncle Graeme had been accompanied to their house by a woman. The girls, having already eaten, were to be put to bed before our meal. 'Uncle Graeme read us a story,' they chanted.

'Actually,' I said, 'we have with us a professional storyteller. Perhaps, if you ask her nicely, she'll tell you a story.'

'But you must come up too.'

The girls shared a bedroom. We sat together on one of the beds. Elaine's story was called 'Jamima's Sticky Day'. The class activity that afternoon was to stick cut-outs into a scrap book. But the glue ran out. Marjorie, the teacher, being busy, asked Jamima to wait, but Jamima, an impatient child, stood on a chair to reach up to the upper shelf of the cupboard for the large glue pot. Unfortunately, the top of the pot was not attached properly and crash! Jamima found herself covered head to toe in glue. Everything that Jamima touched stuck to her and soon she, herself, became a scrapbook covered in all manner of different papers. The children laughed to see her. Marjorie whisked her off to the toilet, took off her dress and washed her down. When her Mummy came to collect her, she found Jamima dressed in Marjorie's cardigan with its long sleeves hanging down to the floor. 'We had a little accident,' Marjorie said, and that was Jamima's sticky day.

The girls loved the story and the accompanying actions. Mia said, 'Daddy's always telling Mummy to screw up the tops of jars.'

Clare cooked and Matt served the meal. Conversation flowed smoothly. Matt asked Elaine where she lived. She said, 'At the moment, I still have my house in Aylesbury but...' She broke off, fluttering her eyelashes at me.

Consummately done, I thought.

All was going well until we got onto a topic in that day's news. A breakthrough in the US had identified those genes particularly associated with proficiency in music and mathematics. It was only a matter of years before parents would be able to select these attributes for their babies. Clare felt this was inherently wrong. 'You love your children however they turn out. It's the random, unpredictable uniqueness that's so exciting. Why mess with that?'

Elaine said, 'It's understandable to be chary of innovation. My mother condemned the contraceptive pill on the grounds it was unproven technology. But if gene selection *is* found to be safe and effective, why would any woman not choose for her baby all the wishes made by Sleeping Beauty's good fairy?'

'Because,' Clare said, 'there's always a bad fairy.'

Matt's objection was sociological. 'The rich can already buy themselves better education, better health, and a longer life. As yet, they can't procure higher intelligence. Imagine if they could. It wouldn't be cheap. You'd entrench two classes: the super-intelligent rich and the stupid poor. At the moment, intelligence and other abilities are widely distributed in the population giving at least some opportunity for social mobility. In this future dystopia, the poor are damned.'

Elaine was about to contest when I pinched her knee. If we were to put to Matt and Clare what for them was a weird request, it would be best not to appear, in their eyes, reckless.

In bed, that night, I asked Elaine what were her first impressions.

'I like them both. Matt is kind, caring, thoughtful and a wonderful father...'

'But...'

'But he lacks the qualities I find in you.'

'Such as?'

'Adventurousness, playfulness, charm.'

'Why, thank you. You've not had much of a chance to see those attributes in Matt. He does have them.'

Saturday gave the opportunity for more interaction. We went walking on The Downs. In the evening, while Elaine put the girls to bed with yet another story, I was quizzed by my brother and his wife.

'Yes,' I said, 'we are serious. In fact, we're trying for a baby.'

Their astonishment made me laugh.

'How long have you been trying?' Clare asked.

'Seven months.'

They silently took this in.

'There's a problem,' I continued, 'it appears I'm infertile.'

'Oh my God! Are you sure? Can't it be treated?'

The conversation ended when Elaine reappeared. Their manner towards her changed subtly, more embracing, gentler.

'You've said something.' Elaine said when we were in bed.

'I've told them.'

'What did you tell them?'

'That we've been trying to get you pregnant and that I'm not up to the job.'

'And their reaction?'

'Delight with the former, sympathetic with the latter. You're a hit. They approve of me settling down.'

'And did you raise the idea...'

'No, of course not.'

'Do you think they'd agree to it?'

'I don't know. Do you want to ask them?'

'Yes, I do. It's better if you raise it without me being around.'

I took the opportunity the following morning while Elaine was playing with the children in the garden.

'You may think this is a daft idea,' I said to them, 'and I'd quite understand if you dismissed it, but how would you both feel if Elaine were impregnated with Matt's sperm. At least our child would then share some of my genes.'

'That would mean,' Clare said, 'that Matt would be the father.'

'Yes, but I would take all the parental responsibility.'

Clare looked at Matt. 'It's a big decision, with consequences.'

Matt said, 'Have you researched the legal implications?'

'Of course. Look, think about it. We quite understand if it's asking too much.'

A week later, I phoned Elaine. 'They've agreed.'

We drove to Bristol the last day of February and were received with hugs and kisses. Giggling, Clare said she'd offered to help Matt at their end. Elaine told her I'd been practising using the syringe.

In tears, Elaine phoned me two weeks later. We made another trip to Bristol to try again. And then Elaine excitedly phoned to say she believed she was pregnant.

It was just after Christmas on 29th December, that I was holding Elaine's hand and mopping her brow as she gave birth to Alexander.

Elaine never did come to live with me. We've kept our two houses, but I see Alex at least once a week, sometimes more often and for longer periods. Elaine is happy. She has her son, her work, and, as much as she wants, a man. We often have sex, it never ceasing to be important to our relationship, a shared intimate pleasure. Am I happy? It's not the close-knit family I had wished for. Elaine has never said she loves me and feels uncomfortable if I tell her I love her. Did I make a mistake ever replying that time to Elaine's letter? Would I have been happier without her? Perhaps, but then I would never have had Alex, my joy, now and forever.

Swan

Once upon a time, there was a woodman who lived alone, remote from the embrace of the village. One spring day, he was walking alongside a lake in the silent heart of the forest when he heard cries of distress. He left the track, seeking the sound and soon found there a swan, its foot caught in a trap. Fearing him, the swan beat its wings wildly but the poor creature, exhausted from its attempts to escape, soon collapsed back down upon the trap. The woodman took off his jacket. He spoke softly to the swan and slowly edged towards it until he was able to drape the jacket over its wings. Talking all the time, the woodman put his arm around the body of the swan. 'I am going to release the trap. It will hurt you as I do so, but you must keep calm.' The swan seemed to understand.

The woodman carried the swan back to his home. He filled a feeding bottle and gave it water and milk-softened bread then laid it on soft bedding in an improvised cot which he placed alongside his bed.

That night, the woodman was amazed to be woken by a beautiful maiden. 'Be not afraid,' said the maiden, 'my name is Olesya. I went to bathe in the lake when the Sorcerer of the Lake saw me and dragged me down into his embrace beneath the water. I cried out to live. The Sorcerer relented but placed me under a dreadful spell. "I will grant you one year," he said, "but only at midnight are you able to assume your human form. At first light you will be transformed into a swan. Next winter you will be drawn down into the dark waters of the lake forever."'

Seven days the woodman nursed the swan and for seven nights, at the stroke of midnight, the swan metamorphosed into the beautiful Olesya. As the day dawned at the end of the seventh night, the swan spread its wings, circled the cottage three times and flew off to the east. The woodman was sad to see the swan leave, but, now and again, he would hear the beating of wings and welcome its return and, at midnight, marvel at its transfiguration.

As winter approached, the woodman became increasingly apprehensive. He went on a journey to find the Wizard of the West Wood.

'The sorcery,' said the Wizard, 'is contained within a gold ring. Only by wearing that ring can the spell be broken.'

'Where is the ring to be found?' asked the woodman.

'It is hidden in the crevice of a rock beneath the waters of the lake. But beware the fury of the Sorcerer. Whosoever steals the ring will discover it is not without its fearful penalties...'

***

Jeremy Bowles never confronted his partner, Jasmin, not even when, after nineteen years together, she threw him out of their bed. Mostly, this was cowardice, she was a formidable woman, and he had learned that opposition was futile, she simply ran you down. But also, he had never felt strongly enough about the issues that divided them to want to be embroiled in argument. He thought of himself as the water in a stream quietly finding a new path when blocked by an obstruction, especially a six-foot, sixteen-stone obstruction. He was five-foot-eight, and thin, with receding, dark brown hair and a gentle face that often appeared reflective as if thinking about some deep problem.

Her reasons were declared in her usual forthright manner. 'You make me too hot. You hog the duvet. You wake me up every time you go for a piss. You fart in bed.'

Jeremy could have questioned all of these assertions but chose not to. He took his clothes, books, bedside radio and earplugs next door into Fiona's room. He was pleased to be in her room, the daughter he adored. She was away studying medicine at Aberdeen. Even now, he could see her doing her homework at the desk by the window that overlooked the back garden. Or she'd be sitting on the bed, her legs tucked beneath her, while they talked late at night. Or he'd catch her scent as he brushed her hair. Her clothes were hanging in the wardrobe. The photographs of her with her school friends were on the bookshelf. He changed nothing.

Jeremy and Jasmin met while working in the health service. Jeremy still had his original job as a podiatrist. Jasmin, endowed with transferable management skills, had left the health service to work in a further education college.

With her billowing long dresses and black boots, Jasmin was as powerful at work as at home. As a dhow, she would sail along the management corridors of Walworth College. The sign on her office door read: 'Jasmin Thrupp, Director of Human Resources'.

Human Resources was a never-ending tug-of-war between the Corporate Agenda and the desires of the workforce. The job of Director, as Jasmin saw it, was to ensure the rules of contest were so framed as always to ensure the victory of the former. Jasmin recognised no need to alter her management style: students were patients, admin staff and part-time lecturers were orderlies, full-time lecturers were nurses, and middle managers were doctors. Consultants were always consultants, to be wooed and give you the strategy you desire. And to the Principal, as formerly in the health service with the Chief Executive, you played the sycophant.

One damp autumnal evening, Jeremy went to a performance by English National Ballet of *Swan Lake*. It was magnificent. Sixty sublime swans softly lit in a blue light dancing in a swirling mist to Tchaikovsky's superb music. As Act Two drew towards its conclusion, one of the swans cried out and collapsed onto the stage. There was a gasp from the audience, then stage hands rushed on and the music and dancing stopped. The poor dancer was carried off. As Jeremy made his way to the performers' door, there was a tannoy announcement that the dancer was being cared for and the performance would continue.

A burly security man barred his way. 'You can't come in here mate.'

'But I'm a podiatrist.'

'A what?'

'My profession, I can help the dancer who fell.'

A manager came up. 'What's going on?'

'He says he's a pod something or other.'

'I'm a podiatrist. I'm sure I can help.'

The manager looked at him then said, 'Follow me.'

Jeremy was shown into a dressing room. He couldn't see the dancer as there were too many fussing around. Jeremy said to the manager, 'Please ask these people to leave.' Then he saw the swan, still in her tutu, laying curled up on a chaise longue, clutching her right foot. An older woman had her hand on the dancer's shoulder.

Jeremy knelt by the dancer. 'What's your name?'

'Anushka.'

'Anushka, I am a podiatrist. Will you let me examine your foot?'

He gently undid the ballet shoe and removed it. Anushka winced. He said to the woman, 'Do you have scissors?' Then he cut round her tights just below the knee and removed the bottom part. He carefully examined the foot often comparing it with her left foot. As he worked he could smell the scent of freesias. Eventually, he said, 'You have cuboid subluxation which is a partial dislocation. Sometimes, it's possible to alleviate the condition with a technique called the cuboid snap. Often that will mitigate the pain but it doesn't always work. Would you like me to attempt it?'

She hesitated, then said, 'Yes.'

He helped her roll over onto her front. He sent the woman off to bring ice in a bag. Then he lifted her right leg so it was bent at the knee. He intertwined his fingers over her foot, manoeuvred his thumbs until they were in exactly the right position, pushed them firmly into her foot then, with a sudden jerk, he extended the knee. There was an audible snap and she cried out.

He gently massaged the foot and, when the woman returned, draped the ice bag over it.

Anushka said, 'That's amazing. That's so much better. I can't believe it. Thank you. Thank you so much. What's your name?'

'Jeremy.'

'Jeremy, I don't know how to thank you. I...' But Jeremy had left the room.

Some days after this incident, at home, before Jasmin got back from work, the phone rang. Jeremy picked it up and before he could say a word, received a torrent of abuse. His first thought was to replace the phone but then decided it was better to discover what this was all about. Eventually, he was able to interject, 'Who is this?'

There was a silence, then the man, educated but not posh, said, 'I suppose you're that cow's husband. Just tell her, she's in for trouble. I'm not going to stand by and let that bitch destroy my wife. I know where you live. Tell her to back off or else.' And then the man slammed down the phone.

Jeremy told Jasmin about the call. 'Forget it,' she said. 'It'll blow over. One of the assistants in my department is turning in a poor performance. I can't be seen to ignore it. I've put her on a disciplinary.'

Jeremy made use of the squash courts in Jasmin's college. Often his partner was a friend, Dave, Manager of the Travel and Tourism Department. After a game, they went to drink water and coffee and Jeremy asked him if he knew about the assistant in the HR Department.

'There was a scene. The husband of Mary, the assistant, came into the College and started shouting. Jasmin called security and they escorted him off the premises. He was still shouting as they threw him out. If you don't mind me saying so, Jasmin has gone too far this time. Mary's a sweet lady, everybody likes her. She's being unfairly blamed for problems in HR. Jasmin has a reputation for first embracing and promoting people she takes to, then discarding them.'

Jeremy got a call on his mobile. 'Hello, you may not remember me. My name is Anushka. You came...'

'Anushka, of course I remember you. How are you? How did you find my number?'

She giggled, 'There aren't many podiatrists in London called Jeremy. I'm calling to thank you.'

Her speech was very precise, educated with a hint of South Asia that could have been Indian.

'How's your foot?'

'It's much improved, thanks to you. But I want to thank you properly. May I treat you to lunch?'

'That's not necessary.'

'Oh, but it is.'

They met in a café in St Martin's Lane. He stood up as she arrived and when she had taken off her full-length red coat and unwound her long, rainbow-coloured wool scarf, he saw a beautiful face, light brown complexion, a long neck and black hair gathered with a red ribbon. They studied the menu. She ordered salad, he a pasta dish.

'I had to meet you to thank you in person. You were fantastic. I've been seen by our orthopaedic surgeon, she approves of what you did. I've been getting treatment from the physio. I'm told I can go back to work next week.'

As they ate lunch, she kept plying him with questions, about his enjoyment of music and ballet, about his work, about his daughter. He melted at the unusual experience of talking about himself and she seemed genuinely interested.

'But what about you?' he said.

She was from Sri Lanka, studied ballet at the Deanna School of Dance in Colombo and then at the Central School of Ballet in Clerkenwell Road. She had mixed-race parentage, her father's family originating from Australia. Her father was tall and lanky and it was from him she inherited long arms and legs that enabled her to become a dancer. He was, she said, 'alternative' with an earring and long hair tied back in a pony tail. He was larger than life, everybody knew him. Her mother was a teacher and she had one brother and one sister.

She lived with other dancers in a flat in Kentish Town. She said how lucky she was with so few jobs available and so many who wanted to be dancers. She had a one-year contract with ENB soon to run out and was praying for another job. She talked about Colombo and the beautiful landscapes of Sri Lanka.

Lunch over, there was a tussle about who paid the bill which he won. 'But the idea was for me to thank *you,*' she complained. 'Which reminds me, I have a small gift for you.' She gave him a little box, beautifully wrapped, and inside he found an exquisite silver figurine of a ballet dancer.

'It's lovely. You shouldn't have, but thank you.' He held her hands and kissed her on the cheek. Her scent reminded him of freesias, maybe it was the perfume she used. 'I've so much enjoyed talking with you. Maybe we could have lunch again some time and talk more.'

'I'd like that,' she said.

Jeremy and Jasmin were eating their evening meal in their kitchen when there was a loud banging on the front door. Jeremy went to see who it was and came back to the kitchen.

'It's Richard Jones. You know, the guy who was abusive on the phone, Mary's husband. He wants to talk to you. He looks angry. Shall I tell him to go away? I've left him on the doorstep and closed the front door.'

Jasmin got up. 'I'll deal with him.'

Jeremy heard a loud altercation and wondered if he should go to Jasmin's aid. He moved nearer the front door and heard Jasmin say, 'I've eaten smaller things than you for breakfast. Take it up with your solicitor if you want to but it won't do you any good.' And then the door slammed.

'Little turd,' she said.

The occasional lunch date with Anushka became

weekly, every Wednesday. Jeremy was pleasurably surprised that she seemed to enjoy his company sufficiently to want to continue meeting. Her presence excited him, made him more voluble, witty even. He was amazed that he could make her laugh. And she began to confide in him, telling him details of the other dancers and the directors and the repetiteurs, the wardrobe, and the technicians. She spoke of her three flatmates who were kind and good fun and how occasionally, on a Sunday morning, she would wander into their common lounge and find a strange man asleep on the couch. She made him laugh characterising the young men who showed interest in her. She shared her fears that at the same time her contract with ENB came to an end her visa expired, and if she couldn't gain an extension she would have to leave the country. She told him of another worry, 'I keep having this feeling that someone is stalking me. That when I leave the theatre at night, I'm being followed.'

Jeremy lay in his bed, in the dark. He could detect a scent, not Fiona's, but the smell of freesias. 'Hello, Anushka,' he said, without moving. He felt the warmth of her body alongside his and her hand reaching to take his hand. They lay in the darkness, side by side, on their backs, holding hands. He pulled off the bed-linen, letting it fall to the floor. They drifted upwards, a hand-span above the bed and began slowly to rotate. Behind the curtain, a string orchestra began to play the waltz from *Sleeping Beauty*. When their shoulders gently touched, a cascade of blue luminescence shimmered through the air. They floated in space, twirling and twisting, playing body against body to sustain the blue fountain of falling stars. The music changed and they floated down to the bed. He lay on his back curved as a bow, like a body in a hammock and she curled into a tight ball, gently rolling, oscillating back and forth on top of him. At the heart of her, a small blue scintillation came into being and within him, a warm orange glow. These lights revealed their bodies to be translucent. They were luminous, a blue ball upon an orange crescent. Slowly, she unwound and stretched out over him. His body was now suffused with orange light. His warmth reached the blue ball at the heart of her and, as it grew, it turned green, then yellow, then, in rising intensity, orange, then, filling her body, red before exploding into a thousand stars.

His bedroom light was switched on. He winced at the violent brightness.

Jasmin said, 'It's that shit, Richard Jones. He's outside in the street. He's roaring drunk and throwing stones up at my window. I'm going to call the police.'

Anushka failed to arrive for their Wednesday lunch. He waited two hours, repeatedly phoning her. He kept phoning during the following week without success and she didn't turn up for lunch the Wednesday after.

He was angry with Jasmin. Not just irritated as normal but distressed. This was a new emotion for him and he struggled how to deal with it. He saw now that Jasmin diminished him.

He went to see *Swan Lake* again, the ninth time. He saw her in the back row of swans and watched her every movement. How beautifully she glided, how graceful her arms, how perfect her pirouettes, how accomplished her congruence with the other swans. After, he went to the stage door with flowers and sent a message that he was waiting for her. She came and brought him to the dressing room and introduced him to the other dancers. She asked him to wait while she removed her face paint. He watched fascinated at the transformation.

She said, 'I'm sorry to have missed lunch with you. So much is happening right now. Oh, and I lost my phone with your number in it. I must give you the number of my new phone. Can we go for a drink? I've so much to tell you. And you know I suspected I was being stalked, well I'm certain of it now. It's horrible. Should I go to the police? What can they do?'

'Do you know what he looks like?'

'He waits, hiding somewhere along the street, keeping an eye on the stage door. A number of times I left by a different exit but I can't always do that. He has a grey wool hat and a black leather jacket.'

'Is that your red coat on the hanger?'

She nodded. He stood up and went to put the coat on. He couldn't get his arms in the sleeves but pulled it round his shoulders. He couldn't button it up but it had a long belt. He wrapped the rainbow scarf around his head and face and neck. As she understood what he was intending, she said, 'No you mustn't, supposing he's dangerous.'

'Just wait for me here,' he said.

He walked along the street trying to imitate how she would walk. He held the scarf over his mouth and chin.

He passed a bright shop window and stopped in the darkness beyond, looking back. And then he saw him, wool hat, leather jacket.

He crossed the road and turned down a narrow pedestrian passage, empty of people. The man followed. Now he was certain.

At the far end of the lane, he turned the corner and stood, back to the wall, waiting. He heard the man running down the passageway. Jeremy's heart was pounding.

He'd never in all his years experienced physical violence, had a horror of it. As the man came out of the lane, Jeremy kicked him hard in the shins. The man cried out and went to put his hands to his shin. Then Jeremy pushed him to the ground and threw himself on top putting his arm across the man's neck. It was all done in an instant. He was a young man, about twenty years old, with a round, fat face.

'You're stalking her, aren't you? Admit it.'

The man nodded. Jeremy relaxed his arm a little. 'I didn't mean no 'arm. I wouldn'ave done anythin'.'

'What's your name? The truth, now, mind.'

'Stuart Metcalfe.'

Jeremy held a fist above his head and looked as threatening as he could. 'Take your wallet out of your pocket and give it to me.'

Jeremy confirmed the name on a credit card. Switching on the video recording on his phone, Jeremy held it above the man's face.

'If you don't want me to go to the police, you do as I say. What's your address? Now repeat after me: my name is Stuart Metcalfe and I have been stalking a ballet dancer.' The man meekly did as he was told. Jeremy said, 'Have you no idea how frightened you made her?' He stood up and threw the wallet down. 'Don't you dare ever do this again. I know where you live.'

When he got back to the theatre, he saw Anushka in the street by the stage door. She ran up to him and put her arms around him. 'I was so frightened. Thank God you're all right.' She was shivering from the cold. He put her coat around her shoulders.

When they were in the pub, he showed her the video on the phone. 'I'd be most surprised if you saw him again.'

'You're amazing, I don't know how to thank you?'

'Just seeing you dance is thanks enough.'

'That's soon coming to an end. My year with ENB is up in a month and my visa runs out at the same time. I applied for an extension but it was refused, ballet dancers are not valuable immigrants. I have 28 days after the visa expires before having to go back to Sri Lanka. It seems my dream of a ballet career in Britain is coming to an end. You must come and see me in Sri Lanka. I'll enjoy introducing you to my parents and showing you all the sights.'

'I know I shouldn't be saying this but people do stay here illegally.'

'What sort of life would that be? I wouldn't be able to apply to one of the prestigious ballet companies. I'm better of trying my luck with the US or Australia.'

'My life is changing also. I'm going to leave my partner.'

'My God, why?'

'I'm irrelevant to her life and I feel suffocated.'

'Where are you going?'

'Dunno. I've got friends. I'll ask them if I can stay until I set myself up somewhere.'

'If you're stuck, there's always our couch, not very comfortable mind. Hey! You could take my room after I've gone. It'll do you for a while.'

Weightless, in the dark, Jeremy floated face down, six foot in the air above his bed. He drifted downwards and found there a body. As he touched it, small filaments of blue light floated like dandelion seeds into the air. He knew it was Anushka. Responsive to his touch, she too rose and floated in the air. They cavorted, producing more and more thistle-down so that the whole room coruscated with tiny points of blue lights. As their bodies dipped and dived like dolphins, the thistle-down swirled about, carried by tides of air.

As their play became more sensuous, their bodies energised and he felt a surge of dynamism. Everywhere was bathed in blue light. Then Anushka's body glowed orange and red. He was a blue planet drawn irresistibly towards an orange sun.

He slowly drifted towards her, and he felt her fire ignite the blue ball within him. How different it all was. The sensations not out there, beyond, distant, but right within the heart of him. The fire within, kindled and grew, and then, when the sensations exploded, shock waves resonated unlike anything he'd experienced before.

Sunday morning and he had come round to see her flat and possibly meet her flatmates. The small kitchen was very tidy, surfaces cleared, even the gas hob had been spotlessly cleaned. The awkwardly elongated lounge had a television and sofa but wasn't an inviting room in which to relax. In contrast, her room was lovely. It was large and full of light, a south-facing Victorian bay window overlooking the quiet street. She had a double bed with white linen and a large wardrobe and bookshelves and hi-fi and it smelt of freesias.

'I'm very lucky, I have the best room.'

They went to the kitchen while she made coffee. A young man, barefoot, dressed in tee shirt and shorts came in.

'This is Michael.'

Michael smiled, filled a glass of water and took it back to his room.

'I've moved out,' he said. 'I'm staying with friends until I find another place.'

'I'm sorry. It must be horrid after so many years together. Have you told Fiona?'

'Yes, she understands. Enough of my worries, what about you?'

'I've told Michael and Julia and Semele that I'll be leaving in just over a month. I haven't yet booked my flight. I'll be sorry to leave this room. I've been happy here.'

'How much do you want to stay? In the UK I mean. Would you have stayed here if your visa hadn't run out?'

'If I could have found work as a dancer, yes. I think there was a reasonable chance ENB would have given me another contract. And I'm sure they'll give me a good reference. I would have applied to other ballet companies as well. But it's pointless to speculate, isn't it?'

'There is one way. You could get married.'

'Married?'

'If you were married to a UK national you could stay here.'

'A marriage of convenience you mean?'

'Yes.'

'Pretending to be married? To a complete stranger? And don't these things cost loads of money?'

'I was just thinking, if it were of any help to you, to your career, you could marry...me.'

'You!'

'We'd need to put on a bit of show for immigration but other than that nothing need change except you'd be allowed to live and work here.'

'But aren't you married already, to Jasmin?'

'We never married.'

'But supposing you met somebody and you wanted to marry? It could happen.'

'Well, that goes for you too. We'd get a divorce.'

'But isn't it illegal?'

'We'd have to pretend we're going to live together.'

'But what about Fiona and your friends.'

'Why do I need to tell them? Eventually, I'd explain to Fiona what happened.'

'It's not the way I ever imagined getting married. Why should you do this for me?'

'I think you're a wonderful dancer and...I've grown very fond of you. Why don't you think about it?'

Anushka consulted her flatmates. They were: sympathetic, concerned, congratulatory, worried, supportive, challenging and everything friends should be. They thought she should: jump at his offer, be very careful, find out more about him, have nothing more to do with him, contact her parents, not contact her parents, look for work in the US, stay in the UK illegally, return to Sri Lanka. But, if she were to get married, then, they insisted, she must invite them to the wedding.

They told her to take her time in making a decision but if she was going to vacate her room they wanted a month's notice so as to find a new tenant, the rent being divided four ways. They said that, for a while, they were willing for Jeremy to be offered the lounge. Julia said that her dance company was about to go on tour and that Jeremy was welcome to her room while she was away. They all thought it would be great to have a resident podiatrist, especially if he could offer foot massage.

Two days later, Anushka arranged to meet him at 6pm

for a drink. He felt every bit as nervous as if he'd proposed a real marriage. Would she accept him? She'd chosen the bar at The Swan at the Globe. Was this auspicious? The sky and the Thames were leaden but the view was magnificent. She had mineral water, he asked for a beer. She looked at him and then said, 'I accept.' And then she burst into tears. He put his arm around her shoulders.

'You've been so good to me,' she sobbed.

Jeremy met Dave for another game of squash even though he was nervous that he might bump into Jasmin at the College.

'Oh don't worry about that,' Dave said, 'she's gone.'

'What!'

'You know that brouhaha about Mary Jones, well Mary took the College to an industrial tribunal for harassment and won. Full reinstatement: damages, legal costs, the lot. Jasmin's position became untenable; nobody would work with her. The Union passed a vote of no confidence, not that that meant much but it showed the strength of feeling. She started applying for other jobs and, with a glowing reference from the Principal, she got one.'

'Who with?'

'You'll never guess. Director of Human Resources, H.M. Prison, Highgate.'

'Good God!'

After their game, Jeremy said, 'I'm getting married.'

'Bloody hell, that's quick. Who is she? Is that why you left Jasmin?'

'No, I didn't leave Jasmin so as to marry Anushka. The thing with Anushka happened after I'd moved out.'

'I've heard of falling on the rebound but this return is faster than a squash ball. How many weeks is it since you moved out? Anyway, how old is this Anushka?'

'Twenty-three.'

'Bloody hell! I didn't think you had it in you. And, don't tell me, she's a model from Eastern Europe.'

'Ballet dancer.'

'You've got to be joking. She'll kill you! Well, put it there, my friend. Good for you, pulling a Russian beauty.'

'Sri Lankan.'

'Ah! I think I'm beginning to understand.'

'No you're not. There's nothing sordid in this. The point is, will you come to our wedding and be a witness.'

'I'm honoured. I can't wait to meet Anushka.'

Jeremy and Anushka went to the Camden Register Office to give notice. They filled up forms and answered questions.

Jeremy had envisioned a simple ceremony: a handful of well-chosen friends at the service, photographs of the loving bride and groom for the record, and then dinner at a suitable restaurant. The first intimation that it was going to be a little more complicated was when Anushka took a phone call and cried out, 'Oh my God, Amma and Dad are coming over.'

Throughout the separation from Jasmin, Jeremy had confided in Fiona, phoning her almost daily. But he shied away from telling her about the marriage. He couldn't say it was a love match but didn't want to admit to a deception. Now that Anushka's parents would be at the wedding, Fiona had to be invited whatever her reaction. He and Anushka had agreed upon a prenuptial contract that upon his death all his estate would go to Fiona, not that he had much estate to leave her.

Fiona's reaction surprised him in its vehemence – 'Bloody immigration laws. Dad, you're a saint.' – and then she asked him for the money to buy a new wedding dress. She agreed that it was best not to let Jasmin know, seeing as how vindictive she could be. Once again, he rejoiced in his daughter.

Anushka said she wanted to invite friends she had made in London and Jeremy invited his oldest friend Duncan to be his best man. That made twelve and Jeremy reserved a small reception room in a well-reviewed Sri Lanka restaurant. He also booked hotel rooms for Duncan and Anushka's parents who were staying for a week. He bought a ring and ordered flowers. He contacted the Register Office again to agree the procedure. With some difficulty, he arranged cover for three days off work.

At Anushka's request, he went with her to greet her parents at Heathrow. Amma and Anushka fell into each other's arms and cried. Glenn, six inches taller than Jeremy, pumped his hand, and in a loud voice said, 'Jeremy, from the bottom of my heart I want to thank you for what you're doing for my daughter. We're so proud of her. All her life she's dreamed of dancing in the Royal Ballet and you're helping her to achieve that dream.'

Anushka said, 'Oh Dad!' then hugged and kissed him.

Jeremy, with most of his stuff in storage, moved what he had into Julia's room. It was very girlie, pink and stuffed toys and soft cushions and a dressing-table laden with make-up and the scent of powder and deodorant. Anushka went off with her parents, sightseeing and shopping and to buy her wedding outfit. Before her ENB contract expired, she had one final performance of *Swan Lake* so that Amma and Glenn could see her dance on the London stage.

Much to Jeremy's relief, Fiona and Anushka liked each other. He offered to book a hotel room for her but she insisted she preferred the couch in the flat. Duncan arrived and they had a stag night, just the two of them. Duncan said, 'You really like this woman, don't you? Be careful you don't get hurt.'

The wedding day was frosty but sunny. Fiona and Amma told Jeremy he was not allowed to see Anushka's wedding dress until the register office, so, in the afternoon, he was sent off to meet the others in a pub in Camden.

They gathered in the Register Office. Thank goodness it was warm. When things were ready, the door opened and Anushka came in with Amma on one side and Glenn on the other. Fiona came behind them. Anushka looked beautiful. A simple, light-blue dress, sleeveless, gathered at the neck and waist and falling to her ankles with matching soft shoes. It showed to perfection her hair, her sinuous figure and her long arms and legs. They walked forward to music from *Swan Lake*. Everybody was smiling. The service was short and matter of fact. There were no speeches. The registrar had a private word with bride and groom and it was all over. They were man and wife.

Following the meal, Dave shouted out, 'What about a speech?'

Glenn stood up, a glass of whisky in his hand, 'I'd like to say a few words in praise of our daughter and this amazing chap here. There's nobody on this planet as obstinate as Anushka. When Anushka was a child, we went on a visit to Yala National Park. We had an exciting guided night trek to a water-hole to see wild boar but they didn't come so we walked back to the visitors' bunk house. Next morning, Anushka was not to be found. We were out of our minds. Eventually we discovered her, fast asleep, by the water-hole. She'd taken a torch and made her way back to the hole to wait for the wild boar. We were so angry with her but you had to admire her persistence. And that's why she's now a rising ballet star.

'And now to turn to this gentleman. We all know how he rushed to Anushka's aid when she suffered her injury. We know how he single-handed took on a stalker – just as well I didn't get my hands on the feller. And, most of all, we all know the great service he's now bestowing on Anushka. He has recognised the gifts she has and it's our great good fortune he should so serendipitously enter our lives. I salute you sir. Please raise your glasses to the bride and groom.'

Jeremy and Anushka were called upon for speeches. Jeremy declined. Anushka stood up. 'I've been saving this news for this moment: English National Ballet have offered me another year! I don't believe in fate, you have to make your own future, but when a certain person walks forward out of an audience and becomes your guardian angel, it's hard not to think that this was all meant to be.'

He was lying in a garden. Everywhere was suffused in a warm light, the pink tint of that brief moment in one-in-a-thousand sunsets when thin clouds coalesce the red of the low sun with the deep blue of the sky. It was very still and quiet until he heard the beating of wings and, from out the sky, came a swan. The swan settled down beside him. He put out his hand and gently stroked the soft down of its long neck. The swan lifted itself towards him and he kissed it. The swan's solidity began to dissolve as if the atoms that composed it were free, like a vapour, to assume new shapes. It slowly transformed, resolving itself into a woman. It was Anushka. They lay together in an embrace so intimate that the love they had for each other flowed together unconfined. The pink light changed to crimson and the sun was gone and he slept.

Julia was soon to return. Jeremy knew he had to look for a place to live. He'd been very happy these few weeks sharing this vivacious household. Then one evening, Anushka, with red cheeks and in high spirits, came into the flat pulling the hand of a beautiful young man. 'Jeremy, this is Pyotr. He's to dance in our new ballet, *La Sylphide*. Pyotr, this is Jeremy who is my loveliest, loveliest friend.' And at that, she took Pyotr into her room and shut the door.

Jeremy lay awake in bed listening to the music and laughter until tiredness overcame him and he was released into a fitful sleep. He woke before dawn, all was quiet. He couldn't bear to be there when they emerged for breakfast. He dressed up warmly and walked up Highgate Road and on to Hampstead Heath. There was frost on the grass and trees. The sky, when it grew light, was grey and opaque. He sat on a bench by the frozen Bathing Pond. In a small pool in the broken ice were two swans. Eventually, with a great swoosh of beating wings, they took off and headed towards the East.

It started to snow and he began to cry. 'Silly bugger,' he said to himself, 'whatever did you expect.'

Frankie Rhodes

I am writing this, my story, while serving my time in Holloway Prison. There are so many falsehoods and fabrications out there that I want to set down the truth. Even now, three months after the trial, I am still the object of controversy. At this very moment, there are three women marching up and down by the prison gates with placards that read, 'Free Frankie Rhodes'. I'm not seeking to exonerate myself. I did what I had to do. I'm guilty as charged and I accept my sentence. I have been accused of hating men. This is not true. I am incensed against only those men who are misogynistic and violent. There are many other untruths directed against me. I now set out exactly what happened, the journey that led me here.

It began with a telephone call from my friend Amanda at two o'clock on the morning of 20th June 2012. She was whimpering and incoherent but I got to understand she wanted me to go, there and then, to her place.

Amanda, at 23, is a good bit younger than I am. She's very pretty: bobbing golden hair to the shoulders, rounded face, soft pale complexion, pouting lips, light blue eyes. Unlike me, she looks like a secretary. Even in blouse and tight skirt and heels, I'm the daughter of a Yorkshire hill farmer. We both worked at the City head office of the Jubilee Bank. We were on separate floors but got to know each other lunchtimes. I bonded with her because she's softer and more serious than the others. We went out together. With her degree in English, she introduced me to gritty contemporary theatre and ground-breaking world cinema. My attraction for her, I guess, is that I brought excitement. I took her clubbing and, being more extrovert with a wider circle of acquaintanceships, got us invited to wild parties. We complemented each other.

When I got to Amanda's, she was red-eyed. 'Whatever's the matter?' I said and put my arms around her. At first, I couldn't make any sense of what she was saying then I caught the word 'rape'. I couldn't see any marks or injury so I sat her down and made us a cup of tea. When she was calmer, I said, 'You were raped? By whom?'

'I don't know as you'd call it rape. I've been very stupid. It was all so sudden.'

'What happened?'

'I accepted his offer of a date. Jumped at it...'

'Who?'

'Michael. Michael Eastwater.'

Michael Eastwater was one of them up there, in the floors above us. Even though he dressed like all the others – short hair, hand-stitched suit, and striped shirt – you couldn't mistake him. He had a film-star face and intense steely blue eyes and a way of looking at you, cool and unblinking. Of course, he was raking it in, and enjoying the lifestyle that goes with the money. No wonder Amanda jumped at the offer of a date.

Amanda's work brought her into regular contact with the likes of Michael Eastwater. Mine didn't, except in the lift. I was mostly responsible for typing up and circulating corporate emails to employees.

Eastwater had taken her to the classy Amethyst Hotel by the Thames. They were enjoying a superb meal, sharing a bottle of wine when Eastwater suggested they delay their dessert so as to watch the second half of the England/Ukraine match. There was a good crowd and everybody went wild when Rooney scored the only goal. In the best of spirits, they finished their meal then danced to a Latin band. He then told her he'd booked a room on the fifth floor. Would she like to look down on the Thames from up there and have another drink in the room? She knew what this meant and was pleased to be with him.

They took their drinks – 'I had a sparkling water, Michael had a beer' – onto the balcony and enjoyed the sounds of the city. The conversation was easy, they got on, Michael was charming.

'We kissed and...you know, I was up for it. We were undressing, I was down to my knickers when suddenly, he yanked them off, threw me face down across the side of the bed and…it was so violent and so painful I was screaming. I begged him to stop. When it was over, he got dressed and left without saying a word.'

I thought, the bastard, if someone's inviting you in, why smash open the door?

'There's no doubt about it,' I said, 'that was rape. What did you do after he went?'

'I wanted to leave that room as fast as I could. I thought he might come back. I got dressed then took a taxi here. I had a shower then phoned you. Thanks for coming.'

'You must go to the police.'

'What's the point? There's no evidence. He'll just deny it.'

'Even if they can't bring a prosecution, your statement will be on file. If he were to do it again, it would add to the case against him.'

'It would be awful. He might even bring a charge of false allegation or something like that. No, I don't want to do it.'

'Well, if such things are possible, will you, at least, swear an affidavit in front of a solicitor and keep it sealed until such time as it might be produced in evidence? We can't let it pass and do nothing.'

'Please don't say anything. At work I mean.'

I stayed the night with Amanda and told her to take the following day off sick.

Over the next few months, every day I went into work I was incensed that Eastwater could get away with it. When I saw him I had to fight the urge to confront him. Amanda was wonderful. An assault like that would make any victim insecure. She was more resilient than she looked. To distract her, I got us as many seats as I could to the London Olympics.

As a girl growing up on the farm, I saw sex everywhere. A hen squawking as she runs from the cock. He clutches her neck with his beak, forcing her down with his weight. Then the sudden release and it's back to farmyard peace, both scratching dust for insects as if nothing has occurred.

Autumn, the ewes, obedient to some strange invisible instruction, wait passively as, one by one, the tup mounts them. With his fat scrotum, swollen with semen, he works his way through the flock. Adding indignity, Dad straps a sack to his chest releasing a smudge of blue dye on the rump of each serviced ewe, a blue badge proclaiming, 'I've had sex.' Neither ram nor ewe seem to enjoy it. The ewes suffering it patiently like they do the rain. The ram, sighing, 'That's another one done. On to the next.' What makes them do it? I wanted to know.

I should have studied human biology instead of accountancy. Sex fascinated me. How was it possible that one collection of cells in abrasion with another group of cells could render a person crazy? I wanted to identify the springs and escape, the gears and levers that made the sexual clock work. I read textbooks to understand the progression from neural stimulation to hormonal dissemination, from vascular tumescence to nerve excitation, from muscular contraction to the release of endorphins. The body mechanism evolved to transfer semen.

My interest wasn't confined to the academic. When I came of age, it was hands on, as it were; I was a conscientious masturbator. I had a flock of boyfriends. I'm now 36 and I've stayed single, not because I didn't have offers of marriage, they came in droves, but because I'd never take a husband. When you want a new bathroom, do you ask a plumber to do the tiling? The tiler to install the electrics? The electrician to trowel plaster? Until I landed up here in Holloway, I'd three men in my life: one, animated, to take me out; another, witty, to make me laugh and the third, indefatigable, to give me sex. All three are brilliant at their trade and crap with any other. Married, your poor man has to be jack of all trades. Single, you pick your craftsman for their expertise.

And my master of sex is a paragon. He knows precisely how to deliver not just the tingling thrill in the groin, but those rippling contractions in the brain that's bliss. You can feel the rush of serotonin and dopamine. Sex is nature's narcotic.

In my way, I too am an expert. I know how a woman becomes multi-orgasmic. I can identify the G spot and the X spot and the most sensitive place on the clitoral head (it's at one o'clock if you would like to know). I love the power sex confers, that look in his eyes when I open my legs and twinkle my sex at him, watching his excitement, as if he'd opened a suitcase to reveal a million dollars. I know how to teach a man to become multi-orgasmic. I know how to give a prostate orgasm. The only sex I didn't have experience of, until Amanda's phone call, was the non-consensual.

I brooded about Eastwater. What made him do it? With the principle, 'know your enemy', I started reading the literature on the subject. I discovered that sexually violent men tend to have an exaggerated sense of masculinity and have a preference for impersonal sexual relationships as opposed to emotional bonding. They may have coercive sexual fantasies. They are more likely to consider victims responsible for the rape and are less knowledgeable about the impact of rape on their victims.

As with most women, I had an abiding fear of violence and especially rape. It was not something constantly in my mind, but an anxiety that would, for example, make me chary of being on my own late at night. There was at the heart of it a horrible feeling of vulnerability and powerlessness. Many of us have a phobia of snakes, ophidiophobia it's called, but in studying them, scientifically examining them, one gains mastery over one's fear. In similar fashion, by coolly studying rapists, I gained psychological empowerment. I understood them. I saw that they were the ones who lacked control. It didn't make them any less dangerous or reduce the need to take care, but I overcame my anxiety.

I made my conclusions about Eastwater. He certainly had 'an exaggerated sense of masculinity'. Investment banking both demanded and attracted men who were non-emotional, aggressively competitive, tough-skinned, and self-confident. He couldn't accept sex as an expression of affection. He shrank from sex as an emotional experience. For him, the thrill was in the depredation; you didn't accept, you seized. And, I imagine, he despised the femininity of women. The only woman he would respect would be one who challenged him.

It was one laugh, one little laugh, that did it for me. I was walking along a corridor and he was standing, talking with a colleague. He looked at me with that cool, calm confidence. The colleague made some remark and, still looking at me, he laughed. Something in me snapped.

The next time I saw him I gave him a broad smile. And the time after that, a nod and a, 'hello Michael'. Then, in the lift, I made a joke about how all the investment bankers like him wore fifty shades of grey. And then, when I saw him turn his gaze to follow a shapely secretarial backside, I said, 'Naughty, naughty, you need to have your bottom smacked.' This did the trick. I got an email from him making a joke about our spanking new coffee machine. A reciprocation of emails and we had agreed upon a dinner date.

I chose the restaurant: Italian, lively, inexpensive, good food. And I insisted on paying half. This was not *him* taking *me* out. He was excellent company, polite, amusing, intelligent, forthright. I asked him how he reacted to the public censure of investment bankers. I said, 'Michael, don't you feel discomforted when everybody labels you selfish and grasping.'

He wasn't offended by the question. 'Why should I? I didn't bring this system about. I take what's on offer in front of me. All them out there: government, press, Joe public, would they stand back and decline the rewards if it were on offer to them? Would they, heck. It's not some higher morality that stops them being like us, it's lack of opportunity.

'They say, we want you guys to work in Britain and keep the billions in tax revenue pouring into the Treasury. Then, having taken the money we've generated, they turn churlish and say, we'd rather you didn't take all that we offered you. Well, screw them. If they don't want us to take the bonus flowing from an incentive, they shouldn't offer it in the first place. You don't sugar the hive to attract the bees then damn them for taking it.

'However, there's something else. Our bonus derives from our performance. But then people take the size of the bonus as a simple indicator of performance. It follows that if you accept a bonus lower than is commensurate with your performance, it leads people to think that your performance is not as good as it is. Put it another way, like it or not, and of course most of us like it, you have to maximise your bonus to enhance your reputation for good performance. We can't be self-denying without injury to our status.'

We got through two bottles of Barolo which stretched my purse but was justified in this good cause. I led him to believe that in sex, I enjoyed control and dominance over my partner. I made it clear that I was up for some 'fun' with him. Before leaving the restaurant (I insisted on parting at 10-30pm saying I had some calls to make), we had agreed that I would organise for him, 'an evening of novel experiences'. Outside the restaurant, I gave him a full kiss on the lips, nauseously necessary.

We exchanged emails increasingly sexually explicit. I wrote I was up for BDSM, that I enjoyed dominance and disciplining, would he care for bondage and submission? He replied that he too preferred the role of dominatrix. I suggested we could take it in turns to play the dominating and the dominated. He snatched the hook and agreed.

I booked a room in a hotel for the following Tuesday and texted him the information. That evening, I heard his knock on the door. When I opened it, he saw that I was dressed head to toe in black leather, that I wore a red fancy-dress face-mask and that I was carrying a matching whip – 'Red suede for fantasy flogging, the ideal accessory for light and sexy bondage play' was the product information that guided my choice when I bought it.

He grinned. 'You're in role already.'

'Your turn comes later. Are you going to be a good boy and do as you're told?'

'Yes.'

'Here are the rules. Do not speak unless you ask for, and I grant you, permission. And when you do so, call me Ma'am. Is that understood?'

'Yes.'

'You spoke without permission. Hold out your hand.' I gave him a light flick with the whip. 'Now, let's try again, is that understood?'

'Permission to speak, Ma'am?'

'Granted.'

'Yes, Ma'am, that's understood,' he said, grinning.

I said, 'Have you explored the pleasures of bondage play?'

'Permission to speak?'

'Granted.'

'No, but I'd like to try it.'

I instructed him to undress then lay spread-eagled, face down on the bed. I had ropes prepared. As I attached the ropes to his wrists, I said, 'You can tie me up later.'

I attached each wrist to the posts either side of the head end of the bed. Then pulled his feet apart and tied his ankles to the legs of the foot end.

'Have you been a bad boy?'

'Yes, Ma'am.' I gave him another light flick of the whip across his back. 'Permission to speak, Ma'am?'

'Granted.'

'I've been a very bad boy. I deserve punishment, Ma'am.'

'So you do.' Then, from out of a bag, I took a dildo and showed it to him. 'You can see, Michael, it's of modest size, not like some cocks that come big and fat. Michael, I don't know if you've had much experience of anal play, it can be extremely pleasurable. Would you like that?'

'Permission to speak?'

'Granted.'

'Yes, Ma'am. I'd like that very much.'

'For it not to be painful, you must give me feedback and I must do exactly what you say. The anus is not under your voluntary control, you cannot make your sphincter muscles relax, so, if it's not to hurt, I have to wait until the muscles relax of their own accord. You have to tell me when it's OK to carry on. Do you want me to do it?'

'Permission to speak, Ma'am?'

'Granted.'

'Yes, Ma'am.'

'Before I do so, I would like to ask you, do you think it'll be clear to me when you want me to keep going and when you want me to stop?'

'Permission to speak, Ma'am?'

'Granted.'

'Yes, Ma'am. I'm sure it will be obvious.'

'Why then, when Amanda was screaming and asking you to stop, did you carry on fucking her?'

'What!'

'Amanda, don't you remember? You raped her.'

'I don't know what you're talking about.'

'You took her to the Amethyst Hotel. You had a meal together. You watched the England-Ukraine match, you took her to a room and then you raped her.'

'Rape? That wasn't rape. She was dying for it.'

'Even when she was screaming and calling on you to stop?'

'Women scream and cry out "God" and "Jesus" and "stop", all sorts of things when they're enjoying it. If she says it was rape, she's lying. Why didn't she go to the police?'

'Why did you leave her abruptly? You had just had sex. No word of endearment. Not even a goodbye.'

'I don't remember that. But what's this got to do with you?'

'You don't get it do you? I repeat my question, can you tell the difference between a person wanting you to carry on and wanting you to stop?'

I pushed the dildo firmly and quickly into his anus. He cried out, 'Fuck! No! Christ! Stop it! Ahhh!'

'Of course, no doesn't mean no, does it, Michael? People scream and cry out all sorts of things when they're enjoying it. You're in ecstasy and want me to carry on, don't you Michael?'

'Please stop. No, stop.'

I didn't want to injure him, just humiliate him. 'You're saying stop. Do you really want me to stop? Does stop really mean stop?'

'For God's sake, no more!'

I retrieved the camera that I had set up to record the whole incident, then I pulled off my mask and gloves and changed my clothes. I left him still tied up and, on my way out of the hotel, told reception that the person in 316 required room service, could they send someone up immediately.

I had taken the video recording with no defined purpose. I suppose in some way I thought I could use it as evidence, but there was no admission of guilt, nothing to show the police. I should have stopped there. I had humiliated him, but I couldn't resist a final thrust. I sent the video to five women at work. That should spread a rumour, I thought, warning that Eastwater was dangerous. I should have guessed what happened next, but I didn't. One of the women put the video on YouTube.

I couldn't be identified because of my mask, but a few days later, I was arrested; Eastwater was preferring charges. The YouTube had gone viral so it was all in the public domain. He had nothing to lose and he had all the evidence needed for a conviction.

I was charged with penetrative assault. I asked my defence lawyer, Rosemary Spiers, what was the maximum sentence I could get. She said, 'Life.' I gulped, surely they wouldn't give me life!

I couldn't deny I was the woman in the video. I pleaded not guilty. From the beginning, the case was a *cause célèbre*. For the press, it was intoxicating – sex, bankers, revenge, a court case – cocktails don't come more potent. Blog and twitter comments were ferociously divided. Some men had vivid imaginings of what they would like to do to me. Many women applauded that the issue of consent had been brought vividly into public discourse. One tweet commented that as the country had been ravished by bankers, it was of no surprise that many of the public wished to emulate Frankie Rhodes.

I was adopted by women's groups. They besieged the court, chanting, 'Now men, get the message, no means no.' And waving placards, 'Free our Frankie.'

One wretched consequence of my action, that distressed me, was the titillated interest in Amanda. Her photograph appeared in newspapers. She was door-stepped, asked how she felt about what I did and was she intending to prefer charges against Eastwater. I would have understood if she had cursed me, but she didn't. Rather, bless her, she offered to appear as defence witness and attest to the truth of allegation of rape. Rosemary Spiers' opinion was that this would only confirm the accusation against me of premeditated vengeance. Amanda was relieved that she didn't need to be called.

The court was full to overflowing. Jury selection was a palaver, each side looking for a type: the prosecution was seeking young cocky men, Rosemary choosing either intelligent, older, married men or young women. She said she would not put me in the witness box because if I told the truth, I'd incriminate myself.

The prosecution condemnation of me was savage. I had feigned friendship to win the confidence of an unsuspecting victim. I had carefully, painstakingly, prepared a vicious trap. It was in the very nature of my plan that, at a certain moment, my interaction with Eastwater would cease to be consensual and become an assault. My purpose, from the outset, was to carry through an act of revenge. In a manner as chillingly dispassionate as any hardened torturer, I had unleashed an horrific assault upon an innocent man. Finally, I had remorselessly set out to crush the victim by exposing his humiliation to his work colleagues and to the world at large.

Interestingly, the prosecution made little of my accusation of rape against Eastwater. I suppose they thought it best not to draw too much attention to that. 'Let there be no mistake,' said the prosecution lawyer, 'injurious penetration is, as the defendant well knew, excruciatingly painful, and is never less that traumatising. The evidence provided by the video recording, taken, pervertedly, by the defendant, is clear and unambiguous. Examine her face as she commits the assault. Consider the thrust of her hand with the object of assault. Listen to his pleas for her to stop while she continues with the assault. There is no doubt, ladies and gentlemen, the defendant intended this to be an assault and made absolutely sure it was an assault.'

I thought, my God, it *is* going to be life. I wanted my

defence to identify Eastwater as a rapist and show my actions were motivated by a simple desire to demonstrate to him what it felt like to be raped. Rosemary Spiers said, 'Do you really want to be a martyr? It's an admission of guilt. Torturing a torturer wins no exculpation. It still earns a long prison sentence.'

Ironically, my defence mirrored what Eastwater had said when I accused him of raping Amanda. It was the defence *he* would have put forward had Amanda taken *him* to court, that what took place was with consent. This, for the women's cause, was a two-edged sword. Like so many male rapists in the past, we too were trying to smudge the line between consent and rape.

Rosemary Spiers addressed the jury. 'I have here in my hand a dildo.' There was laughter. 'It is designed to replicate the shape and size of a large, erect penis. I am reliably informed by the retailer of this dildo that of their wide range of dildos, this is the most popular with their female clientèle.' There was more laughter.

'Would the court please examine exhibit C.' A clear plastic pocket containing exhibit C was handed first to the judge and then the jury. 'Exhibit C is the dildo used by the defendant. Would you please notice that it is nowhere near as big as this the most popular of dildos. Had the defendant used this dildo in my hand, then there might well have been an expectation of pain. But she didn't. She showed the dildo, exhibit C, to Mr. Eastwater and said, "You can see, Michael, it is of modest size." Did he baulk at the thought of being penetrated by this dildo? He did not.

'My Lord, ladies and gentlemen of the jury I would like you to consider carefully the exact exchange of words between the defendant and Mr. Eastwater. I quote: "Michael, I don't know if you've had much experience of anal play, it can be extremely pleasurable. Would you like that?" And his answer, "Yes, Ma'am. I'd like that very much." And then she even repeats her request for his consent, "Do you want me to do it?" she asks. And again his answer, "Yes, Ma'am." Not once, but twice the defendant obtained the consent of the claimant to anal penetration.

'Many people enjoy playing sexual games. They fantasise, indulging even the fantasy of being raped. Michael Eastwater came to that hotel bedroom with expectation of a sexual adventure both sadistic and masochistic. He willingly allowed himself to be tied to the bed. For many people, pleasure and pain are interwoven, the one adding strength to the other. In these situations, it can be difficult to know exactly the point where pain ceases to be pleasurable. Miss Rhodes was uncertain of that limit. As soon as she established that Mr. Eastwater really did want the sexual play to end, she stopped immediately. Reflect on how different this is to rape. How in contrast this is to a person wishing to inflict pain.

'The prosecution allege that the defendant took the video to post it online with the intention to humiliate Mr. Eastwater. That is not the case. She shared the video privately with a handful of close friends. That is all.

'The exchange that took place in that hotel room was a consensual game between two adults who knew what they were doing. Michael Eastwater, for his own wayward pleasure, wanted to subjugate and be subjugated, and, perhaps to some degree, receive pain. As soon as the pain threshold had been breached, Miss Rhodes stopped the engagement. This was no assault. Miss Rhodes is not guilty.'

In his summing up, Lord Justice Siddon-Jones told the jury that the litigant had consented to anal penetration on the understanding that it would take place in a manner that would not cause pain. They had to decide on two issues: whether the anal penetration, in the manner in which it actually took place, was allowed by that consent, and did the defendant reasonably believe she had consent to the penetration in the manner in which it took place.

The verdict came back in ninety minutes: guilty as charged. There were shouts of, 'shame' and 'we're with you, Frankie'. The hearing to pass sentence took place a month later. Again the courtroom was packed with press and public. My Mum and Dad were there to give me support. Judge Siddon-Jones said, 'You have been found guilty of an extremely serious crime that brings with it a maximum penalty of life imprisonment. You aggravated that crime in that it was premeditated and then you set about creating humiliation for the victim.

'In mitigation, you are of previous good character and what took place up to the moment of the assault was with the full consent of the victim. No harm was committed over and above that necessary to commit the offence. Taking all these matters into account, I sentence you to be detained in prison for a period of two years.'

So here I am in Holloway. It *was* the hurt, degradation and humiliation of Eastwater that I wanted. I regret now that I didn't have enough fighting spirit in me to tell the truth in Court and be damned. I did... do want the world to know my reasons for assaulting Eastwater. But now that I've had time, doing time, to reflect, I've come to realise my actions have not achieved what I intended. What drove me to action was Eastwater's lack of contrition and I'd not brought that about. By returning a slap with a slap, I had hoped to bring about an empathetic understanding of what it's like to be slapped. But I didn't get the result I really wanted from him, his repentance. What, I asked myself, would achieve that?

I'm actually well regarded here. There are so many damaged women. They confide in me, seek my advice. I'm taking forward my fascination with sex, commencing a professional diploma course in Psychotherapeutic Counselling, accredited by the Open University. I want to put my interest to some practical use. There's plenty of fieldwork to gain experience in here, Holloway is full of vulnerable women. More than half have, as children, suffered sexual or physical abuse, and many, as adults, domestic violence. They shouldn't be in here. They need comfort and care and counselling.

Amanda comes regularly to visit me. She's left the Bank and now works for Rape Crisis. My three men also visit me, not at the same time! They say they miss me. I miss them. Eastwater has been transferred to the New York Office.

There, I've finished. Time to close the page on this, my story, and turn to another page, in a book concerned with very different matters – my course textbook: *Empathy: what it is and why it matters*. Come to think of it, not so very different.

Papa's Farewell

As with many in advancing years, my thoughts often dwell fondly on the days of my youth. Forty hours after my birth, Sophie entered this world both above and below me. Above, in that she was daughter to Tibor Steiner, the Grand Bailiff of the Esterházy estate, whereas I was merely the son of the flute player in the palace orchestra. Below, because her family's quarters in the palace were directly beneath ours, befitting her higher status.

She was a golden-haired, happy and wilful child and the darling of her, usually stone-faced, father. He delighted in proffering her little presents and took to having her seated beside him on his phaeton as he made the rounds of the estate. The swarthy peasant women clucked over her golden tresses and Sophie took pleasure in giving away her trinkets to their children. This grew to a habit and, on these trips, she always made sure she had something to offer. Disregarding her father's wishes, she gave away all her toys, keeping nothing except her bedtime comfort, an old woollen doll.

My mother was one of the cooks. Soon after I could walk, I was given the job of fetching wood for the kitchen. And then, as I grew older, to make myself useful in whatever way I could. The hour of dusk, before supper, we young lads were given licence to leave our labours and enjoy ourselves. We climbed trees and we played hide-and-seek. However, our favourite game was to hit a ballooned pig's bladder with long sticks and chase it around a field.

An older girl, Zerlina, from a peasant family, took to watching us. Then one evening, she too picked up a stick and started running around. We were outraged. It wasn't right for a girl to join us and she received a good number of thwacks. But she wasn't to be deterred. Long-legged and fast, she soon showed she was as good as the best of us, so we let her stay and accepted her as an honorary boy.

A number of weeks later, Zerlina arrived with a friend. Not only another girl! But the daughter of the Bailiff! It was Sophie. We were appalled and disconcerted. How were we to respond? Was she there with Bailiff Steiner's approval? Was she a spy? What would happen if she got hurt? None of us dared to confront her.

We were all standing round, sticks in hand, looking miserable. This was really going to spoil our fun. And then a servant of the Bailiff arrived to instruct Sophie to return immediately.

'Tell my father I'll be back in twenty minutes.'

Our jaws dropped. To insult the Bailiff was worse than anything we could imagine. She turned to us and, kicking off her shoes, said, 'What are we waiting for? I've only got twenty minutes.'

In the melee of the chase, we soon forgot she was the Bailiff's daughter and she received as many bruises as any of us. No tears, no remonstrances, she whooped and whistled in excited enjoyment.

The following days she came and stayed longer. We were alive to any consequences but there were none. Except we heard rumours of fearful rows between the Bailiff and his daughter. Whatever the matter, she never failed to romp with wild pleasure. We came to trust and admire her and, on occasion, seek her advice on how to behave towards the Bailiff.

Most of my work was in and around the kitchens and I enjoyed singing as I worked. One morning, my father led me out of the Palace and turned left down Klostergasser. A five-minute walk brought us to the house of the master of the palace orchestra, Franz Joseph Haydn, who everybody in the orchestra called Papa Haydn. As we climbed the stairs to his rooms on the upper floor, my father told me not to be nervous. He said Haydn had had a childhood of poverty and only escaped destitution through being recruited to the choir of St Stephen's Cathedral in Vienna. Papa Haydn asked me to sing which I did with a clear soprano voice. And so I was recruited as chorister in the palace chapel, dividing my time between kitchen and choir.

Father encouraged me to learn the horn and within two years I was apprentice to the orchestra. I no longer had time to join the evening games and both Zerlina and Sophie had dropped out: Zerlina, because she was required as shepherdess to livestock, and Sophie had become companion to a number of the ladies of court.

One morning I was told to help load carts with produce – vegetables, fruit and sacks of cereals – needed somewhere in a hurry.

Herr Haydn came to find me. He urgently required a horn player and instructed me to join rehearsal of his newly composed Symphony in G minor for which he had written four horn parts. The superintendent refused to let me go saying the job had to be completed. Haydn insisted and I was just leaving with him when Bailiff Steiner arrived. Usually, such matters were smoothly and privately negotiated to a compromise but in this situation both men were directly responsible for their performance to Prince Esterházy himself. It was a brave man prepared to stand up to the Bailiff. He had a reputation for violently losing his temper. On one occasion he had so roundly beaten a peasant who had crossed him that the man nearly died. But Haydn stood his ground. The argument was protracted and public. The two men both disliked and despised each other. Bailiff Steiner openly reviled the orchestra as an extravagant folly. Haydn thought the Bailiff an uncouth oaf lacking any romantic feeling.

They each expressed their pressing need for my immediate services and, as their argument became entrenched, they felt it impossible to defer without losing face. The stand-off stretched to several minutes. Then the Bailiff spotted a small young kitchen boy who had popped out to see the spectacle. The lad was about to retreat when the Bailiff shouted, 'Hey you. Come here. Load that cart and sharp about it. You can stand in for bugle boy here.' And with that, his face set angry, he strode away.

In April of my sixteenth year, the prince and the court set off for the annual journey to the Summer Palace of Eszterháza. The orchestra was required to follow the prince. I was eager to be taken with my father but this was refused. There were not sufficient rooms at Eszterháza to accommodate the musicians' wives and families so we were left behind at Eisenstadt.

I used much of my spare time in practising the horn, determined to make myself proficient so as to join the orchestra.

One hot afternoon in June, I had a couple of hours of freedom. I set off to climb the oak-covered slopes of Leithagebirge, stopping now and again to listen out for bells. I had a strange feeling of excitement, a sort of breathless anticipation. And then I saw her, Zerlina, sitting under a tree, a herd of sheep grazing nearby. I flopped down beside her.

'What brings you here?' she said, in a low husky voice that she sometimes put on for effect. It had its effect.

'I came to find you.'

'Why?'

I dared not put into words what I wanted. Instead, I stretched out my hand and touched her ankle. She didn't react so I began stroking her calve. She surely understood now what carried me there. Still, she didn't move so I shuffled nearer and extended my hand beneath her long skirt and gently stroked the inside of her thigh. She looked down at me and I noticed her lips had parted. All of a sudden, as if she had finally made up her mind, she threw herself alongside me and put her arms around my neck. We kissed. I hadn't known until then what kissing could do, making me quiver and shake. And, adding to intensity, Zerlina had this personal smell that to me was powerfully erotic. She lifted her skirt, I lowered my breeches and thus I became Zerlina's lover. It was all so simple. It was the most sublime moment of my life; the way all things ceased to exist except the overwhelming pleasure of the act. We lay a long time holding each other close.

Thereafter, we made love everywhere and every time occasion made possible. At the beginning, ours was a relationship characterised totally by lust. She was a warm-hearted generous girl. She almost never refused me. Only on the rarest of occasions did she say she preferred not to do it.

Then one day, after we had made love and were lying dozing in the sun, she said, 'Would you do me a favour?'

I said, 'Of course, anything.'

'Teach me to read.'

I wasn't the only one to have noticed her long legs, slim athletic body, smooth black hair and welcoming dark-tanned face. She could have had more honourable lovers than me, happy to have wed her; it was obvious she would make a fine wife. I cheekily asked her once why I was the only one for whom she lifted her skirt. She laughed and said I had a pretty face and a big cock. And a better compliment I never had.

After six months of loving, I said it was a blessing that so far she hadn't become pregnant. She said her mother had told her to avoid sex at certain times of the month. Now I understood those occasions when she had denied me and felt ashamed of my peevish reaction. I wondered why, if her mother knew about me, she hadn't tried to stop us.

In October, the prince and court returned to Eisenstadt. When my father arrived, we could see he was not well and he became increasingly sick with a fever. My mother attended to him night and day. To give her some respite, I would take my turn by his bedside. The room was dark, lit only by a single candle. Most of the time, Papa was in a sweaty stupor and unresponsive, but suddenly he became lucid and took my hand and fixed his eyes on me. He was agitated to speak what was on his mind, struggling for breath, struggling to bring forward each sentence.

'Remember you are a musician. Things are changing, we won't always be servants. Promise me you will care for Mama. Papa Haydn is a good man, go to him if you need help. I'm sorry I won't live to see my grandchildren. I know you're courting Zerlina. She's not the one for you but deal with her honourably and with respect. Do not let anyone treat you other than with the deference owed to you. Always remember you are a musician.'

Over the next two days, a number of people came to visit Papa, including Herr Haydn, and then he died. The future of my mother, sister and two brothers became uncertain; we had only ever known life in court. Mother petitioned the prince and received a small widow's pension. Papa Haydn took an interest in me and became as a father to me and I came to love him as much as my own dear papa.

Sophie was now the constant companion of the Countess Anna-Maria. She had moved from her father's quarters to those of the countess. I saw them both when they came to concerts. The two young women turned heads: the countess petite with delicate features, brown eyes and dressed in the latest fashion, a green skirt and a close-fitting pink jacket with blue shoulder pads over a red bodice, and Sophie with glorious golden tresses, amber eyes and a sturdy lithe body, more simply dressed. I often thought Sophie was smiling at me as I played but then she might have just been enjoying the music, and anyway, she smiled at everyone.

The countess had many servants. They told me their mistress was as moody as damp firewood: given to sulking followed by a flaring up. Sophie had just one servant, Katerina, who was a distant relative of mine on my mother's side. We had danced together once at a wedding. I liked Katerina. As a child, she had survived smallpox which rendered her pockmarked. However, her vivacity, like sweet music from a bruised instrument, outshone her disfigurement.

That winter was harsh. Zerlina's younger sister fell ill and they feared for her recovery. Zerlina asked me if it were possible to obtain more nutritious food for her. I stole what I could from the kitchen, but this became increasingly difficult. Knowing how generous Sophie had been, I approached her and explained. If she didn't know already of my relationship with Zerlina, she did now. She was immediately concerned and from then on handed me pickings from her table. She had less freedom than before, but one Sunday, she managed to escape with me to visit Zerlina's home. Zerlina wasn't there but her mother welcomed us as royalty. We entered the tiny darkened room where the poor child lay coughing. Sophie held her hand.

When we left, Sophie said to me, 'I have a little money put aside, let's get the Doctor to visit the child.'

And so it is that I fell in love with Sophie. But I was a mouse admiring the moon. She was up there with the princely sun: I, an unregarded servant below stairs. I looked for her on every occasion and I sighed for her like any trouvère of olden days. I even wrote poems to her beauty, some of which I made into songs trying to imitate Papa Haydn.

Even though my heart ached for Sophie, I continued, whenever I could, to walk the hills in search of Zerlina. We even made love in snow. In April, once again, the court moved to the summer palace of Eszterháza. This time, Papa Haydn insisted I stay with the orchestra, so I too made the journey. The Countess Anna-Maria had chosen to stay with the court and I was overjoyed when I discovered that she was bringing Sophie with her. Even though I couldn't make an approach, at least I could observe her and sigh.

It was July and I was now seventeen and often playing fourth horn in the orchestra. Everybody was busy. The servants rushing around servicing the many eminent visitors, the hundred guardsmen away on exercises, the peasants driven to long hours of work bringing in the harvest, especially as they anticipated rain. The weather was sultry with that oppressive heat that presaged a storm.

There being no one else available, Papa Haydn told me I was needed for a job and released from the orchestra for two days. The next morning, I was to drive the countess to the Esterházy Palace in Vienna, stop there for the night and, leaving her there, return the following day.

I was not pleased. Grumbling, early in the morning, I got the carriage ready. It was a light vehicle with one horse, Sabre, to pull it. It had two seats under a retractable hood and a seat in front for me to sweet-talk Sabre. My mood reversed when I discovered Sophie was to accompany the countess. Now I wished it were a week-long trip.

For some reason, Sophie was in irritable temper. I didn't get the customary smile as I helped them into the carriage. We set off and it started to rain. I was soon very wet but I didn't care. As depressions in the track filled with water, the going got more difficult. It was impossible to tell puddles from potholes. Three-quarters of the way into our journey, we were stuck. The rear right wheel was buried deep in mud and trapped in a rut.

I got down and, putting my shoulder to the back of the carriage, whistled to Sabre to heave forward. It moved but didn't release. Three times I tried then gave up. I told the countess and Sophie that I was going to seek help from a farmhouse. It was most unlikely we would make Vienna before nightfall. The countess was infuriated as if it were my fault. Sophie jumped out and said, 'Let me try helping you.'

I said, 'Don't, you'll ruin your dress.'

She said, 'Oh, bother with that. Help me.'

And so I undid buttons and laces and helped her take off the dress which she threw into the carriage.

She said, 'What are you looking at?'

I couldn't look away. Her underclothes, a low-cut bodice and loose fitting leggings of a thin white material, were soon saturated and clung diaphanously to her body.

She took up a position alongside me behind the carriage. I called again to Sabre and we heaved. Nothing happened. Then, suddenly, the wheel broke free and the carriage jerked forward. With a cry Sophie fell. I continued to push until I was certain the carriage would not roll back, then rushed to assist Sophie. She was prostrate in the mud.

'Are you hurt?' I said anxiously.

'I don't think so.'

I helped her to her feet. The rain was now sheeting down in a torrent, running down our faces. I put my arms around her and pulled her to me.

'Sophie, I love you so much.' And I kissed her, tasting mud on her lips.

She seemed astonished then pushed me away saying, gently, 'Go away and don't look.' Then she picked her way down to a nearby stream and washed herself.

The countess, who had remained in the carriage throughout, was aghast at Sophie's behaviour but somewhat mollified by the fact that we could resume our journey. I helped Sophie back into the carriage. Her sodden undergarments left little to the imagination. Did I imagine a squeeze as she took my hand?

On arrival at the Wallnerstrasse Palace, the servants rushed out to conduct the countess and Sophie into the house. I noticed Sophie had put on her dress. Sabre was led off to the stable and I was left to find the servants' quarters. I was given some ill-fitting but dry clothes and a dish of beans. I went to the stable to check that Sabre had been properly cared for. Preferring Sabre's company to the tight-lipped primness of the servants' kitchen, I sat on a stool and revisited that moment when Sophie was in my arms.

Then I heard my name called, softly. It was Sophie. She entered the stable and stroked Sabre's neck.

'You say you love me, but how can you when you're engaged to Zerlina?'

I didn't know how to respond. Anything I said would be to deny Zerlina and I couldn't do that.

Eventually, I took her hand, 'I believe I've loved you all my life. But only in these last months have I discovered my true mind.'

In a breathless silence, we stood very close to each other, almost touching. Then she put her arms around my neck.

My heart beating wildly, I held her close. She lifted her head to be kissed and I was astounded to feel her tongue on my lips. Although I knew her to have a strong and passionate nature, I hadn't imagined her as sexually alive. Yet here she was, trembling with desire.

Eventually, she broke away. 'We mustn't...I mustn't...' And with that she ran. You cannot imagine my joy. To Sabre's wide-eyed wonderment, I whooped and danced around the stable.

The following day dawned clear and much fresher, the storm had passed. At first light, I took Sabre from the stable and hitched him to the carriage ready for my return journey. I was nervous that the connection made with Sophie the previous evening hadn't drifted away with the rain clouds. But I needn't have worried, just as I was about to set off, Sophie ran out and gave me a hug and a kiss.

Back at Eszterháza, I was walking on air and put the energy my love had given me into becoming a more proficient musician. I was determined to earn my place as a full member of the orchestra. Every day I watched and waited for the return of the countess and Sophie. How I cursed that we were so subject to the whim of others.

Somehow the story of Sophie's escapade in pushing the cart got out and circulated; I suppose the countess must have spoken of it. I was the butt of many jokes. I didn't care. I drifted along as light as dandelion seed in a gentle summer breeze, held aloft by Sophie's love.

Then one glorious August day, the countess's carriage swept into the palace yard and they were back. As before, I kept looking out for Sophie but this time, when she saw me, my loving glances were returned. I was praying for the opportunity for us to be alone, but always frustrated. We both seemed to be in constant demand. We began writing notes to each other and seeking ever more adventurous means of delivery. On one occasion I hid a note inside an apple, carefully hollowed out. Another time, I blew on my horn and the resulting squawk led me to find the note hidden in the mouthpiece. My earlier love poems came in useful and her replies, ever more committed, filled me with joy.

In September, news came that my mother was ill. I was given release to visit her in Eisenstadt. I made the journey in deep anxiety but, on arrival, relieved to find her much recovered.

I had determined to finish my relationship with Zerlina. I found it difficult to bring myself to tell her and kept putting off seeing her. A familiar place is never more beautiful than at the moment of leaving it and my appreciation of the exquisite times with Zerlina was at its highest now that it was to end.

I climbed the hill slowly and found her in one of our favourite places, a small grassy shelf on the edge of a sheer escarpment, tucked below the cliff top so that two lovers could not be seen. She embraced me, but immediately sensed my reticence. I told her what a wonderful person she was and I treasured the times we had had together but that now I was in love with someone else.

'It's Sophie, isn't it?'

'How did you guess? I believe she loves me and it's my dearest wish that someday, somehow, we might be married.'

She started crying and I too had tears on my face. I held her in my arms and we kissed, wet kisses and the scent of her and the press of her familiar body was intoxicating. We made love. Stupidity! But it was sweeter than even the very best of times before. With repeated tears and kisses, I tore myself from her and, with a heart filled with mixed emotions, walked back down the hillside. A few days after my return to Eszterháza, I was bent over a desk, copying, by the light of a candle, the parts for Papa's new symphony, when the candle flickered and suddenly I felt a pair of arms around my neck.

'Oh, my darling, I had to see you.'

We held each other close.

'Tell me,' I said, 'tell me you love me.'

'Of course I love you but you too must put my heart at ease. You and Zerlina...'

'I've broken it off with her.'

'How did she take that?'

'I told her I was in love; she guessed it was you. She was tearful but understanding. I hope we can retain her friendship.'

'How I wish I could see more of you. It's very difficult, the countess keeps me very close.'

In the autumn, as customary, we returned to Eisenstadt. From his suite of rooms in the Palace, the prince was able to look down and appreciate, untroubled, the impeccable symmetry of the French Garden with its low hedges, fountains, and statues as tidily structured as the social classes beneath him. At the far edge of this garden, a tall yew hedge divided order from disorder for beyond it, embracing rebellious nature, was the English Garden. On either side of the wide French Garden was a marble gazebo – four Grecian columns supporting a domed roof. Except for the gardeners, servants were prohibited from entering the French Garden. It was *behind* these gazebos that Sophie and I seized our intermittent, hurried embraces. We pushed our bodies forcefully against each other propelled by the strength of our love, desperate to become inseparable. And we drank kisses with a frenzied thirst.

One cold November evening, Sophie, in great excitement, came to find me. 'Oh my darling, I can't wait to tell you, the countess is away tomorrow night. I'm free, free. I'll slip out quietly sometime in the night. Where shall we meet?'

'Do you mean the countess will be away from her room all night?'

'Yes.'

I had a vision of a large comfortable bed. 'Let's meet there.'

'Too risky. What if you're caught?'

'I'll manage it. What time do they all go to bed?'

'They usually play cards till midnight.'

'That late! I'll come at one. Everybody's bound to be asleep by then.'

In the palace, servants were under the strictest orders to go about their work, as far as possible, unseen. Within the thick walls was an entire network of hidden passageways, the digestive system of the palace, through which menials would scurry to deliver to their masters and mistresses wood for stoves, hot water for bathing, food and drink, candles and clean linen, and evacuate ashes and brimming bedpans. The room of the countess, as with many others, was furnished with a secret doorway disguised as a decorated panel which opened into the intestinal servant-ways.

Sophie explained the complicated route emphasising how important it was to remember the markings that identified the countess's door. 'But no,' she said, 'this is too dangerous.'

'I'll be careful.'

I was in a state far too excited to wait until one o'clock. Soon after eleven, carrying a new candle, I slipped into the tangle of passageways. I prayed that I wouldn't meet anybody. Most nobility avoided looking directly at underlings; it was the other servants that were the danger.

I found the door and entered the room. I lifted my candle to see the great bed, a chest of drawers, a table and chair and a large wooden cupboard decorated with painted panels depicting bucolic scenes of happy, dancing peasants. This cupboard, I decided, was my place to hide. It was full of ball-gowns. I snuffed out the candle, squeezed in and sat on its floor.

It wasn't too long before people came into the room. The light from a candle illuminated the gap between the wardrobe doors and I peeped through. It was Sophie and Katrina. I know I should have revealed myself, but I didn't. Katrina was helping Sophie to undress. I watched as the two, lit by the candle, repeatedly crossed my line of sight.

I would dearly have loved to have observed the full disrobing, but the dishonourable nature of my behaviour overcame me. I opened the door. Sophie gasped, grabbed the dress out of Katrina's hands and held it against herself. Then she flung it aside and flew into my arms.

Katrina quietly slipped through a side door which led into a tiny adjoining chamber reserved for a personal servant. I assumed Sophie usually slept in that little room. Goodness knows where Katrina normally had a bed.

We kissed and hugged each other. I was told to hide my eyes while Sophie undressed and put on her nightgown and got into the countess's big bed. Not having a nightgown, I modestly left on my shirt and climbed in alongside her. I was in a rage of desire and, from her responses, so was she.

Finding our clothing a hindrance, we threw them off, freeing our bodies to the delights of wandering fingertips. The urge to penetrate was overwhelming. I rolled over on top of her and tried to part her knees. But she held firm.

I said, 'Don't be frightened.'

'Not yet. If you really love me, not yet.'

I rolled away crushed with disappointment. She turned towards me and placed her hand gently on my chest.

'Don't be upset. I too want to do it, I really do. But I must keep my honour, the honour of my family. You do understand, don't you? I mustn't until I'm married.'

There was nothing I could say. I was cast down by a heavy weight of dashed expectation and felt peevishly angry, and vexed yet more at my inability not to respond as a spoilt child. Fortunately, Sophie was forgiving. She didn't rebound away from my churlishness.

She said, 'Let me show you how I love you. On many nights the countess invites me to join her in this very bed.'

I turned to look at her.

'And we do things.'

'What things?'

'I'll be the countess,' she said, 'you can be me.'

The New Year brought me a wonderful surprise: Papa Haydn confirmed my appointment as third horn. I was now a full member of the orchestra. One January day, we were rehearsing yet another new symphony from Papa. After a particularly beautiful passage, he stopped us, contemplative with an abstracted smile. We waited quietly to see if he would share his private amusement.

'As you know, I've been quite ill recently. In fact, the Doctor insisted I was not to leave my bed. My dear wife had to go out, and she admonished me that I must obey the doctor's orders. You know how she is.'

We did know how Frau Haydn was, she had a tongue like a whip; we were all careful not to cross her. Papa Haydn's relationship with his wife was a strange one. But then I suppose most marriages are strange. It was an open secret that Papa found comfort in the arms of Luigia, the young wife of Antonio Polzelli, our violin player, and Frau

Haydn was brazenly affectionate with Ludwig Guttenbrunn who was in court to paint portraits, including Papa's. In spite of this, there was obviously some caring between them.

'There I was,' continued Papa, 'lying in bed, when this harmonic sequence, the one you've just played, came into my head. I just had to climb out of bed and try it out at the piano. Then I saw, through the window, Frau Haydn returning. You can't imagine how quickly I dived back into bed and rearranged the covers. When she came into the room, I smiled wanly at her, "See, I'm doing what I'm told."'

I don't how Papa came to marry Frau Haydn. I do know, if ever I get to marry Sophie, it will never be like Papa's marriage.

Barely having finished performing one new work from Papa than we started rehearsing the next. A new symphony, concerto or chamber work would only get a few performances for the benefit of the prince and assembled court before the next was expected. In this regard, it was like the court comedian who, if he repeated a joke, however good it was, got booed. Painters sometimes paint over old works to reuse the canvas. Thank goodness you can't do that with manuscript paper. All of this wonderful music had to be saved.

At the end of rehearsal, Papa said, 'I have a wonderful surprise for you all, we are soon to welcome at Eisenstadt none other than Herr Wolfgang Mozart. I am sufficiently immodest enough to believe that some of my works are not without merit...' We all shuffled our feet. 'Thank you, but how inimitable are Mozart's works, how profound, how musically intelligent, how extraordinarily sensitive. Mozart is incomparable.'

Sophie was assigned the job of making Mozart's wife Constanza welcome at Eisenstadt and ensuring her every comfort. From their first meeting, Sophie could speak of nothing but Constanza.

'Constanza says they meet everybody of importance at

Countess Thun's house in Vienna; even the Emperor appears there. Constanza has these wonderful dresses of the latest fashion. Constanza says blue lace is essential. Constanza has this beautiful voice and she's always singing.'

'Oh, for goodness sake,' I said, 'tell me what Herr Mozart is like.'

'I haven't seen much of him. Constanza told me that he gets very jealous if she chats with any of the men.'

The next day, Sophie, rather breathless, came to find me; she was excited with her news.

'I've not got long, but I just had to tell you. Constanze insisted I accompany her when she and Herr Mozart were formally presented to the prince. She actually took me in there with her to the audience chamber. Of course I had to stand at the back and peer over the shoulders of the court ladies. And you wouldn't believe it, the prince actually stood up to greet Mozart as if he were royalty. Mozart was dressed in red, very fashionably, and Constanze was in a beautiful white gown. I've never seen anything like it. Mozart chatted with the prince as if they were old friends. Mozart actually laughed out loud at some remark the prince made to him. Papa Haydn was there and, I'm sure, he too was amazed at the deference shown to Mozart. Of course, everybody at Court is now seeking Mozart's company, and the ladies all want to be with Constanze. She keeps asking me to be near her. I've got to go.'

I got a quick kiss then off she tripped, delighted to be at the centre of animation.

The following day, I too had the chance to see Mozart when he came to rehearse the orchestra. I was shocked. He was not as I imagined. I expected someone distinguished with a strong profile, but he was short, about five foot tall, and had a bland face with a bulbous nose and protruding eyes. His demeanour was, however, self-assured and he had taken great care with his appearance: his hair was well coiffured and his jacket must have cost a pretty penny, red with gold embroidery, and he had a profusion of lace at his neck.

Once we started rehearsing, there was no doubting his authority. He had complete control and knew exactly what he wanted from us and insisted that we deliver it. Working with him was very exciting. He had come to Eisenstadt to oversee a performance of his opera, *The Abduction from the Seraglio*.

I turned to Gustav, who played alongside me in the second horn desk, and whispered, 'What's a seraglio?'

'Rich Turkish men have lots of wives and mistresses. The seraglio is the place in the palace where they're kept segregated.'

When I next met Sophie, I told her the plot of the opera.

'Constanze, she's the heroine – Mozart said he didn't choose the name, it just happened to be that of his wife. Do you believe that? – Anyway, Constanze is captured by Pasha Selim and he falls in love with her. But she loves Belmonte and he loves her, almost as much as I love you. Constanze says that she won't give in to the Pasha even if he were to threaten her with torture or death.'

'Nor would I.'

'So Belmonte decides, in spite of all the dangers, to get Constanze out of the seraglio...'

'What's a seraglio?'

'A place where rich Turkish men keep their many women locked up, presumably to keep them away from other men. But they are discovered trying to escape and the Pasha is very angry. But when the Pasha learns that Belmonte is the son of his old enemy, he decides to repair ancient hatreds and offer the hand of friendship by letting the lovers go free.'

'I wonder if my father could be so kind.'

That winter, Sophie and I met as often as we could. More than once, I tried to go all the way. I couldn't put aside that desperate urge to penetrate. But she maintained her resistance. 'Wait,' she said, 'until our wedding day.'

Avoiding intercourse, we explored every other sexual pleasure two people in love can offer each other. Her favoured method to gain orgasm was to slide her sex along the length of my penis. The movement was delicious to me too but how I longed for the slight shift of angle that would take me into her. Such a tease to be at the door of the one place I most wanted to be and not allowed to enter.

In February, we were in a turmoil of activity for the state visit of the Archduke Ferdinand. The palace, the gardens and the parkland beyond were given over to festivities. Two hundred nobility were squashed into the palace. A raised dais was erected in the garden to provide perspective over a performance arena. And in the parkland, a tented village came into being to shelter two thousand peasants carted in from Hungary and Serbia, brought there to entertain the visitors with their folk songs and dances.

Bailiff Steiner had the job of overseeing the peasant village: ensuring they had sufficient food and water and wood for their bonfires whilst policing illegal poaching from the park's fish and game reserves.

We musicians were intrigued by the strange peasant music and I saw Papa Haydn, more than once, scribbling down tunes that appealed to him.

Following performances, the guests were invited onto the arena to dance their more sedate courtly dances. We weren't required to play; a dance band from the town was hired for the purpose. Provided we didn't have other work to do and didn't chatter too loudly, we servants were allowed to watch. It was a rich spectacle, the women in extravagant ball-gowns of white and red and blue, the tightly buttoned lords in black and red and gold. The value of the costumes on the dance floor would have provided for a full orchestra for a year or more. And then I saw Sophie. She was looking radiant in a simple blue gown needing no lace and muslin to enhance her beauty. She was in a group of young women, daughters of gentry, chatting and laughing and soon they were the focus of men of all ages who competed to dance with them.

Sophie was scooped onto the dance floor and no sooner had a dance ended than a new man would present his arm to lead her back again. I was, of course, jealous, but also proud, proud of her success, proud her heart was mine.

She accepted the offer to dance from a man with whom she had already had one dance. And then, no sooner had that dance finished, she was dancing with him again. This was not right. She should show no favour. And he was a simpering popinjay, gaudy in bright yellow and orange, a torrid butterfly drawn again and again to my blossoming Sophie. I became increasingly agitated, ready to do damage, unregarding of my status. It was obvious this man was taking a great interest in Sophie and she wasn't rejecting him. When they weren't dancing, they carried on talking.

I was on the point of creating a furious scene when Sophie saw me. She smiled and nodded, scribbled a note and gave it to Katerina. 'Meet me in half an hour at the Diana statue by the English Garden.'

It was beginning to get dark as I walked to the English Garden. Access was through a narrow gap in a high yew hedge which screened the garden from the palace. Diana was hidden just to the left of the gateway.

We men are made such fools of by the beauty of the female body. 'Diana' was simply a classical eponym to licence the representation of a woman without clothes. To sustain the pretence, she had an arrow pushed into one hand, a bow in the other, and a quiver of arrows over her shoulder, the strap laying between her breasts. The sculpted object was beautiful. The woman who modelled it must also have been beautiful. The sculptor had been sexually as well as aesthetically aroused; beauty and eroticism married in marble. The choice of huntress was appropriate: ensnared by her beauty, her arrows will pierce your heart.

Sophie bounded through the gap, her bright smile hitting its target and I gasped in pain.

'What's going on?' I said.

Stopped in her tracks, she said, 'What d'you mean?'

'That posturing parrot, that candied confection, that gaudy gasbag.'

'I don't know what you're talking about.'

'That mincing mustardfop you kept dancing with. How could you? It was so degrading.'

'Baron von Humbolt? Is that who you mean?'

'How could you be so vulgar?'

'How dare you! Who do you think you are? You don't own me. I'll dance with whom I choose when I choose and for as long as I choose. How dare you seek to place reins on me. I am not your thing and if you're not man enough to cope with that, find another more willing to accept your controlling jealousies.'

'OK, I'll do just that. There's plenty others who'd be ashamed to throw themselves at a tinselled tosspot.' And with that, I stomped off.

Angry with Sophie, I turned away from the court and its people and sought the dark solitude of the deer park. My eyes grew accustomed to the gloom. Trees stood as black cut-outs in the thin radiance of a half moon. I must have walked for an hour when I saw a distant glow of a fire. As I drew nearer I realised that it was here, in this far corner of the palace estate, that Bailiff Steiner had overseen the erection of the peasant village.

The peasants had organised themselves into circles, each with their own bonfire and cooking hearth. They were singing and dancing and getting drunk on palinka. How natural and joyfully unsophisticated they were after the cloying conventions of the court. I wanted to be one of them; to join arm in arm with the circle of men stepping to the fast irregular rhythm of the wild csárdás, driven forward by fiddle, pipe and drum. I wandered from bonfire to bonfire observing these people briefly released from their harsh lives of hardship and humiliation, now frenzied on bonfire, music and alcohol.

Then, by the light of one of the fires, I saw her, swinging round with a young man in a furious dance. It was Zerlina. I stood back to watch her. Her white blouse shone in the firelight, her long red skirt flared as she twirled and her black boots punched the ground. The dance ended. She curtsied to her partner and joined a group of girls. I could not move. I knew I should smother my desire to go to her but I was unable to make myself turn away.

Then she saw me. Perhaps that's what I wanted, what I was waiting for. She turned and walked away from the fire. I followed her into the shadows.

Zerlina always had this habit of standing very close. Her face was magically illuminated by the distant light of the bonfire. It was all too simple to let my head lean forward to meet her lips. Our kisses became more passionate. I took her hand and we retreated further from the bonfire. We entered the dark shadow of a broad oak tree. I took off my smart servant's jacket and was just about to place it on the deep layer of leaves when she carefully put it to one side. Instead, she removed her voluminous woollen skirt and spread that on the leaves. We lay kissing and stroking each other. Her animal, erotic scent was intoxicating. Now, after Sophie, I was a better lover. I took it more slowly, knowing how to arouse her to a shivering desire. I turned on my back and she rode me with an insistent rhythm, soon coming to climax with a shuddering cry. It was the most beautiful noise I ever heard.

We lay clasped together in those glorious minutes of loving intimacy that follow satiated desire.

I said, 'I would have thought by now you would be attached to some new chap.'

'How do you know I'm not?'

'Are you?'

'Maybe I am, maybe I'm not. What about Sophie?'

'What about Sophie?'

'Why did you come looking for me?'

I didn't know how to answer. Seeing Zerlina was unexpected, I had not set out to find her, at least not consciously, but I didn't want to tell her that.

'I needed to be with a friend.'

'A friend? Is that what I am?'

I suddenly realised that Zerlina was the one person with whom I could talk about Sophie.

'I'm going to lose her.' I said.

'You still love her?'

'Yes.'

'And she loves you?'

'I don't know any more. She's a lady now, in manner and dress and speech, and all the time in the company of toffs. Her father must be contriving an advantageous marriage. He'd do everything to stop her throwing herself away on a mere servant.'

'Sophie has her own mind. When has she ever done what her father wishes?'

'Maybe that's her wish too. Who could blame her for seeking power and wealth?'

'But you have posh clothes.'

'The livery of a servant.'

'And you live at court.'

'In servants' quarters.'

'And you have an easy life.'

'Without independence.'

'What independence has Sophie got as companion to rich ladies?'

'That's it precisely, marrying an aristocrat will give her independence.'

'No, it won't, she'll be dependent on her husband. She'll actually be more independent married to you.'

I squirmed at that comment, thinking of my jealous outburst.

I said, 'You surprise me. You're encouraging me to believe that Sophie will stick with me.'

'Why does that surprise you?'

'It would be more natural for you to wish us to separate.'

'To what purpose? So you'd be free to be with me? You would never marry me, would you?'

And it was true. I was drawn to Zerlina and, in a way, I loved her, but in my position as musician in the court orchestra, I couldn't imagine her as my wife. My silence answered her.

Then I said, 'The one who marries you will be an extremely lucky man.'

'I'd marry to escape poverty. But who with any money would marry a girl from a poor peasant family who spends her days husbanding sheep?'

'You're beautiful and intelligent and the kindest person I know. You will find a man who deserves you.'

We continued to cuddle and kiss for a while then got up and dressed. I brushed the leaves from her skirt and she helped me on with my jacket. She gave me one last kiss then turned towards the bonfire and her people.

Walking back to the palace, my mind was in a fury of deliberation. The conversation with Zerlina forced me to reflect on my situation and behaviour. I saw now, Zerlina had every reason to hate me. She had to have hoped that I might lift her out of an existence of mindlessness and destitution. Without a qualm, I had disregarded her. I resolved to do all in my power to help her to a better life.

My morals were questionable but I had no wish to be a hypocrite. I had sworn fidelity with Sophie and failed at the slightest of temptations. I determined that I could not ask of Sophie what I was not prepared to deny myself. There must be no more lapses of trust. This episode with Zerlina was not to be repeated.

How could I have attacked Sophie for the very qualities I most admired: her spirit and independence? Could Zerlina be right? Could Sophie find happiness with a person of my class? What was my class? Neither aristocrat nor peasant, bourgeois nor worker. A servant, yes, but I had nothing in common with the other servants. My identity was totally contained within the small circle of musicians. That's where I belonged. And even in the isolated world of the court, away from the ferment of Vienna, we musicians sensed the unsettling percolation of change. Our position was no longer that of my father's and his generation. In this new world of changing status, could a bailiff's daughter choose to marry an impecunious musician? Given a nature as wilful and headstrong as Sophie's, it might just be possible. I returned to my quarters with renewed optimism, anxious to make amends with the one who I loved with all my heart.

The next day I was tied up with rehearsals and then, in the evening, with a performance for the archduke and other guests. I saw Sophie at the back of the audience but she avoided all eye contact.

The following day, I had more freedom. I kept an eye open and saw Sophie with the countess and other ladies and a group of gentlemen, including Herr Mustardfop, walking towards the games lawn. This was a large rectangle of flat, low-cut grass enclosed on all four sides by two rows of very tall yew hedges. A space between the hedges allowed gentry to promenade.

I took a wheelbarrow and a pair of hedge clippers and positioned myself between the two hedges but near an entrance gap that enabled me to see into the lawn. Servants carried mallets and hoops and set up a game where the players had to hit brightly-coloured balls through the hoops. Each gentleman paired with a lady to form a team. I noticed Sophie had joined Mustardfop. There was a great deal of laughter.

Pretending to clip the hedge, I waited until, as luck

would have it, Sophie hit her ball in my direction. I waved vigorously and she saw me. I dived back between the hedges, out of sight. Sophie calmly finished her game then came over to seek me. I knew I had little time.

'Well?' she said, coldly.

'I'm sorry. Truly, truly, truly sorry. My stupid jealousy. Forgive me, say you will. It's only because I love you so much.'

Her expression softened. I could hear someone calling her. I hastened my speech.

'I was in despair. I thought I was losing you but then Zerlina encouraged me to...'

'You were with Zerlina?'

She turned away from me. I jumped forward and grasped her hand and, at that moment, Mustardfop appeared. He ran towards us holding up his mallet.

'Is that man troubling you?'

Sophie instantly stepped back by my side.

'Baron,' she said sweetly, 'thank you so much for your concern, but Herr Stumm is an old friend of my family. He was just about to say goodbye.'

And with that, she nodded to me and said, 'Goodbye Herr Stumm, I suppose we won't be seeing you for a long time.' Then she turned and walked back to the game, escorted by Mustardfop.

It was March and we knew we would soon receive the order to migrate to Eszterháza. I learned through gossip that the countess had chosen to remain in Eisenstadt and, of course, Sophie would stay with her. I felt I had a dwindling number of days to win back Sophie's affection. She wouldn't meet me. I turned to the medium of our early courtship, writing poems. Katerina, bless her, agreed to take my love sonnets to her mistress. I received no replies, but they weren't returned.

Most of my poems were poor affairs intended to make her laugh as much as aver my love, but the new one I had just written had more merit. It declared that the fire of my love must melt even the heart of stone.

I went to see Papa Haydn. Luckily he was in a good mood. I told him everything: my love for Sophie, my fear of losing her, my transgression with Zerlina, Sophie's recoil and my determination to win back her love.

He smiled and said, 'I've always had the utmost regard and affection for Sophie. But you have a formidable obstacle in her father. It would give me considerable pleasure to see his daughter marry a musician. But how can I help you?'

I showed him my poem – would he please set it to music?

On the 31st March, the court gathered in the glittering music room for an evening of mixed chamber music to celebrate Haydn's fortieth birthday. There were some keyboard pieces then Prince Nicholas himself took to the stage to play his favourite instrument, the six-string baryton in a trio with viola and cello. This was a new work from Haydn, his 107th baryton trio written, like all the others, to please his master. The applause was thunderous.

After the prince had resumed his seat in the front row, there were three songs for soprano with Haydn himself at the piano playing the accompaniment. The last of these was the setting of my poem. I was in the wings of the stage looking through the curtains. I could see Sophie sitting next to the countess.

Papa Haydn announced the item, 'We have next a new song, "The Heart of Stone", a setting of a poem written by our very own horn player, Johan Stumm.'

I saw Sophie give a little start, bringing her hand to her mouth. She had immediately realised the significance of the word 'stone' for that was the meaning of her surname, Steiner.

At the end of the song, Haydn called me onto the stage to take a bow. I don't know whether it was my poem, or his beautiful music or his public acknowledgement of me but in combination they did indeed melt the heart of stone. Sophie, using Katerina as messenger, arranged to meet me and our reunion was all the more passionate for the heartache that preceded it.

Carts and carriages, cooks and counts, maids and mistresses, ostlers and orchestra, porters and prince, chaos and confusion: we were setting off for Eszterháza. There was a tearful crowd to wave us goodbye. It was April, the prince choosing to leave ever earlier for the Summer Palace, and the wives of the musicians would not see their husbands until October.

I too was in tears. I could not openly clasp Sophie in my arms, Bailiff Steiner was overseeing the expedition, but we managed some kisses in an empty stable. I gave her a ring that belonged to my father and said I would love her forever.

She gave me a lock of her hair and said, 'Don't ever doubt that I love you.'

At Eszterháza, I spent every available hour practising. Gustav, who had been a friend of my father and, in turn, became my good friend and mentor, retired. I was sorry to see him leave; he had, to me, been so encouraging. Soon after, I was ecstatic when Papa Haydn promoted me to second horn.

I wrote often to Sophie detailing my life at court and saying how much I missed her. She replied describing both her love for, and exasperation with, the countess. I assumed they were sometimes sleeping together and, strangely, I never felt jealous. Envious, yes, I wanted to be in bed with Sophie myself, but I suppose I didn't perceive the countess as a competing lover. In fact, the thought of their intertwined naked bodies aroused me and invaded my dreams.

Sophie also wrote of her quarrels with her father over the treatment and squalor of the peasants on the estate. He had retorted, 'How else could the estate revenues be delivered?'

Spring arrived late and its beauty intensified my heartache. Unannounced, whilst at my various tasks, the most profound longing would steal over me and I would lift the locket of hair from beneath my tunic and daydream of Sophie.

By mid-June, I could take it no longer. I went to Papa Haydn, 'I have to see Sophie.'

'It is highly irregular. But you appeal to the romantic in me. If only I were your age. I give you three days away from Court, Tuesday to Thursday. And don't tell the others, they'll all be at me to grant them leave.'

I wrote to Sophie with the news and she replied with joy. 'I've opened my heart to the countess and, you won't believe this, she's offered to vacate her room Wednesday night. We can spend the night together!'

In blithe spirit, I set off on the long walk. I was never so happy, in harmony with nature and blessed by God. Tuesday night I stayed with my mother. On Wednesday morning I sat by the statue of Diana to wait. It was an hour before Katerina arrived. We kissed on the cheek. She said she'd been sent to see if I had arrived and to tell me that Sophie would be with me as soon as she could get away.

It was another hour before Sophie herself arrived. She was dressed in the height of fashion: a dark blue gown that touched the ground, pulled tightly in at the waist, daringly low cut at the breast and all topped with a splendid bonnet. She threw herself into my arms and planted kisses all over my face. In return, I kissed her neck and the exposed top of her breasts.

She pulled away, 'Let me look at you. Have you missed me?'

We sat on the plinth of the statue both talking at the same time and kissing and laughing.

She said, 'I can stay with you only till lunchtime. But we

do have tonight. Go to the countess's bedroom at eleven and I'll join you as soon as I dare.'

I made it safely to the bedroom. It was unoccupied and in darkness. Everything was as I remembered. I wasn't sure what to do so I undressed and slipped into bed. I anticipated Sophie's arrival in a delicious stew of excitement. At last, she arrived and immediately threw herself onto the bed.

Between kisses, she said, 'I've dismissed Katerina for the night, you'll have to help me undress.'

A new pleasure! To loosen laces and buttons and clasps. I jumped out of bed uncaring of my nakedness. She could not but notice how pleased I was to see her. As, one by one, garments were removed, I covered in nibbles and kisses every newly exposed curve and contour, hill and hollow of her body.

We stood at arm's length, each enjoying, by the soft candlelight, the unashamed exposure of the other's nakedness. We moved to the bed and, little by little, began to feed the rising pressure of arousal which we knew would end in an explosion of pleasure.

At one point in our lovemaking, Sophie jumped off me and from a drawer produced a short, leather-handled whip with three cloth tails. 'This is the countess's new toy.' She playfully flicked it on my bum before handing it to me. She crouched on the bed, bottom in the air. 'Not too hard,' she said.

I made a few gentle swipes. 'Harder!' After a few minutes, she was moaning with pleasure. She suddenly cried out, 'Stop, it's too excruciatingly lovely.'

She turned over and placed her bottom on the edge of the bed, feet on the floor, and lay back with a pillow beneath her head. She had no need to tell me what was required of me. I buried my head between her thighs.

She saw him before I could turn my head. The crash of the door and a roar and then a stinging lash across my back. I instinctively shrank away from the onslaught and received the next blow on the arm. I crouched on the floor unable to escape the merciless whipping. It was Bailiff Steiner in a paroxysm of rage wielding a thick leather belt.

'By God, I'll kill you!' he bellowed. And I think he would have done had not others, drawn by the noise, intervened.

He turned his anger on Sophie. 'You whore! You slut! You shameless bitch!' He dropped the belt and slapped her. Then grabbed her by the arm and, as he dragged her out of the room, he shouted, 'Lock him up.'

Two men dragged me to a woodshed, threw me in and locked the door. For a long time, I lay on the floor in the darkness not wanting to move for the hurt. As far as I could tell, no bones were broken but my stomach was in pain, there were weeping sores on my back and my face was a mess.

I had no wish to find out what they were going to do with me in the morning. Eventually, I got up and tried the door, it was solid. My eyes now accustomed to the dark, I could see faint light through holes in the wooden wall. In one place, adjacent to the ground, the planks were rotten. I picked up a log and hammered to enlarge the hole. Chip by chip, splinters broke away until I could wriggle through. I cried out with the pain of it but I was free.

Somehow, I made my way to my mother's quarters. She gasped at seeing me. She helped me in, bathed me and gave me hot milk. She wanted to put me to bed but I knew I could not stay. It was certain they would come looking for me. She found me some clothing, ill-fitting, I had grown, but adequate. I knew, if I could manage it, my best course was to return to Eszterháza, but first I had to know Sophie was safe. I told my mother I was going to hide in the music instrument lock-up room and, in the morning, she should tell Katerina where to find me.

It was mid-morning before Katerina arrived with bread and cheese and news.

'There's a frightful to-do. I got it in the neck for not

staying with my mistress. Bailiff's in a terrible sweat. They're looking for you everywhere. I've had to be so careful coming here. Bailiff's sworn all of us to keep our mouths shut about what happened. He said we'd be in deep trouble if a word...'

I interrupted, 'Tell me Sophie's all right.'

'I didn't know anything until I arrived at the countess's bedroom this morning. I didn't come early because I thought you and Sophie...well, you know. Then I found out Sophie was locked in a room in Bailiff's quarters. You could have knocked me down with a feather. I was ever so scared but I went there and that's when I got an earful...'

'What about Sophie?'

'"You're in cahoots with Stumm," he shouted at me. "No," I said, "I just obeyed my mistress's orders. I know nothing about anything." I begged to be allowed to go into Sophie and eventually he told me to find some clothes and take them into her. Well, when I went in, there she was sobbing and not a stitch on her.'

'Is she all right?'

'She has a nasty bruise on her face but otherwise I think she's OK. She's really worried about you. How are you? What shall I tell her?'

'Where is she now?'

'She's been returned to the countess and told never to see you again. Did you know it was the countess who shopped you? It was her who told the Bailiff.'

'Tell Sophie I love her. That I'm OK and I'm going back to Eszterháza. They will stop my letters. I know this is asking a lot, but if I write to you, will you smuggle them to Sophie?'

'Course I will. That countess is a bitch. Are you going to hide here till night-time?'

'Do you think you can get one of the carters to come into the yard?'

'I'll try.'

Katerina returned an hour later. 'Josef, who brings in flour from the mill, is returning with empty sacks. He says you can hide under them. But if you're caught he'll swear he didn't know you were there.'

'Katerina, you're wonderful!' and I kissed her.

And so I made my escape, lying on the floor of a wagon, covered in flour sacks.

I got back to Eszterháza a day late. When Papa Haydn saw me, he said, 'Good heavens! What happened to you?'

I told him my story.

'Will Steiner come looking for you here?'

'I don't think so. He's sworn the servants to secrecy presumably to protect Sophie's reputation. He'll not be looking to making a public scene with me.'

'Has he hurt your hands? Will you be able to play?'

'They're bruised, that's all. What can I do?' I said.

'Wait for a few days until your face has healed. I don't want the prince seeing you like that.'

'No, I meant about Sophie.'

'About Sophie? Be patient. Wait for things to calm down. You're still very young.'

Weeks passed and there were no repercussions. On the 11th July, I had a letter from Sophie. 'This is miserable, I am watched day and night. How I hate the countess but I have to hold my tongue. Outwardly, I am all smiles. What alternative do I have? I will not go back to my father and I'm not able to seek another placement without the support of the countess. She is jealous of you. She wants me totally for herself. Oh, how I long to see you. Write soon.'

Throughout the Summer we exchanged letters. I kept every letter from Sophie in a recess in my instrument case. One letter from her said, 'I think the countess suspects I'm receiving letters from you. I've warned Katerina to be extremely careful. Your letters are vital to my life. I would not know what to do without them.'

Then, on 4th September, this... 'My darling, something

terrible – Baron von Humbolt has asked my father for my hand in marriage. My father is overjoyed. He came to see me and tell me the good news, that I would be rich and how wonderful it will be for me to enter the aristocracy. I was appalled. The very thought of being Humbolt's wife fills me with revulsion. I'd rather die than marry that man. My father became extremely angry. He has threatened me with all manner of punishments unless I relent.'

I was in turmoil at this news. I felt I had to do something: confront the Bailiff, rescue Sophie, appeal to the prince. What stopped me was the thought that I might make her situation worse. I wrote back saying how much I loved her and we would think of something.

Then there were no letters and after several weeks I heard the news from a haulier that the Bailiff's daughter was engaged to Baron von Humbolt and the wedding was to take place before Christmas. I was distraught. I had to see Sophie.

I went to Papa Haydn to tell him I was going to Eisenstadt. At first, he tried to dissuade me, saying how dangerous it would be, then, when he saw I was determined, he said he would try to cover my absence.

On that Saturday, 20th September, the weather was sultry. Even though wearing a thin shirt, I was in a sweat. As I set off to walk to Eisenstadt, I painfully recalled how happy I had been making the same journey three months earlier.

It was nearly dark when I got to the peasant village. I called quietly to Zerlina's sister and told her to find Zerlina and bring her to where I was hiding.

Zerlina said, 'I thought you were in Eszterháza.'

I took her hand. 'I need your help. I have to see Sophie. I daren't go near the palace but *you* could on some pretext.'

'I heard she's going to be married. Are you sure she'll want to see you?'

'This is all her father's doing. She hates this man. I have

to save her. Oh Zerlina, if you have any feeling for me, please say you'll do it.'

'What do you want me to tell her?'

'I'll wait twenty-four hours by the Willow Brook. If she doesn't come, I'll look for her in the Palace.'

The Willow Brook was two miles from the Palace. A path led through woodland to a dense copse of willows that screened a deep pool. It was there, as children, we would swim. On the nearside, a fallen tree provided a perfect platform from which to jump in, and on the far side, the pool gently shelved to a shallow beach. In the shrubs beyond, I made a bed of leaves and settled down to wait.

It was hot and humid and every now and again I cooled off with a dip in the pool. Sometime, mid-afternoon, whilst bathing, I saw a woman approaching through the trees. I thought it was Katerina. I was conscious of my nakedness. But no, it was Sophie, dressed in Katerina's clothes. I swam towards her. 'Wait there,' she called and straightaway cast off every stitch, climbed onto the log and dived in.

For an hour, that pool became our playground. We were children again, having fun, our cares and concerns cast aside with our clothes. Then we lay in a patch of sunlight to dry off. As our bodies warmed, hot desire seeped into every pore of skin. We moved to the bed of leaves and there, stroked each other to a pitch of arousal that made us scream for release.

We assumed the familiar position with her on top, pressing and sliding her sex on my penis.

But then she said, 'I want you to come in me.'

I was amazed. 'Are you sure?'

'I will not give up my virginity to any other than you.'

'But, so far, at least you've been able to swear truthfully to your father that you're intact.'

'Whatever happens, this will always be a bond between us. I want to do it, here, with you, now.'

I was all too willing to obey her. She wanted to control

it herself. She changed angle and eased down upon me. I had this great desire to thrust but kept very still. She pushed and released, and then again harder, and again until with a cry she had me a little inside her. She stopped in that position for a while then I said, 'I know it must be painful but could you not push me further in?' And so slowly, and with persistence, she eased herself down upon me.

She leant forward to kiss me.

My eyes were wet with tears of happiness. 'I love you so much,' I said.

'You feel very full inside me. It's nice.'

'Not too painful?'

'I'd like you to come.'

I said, 'Stop me if it's too sore.'

I moved as slowly and as gently as I could and she responded, coordinating her thrusts with mine. It had to be painful for her but she encouraged me. When I came, I felt I was overflowing with love for her, this wonderful, beautiful person. She was so right, they could never take this away from us.

What to do? We lay in each other's arms seeking a solution.

I said, 'We have to marry.'

'My father will never accept you. I've tried so hard to make him see sense and he just gets the more angry.'

'Then we must marry without your father's consent.'

'Do you think the prince would let us marry without my father's approval?'

'Wouldn't the countess speak against us?'

'I have an aunt in Graz, maybe we could go there.'

'No place for a musician, but I suppose I might find some other sort of work. You know we'll be very poor.'

'Yes, I know, but I don't care. I'll have you. But you must be happy too. You have to find work as a musician.'

'Then it must be Vienna or Prague or Paris. Papa Haydn might help us; he's always been very fond of you and he approved my coming here.'

'I wish we could run away today.'

'Better if we plan an escape. Pretend to your father that you've relented and now agree to marry Humbolt. He'll relax his vigilance and life will be easier for you. I'll talk to Papa Haydn. We'll all be coming back here in a few weeks then it'll be easier to organise everything.'

I walked back to Eszterháza a happier man than when I left. I was reassured that I retained Sophie's love and we were to escape to be married even if we didn't know how. On my way, the recent humid weather engendered the most dramatic thunderstorm. A mad wind made the trees dance crazily even to destruction. Great flashes rent the black clouds. Fearful bangs followed like the cracking of a monstrous whip. Then the clouds burst releasing their heavy burden of water.

I exulted in the passion and power of these forces to shake and change the world. I wanted a wind that would break the structures that supported the Humbolts above me; lightning that could sever the ties that bound me; drenching water to wash away my servitude. Like a mad thing, I embraced the storm.

Arrival at Eszterháza brought me back to Earth, the reality of the everyday. Papa Haydn had no time to give me. He needed to complete his new symphony, have it ready to perform in November. Soothingly, he said that if the occasion arose he would see what he could do.

As days passed into weeks, I fumed and fretted at my inaction. Then, on 7th October, a letter from Sophie: she had adopted my proposal and offered compliance. Yes, this had eased her relationship with her father but now she had to appear to welcome the attentions of a devoted fiancé. 'I cannot suffer him much longer. And on top of this, preparations are in train for a sumptuous wedding. My father is a mountain of excitement, out to impress the world with the grandeur of the occasion. Invitations will soon be addressed and on the list will most certainly be the prince. We have to act soon before this gains any more momentum. The longer we delay, the bigger the crash that follows.'

I went again to Papa Haydn, this time I was emphatic, 'I'm leaving. I'm going to Eisenstadt, whatever the consequences.'

'Don't do that. It will anger the prince and we're bound to be returning there in a couple of weeks. Far better that you're in Eisenstadt legitimately. You know that a dismissal from this court makes it impossible for you to gain employment with any other.'

The following Monday, at the end of rehearsal of the orchestra, Haydn said to us all, 'I have had an audience with the prince and took the opportunity to raise with his Highness the rumour, you must have heard it, that some of you may have to leave us, that the prince wants to reduce the size of the orchestra. I'm delighted to tell you the prince was categoric, that it is not his intention to lose any of the orchestra for the foreseeable future.'

There was an audible murmur of relief at this news.

'But,' Haydn continued, 'his Highness shared with me that he sees little reason to return to Eisenstadt until a few days before his name day on the 6th of December which he will celebrate there as usual.'

This was received with consternation. 'Are we not to see our wives and children until December?' they asked. 'The prince is a humane man, could you not plead with him that we wish to be reunited with our families?'

Haydn replied, 'Should a prince determine his life by the wishes of his servants?'

After that there wasn't much could be said. It was an unhappy orchestra that left the music room.

Haydn detained me, 'I know what must be in you mind. This is the very pickle of a situation. I have been thinking how to help you and I have a stratagem that might get you to Eisenstadt early in November. You will then be there under my and, more importantly, the prince's protection until you work out what to do. I beg you not to act precipitately.'

'November! Just think how advanced the preparation will be just six weeks before the wedding. Think how Sophie will be feeling. She'll conclude that I'm standing by and doing nothing, that I've abandoned her.'

'If you wait just these three weeks, I promise I will then intercede on your behalf with the prince. I will ask him to stop this marriage on the grounds that Sophie is being forced into it against her will. You must write to Sophie to reassure her and you can tell her what I've just said.'

'You are very kind. Thank you.'

'Actually, I thank *you*. Your problem has led me to think of how, without being impertinent, we might prompt the prince to return to Eisenstadt. And this has led me to a new delightful idea that excites me. Now you must excuse me, I'm in a great hurry to complete the new symphony. By the way, I've chosen to write it in F sharp minor. I don't think that key has ever been been chosen for a symphony before. I know you cannot play the horn in that key. I'll order crooks to be made for you to insert in your horns. In fact, I must remember to do that straight away so they will be ready in time. I want you to play in my new symphony, so don't go and disappear on me.'

I wrote to Sophie immediately. Days passed without a reply. Papa Haydn had mentioned early November. I determined that I would give it until the end of the second week of November and then run to Eisenstadt whatever trouble that might bring.

Wednesday 22nd October was a special day: we horn players received our new crooks and immediately tried them out. It took some getting use to, adjusting the intonation for playing in the new keys. Although Haydn hadn't completed the symphony, he handed out parts for the first two movements and we began rehearsing them.

The last day of October, I finally got a reply from Sophie, 'I'm drowning in the horror of it all here. Oh why don't you come? I can't take much more of this.'

I longed to set off immediately but I loved Papa Haydn and didn't want to go against him and he was our best hope. And, I have to admit, the opportunity to play in the first performance of the new symphony was irresistible. One more week, just one more week.

The following day, November 1st, was All Saints' Day. I went to mass and prayed for God's help to unite me and Sophie in holy matrimony. I remembered my father and prayed to him. I thought of his last words to me: 'Zerlina, she is not the one for you.' How perceptive he was.

A frisson was exciting the court, word had got out that something different was to happen at the performance of the new symphony. We arrived early at the music room that Saturday 11th November. We warmed up our instruments and lit our candles. The hall filled, then everybody stood up as the prince and the princess Marie Elisabeth took their seats in the front row. Papa Haydn was playing violin, he raised his bow and we started.

The first movement, *Allegro Assai* (quite fast), was turbulent in character and received warm applause. The second was slow and meditative and was also well received. The Minuet, third movement, was applauded and then there was an audible muttering. So far, a brilliant new work, they concluded, but where was the surprise? Was it reserved for the final movement? They settled down in anticipation. The last movement was *presto* and jolly good it was too. After three minutes, it came to a stop, then, when the music started again, there was something completely new. Haydn had changed the metre from three to two and the music was slow again. Was there to be a second slow movement?

After another minute the music came to the end of a section. There was a pause and the oboe player stood up, gathered his music from off the stand, blew out his candle and walked off the stage. This was unheard of. There was a gasp of amazement in the auditorium. Then it was my turn. In my part, the second horn, Haydn had written, *'nichts mehr'*. Feeling very excited, I got to my feet, blew out my candle and walked off the stage. There was another gasp from the audience.

I watched everything that followed from the wings. The rest of the orchestra carried on. After another minute, the bassoon player came off. The only wind left playing were the second oboe and the first horn and they soon made their exit. Now there were only strings. The music continued, soft and mysterious. After half a minute more, the music came to another pause and the bass player joined us in the wings. We peeped at the audience through the curtains. They didn't know how to react. Many had their hands at their mouths in amazement. Quite a few were laughing.

The theme that started this slow section was now repeated in a different key and with just the remaining strings. It sounded so strange without the oboes and horns. The two cellos stopped and now there was just five violins and a viola. When three of the violins blew out their candles, the stage was almost in darkness. Papa Haydn and Alois Tomasini, the leader of the orchestra, had put mutes on their violins and now they played softly to the viola accompaniment. The effect was magical. The viola tiptoed off and finally, alone, Haydn and Tomasini brought the symphony quietly, breathtakingly, to an end. They blew out their candles and the stage was now left empty and in darkness. Musically, it was a supreme inspiration. Theatrically, it was a master-stroke.

There was a silence. We were all waiting to see the reaction of the prince. Then he burst out laughing and everybody broke into loud applause. The new symphony was a hit. We all trooped back onto the stage to take a bow. Haydn was received rapturously.

The prince approached the stage and said, loud enough for all to hear, 'Herr Haydn, are you by any chance trying to suggest something to me?'

Papa Haydn bowed low and said, 'Your serene highness, I hope you enjoyed my little joke.'

'A very clever little joke, but barbed, barbed. However, you have hit your target, on Monday, we shall leave for Eisenstadt.' There was loud applause from the musicians. I was overjoyed. I rushed over and pumped Papa's hand.

The next day, even though we were in a confusion of packing, I had the opportunity to have a brief word with Papa Haydn. I said, 'What amazes me, is the unity of your symphony. The conclusion is no mere tacked on afterthought. It's as if you knew the ending even before you began work on the first movement. But you couldn't have done.'

He said, 'As I composed, the music led me to an end, soft and gentle. But then I had the idea of the pantomime, using the symphony to nudge the prince, and I realised I could marry one with the other, both create a perfect final movement to the symphony and have it fit for its ulterior purpose.'

'You are truly a genius.'

'When we get to Eisenstadt, I'll carry out my promise to speak to the prince on your behalf. I don't have to tell you to be careful. Keep well out of the way of Steiner.'

I was so eager to get to Eisenstadt, I persuaded the wagoner of the leading cart to let me ride beside him. We were five miles distant from the palace when a man on horseback came riding furiously towards us.

He shouted at me, 'Right, you bastard. Where is she?' and before I could respond, his whip drew blood from my arm.

I cried out at the pain and the sudden violence of the attack. It was Bailiff Steiner.

'Sophie, where is she? Tell me or by God I really will kill

you this time.'

I shouted, 'If I knew where Sophie was, I wouldn't tell you.'

I grabbed at the cudgel that lay at my feet and managed to lessen the impact of the flying whip tail as it seared my back. I jumped from the wagon and ran into the woods. In a moment, he was off his horse and after me. I would have outpaced him had I not tripped on a root and fell to the ground. I had just time enough to pick up the cudgel when he was on me. The blow cut my thigh. I held up the cudgel to protect myself from the next strike and the tail of the whip lashed itself around the wooden staff. With a yank, he pulled my weapon from my hand. As he shook the whip to free it, I lunged forward and, with all my strength, kicked him in the balls. He doubled over in pain and then I threw myself at him knocking him to the ground.

He lay writhing at the pain in his groin. I stood over him and said, 'You're a bully and contemptible and I hope the prince comes to see what an ugly man you are. Wherever Sophie is, she's best well away from you.'

I left him, found his horse and rode as fast as I could to Eisenstadt. If Sophie had escaped, I needed to find her. First, I had to speak with Katerina.

I went to my mother, 'Have you seen Katerina?'

'She's disappeared along with Sophie. The Bailiff's in a fury. He even came here, demanding to know if I'd seen you.'

'When did this happen?'

'They must have left in the night. Bailiff came this morning after he'd discovered she was gone.'

I spoke with the ostlers and they told me two horses were missing, one of them being Moonshine, Sophie's favourite. There were no clues as to where they were heading. It was getting dark. It was too dangerous to stay overnight at Eisenstadt. Hoping to find a barn en route that would shelter me for the night, I set off to walk 25 miles.

My destination was Vienna.

I made my way to what had once been the centre of the Jewish community and found what I was looking for: Number 3, Judenplatz. I ran up the stairs to the second floor and used the knocker. A dog started barking. A man opened the door whilst holding back the yapping dog.

'Shut up, Gauckerl.'

'Good day,' I said, 'my name is Johan Stumm. Could you please tell me if Sophie Steiner is staying here?'

The man, obviously a servant, looked me over with slow deliberation and visible distaste.

'You'd better come in and wait.'

He bid me sit down in an ante-room. Gauckerl also sat, eyeing me with suspicion. It was very quiet, then Gauckerl, growing bored, stretched and padded over to a door slightly ajar and pushed his way into the adjoining room. I saw a man bent forward, working at a desk, and heard the scratch of quill on paper. It was Mozart. I wondered what sort of work he was composing, maybe a symphony, or a new piano concerto or another opera. Every now and again, he would raise his gaze to the ceiling as if listening to music from heaven. I dared not make a sound.

Eventually, he stretched, swinging his arms in the air and over the back of the chair. He turned his head and saw me and jumped up.

'Hello. Who have we here? What can I do for you?'

I bowed low. 'It's Johan, Johan Stumm. I play horn in Prince Esterházy's Orchestra.'

'Oh, yes, of course, we met at Eisenstadt.'

'Forgive me for intruding, Herr Mozart, but is Sophie here?'

'No.'

My heart sank. I had chanced everything on the idea that she might have expected me to come looking for her here. Now my expectations were dashed.

Forlornly, I said, 'You wouldn't happen to know where

she is, would you?'

'Not precisely.'

'Not precisely?'

'No, she's probably somewhere near the market, with Constanze, they should be back in half an hour.'

'In half an hour! Thank God!'

I told him of Papa Haydn's device to return me to Eisenstadt. He laughed with gusto, 'That's so good. Haydn's a genius.'

I told him of the fight with Sophie's father. 'I didn't know where Sophie was heading for. Frau Mozart was very kind to Sophie. I made a wild guess that she might have come here.'

'What would you have done if she hadn't?'

'She made mention of an aunt in Graz. I'd have gone there. I would have carried on searching for her until I found her.'

'Now you have, what do you want to do?'

'I want us to be married as soon as possible.'

If I had been less anxiously impatient to see Sophie, I would have paid more attention to Mozart's chat with me. I wish I had. He said he too had to deal with parental opposition to his marriage. He and Constanze had put off their wedding day waiting for his father's blessing. Eventually, giving up on this, they got married anyway and then, the very next day received the desired approval.

He said he wanted to write an opera about two young lovers. The background story would involve the Freemasons. He himself was a member of the lodge, Zur Wohltätigkeit. He said the Freemasons united all those who believed in the spirit of the Enlightenment: scientist, artists, writers and doctors. The young man in the opera would apply to join a lodge and would be given three tasks to undertake. These would both prove his worthiness to join the lodge and win him the love of his lady.

'You, Johan, have overcome many obstacles to gain

Sophie's love. You'll make a good model for the hero of my opera.'

Sophie returned and we rushed into each other's arms. When I recovered my manners, I bowed to Constanza and kissed Katerina. We had a joyful meal together, Sophie relating the story of their escape and Mozart entertaining us with anecdotes of musical life of Vienna.

When he learned I had nowhere to stay he said, 'Sophie and Katerina are in the spare bedroom, but you're welcome to a mattress on the sitting-room floor.'

The Mozart household was always busy with the comings and goings of friends and musicians and singers and the intellectual elite of Vienna. It was full of laughter and chatter. Mozart himself often sat and composed in the middle of this hubbub quite oblivious to all the noise. It was as if he needed people around him in order to work.

One group that often came was a small party of music enthusiasts from England. I found their language most strange but they spoke excellent German. They always arrived with crates of wine. They particularly enjoyed Sophie's company, teaching her the strange English dances.

I wrote to Papa Haydn, telling him of our intent to marry and where we were housed, asking him to keep that information to himself. He replied that he was delighted we were staying with his esteemed friend and please to convey his respects. He said there had been a great furore at the cancellation of the wedding but the prince had declared that he did not wish to become involved in the matter. 'I think it best, at least for the foreseeable future, that you do not return here. I trust you will find work in Vienna. Should you require references, I will be happy to oblige. Please convey my fondest best wishes to Sophie.'

Daily we expected a visit from Sophie's father, but, to our relief, he never came. A month after my arrival in Vienna, we got married in St Stephen's Cathedral. It was a small affair. I was very nervous as I waited at the altar and I was not helped by Wolfgang, my best man, who kept making rude jokes. I turned and saw Sophie, who was radiant and beautiful, supported, to our delight, by Papa Haydn. Constanza and Katerina followed behind as bridesmaids. The only witnesses were the English who were most anxious to meet the famous Joseph Haydn.

The reception was back at the Mozarts'. Everybody was so happy. The English took the opportunity to try and persuade Papa Haydn to go to England.

'In London,' they said, 'there is enormous appetite for music. Your works are already well known there. You will be acclaimed wherever you go. Their Royal Majesties will be delighted to receive you. They give special honour to German and Austrian artists and musicians. Queen Charlotte is, herself, from Germany.'

'I was there when I was eight,' Wolfgang said. 'I accompanied Queen Charlotte as she sang an aria. I dedicated six sonatas to her and she gave me fifty guineas. You should go. I might even make another trip there myself.'

Haydn declined, 'Thank you, but I am much indebted to the generosity of my noble benefactor Prince Esterházy. I will not leave while he wishes to retain my services.'

'Well,' said an Englishman, whose name was Thomas Attwood, 'if you change your mind...What about you Johan, there's plenty of work in London for a good horn player?'

Sophie said, 'I've heard such exciting things about London.'

One of the English women, Nancy Storace, said, 'You would love it; I could show you all the sights. London is a huge city, there's so much going on.'

And so it was, when Thomas and Nancy, and her husband Stephen, were to return to their native land, they generously offered to take us in their coach. Sophie and I agreed to go with them to seek a new life in a new country.

On our last evening, as we sat with Wolfgang and

Constanza, drinking wine by a roaring fire, Sophie said, 'How did you two fall in love? Was it love at first sight?'

'I was sixteen when I first met Woferl. My father was a musician in Mannheim. We were very poor.'

'Did he fall for you then?'

Constanza laughed. 'He did not. He only had eyes for my sister Aloysia. He wanted to marry her but she wouldn't have him.'

Wolfgang said, 'She did me a good turn, rejecting me. But even if she had accepted me, my father would have put a stop to it. He didn't approve of the Webers.'

'Why ever not?' I asked.

'For him, my perfect wife would be well off, have connections with the nobility and enhance my career. Love didn't enter into it.'

'Not so different from *my* father,' Sophie said.

'So how *did* you two get together?' I said.

Constanza said, 'After my father died, we moved to Vienna because Aloysia got a job singing with the National Opera. She provided the income for the whole family.'

'Then,' Wolfgang said, 'when I escaped servitude with the Archbishop Colerado, I needed a place to stay in Vienna.'

'And we provided the perfect home. We shared our meals, waiting impatiently for him to arrive at table until he had finished what he was working on. We gave him use of two pianos and we four girls entertained him with singing and dancing.'

'Much more pleasant than living on my own. Father was incensed. He believed I would be trapped by one of the sisters, and so indeed I was.'

'It was when he was a guest in our house that I fell in love with him. He's such fun to be with. I was just nineteen. He says he fell in love with my dark eyes...'

'And your glorious figure.'

'But, if truth be told, he saw I was the only one in the

family who showed any skill in managing the household.'

'After her father died, a friend of the family assumed the role of guardian. When he perceived my interest in Constanza, he made me sign a document that, if I didn't marry her within three years, I would have to pay her three hundred florins a year. It was outrageous, but I was happy to sign because I knew I'd never have to fork out the money. When Connie saw the document, she was so angry she tore it into little pieces. And that made me love her all the more.'

'We couldn't get married because we had no money. It was only when Woferl finished writing *The Abduction* and it was a great success that we had the wherewithal to set up on our own. We nearly didn't make it. Three months before the wedding, we had a terrible row. I had gone to a soirée at Fanny Arnstein's when a bet was proposed by the young men as to who of the ladies had the most prominent calves. We hitched up our skirts and allowed them to measure us. When Wolferl got to hear of this, he went wild. "How could you be so loose," he shouted at me. I told him if he was going to be so jealous, I would have nothing more to do with him.'

Sophie gave me a knowing look and I blushed at the memory.

'And what about you two?' Constanza said. 'When did you know you were intended for each other?'

I laughed and told the story of Sabre and the stalled carriage and the mud.

Sophie said, 'That's when you said you loved me. I had my eyes on you long before that.'

'I didn't know. Why didn't you tell me?'

'You were with Zerlina. I went to see your father shortly before he died.'

'Did you? I didn't know that.'

'He was very ill but calm and lucid. He took my hand and said, "Johan has this affair with Zerlina but it won't last. Give him time. He will eventually come to see that you two are made for each other. Do not despise the love of a poor musician, he will make you a good husband." And I saw that was true. I was yours long before you ever declared your love for me.'

'My father,' I said, nodding my head, 'was a far-sighted man.'

Early the following morning, Thomas Attwood arrived to usher us to his coach where Nancy and Stephen Storace were there to welcome us. The Mozarts came down to wave goodbye, and we were off to a make new life in England.

Serendipity

Hi there, my name is Haydn Jones. I was born and bred in Nantgarw, a little village five miles south of Pontypridd. I was appropriately named because I was always good at the music. My Da was a musician, and his Da before him. They insisted I should follow in the family tradition, but I was a big strapping lad and wanted something manly and physical. I would have gone down the pit if Thatcher (spit) hadn't closed them all. So I chose the construction. Da said, 'Don't be daft lad, stay away from that airy-fairy stuff, get a real job – music technology, now there's the future.' But I wouldn't listen.

And then there was a recession and no work, so my fate was inevitable. What else could I do? I enrolled for a music degree at the Welsh College of Music and Drama in Cardiff.

It was my first day there and I went to the student refectory and sitting on her own at a table was a young woman. Oh, she was so beautiful. Most people have an angle at the bridge of their nose but with her it was a gentle curve just like a baby. A baby face, that's what she had, with large cooing eyes. And her hair, tumbling in chestnut luxuriance.

'Hello,' I said, as I sat down beside her, 'my name's Haydn. Are you new here like me?'

She smiled and said, 'Shwmae. Fy enw i yw Seren.' She carried on speaking in Welsh. 'Are you music or drama?'

'There's always some drama where I'm concerned,' I said, 'but I'm here to play on my horn.'

She giggled.

I said, 'You're music too, aren't you?'

'How did you know?'

'I have psychic powers. I can even tell which instrument you play simply by examining your hand.'

She put out her hand and I took it in mine. I carefully felt her palm with my fingertips. I looked into her amused eyes. 'You play the oboe.' I solemnly pronounced.

Her eyes widened, 'How could you know that?'

I gestured with my hand to bring her head forward, took my lips to her ear and whispered, 'I can see your instrument case under the table.'

She rocked back away from me, laughing.

'Seriously,' I said, 'you're from Llandovery.'

'How the hell did you know that?'

'My Aunt.'

'Your Aunt?'

'My Aunt Beti. She has a cousin in Llandovery with a daughter called Seren who's into music and very beautiful. Never having seen her, I couldn't vouch for her beauty, but now, having met her, I can.'

'So we're related?' and she laughed again.

I thought, this is going very well, then this chap came and sat down beside her. Seren switched to English and said, 'This is Richard.'

There were other young women during my years at the College, but I never stopped loving Seren. Behind her soft features, she had a steely determination to succeed and a surprisingly subversive spirit that prompted her, sometimes to her own disadvantage, to elegantly and hilariously deflate the posers, the pompous and the smug. We were often alone together when Rich was off somewhere playing fiddle in his ceilidh band. So many times it was on the tip of my tongue to tell her how much I loved her but what was the point, it could only make things awkward between us.

In our final year, we had to write an extended dissertation. I told my tutor, for obvious reasons, that I'd like to do something on Haydn. He suggested that an interesting debate was to be had on the final movement of the *Farewell Symphony*: was the unusual ending an afterthought or had Haydn conceived it from the very beginning.

The more I researched, the more I warmed to the subject. I discovered the issue was much wider than this particular symphony, extending generally to Haydn's process of composition. Using search engines, I read widely and turned up a short paper scanned from a London music journal of 1833 with the snappy title: *A personal account of the first performance of Franz Joseph Haydn's Symphony No 45 in F# minor known as 'The Farewell'*. The article was written by one Johan Stumm in a style dry and academic. It was valuable in being an eyewitness account of the occasion, Stumm being a horn player in the orchestra. Particularly intriguing was that Stumm said he raised with Haydn the very question that formed the basis of my thesis. He wrote, 'It's as if you knew the ending even before you began work on the first movement.' Haydn's response, 'The music led me to an end soft and gentle.' suggests Haydn's primary concern was the unity of the work in form and content.

A footnote to this article made mention of a longer, more personal memoir published in an anthology, *True Tales of Love Requited*, dated two years earlier, 1831. I eventually tracked this down to a book stored (and scanned) by the British Library and catalogued within the section "Nineteenth Century Erotica". Apparently, there had been a companion volume, now lost, *True Tales of Love Unrequited.*

Stumm's memoir didn't contribute much to my dissertation which required a musical analysis of Haydn's symphonies, but the story spoke to my heart, even if some of it was invented.

'Invented?' you ask. 'What was invented?' Well, much of the story has the ring of authenticity; for example, the details of the Esterhazy court and the friendship and high regard between Mozart and Haydn, but the *Farewell Symphony* was written in 1772 when Mozart was sixteen years old and he married Constanza ten years later.

Stumm was 77 when *True Tales* was published so either it was the confused memory of an old man or the story had got embellished over the years. Having the *Farewell Symphony* written to help you win the love of your life is wonderful: having Mozart as your best man is triumphant. Neither was necessarily untrue, they just couldn't happen in the same year.

But none of that matters, it's the story that made me want to hug Johan Stumm. Like me, he was a horn player, like me his heart ached for the woman he loved. I knew in my bones, Seren and I were made for each other. Was there not a moral for me in the way Sophie patiently waited until Johan had got over Zerlina? Did I too not have to wait until Seren woke up to the realisation that Richard was not going to be her life partner?

We three graduated successfully and were looking for work. We continued to live in Cardiff; Seren was with Rich and I shared a flat with another chap. Both Seren and Richard separately confided their niggles about living with the other. I told them not to be silly. 'When you live with someone, there's always something about them you're going to find irksome. That's of nothing when put against the joy of living with the person you love.'

Seren said, 'You sound like an unmarried vicar instructing a couple about to be married.'

Along with scores of others, we applied to orchestras. Along with scores of others, we were unsuccessful. Teaching seemed to be the only alternative. But we hankered to play in a professional orchestra and that is how the South Wales Chamber Orchestra was born. We joined with other graduates to create our own orchestra. And we picked up bookings, playing in all sorts of small venues throughout South Wales.

One day we had a policy meeting, dreaming up ideas to reach new audiences. I suggested the *Farewell Symphony*:

recreating that first performance: wearing wigs, waistcoats, breeches, and stockings, blowing out candles and walking off the stage. I read to the orchestra Stumm's account of the first performance. Initially, there was enthusiasm for the idea, but then Rich said the pantomime undermined the seriousness of our intentions. The music spoke for itself. It was our playing that was most important and we shouldn't let this fooling around detract from our performance. He said he had no intention of dressing up in stupid clothes.

I think his opinion might have prevailed if it hadn't been for Seren.

'What a load of piffle,' she said. 'Where's our future if we're unable to attract new audiences? What good is our "seriousness" if people don't come to hear us? Where's your sense of fun? Haydn loved a joke. If it's good enough for Haydn, it should be good enough for you. It's a brilliant idea and our own Haydn deserves applause for suggesting it.'

Rich walked off in a huff.

We got a grant from the Arts Council for this project and we took it on tour. It was a huge success. Often fire prevention officers gave us permission to use real candles. When this was impossible, we used desk lights with a candle shape, which was OK but not as good. In alternate performances, I and my fellow horn player swapped first and second horn parts.

One evening we were booked to play in the hall of the little village of Ponthir. Something happened to me that evening. An urgent feeling of discontent swept through me. I felt I was boxed in and had to break free. We arrived late, no time for a rehearsal, not that we needed one. We changed into our Haydnesque costumes on the coach and grouped together in the kitchen. Our roadie had set up the stands with the music and the candles. A hundred people filled the hall. They must have come from miles around. We trooped onto the stage through a door on stage left.

As a warm up and to fill the one hour programme we played Haydn's Twelve German Dances. They received warm applause. Then it was the *Farewell*. Seren, as first oboe, was first to blow out her candle and walk off. Except she didn't go to the door through which we had come onto the stage, but to an identical door on the far side. I was second horn that evening, so next it was my turn. I placed my horn on its stand and blew out my candle. I thought it would look odd to be exiting by a different door to the one taken by Seren, so I followed her to stage right. I walked into blackness.

'Seren,' I whispered.

'I'm here.'

She touched my chest. I couldn't see her, but I put my arms around her.

She giggled and said, 'I think it's a store cupboard.'

'Seren,' I said, 'I love you. I've loved you from the moment I first set eyes on you.'

She didn't react. Didn't move. Didn't speak. Just stood there close against me, letting me hold her.

The door opened and another person came in. I knew who it was, Lucy, the bassoonist.

'Fuck, what's this?' she said.

We both giggled. 'Come and join the party,' I said, and we reached out to touch her. One by one the others come into the black hole. Each new arrival providing an exclamation that made us cackle anew. By the time the last of the tutti violins arrived, it was a tight squeeze and she had trouble pushing herself in and shutting the door. There were only two players now left on the stage. I still had my arms around Seren and our bodies were pushed firmer and firmer against each other. My lips were just next to her ear and I whispered over and over again, 'I love you, I love you, I love you,' and then I bent my head down and gently kissed her on the neck.

The music stopped, the symphony had come to its

sweet end. The last two came towards the door. The audience chortled and began to clap. When the door was opened, we tumbled out onto the stage with an explosion of laughter. Then the audience, realising what had happened, burst out laughing anew and applauding even louder.

The following day, we, the orchestra, met up in a pub and enjoyed sharing in every detail the experience of the previous evening. Seren said that when she opened the door she knew she had made a mistake but thought it best to go in rather than turn and walk back across the stage. I was very quiet. Then, when people had stopped talking, I said, 'I'm going to leave the orchestra.' Everybody was amazed and concerned. 'Why?' 'You can't do that.' 'We need you.' 'What's wrong?' 'Have you got another job?' 'What are you going to do?' 'Where are you going?'

I said I didn't know what I was going to do but I thought I might go to Berlin.

When we all parted, Seren hurried after me.

'Are you leaving because of me?'

I felt very emotional, there was a lump in my throat. 'I can't...I can't be near you any more.'

She stood very close and put a hand to my face. 'I didn't want to announce it to the others until it was finally settled, but I have to tell you, Rich and I are splitting. He's going to leave the orchestra. He's applying for jobs in London. Do you really want to go?'

For answer, I simply kissed her.

Mama Mia!

It was just bad luck, Panigatti falling ill a month before the onset of Antarctic winter. Dismissive of his illness, he had wanted to stay but Sergio, the medic, was blunt; it would be crazy to risk having him stuck on base for months, unable to fly him out should he require hospital treatment.

There was barely enough time to find a replacement Head of Base. The three men left on base, Sergio Foresti himself, together with Luciano Vittoni and Piero Ripandelli, would be woefully under-manned without a chief. PNRA (Programma Nazionale di Ricerche in Antortide) appointed Sergio interim Head while they urgently sought a replacement. Sergio, at forty-six, self-assured with a wealth of experience, believed he should have been promoted to party chief years ago. The fact that he was always passed over, rankled. He hoped they would send out a new chap but leave him in place.

The three men carried forward their research whilst enjoying the easy, jokey, very male friendship between them. Sergio's interest was micro-organisms in ice at sub-freezing temperatures. Luciano was thirty-two. Unlike Sergio, he had a calm, considered manner. A climatologist, he had the temperament to take infinite pains in his work and had earned a solid reputation for meticulously recording meteorological data. Piero at twenty-seven was already an expert on snow. His Ph.D. thesis on the morphology of snow under pressure had appeared in a prestigious academic journal and attracted more than the usual number of citations. He was intensely dedicated and ambitious, looking forward to an academic career ending up with a professorship.

Director of PNRA, Carlo Masagni, acknowledged that Sergio had the qualities to make a good party chief, but the fellow could never hold his tongue. He couldn't help but speak his mind, and his impolitic comments had earned him resentments.

They wanted a geophysicist and found three who could do the job and were willing to leave in a hurry. Two of them were solid men, predictable and safe. The third candidate was exceptional, but not without problems: she was a woman and, furthermore, a woman who attracted controversy.

None of those on the Appointment Committee considered themselves sexist, but one had to think of the practical considerations. The controversies were more serious: Giacinta Vagnussi had brought upon herself the ire of the oil industry. Rich gas and oil deposits had been discovered east of Rome. To many, this was the miracle solution to Italy's long-standing financial woes. Giacinta Vagnussi went public with a survey suggesting that fracking would endanger Rome's supply of water.

Captains of oil set about undermining Vagnussi's survey. They found it impossible to contest its method and procedures but a number of 'experts' attested that the results didn't warrant the conclusions. Coming to Vagnussi's support, respected hydrologists protested that the Government could not take such a risk with the City's water supply.

Suddenly, articles started appearing in newspapers and journals re-working colourful chapters in Vagnussi's life. In particular, to the envy of many women, the fling she had with gorgeous film star Cosimo Mastrogiovanni. Their subsequent split was a brief sensation. 'Hardly,' said the oil lobbyists, 'the life of a cool-headed scientist. Could one take seriously the work of a person with a life so sordid?'

But, for PNRA, Vagnussi had one outstanding attraction: the months she had already worked in the

Antarctic when she had laid the foundation for promising future research and, more importantly, impressed everybody by her qualities for leadership. The announcement of her appointment was newsworthy. The Committee and the Director, Carlo Masagni, watched the television interview with interest. Wearing a bright red dress, she looked good – her mass of short curls, her open laughing face, her beautiful teeth.

Was she surprised at her appointment?

'Being a woman, you mean? Does this surprise any more? The British appointed a woman to head their Antarctic camp. Two of the five crew of the forthcoming Mars mission are women. Any sensible organisation chooses the best person for the job regardless of gender.'

But how did she think the three men at the Camp would react to being isolated with a beautiful thirty-five-year-old woman for seven months?

'Sergio Foresti and Luciano Vittoni and Piero Ripandelli are brilliant scientists. It's an honour to be chosen to work with them. There is much we want to achieve particularly in furthering understanding of the complexities of climate change.'

She was on record as being concerned with environmental issues. Wouldn't her work contribute to opening up the continent to oil and mineral extraction? Did this worry her?

'This is a good question and I've had to think deeply about it before accepting the appointment. But there's no gain to be had in ignorance. Knowledge of our planet brings great rewards as well as risks. It isn't the knowledge itself which is threatening but the sacrificing of long-term sustainability to short-term greed.'

As a former friend, would she like to comment on Cosimo Mastrogiovanni's affair with Lori Micheli?

'Cosimo's a sweetie. I wish him every happiness.'

Members of the Appointment Committee looked at

each other and nodded: PNRA couldn't wish for a better telegenic presence. A bit of controversy wouldn't do them any harm.

Sergio received the news with a mixture of disappointment and excitement. Vexed that he was not to remain Head of Base, yet thrilled to be living and working alongside a beautiful woman. Luciano was impressed by her work as a scientist. Passionate about degradation of the environment, he admired her courage in taking on the oil industry. Piero would have preferred a man, not because he thought a woman any less capable, but she was bound to inhibit their free bantering, free farting, male camaraderie.

As she stepped from the helicopter, Sergio was the first to greet her. She saw a man with a large, powerful body-shape, dark eyes, a rugged face with an imperfection on the cheek and a trim black beard.

He said, 'I'm Sergio. I'm delighted you're here to join the team.'

'Thank you, Sergio. I've read a lot about you. I'd be grateful for you to show me the ropes until I've settled in.'

'Don't believe all you read.'

He introduced her to Luciano who was much shorter in stature with a smooth, round, vulnerable face, prominent cheek bones and brown eyes. Even though younger than Sergio, his hair, unlike Sergio's, was receding. Although quietly self-confident, he was more restrained than Sergio.

Luciano said, 'I hope you're happy here. We need someone like you to arouse the public to demand that political leaders around the world act on climate change.'

'And we need you, Luciano, to provide the data ammunition.'

Finally, Sergio introduced Piero. He was as tall as Sergio but lanky, with a thin face, long neck and prominent Adam's apple. With his curly light-brown hair and soft beard, he looked surprisingly young; you could still see the boy that he once was.

Giacinta said, 'I read your paper. Very impressive. You're now taking that forward. Is it going well?'

'I wouldn't wish to be anywhere else.'

Giacinta, aware of Sergio's position, was wary of asserting authority and making changes, but there was one issue that she couldn't avoid and when she took action, met with resentment and resistance. Panigatti had left them free to sleep as and when they wished. After all, it was not so important during the season of twenty-four hours of sunlight, but this laxity would not do during the winter months. Giacinta arrived on 23rd April, austral autumn when the decline in daylight hours was at its most extreme. On that day there were six hours of sunlight, 11am to 5pm.

A week later, the sun departed and would not return for a hundred and six days. That last day, they watched as the light increased in intensity until, suddenly, the golden tip of the Sun's orb rose dazzlingly brilliant. Ten minutes later, it had gone. In the days that followed, with the long hours of daytime twilight, it was natural for the body to suppose that the mid-day glow in the northern sky was dawn and, left to itself, wake up later and later in the day. Many had experienced the resulting complete confusion of the body-clock and the loss of regular sleep. Giacinta set her alarm clock at 8:30am and if the men were still asleep at 9am, she roused them. With this new rule they were not happy.

Soon after she arrived, she was alone and cooking when Piero came in.

'What the hell are you doing?' he said.

'I'm making you *fagioli all'uccelletto*. Why?'

'You've put these beans in water!'

'How else do you make beans in the style of little birds?'

'But they're our chips!' Piero exclaimed, quickly straining the water from off the beans.

'You can't make chips out of beans.'

'No, no, you don't understand. They're our poker chips. You were about to destroy ten million Euros!'

To Sergio, Luciano and Piero's discomfort, Giacinta took a much closer interest in their work than they were used to. They reacted defensively: fearing interference, anticipating criticism, suspicious that she might claim part of their work as her own. However, they were impressed by how quickly she grasped the essence of their research. Her questions were intelligent and of increasing value to them. What did they think that meant? Had they thought of...? Why was that happening? As they saw that her interest was benign, they began to look forward to the regular briefing sessions she had insisted on.

She didn't waste any time before initiating her own work: to measure changes in depth of ice cover in a number of locations near the Camp. She often needed help from one of the others and this increased their comradeship.

She enthusiastically entered their table-tennis tournament and encouraged them to join her in daily yoga. She didn't care for their noisy card games, but sang, as loudly as they did, popular operatic choruses:

Va, pensiero, sull'ali dorate; va, ti posa sui clivi,

sui colli, ove olezzano tepide e molli l'aure dolci del suolo natal!

Fly, thought, on wings of gold; go settle upon the slopes and the hills, where, soft and mild, the sweet airs of our native land smell fragrant!

And they thought of springtime at home.

***

Giacinta had a feminine curiosity, was not afraid of asking personal questions and was an attentive listener. They soon succumbed to talking about their private lives. Sergio had been married but his wife, tiring of life as an expedition widow, left him to have babies with another man. He was endlessly entertaining with stories of past assignments and the extraordinary people on them. Prompted by Giacinta, he told her he had a friend, Anna, in

Bologna whom he visited occasionally. She was an actor who, when young, had plenty of work on stage, but now, at fifty, more often worked as a tour guide.

Luciano, unlike the other two, was a devout Catholic. He loved his wife, Beatrice, and was besotted with his little daughters, Rosa and Sophia, saddened to miss the almost daily changes in them as they grew older.

Intensity was a key feature of Piero's personality. He was engaged to Isabella, a mathematician, but in no hurry to get married. When relaxed, he was great company, with a repertoire of very good saucy jokes. He was touchingly attached to a long woollen scarf his mother had knitted for him. He was teaching himself to play classical guitar on an instrument generously left by a previous occupant. He played very softly, ceasing altogether if someone had a headache.

Between blizzards, even in temperatures of over minus forty, all four of them delighted in being out in the snow, for work if that was required, for fun if it wasn't. On the best of days, there were clear, starry skies when even sound was frozen so you could hear your heartbeat. Giacinta's work involved establishing the exact location of a test site, laying out an array of geophone pick-ups, boring a hole, detonating a charge of dynamite and recording the subsequent seismic shock-waves.

To drill the hole in the ice, Giacinta had a petrol-engine hole-borer with a helical auger. It required two people to hold the drill and swing it, in tandem, rhythmically and rapidly, up and down so as to clear the ice from the hole. It was tiring work but warmed you up and kept you fit.

Piero, as much as the other two men, grew more and more fond of Giacinta. He admired how, without embarrassment, she could talk freely of sex and love. He confided that during all the times with his fiancée, Isabella, he had never known her to have an orgasm.

Giacinta was touched by his confiding in her. 'Have you

asked her?'

'No. She's never seemed unhappy or dissatisfied with our love making.'

'You must talk to her about it. Every woman is different, physiologically and psychologically. One cannot generalise, but few women would resent a lover being concerned for their sexual fulfilment. So often, the opposite is the case, unsatisfied women pissed off that their men aren't bothered.'

Giacinta looked down the microscope.

'Can you see them?' Sergio said. 'Held in the ice for hundreds of years, and they still live.'

Giacinta, smiling, turned to look at him. His face was inches away. He leant forward and kissed her on the lips. She didn't move away. She lifted her hand and stroked the side of his face. She said, in a gentle voice, 'It's not a good idea, is it? Think of the other two. How would *you* feel and react if I formed a relationship with one of *them*? The four of us are very happy together, I don't want that to change.'

***

She was puzzled by some of her results. She showed Luciano. 'You see here and here, these low intensity, intermittent vibrations of a different frequency. Sometimes they appear, other times they don't.'

'Most likely it's a fault in one of the geophones.'

Giacinta tested all the geophones. She examined more closely the paper print-out from the seismometer. The Earth, from its seismic activity, rings like a church bell. A larger strike, such as an earthquake, sets it vibrating more violently, the nearer to the site of the shock, the stronger the signal. Her test detonations were, of course, evident on the seismometer read-out, but so also, upon examination, were the, easily missed, mysterious other vibrations. She said to the others that she wanted to explore the matter further and take readings over a larger area, but the weather turned against her. Visibility was reduced to tens of metres as high winds filled the air with ice particles.

***

Sergio couldn't restrain himself from speaking to Luciano and Piero about his feelings for Giacinta. 'I feel this electric charge whenever I'm near her. She's the most sexy woman I've ever come across. She sets my heart racing.'

Luciano and Piero said nothing but the sentiments diffused like hot whisky into their blood. As scientists, they never ceased being excited working in Antarctica. Now the atmosphere was more than excited, it was charged. Giacinta sensed the change but gave it no acknowledgement, attempting to retain the easy-going way of living with them she had established.

Relaxing after a meal, Sergio said, 'I wonder if the boys and girls on the Mars Mission will have sex.'

There was a brief silence then they all laughed.

'Well,' Sergio continued, '*we're* just here for a year. Three years is a long time to go without sex.'

Luciano said, 'That goes for their partners as well. Don't you think they would hope and expect their loved ones to remain faithful during that time?'

Giacinta said, 'With three men and two women, the one thing they can't do is couple up.'

'Even if two of the men were gay,' Piero said.

Giacinta said, 'Knowing the propensity for human beings to get themselves into trouble, one hopes they have the sense to pack contraceptives.'

'And a pill for abortion.' Sergio said.

Luciano said, 'Maybe abstinence is the best policy.'

Sergio said, 'They're intelligent, they ought to be able to arrange it to everybody's satisfaction.'

Giacinta said, 'Scientist we may be, rational we're not.

Hearts become entwined and then it's painful to disengage.'

***

Alone with Giacinta, Piero said, 'D'you think it's possible to remain happily married to the same person for life?'

'You're the sort of person who might manage it.'

'If I got married now, I think I'd always regret missing the experience of getting to know, intimately, a variety of different women.'

'I believe people in long-term monogamous relationships are happier.'

'Are you happy?'

'My work means a lot to me. I couldn't settle down with any one man for very long.'

'Don't you want children?'

'Ah! The motherhood crave: it's the curse of the free woman.'

Piero was thoughtfully silent for a few minutes then put the question he had hesitated to ask. 'Would you teach me to be a good lover?'

'You're very sweet. How would Sergio and Luciano react if I took you to my bed?'

***

The weather improved and, with help from the others, Giacinta made a series of readings. She poured over the data.

'It's as if,' she told them, 'there's some intermittent seismic activity originating from a source fifty or so kilometres away in the direction 072 degrees. I would like to travel there and investigate.'

They knew such a journey in mid-winter was hazardous. Sergio said, 'It could all go horribly wrong.'

Luciano said, 'It might be a wasted trip but we can't ignore these strange readings. We'd kick ourselves if we passed up on something that turned out to be important. I think we should go.'

Piero said, 'Count me in.'

Sergio said, 'Well, if you're up for it, so am I.'

Giacinta said, 'I knew you'd support me. But one of us needs to stay here.'

They all wanted to go. Giacinta had to go. Sergio argued the necessity of having a medic on the trip. Luciano and Piero picked straws: Piero won.

***

They would be entering an area into which neither they nor any before them had travelled. They studied the aerial photographic survey of Antarctica. After traversing some low foothills, they would need to find their way over a col between two mountains, both peaks over three thousand metres. Then descend to, and cross, a plateau towards a second range of mountains. They estimated three days for the trip, a day's travelling each way and a day to locate the centre of the seismic disturbances and take measurements.

They got themselves ready to leave but waited for clear sky and no wind. Although the weather, always changeable, could never be predicted, statistically, fifty-per-cent of days at that time of year had gentle winds and clear visibility. They packed three scooters with care: scientific and navigation equipment (including Giacinta's geophones, hole-borer and dynamite), portable satellite phone, medical kit, fuel, one tent, sleeping bags, food and a stove. On 27th May, in bright moonlight, they set off. Luciano, looking miserable at being left behind, waved them goodbye.

***

Running over familiar territory, the first few hours went well, the moon illuminating the route ahead. But the journey up to the col was beset with difficulties: a fragmented landscape of large boulders and deep hollows that could swallow a scooter. More than once, they arrived at an impasse and had to turn back and detour.

The view from the col, when they got there, was stunning. The plateau lay before them and, beyond that, the far range of mountains with some distant peak spinning swirls of cloud across the sky. But they couldn't stay long to admire the scene; the wind, funnelling through the col, was painful.

The descent from the col raised adrenaline. Piero, in the lead, disappeared over a ledge. Cautiously, Giacinta approached the edge and looked down to see a twenty-metre drop of terrifying steepness. At the bottom, the slope curved, like the interior of a bowl, onto a flat area of snow. And there was Piero, standing away from his scooter, looking up at her. She walked around to see if there was an alternative descent. A rock wall either side made this impossible. There was nothing for it, she would have to drive down. Heart pumping, she let the scooter slide slowly forward. Then she was hurtling down. Then violently thrust away from the cliff onto the flat area. Shaken, she closed her eyes to recover. Piero put his arm around her. 'Well done,' he said.

They looked up towards Sergio. He clearly didn't like it. After what seemed like an age, he let the scooter roll forward. He wasn't square on and at the bottom of the slope, the scooter pitched over, throwing Sergio off into the snow. They ran over to him. He had an abrasion on his face where his goggles had cut into him but, otherwise, he was unscathed. Although the scooter was readily re-started, its headlight was smashed. Sergio said, 'How the hell do we get back up there?'

They proceeded cautiously to the plateau below and

there stopped to eat bread and tinned sardines and drink the water they had melted on the stove. Speeding across the wide plane, they made up lost time. They circled clockwise round the base of a large conical-shaped mountain and found themselves ascending a valley towards another col. The moon had set and they had no idea of the territory ahead. Sergio, without headlight, was placed in the middle of the three. Giacinta, worried about being able to navigate to the right place, thought they would have to stop and camp and wait for better light.

When they reached the top of the col, they knew they didn't need any instruments to find what they were looking for: it was there before them. Five kilometres ahead, in the dark frozen waste, a great banner of fiery red swirling into the sky with fine jets of orange light spraying upward, tracing parabolic arcs before falling back to earth. They stared in disbelief. Volcanic activity? In the heart of Antarctica? It was unheard of. There was only one active volcano in Antarctica, Mount Erebus, seven hundred kilometres away. With mounting excitement, they drove closer. Now they could smell it. And the stars were lost in smoke. Pouring down the side of a hill was a broad stream of bright golden-red molten lava. How dangerous was it? Could the volcano blow its top? They didn't know. They went as close as they dared, the air hot and sulphurous. There was a continuous roar and hiss as the hot lava met the ice. They took photographs and video.

Giacinta knew the importance of this event and that it was newsworthy. Sergio set up a satellite link with Luciano, told him to record the video and send it on to PNRA. They formed themselves into a TV crew, Piero holding the camera, Giacinta facing camera with the volcano behind her and Sergio holding a torch to illuminate her face. Giacinta composed in her head what she was going to say, then told the world in Italian, Spanish, English and Mandarin that Antarctica had a second live volcano.

***

Anna poured herself a glass of very cold Verdicchio and rested her sore feet. It had been a demanding day, hot and, in spite of her passion for Bologna, her native city, the party of English remained unenthusiastic tourists. She wondered why they bothered. They were also mean with their tips. Half watching, she was jolted to attentiveness when she heard Sergio's name on the television evening news. 'A major coup for Italian science...the discovery by a team of Italian scientists of a newly erupted volcano in Antarctica...' There followed a dark screen with a difficult to define glow which viewers were told was the volcano. And then, torchlight on her face, Giacinta, clearly excited but in a controlled voice describing the extraordinary scene of the volcano. She said it was probably a Strombolian and made an estimate of its magnitude, size of ash plume and rate of lava flow. She outlined the journey they had undertaken to get there. She named her colleagues and said how delighted they were to be the first to set sight on this totally new volcano. The newscaster said that as the volcano was as yet unnamed, maybe it should be called Vagnussi.

Anna thought to herself, my God, she's pretty. Sergio's bound to fall in love with her.

***

Isabella never saw the broadcast, she was in Beijing. Although her degree was mathematics, she had taken a masters in economic modelling and now worked for the Italian Treasury. Her mother was Italian but her father was Norwegian and from him she had inherited her long blonde hair. It was her ability to make rapid calculations that prompted her boss to include her in the delegation to beg (negotiate, one should say) financial support from the

Chinese. It was her mother who phoned to tell her Piero had found a new volcano and everybody was very excited.

Isabella felt guilty. It was some time since she had last skyped him. Although she was sure she loved Piero and she really did miss him, she also loved her work and was thankful that he was not around to distract her. She resolved to contact him as soon as possible and congratulate him.

***

'Marco, come and stand next to me and let's see you in the mirror with these funny hats on.' Marco was Beatrice's last interview of the day. She was anxious to go: a child-minder had collected Rosa and Sophia from school but it was soon time to take them home.

Marco's mother said, 'Please, Marco, come and stand next to Beatrice.'

'What do you think of this Superman mask?' Beatrice said.

Marco had been referred to the Institute with long-term behaviour problems. Beatrice diagnosed an impairment in the development of self-awareness. By the age of four to five, most children acquire self-conscious emotions: shame, pride, guilt, envy, embarrassment. In Beatrice's tests, Marco, now seven, showed an absence of these emotions. A brain scan had revealed medial prefrontal damage. Beatrice was looking for signs that Marco was responding to a new drug treatment.

Phoebe, a serving lady in the canteen, popped her head around the door. 'Quick, it's about your hubby, on the box.' Beatrice ran into the canteen followed by Marco and his Mum. The television, always on, was high up on a shelf. Beatrice was disappointed that the clip didn't show Luciano. But she was pleased when she heard Giacinta say his name. He would be pissed off that he had been left behind to man the Base. She was overcome with emotion. She missed him desperately. She would spend the evening phoning everybody with the news.

A glass crashed to the floor of the canteen. Beatrice, Phoebe, and Marco's Mum turned around to see Marco standing by the splintered glass. His face was flushed and he was biting his lip. Perceiving his embarrassment, Beatrice swept him into her arms and said, 'You wonderful boy.'

***

They found a place to camp, in a sheltered hollow, well away from the volcano. They ate, with rice, a dried packet meal reconstituted with hot water that tasted of flavoured mush and was labelled, 'Duck à l'Orange'. Much more to their enjoyment was the drink of hot chocolate. Their tent, pyramid in shape with steep sides, was all right for two, a tight squeeze for three. They slept in their clothes inside their sleeping bags on top of sheepskin rugs on top of insulating mats on top of self-inflating air beds. The temperature was minus forty-two.

The following day the weather still held fine. They had an instant oatmeal breakfast. It was vital to eat sufficient food energy to keep body core temperature normal. Using midday twilight and moonlight, they made a thorough survey of the volcano including recording its seismic activity. Sergio collected samples of ice. Piero examined the interface between lava and snow. They measured wind speed and made estimates of the volume and rate of lava flow. Keeping to windward, they climbed as high as they dared towards the edge of the crater. Giacinta remembered her volcanology training: it's vital to keep your attention on the crater. Always look for the lava bombs that track through the air and try to pick out the ones that might be coming towards you and step out of the way. If you hear an explosion, do not turn away or run or crouch down. Keep your attention on the crater.

A number of times she had to step aside as a ball of hot lava sizzled into the ice where she had been standing. Giacinta thought how extraordinary was that interface of ice and fire. How the, so solid, two-and-a-half thousand metre depth of ice covering most of Antarctica together with the rock below was but a thin crust over such a fiery liquid tumult. They took more photographs. Piero wanted to go higher but Sergio said, 'Let's get out of here, we've no idea if it will explode.'

The light too dim to do any more surveying, they returned to the tent. They ate, again with rice, Boeuf Bourguignon, tasting no different from Duck à L'Orange. Tucked up in their bags, and on the point of drifting to sleep, repeatedly, they would burst out laughing as one or other of them would let loose a loud fart. They blamed the Boeuf Bourguignon.

Refreshed and in high spirits and with a following wind, they set off to return to Base. They stopped at the col to look back at the volcano. It was magnificent. Belching smoke and ash lit by flashes of incandescent sprays, it was the allegory of power and menace, the disturbed god of the underworld in angry mood.

They descended slowly to the plateau where they were able to double their speed. It was exhilarating. The mountains ahead were gaining in clarity in the softly luminous sky. At the far side of the plateau, they began the ascent of the mountain towards the col. They came to the wall and stopped there to eat, staring up at the impossible incline. It was out of the question to try and ride the scooters up the ice wall.

Giacinta said she had a plan they could try. Piero cut steps in the ice, carried a rope to the top and hauled up the ice drill. On the flat, some metres beyond the edge of the wall, he and Giacinta drove the hole-borer deep into the ice. They unloaded the scooters. They looped the rope around the auger and attached one end to the front of Piero's scooter and the other end to the rear of Sergio's scooter. Using the auger as a pulley, Sergio drove away from the incline as Piero drove up it. Their fear was the auger might bend or break or pull out of the ice. But it held. Piero made it onto the flat area above the wall. Then they used that scooter to assist the other two and haul up all the gear.

It all took a long time. They were so completely absorbed in their task, that it was only when they were ready to set off again they became aware of how much the wind had gained in strength. By the time they reached the col, they were in a gale. It was better on the lee side, but ice particles whipped into the air made it difficult to see ahead. And below them, they had to traverse *La Valle di Grossi Massi* as they called it – The Valley of Big Boulders. But more dangerous still was the wind chill and the threat of hypothermia. It was madness to try and continue. They looked for some shelter from the wind and with great difficulty erected the tent and got the necessary gear inside. They carefully tied down everything that was left outside.

Piero went into the tent to sort out the bedding while, shivering, Sergio and Giacinta cuddled together trying to retain warmth. When they were squeezed inside, lighting the stove meant keeping open a vent of the tent and this allowed the ingress of ice particles. With cold stalking as a killer, they tried to keep clothing and sleeping bags as dry as possible. Sergio attempted to make contact with Luciano but it wouldn't work. Fuel was another worry. Essential for preparing food and, more importantly, water. They had enough for three more days.

Against the fearful noise of the wind madly shaking the tent, they lay in the dark telling each other stories. Stories of their lives and the people they had met. Stories about their families and childhood. Stories of past loves. Intermittently, they slept. They played a game: attempting to recall in exact detail the plots of films and books and plays and operas (*Romeo and Juliet*, Chekhov short stories,

Sorrentino movies, The *Marriage of Figaro*, Montalbano mysteries).

Leaving the tent was a horror but, on occasion, necessary. Each time they had to dig themselves out through the accumulated drift. When outside, they knew how easy it was to become disorientated. Failure to find your way back to the tent was a death sentence.

At times, they switched on a lantern and prepared food. A day passed and still the storm raged. Sergio had an extraordinary memory for the lyrics of popular songs and got the other two to sing along. They got stiff from lying down and had to stretch. To warm up, they played a game: rolling into the middle of the three bodies alternately from left and right. They lost all sense of time.

***

Luciano had a nightmare followed, later, by a dream. Both were enacted in unearthly silence as if in a world without sound. He knew she was there ahead of him. The snow, like small shot, dashed itself into his face. The wind tore at him, railing at his refusal to release himself to its power. He forced his legs forward, the drifting snow over his knees. Inside his head, he could hear her crying out, 'help me, help me.' But he couldn't find her.

He struggled forward, energy draining, increasingly weary. More than anything in the world he wanted to lay down in the snow, close his eyes and release himself to sleep. But he knew if he did so, he would die and so would she. He tried to cry out to her, 'Giacinta, Giacinta, I'm coming, I'm coming,' but could make no sound.

Suddenly, he found her, unconscious, lying in the snow.

He hauled her onto his back and turned to make the journey to the safety of the tent. Soon, he knew the effort was beyond him. To save himself, he would have to abandon her. Tears freezing on his face, he held her stiff frozen body.

He awoke to the scream of the blizzard rampaging outside and the overwhelming relief that it had been but a bad dream.

Frustration drove him to pace about the cabin. He imagined they needed help but he was powerless to do anything. Nothing to be done except wait and pray. He decided to try and get more sleep, he wanted to be as fresh as possible for what may lay ahead.

He was in an examination room, bare, grey, sitting at a small square wooden table. Similar tables, arranged in neat lines and rows, filled the room and at each table, sat an unclothed mannequin. There was no sound. The door opened and Giacinta walked silently to the front of the room. She was naked. She picked up a blue board-pen and began writing mathematical equations on the whiteboard. He couldn't take his eyes off her, the way her body flowed and reshaped as she twisted to face him then turned back to the board, her weight on her left foot, her right arm extended. She put down the pen and slowly walked between the rows towards him. She stood beside him and he twisted in his chair and looked up into her face. She extended her arms and placed them around his neck then bent down and kissed him on the lips. The kiss was beautiful, an affirmation. He stood up and put his arms around her and pulled her close then saw, through the open doorway, Beatrice, motionless, regarding them with a look meditative and dispassionate.

He awoke suddenly, recalling his dream in immaculate detail. He knew it was significant, that it was offering some important truth and he held on, as long as he could, to the erotic charge of her kiss.

***

Another day in the tent, then the capricious God of

Wind chose to release them. As if emerging from hibernation, they dug themselves out of confinement. The pink glow in the northern sky proclaimed it to be late morning. The first job was to find the shovel, cursedly buried with the scooters. It was a joy to be out of the tent. They relished their large bowls of oatmeal porridge. It took two hours to dig out the scooters and pack up. Then they set off to navigate L*a Valle di Grossi Massi* which they found to be much altered by new accumulations of drifted ice.

Reunion with Luciano was emotional and exuberant. Whooping and crying, he hugged them close. 'Thank God! Thank God!' He kept repeating.

'Did you get the video?' they said.

***

Anna, Isabella and Beatrice phoned their love, speaking of how they first heard the news. Messages of congratulation came in from a variety of scientific and political leaders including the Prime Minister.

Luciano could see that a new bond of shared adventure had grown between the other three and regretted he had not been part of that. As if sensing this, Giacinta was particularly warm towards him, giving him more of her time.

When he was alone with Sergio, he said, 'I know that when people tell you their dreams it's intensely boring, but in spite of that, I want to share this one with you.' He then told Sergio of his dream. 'What d'you think it means?'

'It's blindingly obvious, isn't it? It's your wish fulfilment. You lust after Giacinta, don't we all? You're worried about being unfaithful to Beatrice and you wish her to give you permission to fuck Giacinta.'

'What about the mannequins?'

'Oh, that's us, me and Piero. You want Giacinta to single you out for her affection. The examination room is our base here, where we're confined.'

'And the maths on the board?'

'You admire Giacinta's intellect as much as you're aroused by her body.'

'You make it sound sordid. That's not how I felt it.'

'Only if you think desire is sordid. Sex is the most wonderful gift in the world, yet we invest it with so much angst. Providing we don't hurt each other, emotionally I mean, why can't we just enjoy it and celebrate it?'

'I wouldn't want to hurt Beatrice.'

'What the eye doesn't see... The question is, how would you feel if you had to share with two of the dummies?'

***

It was 5th June, Giacinta's birthday. The three made a fuss of her: breakfast in bed, a bunch of home-made paper flowers, a bottle of champagne and a cake made of chocolate and biscuits. In the evening, they said they wished to offer her the finest presents in the world. They cleared a space to create a stage and placed a chair for her as audience.

Sergio said, 'We're offering you three presents, one from each of us, but you're only allowed to choose just one of them.'

'But what if I want all three?'

'Uh-uh, not permitted. In choosing one, you reject the other two. And you must kiss the one of us whose present you choose.'

The three left the room then, wearing woollen hats, re-entered, walking behind each other in a line very erect and dignified. Piero carried a script, Sergio a plastic bottle wrapped in gold paper. Sergio and Luciano sat down, again holding themselves erect and attentive.

Piero bowed to Sergio and Luciano and said, 'Your Majesties, Your Royal Highnesses, Ladies and Gentlemen. Today, we celebrate the achievements of Professor

Vagnussi. This Prize recognises the numerous seminal contributions to theoretical, computational and interpretational methods of seismology made by Professor Vagnussi. A sequence of influential papers led to the Chiernov-Vagnussi seismogram algorithm, an outstanding achievement in one so young. Professor Vagnussi participates to a quite staggering extent in the life of the international geophysical community through her intellectual input and leadership. We salute her single-minded dedication to a life of scientific endeavour.'

Turning to Giacinta, he continued, 'Professor Vagnussi, on behalf of the Royal Swedish Academy of Sciences it is my privilege to convey to you my warmest congratulations for your outstanding work. I now ask you to step forward to receive, from the hands of His Majesty the King, your Nobel Prize.'

Sergio stood up. Smiling, Giacinta rose and bowed to His Majesty. Sergio handed her the prize and they shook hands. Luciano took photographs.

Giacinta said, 'Thank you, your Majesty, you do me a very great honour.'

The three left the room again. Sergio came back, turned off the lights and shone a spot lamp on the doorway. With his arms held tightly around Piero and staring up into his face, Luciano sauntered into the room. He was wearing a long shirt as if it were a dress. He was barefoot and without trousers. Thrusting from beneath his shirt were two lumpy breasts. Giacinta burst out laughing.

Sergio said, 'Observe. She is glued to her man. She will not release him. She gazes wonderingly into his face. She can think of nothing but him. Her whole being is in a rapture, her mind suffused with ecstatic joy. She knows this is why she was born. She knows now she is truly alive. She does not tire of being held by him. One kiss ended, she is impatient for the next. Her everyday world is freshly coloured, the dull and jaded are made vivid and joyous. Her step is light, her senses enhanced. The scent of a melon, the taste of a cherry, the flavour of wine, the catch in the voice of a singer, all are newly intense. She wants to sing out loud. She wants to hug everybody. And when he tells her how wonderful she is and that they must never part and he will love her forever, she is ecstatic and knows that nothing is as important as this, not even a Nobel prize.'

Sergio presented her with a big heart-shaped card and said, 'Giacinta, my present to you is...love.'

Giacinta said, 'Oh it were that simple.'

The three left the room again. Giacinta settled into the chair wondering what would come last.

Luciano came in without the other two, closing the door after him. He addressed Giacinta. 'I also give you love. A love which, when you dwell upon it, makes you cry. You cry when you're hurt, yes, but you cry also when overwhelmed by emotion. And it's pregnant with emotion you are, when you think on your love... for a child.'

Luciano had to stop, even talking about it in a matter-of-fact way affected him.

'We are tensioned like cellos with strings of emotion. Mute when unplayed, but when the bow of love for a child is drawn across our strings, we sing.'

He walked across and opened the door. Piero wheeled a trolley into the room and in it sat Sergio naked except for a little cotton cap, a towel wrapped over his loins as a nappy and, in his mouth, a dummy. Giacinta again burst out laughing.

'Behold,' Luciano announced, 'your child. And from the first moment your baby is placed squealing into your arms, to the end of your life, you will not cease to possess that love which makes you cry. My gift to you is... love for a child.'

Giacinta said, very formally, 'I thank you for your gift. One could not wish for a more sturdy child.'

Sergio said, 'OK, you've now got to choose and one of

us gets a kiss.'

Giacinta said, 'Go and get dressed. How can one possibly think straight looking at you like that?'

When they came back, Giacinta said, 'So, the choice before me is this: from you Piero, success in my career, intellectual fulfilment; from you Sergio, to love and be loved by a man, romantic fulfilment; and from you Luciano, having and loving a child, emotional fulfilment. And I can't have all three.'

'Nope, they're mutually exclusive,' Piero said, thinking of himself and Isabella.

'Some women manage it, with a bit of compromise here and there,' Giacinta said.

Luciano silently agreed with her – with compromises, Beatrice had all three. He said, 'Think of it as which of these three you would prioritise.'

After a little time, Giacinta said, 'Intellectual, romantic, emotional fulfilment – I can't choose. I refuse to choose. We women need all three.'

'What d'you say, lads?' Sergio said. Then he turned to Giacinta, 'All right, but you're going to have to kiss all three of us. And I don't mean a peck on the cheek. I mean a proper kiss delivered from the heart.'

Giacinta said, 'I knew I was right to persist, now I get three kisses instead of one. But I'm not going to kiss you while I'm being watched, two of you clear off.'

Piero was first in. A foot taller than her, he appeared gauche, uncertain how to begin. Giacinta took him by the hand, led him to a chair and sat him down with herself on his lap. They kissed. Then, smiling, they looked into each other's face. Piero gently pulled her towards him again. This time, they relaxed more fully into the pleasures of the kiss. Giacinta was surprised by how it aroused her.

Sergio, on his turn, wrapped her in his arms and held her close, their bodies pressed together. Then he closed his eyes and waited. Giacinta put her hands behind his head and pushed her lips on his. Their kiss became all-consuming. They felt themselves tumbling into a dark space where nothing exists except the kiss.

Luciano held her hands and looked at her. 'You're very beautiful.' He kissed her gently, lovingly, investing the moment with great significance. He indulged the kiss as if it were warm sunshine.

He said, 'Can I ask you something? When people form friendships, invariably they're attracted towards one person more than another. We cherish all our friends, but some are more special. Yet I've noticed you're very careful to show no partiality between us. Is that because of your position as Head of Base?'

'Possibly when I first arrived, but now I don't need to be careful, I genuinely like all three of you. You're all special. Is that what you wanted to know?'

'No, that's not my question. Can I be frank? I think Sergio and Piero are under the impression that you would agree to have sex with them providing it were with all three of us. Is that right?'

'Has Sergio been talking to you?'

'No. No, he hasn't. I've just sensed it. Things said, and your reaction to them.'

Giacinta was alarmed. 'Oh, I'm so sorry. I can see now this has placed you in a difficult position. I should have been more circumspect. They've not tried to press you? Nothing is as important as we four retaining the happy relationships we've established.'

'No, you don't understand. I'm not complaining. I needed to know whether my sense of it were right so that I could tell you that if you were to...you know...What I want to say is, if this were a possibility, I'd be thrilled to be involved.'

At that moment, Sergio and Piero burst into the room, 'Hey! What's going on? That must have been some kiss.'

***

The following evening, after dinner, Giacinta, speaking softly, said, 'All three of you have, in one way or another, led me to understand that you would like your relationship with me to – how shall I put this? – become more intimate.'

Sergio and Piero looked with surprise towards Luciano but held their tongues.

'I've been thinking about something Sergio said: that intelligent, rational people ought to be able to arrange it so it works. We all know the dangers. If we're clear about what we're doing and organise it carefully, why shouldn't we enjoy something that could provide us with so much pleasure, without harm.'

Sergio said, 'Am I hearing this right? You're proposing to have sex with us, all three of us?'

'If that's what you are happy with and you accept certain ground-rules, then yes, that is what I'm suggesting.' Giacinta laughed. 'All three of you look as if you can't believe your luck.'

Piero said, 'You're right, we can't.'

Luciano said, 'What are your rules?'

'I've had my fill of sensational media coverage of my private life; you can imagine what they would make of this. We all have good reason to be discrete. We must solemnly swear that our arrangement remains a secret between us.'

They placed their right hands together and each of them, in turn, declared their commitment to secrecy.

'We're either all in this together or not at all; if one of us is unhappy with it, it will stop. Also, our arrangement ends the moment we leave this place to return home. Also, I enjoy sex but I'm not kinky, so no three or four in a bed.'

'What a shame,' Sergio said. They all laughed.

'I would like my room to remain my personal space so, if you don't mind, you can entertain me in your rooms. I like you all equally and I'm determined there'll be no preferences, so I'll not choose which of you I'll be visiting. We'll have a rota and I'll make an assignation with you to visit you according to the rota. What happens between me and each of you must remain private. It's hard not to chat. You might be tempted to share notes, but that could lead to upsets.'

Turning to Sergio, she said, 'Am I right that the medical tests we had before we came here mean that we don't need to take precautions?'

'None of us has any STIs, if that's what you mean, they would have shown up in the tests. Providing you're on the pill, it's fine.'

Luciano laughed, 'It sounds as if we're planning an expedition to the Pole rather than having fun in bed.'

Giacinta said, 'I'm sorry it's so unromantic but we do need to set the ground-rules then we can enjoy ourselves. Oh, and one last thing, this is an affair of the body not the heart. I'm not going to fall in love with any of you and you're not going to fall in love with me.'

Piero said, 'Who's first on the rota?'

Sergio said, 'Eager, aren't we? We could play poker for it.'

'No, no, no,' Giacinta said. 'I'm not going to be a prize in your poker game.'

She removed all the hearts from the pack of cards, shuffled them, and laid them face down on the table. 'Pick a card, highest goes first, ace is high.'

Luciano leant forward and turned over a card, it was the ten. Sergio flipped over the eight. Finally, Piero picked his card, it was the king. Giacinta turned to Piero, 'What d'you think. Why wait? Do we have a date this evening?'

***

Giacinta entered Piero's bedroom. It smelled of

deodorant and she could see he had made an effort to tidy up, clothes stuffed into a cupboard. They both felt awkward.

'Come and give me a hug,' she said. She had to tilt her head back to look up at him. 'So, you want me to be your mentor? Guide you in the skilled art of lovemaking.' She adopted the tone of a sports coach. 'Three P's: patience, practice and persistence. Have you ever hand-whipped cream to make it thicken? You whisk and whisk and your hand starts hurting. And then negative psychology kicks in. Maybe it's not cream, or at least, not cream that thickens. Pointless then to continue. Fight that. You have to believe it's cream and that it will thicken. Women are cream. Give her time. Have the right touch and she will get there.'

They undressed and she lay down on her back on his single bed. 'Imagine I'm Isabella. Are your hands warm? Gently stroke the inner part of her thighs. No, not up and down, always upwards. Start at the knees. Short strokes, ending each time a little nearer her groin. You must tantalise her. Get her to desire more than anything in the world, your fingertips on her clitoris.'

Giacinta closed her eyes and concentrated on the sensations. As she rose in arousal, she took hold of his hand and moved it for him until, with a little cry, she climaxed. When she had recovered, she grinned and said, 'Well done. I'm now super thick cream. Come on top of me and let me hold you.'

***

Two days passed before Giacinta tapped on Luciano's door.

As always, he had music playing: a folk tune sung to a lively dance rhythm, thrumming guitars, a warbling clarinet and a male vocalist. He was lying on his bed. On seeing her he waved her in.

'That's nice,' she said.

He got up, took her in a ballroom dance hold and sped her round in time to the fast waltz rhythm. He sang along:

Di chiare nubi è l'aria serena
Di gioia piena il giorna sorà;
di luce ardente si tinge la sera
e la natura nel sonno cadrà.

(The sky is cloudless and clear,
The day will be full of joy;
The evening takes on a glowing tinge
And nature is about to fall asleep.)

Out of breath, they hugged each other close. He then carelessly threw off his clothes and chucked two pillows onto the carpeted floor. Giacinta undressed and, intrigued, allowed herself to be seated on a pillow facing him. He shuffled forward, intertwining his limbs with hers so that they were close enough to kiss. He was a carefully deliberate lover. She had, in her past, explored most of the repertoire of pleasures her body was capable of, including a flirtation with tantric sex, which didn't inspire, but Luciano was a maestro. He brought her again and again to an intensity of sweetness she had not believed possible. She lost all sense of time.

Later, much later, she awoke, still on the floor, curled into his side, her head resting on his arm.

'You're very responsive.' he said.

'And you're an asset to womankind. Beatrice is a lucky woman.'

'No, I'm the lucky one.'

'I was surprised when you agreed to join Sergio and Piero.'

'I think Beatrice would understand.'

'What would she understand?'

'Here, we are displaced. A nether world where the old rules don't apply. Constantly, you appear erotically in my dreams. I don't think she would blame me for stepping into my dreams. When we get back, we will re-awaken to our real lives and our time here will then seem like an amazing sleep.'

***

Giacinta waited three days before making an arrangement to see Sergio the following evening. There was a sudden improvement in the weather, the wind calmed and there was almost a full moon. Weeks without sun with just a brief twilight at midday, the moon in a clear sky was enormously important to them. It was incredibly beautiful: moonlight reflecting from the pinnacles and crevassed ice of the glacier, the mountains standing in bold relief against the sky. Sergio was out late helping Luciano with observations. When he got back, Giacinta asked him if he wanted to put off their assignation.

'Sono stupido? Give me ten minutes to have a shower and I'll be with you.'

Giacinta went into his room. She switched on the rose-coloured bedside lamp and turned off the harsh ceiling light. A Camilleri paperback lay on the bedside table: *Gli arancini di Montalbano*, one of the few she hadn't read. She'd ask him to pass it on when he'd finished it. She undressed and got into his bed. It had a slightly stale but not unpleasant smell. He padded in, his loins wrapped in a towel. She laughed, 'Wearing your nappy, I see.'

'Are you in the nude, in that bed?'

'Yes, I am. Come on, let's see what you have to offer behind that towel.'

Holding the towel in front of him to hide his cock, he did a little dance. 'Am I seductive?'

'As a stewed prune.'

'More like a banana,' he said as he whipped the towel

away to expose his hard on.

Sergio's style was missionary position. It didn't take long. As he came, he cried out, 'Fuck, fuck, fuck.' Afterwards, he said, 'Excuse the expletives; it was rather good.'

'You all three have different climactic exclamations.'

'Why, what do they say?'

'Should I be telling you this? Piero invokes, "Cristo, Cristo", and Luciano cries out, "Mama mia, Mama mia". But I like "fuck" – down to earth, unrestrained and descriptive.'

'And what d'you shout?'

'You'll have to find out.'

Sergio slid down to get his head between her legs. She pulled him back up again. 'No, it's fine. Just hold me.'

'But I want to see you come.'

'Next time. Sex is so strange isn't it? A mixture of science and magic, like an aeroplane. You take a shaped wing, move it fast through the air, and hundreds of tons rise into the sky – magic! You take a six inch sausage, stick it in a vagina, jiggle it about and both parties take off into clouds of pleasure. It's all magic.'

She asked him if, in the Camilleri stories, he thought the relationship between Montalbano and Livia was analogous to his relationship with Anna.

'How do you mean?'

'They live apart. She loves him and wants to marry him. He won't commit because he's attracted to the beautiful women he meets. Deep down, he really does love Livia but doesn't want her around too much to spoil his fun. When they do get together, they have a good time. Does that describe you?'

'True, Montalbano won't commit. It might be because, as you say, he loves Livia but wants to flirt. Or is it that he knows their relationship is flawed and lives in hope of one day meeting "the right woman"?'

'Well, which is it for you and Anna?'

'"Ho un cuore d'asino e uno di leone."'

'I don't understand.'

'It's a Sicilian expression Montalbano uses: "I've got a heart like a lion and another like a donkey." It means I'm in two minds. After a period of separation, I long to see Anna. We often phone or skype and I think, why aren't we together? But after some time being with her in Bologna or when she joins me in Rome, I have to admit, it's quite a relief to say goodbye. Camilleri keeps Montalbano eternally in that state of indecisive tension. Maybe that's the place I, too, choose to remain: betweendom.'

***

Suffused with pleasure, the Italian Antarctic Base became perfumed with quintessence of happiness and harmony. The men, eschewing jealousy, possessiveness and exclusivity, celebrated their mutual good fortune. They were bound together by Giacinta in the way a beautiful piece of music both exalts each individual listener and unites them in sharing exultation. Giacinta felt increasingly tender towards them with a strengthened conviction that she had made a good decision. They felt they were embarking on a new adventure, a *ménage a quàtre*, fraught with potential for disaster but so exciting if they could succeed. They returned to their scientific tasks with renewed vigour.

***

Together again in Piero's room, Giacinta taught him how to massage. 'D'you think you'll like doing it to Isabella?'

'Yes, but I think she might fall asleep.'

'Then do it on a Sunday morning. Now come and make love to me and I'll show you how to delay your orgasm. Eventually, with loads of practice, you'll get Isabella to come before you do.'

After they had made love, Piero said, 'Is it better for you if your lover has a big cock?'

'What do you think?'

'I think women like a man with a big cock.'

Out of consideration for his insecurity, her response was circumspect. 'Seeing a big cock, as opposed to a small one, is exciting, like seeing a big tiger rather than a small one, but when it's inside you, you can't see it, so it's not necessarily the actual size that counts but it's how big you can imagine it to be. I want to be able to imagine an impossibly large cock inside me. No man can measure up to my imagination.'

***

Two days' later, with Luciano, Giacinta was happy to swap roles: now the inductee rather than, as with Piero, the instructor. He arranged postures and pillows for them to be conjoined and comfortable. It was surfing in California. He showed her how to thrust out, and out and yet further out. Then, anticipating the incoming wave, rise up, balance, and with the most gentle, graceful, nuanced of movements, ride the crest, ride the crest and still ride the crest of orgasm until the very shallows. There to rest and then turn to push out again towards a new wave.

After an hour, in her mind the allegory changed. Tight together, they were hardly moving. She felt as if their bodies, between waist and thigh, had fused together. Penis and vagina united as a single internal organ that they shared. No longer giving rise to two distinct sensations experienced separately, but one and the same, coursing through both of them. Other than in the womb of her mother, it was the most profoundly intimate she had ever been with anybody. A slight contraction of the pelvic muscle was all that was needed to keep them permanently dancing on the very edge of the orgasmic precipice.

Another two days, and with Sergio it was all change again: neither teacher nor taught but at play. It was with Sergio that she was at her most relaxed. She revelled in his masculine strength: the man smell of him; the matt of hair on his chest, thick, black; the broad muscles of his thighs. One game involved chocolate mousse and another a ping pong ball. Or, impishly pretending to ignore him, she would start reading his book aloud, and he set about distracting her. Finally, unable to bear it any more, she would collapse in giggles and lay down on top of him plying him with kisses.

Giacinta thought of her vagina as shaped like an egg-timer: two rounded enclosures joined by a narrow waist. There was much loveliness to be had as the penis entered the first enclosure but the ultimate pleasure came when the head of the penis was trapped within the second. She held it there and, with tiny pelvic movements, polished it until she resonated, singing out at the pleasure of it: 'Bellissima! Bellissima!'

She said, 'You stand on a rock and look at the sea below. From experience, you know how it is to be in that sea: the holding of your breath, the coldness, the buoyancy, the translucent light. You stand on the rock, in the warm sun, with a gentle breeze and the sound of waves on a beach, and you dispassionately consider the water. Then you dive and, in an instant, you enter a different universe where there is nothing other than being immersed. I think sex is like that. It doesn't make sense until you're in it and then it becomes totally compelling.'

Sergio said, 'You make love as a man makes love.'

'How do you mean?'

'A man may, or may not, pleasure his partner. He may enjoy being pleasured by his partner but, at some stage, he wants to take hold of his partner to give himself pleasure. Women will give and receive pleasure but rarely use a man to pleasure themselves. You do.'

'Is that reprehensible – in a woman?'

'On the contrary, it's fantastic. You become ecstatic without me having to do a thing.'

'Women are more reticent because they feel vulnerable. For a woman to cut the cords of control and abandon herself to sex, she has to have complete trust in her man. When you use a man's body to lose yourself in waves of pleasure, you cannot but believe that he loves you.'

***

Midwinter's Day, 22nd June, was given over to celebration. The day was blessed with fine weather. It began with a pre-breakfast race: twice around the Base wearing nothing but boots and a woollen hat. After breakfast, they went skiing: a circular tour of the hills nearby. The twilight extended over a period of about nine hours that day, a northern glow with wisps of beautiful pink cloud along the horizon. For dinner, rather than have their usual frozen pre-cooked meal, they opted for each to prepare a dish. Inventively raiding their stock of frozen, dried and canned food, Giacinta made *Fave e Spinaci con Acciughe Marinate* (Broad Beans with Spinach and Anchovies); Sergio opted for *Conchiglie al Pomodoro e Porcini Secchi* (Pasta Shells with Tomatoes and Dried Mushrooms); Luciano, a skilled cook, prepared *Branzino Arrosto con Lenticchie* (Sea Bass with Lentils) and Piero made dessert *Sorbetto di Cilege* (Cherry Sorbet).

After dinner, they played silly party games and, with low lighting, danced. They opened bottles of champagne, reserved for this occasion, and toasted the passing of the winter solstice.

Drunk, they decided upon a contest of wrestling. They cleared a space in the living room and placed mats on the floor. They stripped to their knickers. Giacinta wrestled well but was too light to offer any serious opposition. The real contest was between the men. Piero was the fittest, Luciano was quick on his feet and Sergio had the weight. Luciano was soon eliminated. What began as a joke now turned serious: the young stag challenging the leading male for dominance. They agreed on the best of three bouts. There was a lot of huffing and puffing.

Luciano and Giacinta started dancing, then smooching, then kissing that evolved, like the wrestling, from jest to earnest. Luciano sat down on a chair and Giacinta straddled him. Before they had time to think about it, they were making love. Sergio shouted, 'Hey, you know, that's seriously distracting.'

Piero said, 'I didn't think Luci was next on the rota.'

Giacinta called out to them as they continued to wrestle, 'Don't worry, I'll console whichever of you loses.' She whispered in Luciano's ear, 'You really are the most adorable man.'

When they'd finished, Sergio and Piero lay side by side on their backs breathing heavily. Giacinta came over to them. 'OK, which one of you won?'

Together, they chanted, 'He did.'

Giacinta laid herself down alongside Piero. Sergio got up, put his arm around Luciano and together they went to the kitchen to drink water. Sergio said, 'If you were a woman, I'd fall in love with you.'

Luciano said, 'If I were a woman there's nobody I'd rather be fucked by.'

When they returned to the living room, Giacinta was asleep in Piero's arms. Sergio slapped her on the bum to wake her up. 'Come on,' he said, 'it's time for bed. I too need consoling.'

***

Giacinta woke up the following morning, in her own

bed, with a hangover. She felt ashamed of herself, to have been so dissolute. Retaining authority, she knew, entailed clarity about the limits of familiarity. Her intimacy with the men blurred constraints which is why she had taken so much care to define rules of sexual engagement. And now she had broken her own rules. She had invited disorder.

They all came to breakfast with fat heads. Strong coffee helped. They tidied up the mess from the previous day. Then they went for a brief walk. It was still fine and the cold air helped to revive them. In the afternoon, they worked at their individual tasks. Whatever else was going on in the Base, none of them was going to be distracted from pursuing their scientific work. Giacinta was relieved. She needn't have worried. Nothing untoward resulted from the festivities of Midwinter's Day.

If anything, their sexual lives settled into a more regular pattern: a weekly routine. Giacinta bedded with Piero on Mondays, Luciano on Wednesdays and Sergio on Fridays. The upkeep of the Base had always been good, now it was even more orderly. When weather allowed, the daily tasks outside (clearing ice, maintenance of equipment, storage of waste) were completed efficiently. Inside, everything was tidier, more cared for. There was no prompting from Giacinta in this: it came about naturally and spontaneously.

***

It was 7th August when Sergio confirmed Giacinta's suspicions. 'Yup, there's no doubt about it, you *are* pregnant.' Then, after a pause, as he pondered on the implications, 'Have you worked out which of us is most likely to be dad? Working back through the rota.'

Speaking slowly, significantly, Giacinta said, 'I think it's a bit more complicated than that. I think it was Midwinter's Day.'

'Oh!'

'There you go.'

He said, 'You wouldn't, by any chance, have deliberately stopped taking your pill, would you? You're thirty-five and women at that age without children...'

'Oral contraceptives do fail sometimes, don't they?'

'Oh yes, the failure rate is about nine percent, but...' He shrugged, failure of the contraceptive wasn't impossible. 'I've nothing here to bring on an abortion.'

'What! I've no intention of terminating my pregnancy.'

'Are you going to tell the others?'

'Of course, after dinner this evening.'

Giacinta was vomiting. Luciano and Piero fussed around, worried about her.

'Luciano,' she said, 'what was your present to me on my birthday?'

'I wished you the happiness of loving a child.'

'Well, your wish is about to come true a little earlier than we might have guessed.'

It took them five seconds to comprehend.

Luciano cried out, 'Meraviglioso!' and gave her a warm hug.

Piero said, 'Which of us is the father?'

'I don't know.'

Sergio said, 'I've been thinking about this – blame me.'

***

Monday, 14th August was a big day. At mid-day they went outside and stood in a line, their arms around each other's shoulders, looking north. The sky lightened and whitened until suddenly the first dazzling, unsurpassable rays made them whoop with joy. The few seconds' difference between the bright sky and the now sun-filled sky was astounding. And this was but the merest tip of the sun.

They performed a jig in the snow and then it was all over. Five minutes and the sun had sunk below the horizon, but it filled their hearts. After over a hundred days, the sun had come back.

***

The men became touchingly cosseting. They wanted to lift work from her but, even though she was more readily tired, she would have none of it. Eventually, Sergio, as her doctor, had to instruct her to be sensible. They took on all the everyday tasks of their household. The mere smell of their usual meals sent her retching to the toilet, so they devised simple, plain dishes in the hope she could face eating them. Sergio told her to try and eat the brown rice because of the folic acid. They encouraged her to sleep longer and more often. She became increasingly grateful as she experienced an overpowering fatigue.

When she was with Piero, he asked her if it was safe to continue with sex during pregnancy. She laughed, 'You betcha! In the days before contraception, pregnancy was the safest contraceptive.' She often asked him to give her massage. He became very proficient at soothing her back.

Locked in embrace with Luciano, he told her how, if it were possible, she had grown to be even more beautiful, her skin glowing and her face radiant.

When she was with Sergio, he said, 'I'd hate this to stop, but you do know if that's what you want, we would immediately concur.'

She kissed him. 'I've no experience to go on so I don't know how my body and my feelings will change but, at the moment, it's all just wonderful and I love you holding me.'

***

Giacinta was woken by loud laughter. She went to investigate the cause and the three reacted guiltily as if they were up to something they'd prefer her not to know. Sergio grinned, 'We were looking at slides in the microscope, trying to decide who of us was most likely to be dad.'

'And the result?'

'Inconclusive.'

***

On 23rd August, the first helicopter arrived bringing fresh food including, on Sergio's recommendation, avocados, eggs and yoghurt for Giacinta. There were supplies of all kinds and letters and newspapers. Excited, they greeted the two pilots, calling for news and gossip. Giacinta wondered if they could tell she was pregnant. If they did, they didn't say anything. All four were disconcerted to have their enclosed world entered by others. It made them feel more protective of their closeness.

***

'What are you going to do about going back?' Sergio said. Giacinta's tour was for a year, finishing in March, at the end of the austral summer. The tour of all three of the men was to end in November.

'Assuming all goes well, I'll go back with you. I'm sorry to miss out on summer here. I suppose we'd better let Head Office know.'

'No rush.' Sergio said. 'Let's see how you get on.'

***

Giacinta felt she was growing huge. Sergio said everything was normal. On 15th September, she sent an email to Head Office: 'I am 14 weeks pregnant. I wish to return with Sergio Foresti, Luciano Vittoni and Piero Ripandelli on 23rd November. Until then, I will continue to carry out all my duties as Head of Base.'

Head of Human Resources took the email to PNRA Director, Carlo Masagni. He shrugged, 'These things happen. When she gets back, do we honour her, or hide her? Tell her we'll arrange for her to return earlier if there's the slightest problem.'

***

In early November, Sergio, anticipating that, after their return to Italy, Anna would hear of Giacinta's pregnancy and of his role in it before he had an opportunity to see her and tell her himself, wrote her an email.

Mia Cara Anna, my closest friend. What I'm about to tell you will upset you and for that I'm sorry. Giacinta is pregnant by me. There, I've said it.

I don't know how this will turn out. I do know that I want to be a true and loving father to the child, but also...I haven't told anybody this, least of all Giacinta...I am in love with her.

There, I've opened my heart to you. That she's fond of me, I'm certain. That she might love me – I don't know. Maybe we'll go our separate ways on our return. She's a very strong woman: my being the father of her child will have no sway on her affections. But...I have to take my chance.

I would have preferred to have seen you in Bologna and tell you all this in person, but you're sure to hear of it before I can do that. I treasure our relationship and I'm sorry to cause you distress. I hope we can remain close friends. Sergio.

He didn't have to wait long for a reply.

You're a complete and utter bastard. You're also a fool. She's trifling with you. Once she's back in Italy, she'll dump you as readily as you've dumped me. Oh, of course she'll keep you dancing around while she has the baby, but she'll be off with a new boyfriend as soon as she regains some of her figure. She'll look to you to support the child but that's all she'll want from you. When I think of all the wonderful times we had together...how could you!

***

Giacinta said to Sergio, 'I hate telling lies but, for Piero and Luciano's sake, it does seem that's what we have to do. But it's hard on you. When we get back, what will you say to Anna? I really don't mind what you say to her about me. Tell her I got drunk and seduced you. You're going to have to row hard to make your way back to her forgiveness.'

'I've already written to her.'

'Jesus! What did you say?'

'That you were pregnant and I'm the father.'

'And?'

'That's it.'

'Oh, the poor woman! Didn't you tell her you loved her and this was a sorry mistake?'

'She wrote back calling me a bastard.'

'I'm not surprised. Oh, Sergio, I'm so sorry.'

***

Because Giacinta was leaving with the men, it was arranged that the replacement team would arrive, for a brief induction, three days earlier than originally planned. They were four men and, for those three days, the Base was very cramped. There were a lot of handing-over procedures to be completed and much laughter and good banter. Gossip about Giacinta had circulated, so they weren't surprised at her condition, but they were piqued, and playfully attempted to coax the full story from Piero and Luciano who manfully kept to the agreed prevarication: Sergio and

Giacinta had developed a relationship. That wasn't something they felt uncomfortable about. They didn't feel they had to make a judgement about it. Giacinta was a wonderful Head of Base.

***

Carlo Masagni was at Rome airport Fiumicino to meet them. The three men gave Giacinta a brief hug goodbye then, on seeing the large crowd of press, quickly left; Piero with Isabella and Luciano with Beatrice and the two girls. Masagni took note of Giacinta's swollen belly and asked her if she could face a short meeting with the press. They made their way into a small, overheated room. It soon became crowded with reporters, cameramen and television crew. Giacinta removed her coat. She was thankful she had the foresight to have pre-arranged for maternity clothes to be ready for her in Christchurch. Between flights, there had been just time enough for a hurried fit. Now, with bright red lipstick and flowing cream maternity dress, she looked the personification of fecundity.

After a castanet clicking of cameras, Masagni opened the meeting. He paid tribute to Giacinta's 'superb science and courageous determination'. He said that the journey to and from the volcano was a hazardous adventure in keeping with the history of Antarctic exploration and a tribute to her skills of leadership. He said the discovery of the volcano was a supreme achievement for Italy's Antarctic programme. 'Ladies and Gentlemen of the press, please welcome home, as I do, the discoverer of Volcano Vagnussi – Giacinta Vagnussi.'

Giacinta stood up to applause. 'In Antarctica, as you can see, I encountered more than one eruption.'

There was a moment of complete silence and then a huge guffaw.

'I thank Carlo for his kind words but, as with many

discoveries, so much has to do with good luck – being in the right place at the right time. I want to acknowledge the contribution of my colleagues: Sergio Foresti, Luciano Vittoni and Piero Ripandelli. Without their help, nothing would have been achieved. It was exciting and wonderful to have been the first to find the volcano, but the more important legacy of our scientific research in Antarctica is the contribution we make to the further understanding of the mechanisms of climate change. It's vital that Italy continues to play its part in the global effort to address the threatening temperature rise of our earthly home and, for that, our work in Antarctica is essential. I'm happy to answer any questions you have.'

Masagni said, 'I'm sure you'll appreciate Giacinta must be very tired from her long journey. I hope you understand if I impose a limit of two questions. I would remind you that we have placed a great deal of information on our website.'

From a hedge of upright arms, he chose a reporter from a more serious newspaper. 'Did you return to Volcano Vagnussi?'

'No, we didn't. I considered the journey too hazardous for what it would have achieved. Other teams have now made helicopter visits and the Americans have set up an unmanned web-cam permanently monitoring the volcano. I continued to record the seismic vibrations emanating from the volcano and I'm now preparing a paper marrying my recordings with the activity of the volcano as captured by the web-cam.'

Masagni chose next a female television reporter: 'You mention the word "marrying". Would you like to make a comment on your pregnancy?'

'Needless to say, it was accidental: the Antarctic in winter is not an ideal place to become pregnant. Having said that, I'm absolutely delighted. Sergio Foresti and I are in a happy relationship and I'm looking forward to having his child.'

***

'So we're in a happy relationship, are we?'

'What else could I say – that we had a one-night stand?'

Giacinta was on the phone to Sergio. She had just been contacted again by TV channel RAI 1. They were finalising arrangements for 5th December, an evening devoted to a pre-Christmas appeal for the benefit of deprived children. There would be reportage of the plight of children world-wide intermixed with screenings of classic comedy clips and live guest shows. Many celebrities were gifting their involvement, would Giacinta and her three colleagues join the six-o'clock show? Luciano and Piero had categorically declined. Sergio had been more hesitant. The TV researcher had got back to her: having one of the men with her would make a huge difference, could she persuade Sergio to reconsider.

'Tell her,' he said, 'strictly Antarctica. No prying about paternity.'

***

The following day, Sergio collected Giacinta from her flat and drove her to the hospital for an ultrasound scan. They kissed warmly on meeting. As agreed six months earlier, sexual intimacy ceased from the moment the relieving party had arrived at the Base. Sergio's companionship with her now was not as her lover but as the putative author of her pregnancy.

They stared into the blue, shimmering screen. The technician said, 'Hey, what d'you know? There's two. Definitely. Twins it is. Yep, definitely twins.'

Giacinta said, 'I knew it. I just knew it.'

The technician said, 'Hang on, let's try to get this clearer.

Maybe I'm wrong. Yep, it's not twins. No. No. Don't you see? There – there's a third one. You're carrying triplets.'

***

A spirited audience filled the small studio theatre. When it came to their turn to be interviewed, the presenter said, 'Let's again see that amazing scene of Giacinta broadcasting to the world the discovery of the volcano.' They showed the clip and the audience applauded wildly. When prompted, Sergio explained that he was holding the torch to illuminate Giacinta's face. Together, they retold their story of the journey to the volcano. A man from the audience commented that the anomaly in the geophone readings was surely poor foundation to risk the lives of three people in a wild escapade. Giacinta replied, 'Anomaly is the activator, the stimulant of science; maybe leading to nothing, but not to be ignored. We weren't rash. We assessed the risks and believed the odds were in our favour. We were fortunate and the results confirmed our confidence. But, in my view, we should have received no less approbation had our journey led to nothing. Science is the activity of investigation and is no less estimable when, on occasion, it leads to a blank wall.'

A little girl asked, 'What do I need to do to become an explorer in Antarctica?'

Giacinta said, 'Be determined. Science is every bit as fulfilling for women as it is for men. Men are single-minded, women use *all* their brains. Study science and see, in every sense, the world.'

The presenter turned to the audience, 'Ladies and Gentlemen, just before coming on to this programme, I learned a wonderful piece of news – Giacinta is going to have...triplets!'

There followed whooping and loud applause. 'Sergio, how do feel about being the father of triplets?'

'Thrilled.'

'But a bit of a shock, yes?'

'Yes.'

'Are you planning on getting a bigger house together?'

There was a long pause. 'I'm not sure...'

'You're not sure...?'

'That we'll be together.'

There was a hostile gasp from the audience. The presenter had sprung a hare and set off in glorious pursuit. 'You're not sure you'll be together?'

He looked to Giacinta to rescue him, she held back.

'I...we...haven't discussed it.'

'You haven't discussed it? You're proposing to abandon the poor woman – with triplets!'

'That's not true. I...' There was a monumental pause with a hushed and expectant audience. 'I love her. I adore her. But I don't know how she feels about me.'

All eyes turned to Giacinta. She reached out and took hold of his hand. 'I think Sergio and I need to have a talk.'

***

When they were alone together, Sergio said, 'God! How did that happen? Declaring one's feelings in front of the nation. What made me do that? But there, I've said it, do you think you could love me?'

'Tu asino stupido! Of course I do. Isn't it obvious?'

'As a cat in the clouds. Why didn't you tell me? I'd no idea you felt differently about me than you did about the other two.'

'I wasn't sure how you felt and I didn't want you to feel obliged to help me with the babies especially as we don't know they're yours.'

'Ecco, Anna!'

***

Piero bought a book: *Making Love: How to Please Her* and left it in his sock drawer where he knew Isabella would find it. He now gave her more of his time. When she got home to their flat, frazzled from counting the nation's money, he would offer her massage with, initially at least, no amorous intent. He imagined his energy flowing down his arms, flowing through his fingers, flowing into her body. He thought of himself as a potter, taking the cold unyielding clay of her body and kneading it to become soft, malleable, alive; imbuing her, like the clay, with potential for transformation. What began solely as a physical activity, increasingly engaged him emotionally: she became more precious to him.

Isabella found the book, smiled, and left it where it was. She knew he intended her to find it.

***

Luciano, formerly a devoted husband and father, was now even more so. He got the girls up, dressed and breakfasted in the morning, giving Beatrice precious extra minutes in bed. He negotiated his work time so as to be with Rosa and Sophia after school before Beatrice returned from work. Above all, he was tender and loving to Beatrice. His devotion was absolutely genuine, he loved her, but pricked on to a new intensity by guilt.

***

Neither of their flats being suitable for one child let alone three, Giacinta and Sergio made plans to rent a flat together more appropriate for a family. Even as they did this, she kept seeking reassurance from him that, even if it turned out the babies were not his, he really wanted to commit himself to care for them as their father.

She said, 'You don't have to, you know. I got myself into

this. I could manage alone.'

He replied, 'My wife left me because I didn't want children, and now I'm going to have three and I couldn't be more happy.'

He steadily transformed from professional to protective, from supportive doctor to expectant dad. His anxiety was heightened from knowing the increased risks associated with multiple pregnancies: the likelihood of prematurity, increased congenital abnormalities, higher rates of perinatal mortality and complications in labour. Giacinta was put in the care of consultant obstetrician, Andrea Novelli. She spelt out the risks and offered the choice of a termination which Giacinta adamantly refused. Novelli said they should be prepared for the babies to arrive early.

Piero and Luciano were constant visitors to Giacinta's flat, arriving every time with small gifts. Beatrice said to Luciano, 'One would think it's your babies she's having.'

Sergio received an email from Anna, 'I miss you. You are my closest friend and it's such a loss not being able to talk with you, confide in you. I feel very lonely without you. I don't know how I'm going to cope without your love.'

Sergio phoned her. It was a long, hesitant, tearful conversation in which he kept repeating how much he valued her as a friend and hoping that they could move on to a new friendship, one that accepted his life now was with Giacinta.

***

Giacinta entered hospital on 15th January, in her thirty-first week of pregnancy. Four days later she went into labour. It was long and complicated. Sergio was with her all the time, holding her hand and wiping her face. A girl was successfully delivered and then, hours later, a boy. The life of the third baby hung in the balance before it too arrived, extremely weak; it was a boy. All three babies were rushed to intensive care. Giacinta was utterly exhausted.

The hospital issued a brief press release. Giacinta's return from Antarctica being now old news, some, not all, papers carried it. Piero and Luciano came to visit her, Piero with a huge bunch of flowers and Luciano with a bowl of blue and pink hyacinths. They went to look at the babies lying asleep in their little space-age cots.

Luciano said in a whisper, 'It's impossible to tell who's the father.'

After four days, reluctantly leaving the babes, Giacinta went home. Luciano and Piero came again to see her, this time with champagne, immediately uncorked in celebration.

Luciano made a speech saying how wonderful it was that Giacinta and Sergio had got together. He asked when would they know who was the father.

Sergio said, 'It's better not to know. Although I'll be "Dad", you must be close uncles.'

'No, no,' Luciano said, 'we must find out who's the biological father. It completely changes things for me if I know they're mine.'

There was a silence, then Sergio said to Piero, 'What do *you* think?'

'I...It's better not to know. It would complicate things.'

Luciano said to Giacinta, 'Surely you agree with me?'

She said, 'I do understand you would wish to have more involvement if you knew they were yours.'

Sergio shrugged, 'As you like.'

***

On a visit to the hospital, Giacinta took the opportunity of meeting Andrea Novelli to confide in her that the chance of Sergio being the father was but one in three.

She said it was important to all four of them that they knew who was the father. Could she arrange DNA tests?

The three men went to the hospital together. All three babies were doing well and Giacinta encouraged each man to cuddle one of the babies. The sight drew broad smiles from the nurses.

A few days later, Novelli came to Giacinta's flat. She said a journalist had phoned her to verify a story he had just been given. It was to her great regret that she believed someone had leaked this most highly confidential of information. In these circumstances, it might be more dignified to jump rather than be pushed and issue an official press release.

It was the main item on RAI early evening news:

'Giacinta Vagnussi, who last year discovered a completely unknown volcano in Antarctica named, in her honour, Volcano Vagnussi, astonishes the world yet again. She has become the very first documented case in medical history of a woman giving birth to triplets where each of the three babies has a different father.

'Although accepted as theoretically possible, it was believed to be too unlikely ever to actually occur. Our science reporter, Giulia Fabrizi explains.'

'Giacinta Vagnussi's triplets have come about through the simultaneous occurrence of two exceedingly rare events. Non-identical twins are formed when two sperm fertilise two eggs at the same time. For identical twins, one sperm fertilises an egg which subsequently divides. However, in about one in a hundred conceptions two sperm fertilise the same egg. Very few embryos formed in this way survive, but it can happen.

If the embryo subsequently divides it can result in, what are called, semi-identical twins. These are extremely rare but not unknown. A woman in the United States in 2007 did give birth to semi-identical twins and they are now happy healthy children.

'Vagnussi's triplets are a combination of semi-identical twins with a non-identical twin: one egg fertilised by two sperm while at the same time a second egg is fertilised by a third sperm. This is an exceedingly rare occurrence.

'But that's not all. There are documented cases of what is known as heteropaternal superfecundation in which the two eggs that give rise to non-identical twins are fertilised by sperm from different men; in effect, giving rise to twins with different fathers. In Giacinta Vagnussi's extraordinary case, each of the three sperm that gave rise to her triplets came from different men.'

'And how would that happen?'

'Well, there's only one explanation. Within a very short period of time, a day or so, she must have had intercourse with three men. And since she was isolated in Antarctica at the time with just three men, it's not difficult to work out who are the fathers of her three babies.'

'An extraordinary case.'

'Indeed. It has only come to light because of the availability of DNA testing. Since DNA testing is a relatively recent scientific breakthrough, we have no idea how frequent it was, in past centuries, for women to give birth to twins with different fathers. Medical opinion is that the probability of the occurrence of triplets with different fathers is less than one in a hundred billion pregnancies.'

***

'Rutting weasel! Pustulous prick!' Piero dodged the book aimed at his head. Isabella picked up a large glass vase of flowers. 'Treacherous toad!' And, displacing her anger away from him, threw it against the wall. 'Where's the trust. Why? Why did you do it?'

'Believe me, I did it for you.'

'You did it for me! You fucking men, you're all the same.' She fled the room, slamming the door. Two minutes later, she was back again. 'What d'you mean, you did it for me?'

'I...I felt I was inadequate as a lover. I asked her to

help...help me be better at sex – with you.'

'You're pathetic!'

A minute later, he heard her slam the door of their apartment – hard.

***

Carlo Masagni heard the news and groaned. 'This is too much; we'll have to cast her adrift. Just think of the headlines: "Antics in the Antarctic", "Sex in the Snow", "Three with her Favours", "Programma Nazionale di Riproduzione in Antortide". You couldn't make it up.'

Anna heard the news: 'Oh Sergio, what have you got into?'

Beatrice heard the news and wept. She told Luciano she couldn't bear to have him touch her. 'The three of you...it's disgusting!' He moved into the little spare room with the baby cot, baby bath, old pram, buggies and children's high chairs.

Isabella didn't return until after midnight. Piero was asleep.

'Come on. Show me, lover boy.'

'You're drunk.'

'Of course I'm fucking drunk. Come on. Show me what you can do. Show me what she taught you.'

'I don't think that's a good idea.'

'You don't think that's a good idea! Do it. Do it or I'll scream. Do it to me doggy style. That's what you did with her, isn't it?'

She collapsed on the bed and vomited. Piero washed her and cleaned up the mess. She fell asleep. He lay down beside her with his arm around her.

Luciano came into the kitchen, the three of them were at breakfast. As on previous days, there was silence, no acknowledgement, no greeting. Rosa and Sophia were attending to their bowls of cereal. He was anticipating this iciness from Beatrice and hated it, not knowing how to bring about a thaw. He poured himself a coffee and sat opposite her, staring into his cup. Beatrice had already, in her head, forgiven him, but she wasn't going to let him know that, yet. Let him suffer a little longer.

***

Giacinta went everyday to the hospital. She was told that, with their progress, she shouldn't have to wait too long before taking the babies home. It seemed at last that the media interest was beginning to abate. After a visit, she sat in the hospital foyer waiting for Sergio. It was then she noticed the magazine on display in the hospital shop. It was Cosmopolitan Italia. The photograph, scooped on the front cover, depicted Giacinta seated, Sergio standing behind her, Piero to her right, Luciano to her left, each man holding a baby, and below, a great banner headline: 'Mama Mia!'

Undergrowth

An Account of the Manner of my Departure from Her Majesty's Civil Service

Following long service with an employer, anyone would wish for a dignified departure: a gathering of colleagues, speeches, recognition of achievement, a gift presented; to retain the memory of a warm, happy occasion. That my leaving was not like that, still rankles. By setting down an account of the manner of my departure, I hope to distance myself from what remains, a year on, as a sore.

Nearly forty years ago, I received a first-class degree in sociology from Hull University and then trained as a social psychologist. Immediately following that, I joined the Civil Service in Whitehall. I was competent, I moved up the ranks, my judgement was trusted and, eventually, I ended up attached to the Government Social Research Team from where, after a lifetime of service, I looked forward to a happy retirement.

The general election in 2010 brought David Cameron into power leading a coalition of the Conservatives and the Liberal Democrats. Whatever ministers may wish to achieve, their everyday occupation is fire-fighting. There are always frictions and hot discords that, given a little ill wind, ignite into serious incidents. Their task is to placate the three 'p's: public, party and press. The election added a fourth 'p' – 'partners', as in 'coalition partners'.

In contrast, the fleshing out and implementation of policy is the province of the civil service. Overseeing that process is the No 10 Policy and Implementation Unit. The PU used to be manned by the civil service but, increasingly, governments wanted to take control and they would appoint a number of trusted party officials to serve on the unit. However, with the incoming coalition, the Conservative and Liberal Democrat partners fought each other to manoeuvre into place their own people. Unable to conclude a peace treaty, they vacated the field and invited in the civil service as a neutral force. Suddenly, my boss, Peter Russell, found himself serving on the PU.

The Prime Minister was faced with a demand from the Liberal Democrats for a new freedoms bill to, 'cut state intrusion in everyday life'. It wasn't a proposal that excited him but, on the other hand, there seemed no harm in exploring the idea. After all, he believed, aspirational people would be much better off if government got out of the way and let them get on with bettering their lives.

September 2012, there were nine of us at the meeting.

'OK,' Peter said, 'the instruction from our masters is to go forth and create proposals to enlarge personal freedoms. This is,' he continued, 'a blue skies session. Feel free to be creative.'

I knew what that meant, you open your mouth and get howled down in a deluge of derision. I kept my eyes on the floor.

'Drugs,' someone said, 'It's got to be drugs. What else comes near it in restricting personal freedom?'

'Ruled out,' Peter said. 'We can come forward with any proposals we choose except to change the law regarding drugs.'

There was a silence then another person said, 'I suppose euthanasia is being dealt with as a private member's bill.'

'What about relaxing planning regulations? Let people do what they want with their own land.'

'Strengthen regulations on CCTV cameras.'

'Ban wheel-clamping.'

'Give people the positive right to be naked in public. It's shameful the way that guy, what's he called, the naked rambler, was harassed – imprisoned in Scotland, wasn't he?'

'Get rid of the licence that restricts live music in pubs and other small venues.'

And so on. There were a couple of dozen suggestions. Peter said, 'Tom, you're very quiet.'

I should have held to my resolve and kept my mouth shut. Stupidly, I said, 'A third of young people today are engaged in an activity we make illegal. Why not enlarge their personal freedom, recognise the changing patterns of behaviour in our society and lower the age of consent?'

'Encourage young kids to have sex, you must be joking.'

'Think of the exploitation.'

'A paedophiles' charter! That's what that is.'

I put up a brief defence of the idea then shrugged my shoulders.

Closing the meeting, Peter said, 'Thank you everybody. I'll draw up a list of half-a-dozen of your suggestions and we'll prepare a briefing paper for the PU.'

When we were alone, he said to me, 'I wouldn't rule out your suggestion. Could you draft something? The usual thing, pros and cons and all that.'

The age of consent for sexual intercourse in the UK is 16 years. If a 60 year old person and a 16 year old both consent, it is perfectly legal for them to engage in sex. If the people having sex are 16 and 15 years old, it is not legal, even with consent, and treated as a serious offence incurring the possibility of up to five years in a detention centre and being placed on the Sex Offenders Register.

This law would not be in question were it not for the fact that many young people below the age of 16 are engaging in sexual activity. How many is 'many'? I studied the research. The most credible survey undertaken in the UK is the Second National Survey of Sexual Attitudes and Lifestyles, known as Natsal 2000. This states that of those interviewed in the 16 to 19 years age band, one third of men and one quarter of women had sexual intercourse before

16. What other law is broken by so huge a portion of the population?

I had a living illustration close to home. My niece, at the age of fifteen, formed an attachment with a nice lad in her class at school. When my sister discovered they were having sex, she said she would rather them spend time together safely at home than have them facing risks God knows where.

I consulted professional opinion (legal, medical, educational) and the views of organisations involved in working with young people, including the churches. The responses were as mixed as one would have predicted. There were two particularly strong arguments for keeping the bar at sixteen. First, to protect the young from predatory adults, and second, that it gives girls who feel they are not ready for sex, support in resisting peer pressure. The opposing view was that there are ways to protect girls other than by criminalising whole swathes of the young population.

I investigated the Age of Consent (AoC) laws of other countries and discovered considerable variation. I was particularly interested in Canada. They wanted to protect young people so actually *raised* the AoC from 14 to 16. However, they recognised the problem this created and allowed for "close in age exemptions" whereby a 14 or 15 year old can consent to sexual activity with a partner as long as the partner is less than five years older and a 12 or 13 year old can have sexual activity with another young person provided they are less than two years older.

In preparing policy papers, I always liked to include a number of illustrative cases. I looked for people whose lives had been affected by the current law. For this paper, I chose two. One was a girl from a white working-class family in London who had featured in a television programme. When I interviewed her, she spoke articulately of how her friends, girls, at the age of fourteen were suborned into sex by the demands of the gang of lads they went around with. Join in or be outlawed was the rule. She didn't want to have sex but felt she couldn't give this as her reason for refusing. The issue had been discussed in school and teachers had emphasised that under-age sex was illegal. She felt this had given her support in opposing the gang culture.

The other of my two illustrative cases was Mr. Josh Tyler. He had a letter published in the Times cogently making the case for reducing the AoC. Implicit in his letter was that he himself had suffered as a result of the law. I contacted Mr. Tyler by email and then followed this up with a telephone call. Our conversation was of sufficient interest for me to ask him if we could meet. He said he was happy to talk to me but, as work was particularly demanding at that time, he didn't want to take a day out from his work in Sussex to travel to London.

Now I must admit to a little ulterior motive. I spent my childhood in mid-Sussex and the area has happy memories for me. The idea of an afternoon trip to that beautiful county was too much to resist. It was a fine Autumn day when I caught the train to Groombridge and walked the mile to Mr. Tyler's house. It was a small detached cottage on the edge of a wood. Alongside, was a wide barn and a large dirt yard with great logs, some untreated, others cut into planks and stacked. It was there I found Mr. Tyler driving a dumper truck.

He was a young man, about mid-twenties, tall and well-built, curly fair hair and a way of looking at you that was half amused, half quizzical. He shook my hand.

'This is our mill,' he said, gesturing towards the barn. 'Would you like to see?'

We walked through huge doors into the barn. The noise was horrendous. There were a couple of chaps wearing earmuffs working the machines. They nodded as we walked round. He shouted into my ear. 'These machines cut the felled trees into planks. They're then stored outside for one, two, three years to reduce the moisture content below twenty-five per cent, after which they're put in the kiln to be dried.'

He ran his hand through sawdust extruded from the machine into a large bag. 'Nothing's wasted. We compress this stuff into briquettes.'

Thankfully, we then escaped the noise and walked towards the house.

'Where do you get your wood?' I asked.

'Local privately-owned woodlands. It's all English hardwoods, mostly oak, ash, chestnut and a small amount of walnut. We're not denuding our country of these woods. It's all part of natural woodland management. With our suppliers, we make sure felled trees are replaced to ensure stocks will be available over the next hundred years. Would you like a drink, a tea or a coffee, or a beer?'

I asked for a coffee and we sat outside the house on a bench in a sheltered corner. I explained in more detail what I was working on. I said that I was impressed by what he had to say on the subject. Would he like to develop his views?

He asked me lots of questions about the government's intentions, the PU, and my role.

He asked me for my personal opinion regarding lowering the AoC. I said that, in my view, the law had to protect the young from predatory adults. However, society should recognise that, following puberty, many adolescents would engage in sexual activity and there seemed no good reason to criminalise them for doing so.

He said, 'Do you support a change in the law?'

'I am inclined towards the opinion that the government should prepare a carefully drafted bill to put before parliament to discuss changing the law regarding the age of consent.'

This seemed to satisfy him. 'My interest derives from personal experience.'

'I thought so.'

'Is this relevant to your enquiry?'

'Of course. I've received a lot of evidence from interested organisations but it would be advantageous to flesh-out the generalisations with individual life stories.'

'If you use my story, can you keep my name out of it?'

'Of course.'

'Just a minute.'

He went into the house and returned five minutes later. 'Sorry to keep you waiting, I had trouble finding it.' He handed me a plain exercise book. 'It's my story, written when I was seventeen. I never typed it up. It's a bit overblown, I've mellowed somewhat since then, but it's how I felt at the time. It shouldn't take you too long to read. I'll get on with my work. Call me when you've finished.'

Even to this day, I feel angry. What justice is there in humiliating young people for being in love? This country is sick. The law is crass. Politicians, who have the power to change the law, run scared rather than choose what is right because a handful of billionaires, mostly living abroad, with naked self-interest spread their intolerance and bigotry across the land.

Only the young can live a new way. Only the young defy social conventions. It's the young who campaign for social justice. It's the young who place harmony with nature over greed.

I want to keep viscerally fresh what happened to me. I want to capture the touch, sight, sound of my experience. Passing years scour the memory. Not to forget, that's my intention, that's why I write; to capture the recollection as vivid as if it were yesterday.

I built my first pod at the age of twelve years, three months. Built is too grand a word, gouged more exact. It was the Easter holidays. Dad was at work. Mum had taken Sam, my younger brother by three years, to a funfair. I refused to go. When Lydia, my sister two years older than me, was told to keep an eye on me, she grunted in reluctant acquiescence. She was looking forward to time alone with her friend Chloe. I didn't mind, I was happy enough on my own.

I pedalled my bike to The Wood. It was one of those days

remarkable for April, hot in the sun, cool in shade. I love woodland, its dappled light, its hidden ways, its distinctive smell; the territory of Robin Hood. Our Wood, covering most of Saxon Hill, was divided by two broad tracks and threaded by a multiplicity of little paths. It's the place to unleash your dog or, in one grassy flat clearing, enjoy a picnic.

I pushed up to the Humps and Ditches, the place where, five thousand years ago, men and women had built themselves a home. A home in the wood, what could be better than that? It suddenly came on to rain, an April shower. I stood against the trunk of a high sycamore then looked for a better place to shelter. There was a dense clump of laurel. With a stick, I beat a hollow into the dark, dead interior beneath the broad evergreen leaves and crawled in. The shower turned into a downpour. I thrilled at the experience: the great shooshing noise, the onrush of released scent, the enclosed security and, above all, being completely hidden, a privacy I yearned for as I share a bedroom with Sam. The privacy was erotic. In the confined space, I struggled out of my shorts and stroked myself to a satisfying conclusion.

What are the ways of sexual awakening? Perhaps suddenly, from the boastful talk of our peers. Perhaps incrementally, a slow greening in the April of our lives. For me, my first arousal was literal as well as sexual. In my dream, Sebastian's soft, tortoiseshell-haired head repeatedly butting my groin brought me, shuddering with pleasure, to wakefulness. I was just twelve. From that time, I experimented with one of Mum's furry gloves. That innocent glove soon acquired a smell, fetid and pungent. I washed it and when dried it looked like a dead cat. Mum never did discover how she managed to lose her gloves.

The school bus circulated the bottom of Saxon Hill. In the morning, Chloe would get on at the stop before ours and always look out for Lydia. They were united in contrast. Lydia, like me, fair-haired and pink-skinned, easily burned in the sun; Chloe, dark eyed with long, sleek, black hair and skin the colour that the fair-skinned hope to attain by the end of their summer holiday. Lydia, clothing deliberately awry in usually unconscious, occasionally rancorous, protest; Chloe, neat, as if modelling the school uniform. Lydia impassioned and opinionated; Chloe, cool with a gentle smile. And they were inseparable. Chloe got on the bus with her younger sister, Anna, but the seat next to Chloe was always reserved for Lydia.

Maggie drove the bus, usually with her spaniel, Francis (as of Assisi). Only Maggie could name a dog after a saint. Maggie was a spinster and had a gap tooth so when she told you off for being late, she whistled through her teeth. My mate, Ryan, could so mimic this as to have us weeping with laughter.

When I missed the bus (Lydia was always there on time), I had to take my bike up and over the hill through The Wood and I would be in trouble for being late. One such day, on my way home after school, with sex on my mind, I sought out my pod. Afterwards, I lay naked on my back in pleasurable relaxation. Then I heard a dog. Damn dogs with their compulsive curiosity and acute noses. I lay perfectly still, aware that, upon me, there were smells of interest to dogs. There was a shout of 'George' and, fortunately, the dog ceased to snoop around. My pod was too near a pathway. I would have to penetrate deeper into undiscovered Africa.

Over dinner that evening, Lydia said, 'I don't see why I have to be at the end of Maggie's invective just because you can't get up in the morning. She waited two minutes before giving up on you. And, all the while, she was complaining to me, as if it was my fault.'

I grunted and muttered, 'Maggie's an idiot.'

Mum said, 'Don't you mock Maggie, she's a good soul. Sam likes her, don't you Sam?'

Sam goes willingly to Maggie's Sunday School Class. I tried it once and decided it wasn't for me.

I chose the site of Pod Two with great care: far from the main paths, no obvious way to it, screened on all sides and with a place to hide my bike. I carried up a saw and secateurs and within a thick evergreen laurel shrub, created a big hollow space, triple the size of Pod One and high enough to almost stand. I attached a sheet of polythene for ceiling and laid a square of carpet for comfort. I wove branches into a small door with hinges of string. I came (both meanings) there whenever I could get away. Afterwards, I would lay on my back (I soon acquired an old pillow for my head) and listened to the birds.

To escape to The Wood, I needed a cover story. After my guitar lesson on Saturday morning, Mum took us all to Tunbridge Wells. To Mum's surprise, I dragged them into a bookshop. I found what I was looking for. With pocket money, I bought the Collins Field Guide to Bird Songs and Calls with CDs of signature bird calls. I was going to become a twitcher.

Dad regarded my new hobby with amused and unwanted interest, 'Anything new today?' Embarrassed and paranoid about my sexual proclivity being discovered, I blushed, surely he knew what I was really up to, and mumbled something about 'woodcock'.

I was going to have to become more convincing. Post-tumescent, relaxing in my pod, I opened my ears. The bird calls that formerly passed unheeded, I now found soothingly magical, exuberant with life. Once I could separate individual songs, I was amazed at the number of different birds and the variety of their voices. I soon learned to identify all the common birds. Proudly, I told Dad that although it was very difficult to distinguish visually a Willow Warbler from a Chiffchaff, the Willow Warbler's song was a liquid cadential hoo-eet, whereas the Chiffchaff was with an alternating 'chiff' and 'chaff' at a steady relaxed tempo from which the bird 'Phylloscopus collybita' acquired its common name.

I grew in confidence. Not only could I distinguish birdsong I'd not heard before, I became proficient at mimicry. It became a new game, my family naming a bird, and challenging me to provide an imitation of its song. Dad came home with a smart leather-bound hardback book with blank pages. 'You might like to make a log of the birds you see and hear,' he said. 'Record everything: date, time, place, every particular.'

One great piece of luck was to find, underneath the seat in the bus shelter, a soft-porn magazine. This gave my pleasurings a whole new focus. I couldn't understand how the simple spread of coloured inks on a two dimensional surface could produce in me such excitement. I felt a deep gratitude to the women in the magazine who had allowed themselves to be photographed. The associated text I thought crass and disgusting.

One day, early May, after school, I told Lydia I was staying to play football. Kids at school thought I was a nerd, having guitar lessons and actually enjoying maths and I could easily have been picked on by bullies. But I was broad-shouldered and prepared to stand up for myself. What really gave me credibility, however, was football. I was good at it.

After the game, I started on my walk home through The Wood looking forward to stopping off at the Pod. I didn't hurry, it was a beautiful evening, early bluebells had opened. I leaned down to smell them. Soon The Wood would be gloriously perfumed by its dense blue underlay. I lay on my back, naked in the pod, with the door open, floating in a pleasurable heaven when a face appeared. It took some seconds for me to recognise who it was and for them to take in what I was doing. It was Chloe. She must have followed me from school.

'Oh, I'm so sorry,' she said. And then she was gone.

Would she tell Lydia? When we got on the bus the following morning, she said, 'Hi Josh.' I blushed. Lydia flopped herself next to Chloe and they then both ignored me completely.

Even though it was May Bank Holiday Monday, there was no holiday for Dad on duty at some festivity, or for the shop workers in Tunbridge Shopping Centre. Mum had taken Lydia to shop for yet more clothes and Sam for a new pair of shoes. I opted out and, on my bike, headed for the pod. I was just about to dive in when I saw Chloe lying there.

'Hey!' I said, 'This is my pod, get out.'

She quickly covered herself with her jeans. On the carpet, were her white knickers.

She said, 'I thought you were shopping in Tunbridge.'

'What are you doing?'

'Exactly the same as what you do here.'

Of course. Like me, Chloe shared a bedroom. I was angry, but also intrigued by her purpose in being there. It hadn't occurred to me that girls also did it.

'I'm sorry,' she said. 'I've invaded your private space. I'll go.'

I was blocking her exit. 'Do you want some lemonade?'

She made room for me, laying her head back upon the pillow. Shit! She must have seen the porno mag, it was under the pillow. I took delight in those pictures, but it was embarrassing to have them discovered in my possession.

'It's cosy in here,' she said.

'You can come here again if you like.' But then added as an afterthought, 'You won't tell Lydia, will you?'

She smiled, 'I won't tell Lydia.'

She looked at me as if trying to make up her mind about something. I looked back at her enquiringly.

'I've never seen a real penis. Not up close. I've seen pictures, of course, but never...you know. Would you let me see yours?'

'No way!' I said. But then the thought of exposing myself, of her looking at me, was intensely arousing. I undid my belt and wriggled out of my jeans and underpants. She leaned forward.

'Can I touch it?'

I nodded and she prodded it gently with her forefinger and then held it lightly between thumb and fingers. She gently squeezed, testing its resilience.

'It's a bit like a sausage,' she said, 'firm, like a cooked sausage.'

'Show's over,' I said, pulling on my underpants.

She crossed her arms and pulled her top up and over her head then unclasped her bra. I had never seen anything so beautiful and I felt grateful and...honoured.

'Can I touch them?' I cupped my hand over one then the other. 'You're beautiful,' I said. I was too shy to ask if I might see her lower parts.

'I must go,' she said. 'Would you go outside while I get dressed.'

We walked back together through The Wood until our paths diverged. Other than playing games with Lydia, this was the first time I enjoyed the company of a girl, even though I didn't know what to talk about.

On the bus the following morning, there was the merest of greeting: 'Hi Josh,' and then a look and a smile. I was overjoyed. In lower school, out of class, there was the strictest of self-imposed segregation by age and gender, you simply never talked with someone not your own age and sex. This separation began to break down in upper school as the sexes became interested in each other.

Going home on the bus Tuesday evening, Chloe said, 'Would you like a sweet, Josh?' And then, as she pressed a toffee into my hand, it came with a folded note: 'I would like to go to the pod, tomorrow after band practice.'

Chloe played drums in the year-ten rock band. I studied the words. This was the first time that textual analysis had any importance for me: was this a request or an invitation. Did she want to be on her own without the embarrassment of my arrival or did she want to meet me again?

Stupidly, the following morning, I missed the bus and wasn't able to ask her. After school, I stayed for a game of football. I walked around to the music room. It was all locked up. At the pod, I quietly called out, 'Chloe, are you there?'

'Yes.'

'Do you want me to go away?'

'No.'

And so began our relationship. In due course, we became lovers. We both claim the credit for being the one to first bring a packet of condoms to the pod. Initially inept, we soon gained experience. Afterwards, we would lie together listening to the birds, Chloe asking me to name them.

And then a piece of luck. The rock band was rehearsing to play a few numbers at a meeting for year-ten parents to discuss GCSE options. Their guitarist broke a finger playing rugby. Mrs. Mason, the music teacher, asked me if I would help out. Jack, my guitar teacher, was given a recording of the numbers and he showed me what to do. I joined the after-school practice sessions.

Chloe and I would walk together to the pod. We talked about the other members of the band. We talked about the teachers. We talked about Lydia. She asked me about Dad and his job. We discussed her GCSE options. I asked her about her parents and Anna. We argued about the music we liked. She wanted me to listen to her favourite bands.

One wonderful June evening with the late sun slanting through the trees, Chloe said, 'You got rid of that porno mag.'

So she had seen it. I didn't want to lie. 'I've hidden it in my bedroom.'

'What would you think if I or Lydia were in a mag like that?'

'You're not serious. That would be awful.'

'But the women in the photographs have boyfriends, mothers and fathers.'

'I don't know those women, do I? I just see the photographs. It doesn't make a blind bit of difference to those women if I, Josh Tyler, look at those photographs or not.'

'Don't you think you look at me differently because of them?'

'No, I don't. You're a complete person, not an image.'

'You don't compare me to those women.'

I had to think about that one. 'It matters to me that you're beautiful.'

'So you wouldn't want to be with me if I were ugly?'

'Now I know you, I want to be with you all the time and I'd still want to be with you even if you were ugly.'

'That's very sweet.' And she kissed me. 'Why do you feel you need to hide the mag from me, from your mother?'

'I suppose I think you find it offensive. Do you?'

'I think it's unpleasant.'

'Would you find pictures of naked men unpleasant? Or would you find them arousing?'

Now it was her turn to consider her feelings. 'Yes, I would find them arousing and, yes, I would prefer to keep them hidden.'

Year-ten Rock Band were too loud and too aggressive, but the parents applauded anyway. Being two years younger, it gained me a lot of street cred. That evening over, liaisons with Chloe became more difficult to arrange. I was not looking forward to the summer holidays. I couldn't see how I could be alone with Chloe. I'd be expected to play with Sam, but Lydia would be the biggest problem.

It was a Sunday just before the end of term. We had managed to slip away. We were lying in the pod, naked in each other's arms, carelessly leaving the door open. We heard a scuffling noise that might have been a dog and kept very still. Then a face appeared at the doorway. It was Maggie. She quickly came to the correct conclusion and shouted, 'fornicators!'. The explosive 'F' came with a whistle and we couldn't help but laugh.

'Laugh, would you? I'll teach you to laugh. Chloe Seaton and Josh Tyler, you just get dressed and get out of there. You shall hear more of this. May the good Lord forgive you.'

We didn't have to wait long to know the consequences, they came with a rush. Dad interviewed me that evening – was it true? It wasn't that I was incapable of lying; I couldn't deny something I didn't believe to be wrong.

'I love her,' I said.

Dad got exasperated. 'For God's sake, Josh, don't you understand, it's against the law! The penalties are really harsh. They can put people in detention centres and name them on the sex offenders register for life.'

Mum was crying, 'He's just a child, he's just a child.'

Dad said, 'I know you're not to blame but you have to see that what you've done is wrong.'

A social worker came to interview me. It was horrible. I was very quiet. Did I have sex with Chloe? I nodded. Did I know that it was against the law? Again I nodded. Had I had sex with any other girl? I shook my head.

The social worker put questions to Mum and Dad about how much I was left unsupervised.

There was a meeting, ten of us: an official of the Court, a child specialist, advocacy for Chloe and myself, and our parents. Chloe smiled at me. She looked beautiful. The official read out the facts: 'The allegations are that, between April and July this year, unlawful sexual intercourse took place between two persons of an age of minority. The allegations are not disputed.'

There was a discussion. The official asked Chloe and me if we understood the seriousness of our misbehaviour. We both nodded. He said he wanted us to answer in our own words.

Well-rehearsed, I said, 'I now realise that what we did was seriously wrong.'

Contrition is what they wanted, contrition is what they heard. What I wanted to say was that if the law says loving each other is wrong, the law is crass. I wanted to say that this had been the most wonderful thing to have happened to me and where was the hurt to anybody? I wanted to say that I loved Chloe and regretted nothing. But I didn't and I felt a complete coward.

Chloe looked at me, then she said, 'I understand loving Josh is against the law. But I don't understand why the law should make illegal something so beautiful.'

The official frowned and said we should receive counselling and that the specialist was to report back to him in a month. Addressing Chloe and me, he said any further misbehaviour would be held against us. And that was that.

The whole process left me feeling humiliated. I was instructed, on pain of severe punishment, to keep well clear of Chloe. I felt sorry for Lydia, she'd lost her best friend. I couldn't bear going back to the pod and I destroyed it. But I never lost my love of woodland and my knowledge of birdsong.

I was never damaged by my relationship with Chloe, only by the stupidity of social intolerance. Where was the harm to me, Chloe or anybody else in what we were doing? I don't regret having sex with Chloe, on the contrary, I want to be able to recall every moment.

Once, gays were criminalised for engaging in a healthy, natural behaviour. We now live, in Britain at least, in more understanding times, but not sufficiently enlightened to cease criminalising teenagers for their healthy, natural behaviour. The change in law on homosexuality was brought about because there were homosexuals in parliament and the judiciary. Who is there to speak up for young people?

***

After I finished reading, I went to look for Mr. Tyler. He was again on his fork-lift truck. He jumped down and we walked away from the noise of the barn to the seat in his garden.

'Thank you,' I said. 'Such an open and honest account. Personal testimony always has a vital place in defining policy. They provide points of colour in the grey of generalisation. One cannot be unmoved by your experience but the law exists to protect young people and although inappropriate in your case, the Court saw that and dealt with it in a wholly humane and restrained way.'

'Humane and restrained! After I graduated, I applied to join the 'Teach First' programme to gain a PGCE qualification. As with all applicants, they ran a criminal record check, and I found out I was listed! I had no idea. How could I apply with that on my head? Is that humane? Is that restrained? The law is interfering in an area it has no place. As in other countries, we are quite capable of writing legislation which both protects young people and allows them personal freedom. Why criminalise thousands of young people for doing what comes naturally? If the intention of the law is to deter under-age sex, it's failing abysmally.'

'How do you respond to the argument that the law gives reinforcement to the young woman who doesn't want sex but is being coerced into it by peer pressure? She can say to a demanding male, "It's against the law."'

'That's a cultural issue, not a legal one. Women are growing in empowerment, we have to continue to change attitudes. That's why your work is of such importance.'

As we were talking, a small red Renault drove into the yard. A woman carrying a child came towards us. She was beautiful with long black hair, dark eyes and sun-kissed complexion. I looked at Josh, 'This couldn't be...Chloe?' I asked.

He laughed. 'No, Chloe met her husband at university. They now live in Australia. This is Anna. Anna, come and meet Mr. Tom Rutherford.'

I wrote up my report. I listed the different policies of a number of countries. I defined the options relevant to the UK with arguments for and against each one. I outlined the history of legislation and the present social context. I summarised the opinions of interested organisations including child welfare and medical services and the different churches. I stated the likely response of different media and the other political parties. Finally, I concluded that if the Government wished to enlarge personal freedom, they should consider changing the law to allow sexual relations between near-age minors, fourteen years and over.

My report went to the PU in January 2013. Someone leaked it to the press. The tempest was instant and ferocious. 'Who in their right mind...?' screamed the Daily Mail.

David Cameron immediately denied the government had any such intent. He said he was appalled that the idea had ever been considered. Privately, he was furious, 'what an effing stupid proposal.' He demanded that whoever was responsible should 'get a big kick up the backside'.

Equally embarrassed, Nick Clegg said it was, 'categorically untrue that the Liberal Democrats had in any way been pushing the idea of lowering the age of sexual consent.'

I was quietly moved to areas of less sensitive policy and then, in accordance with the ongoing drive to cut government expenditure, offered redundancy with a reduced early pension.

So, no honourable send-off for me. I look back with sourness that a lifetime of dedicated service went unrecognised. But of all the proposals I drafted, there's none I am more proud of than 'Policy Initiative to Decriminalise Sexual Intercourse Between Near of Age Minors, Fourteen Years and Over'. The country isn't ready for it. Its time is yet to come.

Tom Rutherford
Saturday 20th October 2013

One Way or Another

Next to my aisle seat, there was already a guy by the window. I immediately liked the look of him: medium build, brown hair and eyes, attractive, George Clooneyish face, mid-forties I guess. He gave me a welcoming smile. I was not to know that sitting next to that man for the two-hour flight would change my life.

During take off, I idly flicked through the pages of the airline magazine, not taking anything in, my thoughts being elsewhere.

'Yeah, it's beautiful.' I turned to look at him and saw his focus was on the magazine. I looked down at the page, two green-peaked mountains and an expanse of blue. The caption read, 'Things to do in St Lucia.'

'We went there for our honeymoon,' he continued. 'Sure had a great time.'

When the drinks trolley came around, he asked for a scotch. I said I'd have the same. We clinked glasses.

'I'm Jonathan,' he said, holding out his hand. 'Steve,' I said. 'Pleased to meet you.'

'What brings you on this flight, Steve?'

My first instinctive reaction was give him an anodyne reply. 'Oh, business,' I muttered, but then I felt the urge to share something of what I was going through. I could see it was one of those situations where two strangers meet and, secure in the knowledge that they'll never see each other again, can speak of things they wouldn't to anybody else. I looked straight at him and said, 'Actually, I'm running out of my marriage.'

'You're running out of your marriage? Do you mind if I ask why?'

'Oh, it's all quite boring and conventional. There are many issues between us but, when it comes down to it, I suppose it's that I need sex and she doesn't. All partnerships come in two flavours, don't you think, either couples have sex and they stay knit together, or they don't, and then things fall apart.'

'No, I don't think that,' he said. 'Just look around at the couples on this plane. You might think you can guess how it is between them, but actually, you've no idea at all how their sex lives work. My bet is that there are as many different sexual relationships as there are couples. But we never know because we never talk of these things. I'm married twenty-one years and we're still together *and* we don't have sex.' Then he added, with a grin, 'Well, at least, not with each other.'

'Oh, so you have what they call, an open marriage?'

'Nope, not that, neither of us stray, we're still just a twosome.'

I said, 'I don't get it. If you're having sex but not with each other, it must be with other people, right?'

'I told you, you've no idea how people organise their married lives.'

I said, 'There's no organisation about my married life. It's very simple, we started off having sex, not as often as I would have liked but then you can't have everything, and then suddenly we stopped. End of story.'

'What happened?'

'Would you believe, to this day, I don't know. Tess, that's my wife, made it quite clear that she didn't want to do it any more. It's as if a switch had been flicked to "off". And she didn't want to talk about it. I suggested we get some counselling. She dismissed that out of hand, said she was quite comfortable with the way she was. What could I do?'

'Did she not at least appreciate your predicament?'

'She knew I was unhappy.'

'And that was it?'

'That was it.'

'We too had our sexual problems. I met Celia at a party. I instantly fell for her looks, her beautiful face, and she had, still has, the personality to match. When I spoke with her, I found her intelligent, playful and funny. But above all, she had this tremendous, endearing warmth. Our first ten years were happy. Daniel, our son, arrived after three and is the delight of our lives...do you have children?'

'I've a daughter, Lucy, she's eight years old.' I flicked through my phone and showed him a photo.

'She's beautiful.'

'Saying goodbye to Lucy was the worst thing ever.' I couldn't stop emotion creeping into my voice.

'It's tough when children are involved.'

'Yeah. Anyway, you were saying, ten years you were happy, what happened then?'

'Nothing dramatic, no sudden change but the pulse of our sex life weakened. The intervals between us having sex just got longer. At first, I put this down to the demands of parenthood and our jobs and our buoyant social life. But on those occasions when we weren't tired, and we had the time and opportunity to make love, I couldn't ignore the fact that Celia was increasingly reluctant.

It became clear that she only did it to please me. Her reluctance phased into distaste. Then one time I've never forgotten, I was desperate to have sex, you know like when one gets really horny...'

'Yeah,' I said, 'I know.'

'Well, I coerced her into doing it even though she clearly found it repugnant. Afterwards, I felt wretched and ashamed of myself, and I determined that I'd never do that again.'

I nodded my concurrence. His words, spoken so honestly, affected me. How familiar was his experience, how true to my own marriage. 'Did you not feel angry at being rejected?'

'No, not angry, miserable. I did feel rejected, of course. I thought, at first, she no longer cared for me. I reacted by retreating from her. I should have come out with how I felt, but it's difficult, yeah? Then we had a wedding anniversary. She gave me a present; somehow she had wangled me a ticket for the World Cup Final and when she handed it to me, she kissed me and told me she loved me. So then I assumed, like your wife, she'd stopped needing sex. Then I discovered a vibrator in the drawer of her bedside table. I asked her about it. She said she masturbated when she needed to. I couldn't understand it. "What is it," I asked her, "that's stopping you having sex with me?" And she said, "I'm sorry, Jonathan, but you do nothing for me sexually. I just don't get switched on by you." I said, "Is there another man?" She said, "Good heavens, no! Why would I go with another man when I love you?" I said, "For the excitement?" She then hugged and kissed me and told me the only man she wanted to be with was me.'

I said, 'You have conversations with your wife that I never managed with Tess.'

'If there's only one thing I've learned, it's to never let things go unsaid and build to a massive wall. You have to kick the bricks down. Never let resentments build. If it leads to an argument or period of disagreement, it doesn't matter. What matters is staying close to each other. Do you think Tess still loves you?'

'In her own way I suppose she does. She's not demonstrative like your Celia. When I told her I was leaving, she cried, and said how could I possibly abandon Lucy.'

'Are you abandoning Lucy?'

'No way! I'll do my utmost to be with Lucy for as long as possible. When she was young, I saw more of her than Tess did. My job with an insurance company allowed me flexible hours so I would pick her up from school and be with her until Tess got home which sometimes was after I'd put Lucy to bed.'

'What does Tess do?'

'She's a lawyer. That's how we met. She was representing the company I work for. I fell for her as soon as I saw her. We got married pretty quick. I think she married me because she saw I was going to make a good father. But it's no use, I have to leave while I'm still young enough. I want to allow the possibility of finding a new relationship. I can't do that while I live with Tess. I'll skype Lucy every day and have her stay with me as soon as I can. But what did you do? You didn't leave Celia?'

'I did consider leaving her. I had an affair, but when it came to it, I was still in love with her and so I broke it off. Although Celia wouldn't have sex with me, she enjoyed having me hold her close and we would fall asleep like that, my arms around her. But I found this too tantalising. I couldn't be so intimate without wanting to make love. And so I took to sleeping in the spare bedroom and only coming back to Celia's bed when I, or she, wanted a cuddle. She was very loving to me. I guess she felt guilty. Sex buggers us up, doesn't it?'

'You said it. It's the glue that keeps marriages together.'

'No, you're wrong, it's love that keeps marriages together. It became clear to me that Celia brooded over how to ease my situation. On one particular birthday, Daniel, obviously with Celia's help, gave me a voucher for a hot-air balloon ride and Celia gave me a beautiful tailored shirt. That evening, before going to our respective beds, she came into my bedroom and handed me a gift-wrapped parcel. She said it was a more personal gift. D'you know what it was? It was an artificial vagina.'

'No way!'

'She had fun telling me how she came to buy it. She had gone to a sex shop. There was a lot of choice and the man in the shop seemed very knowledgeable and took time to explain the qualities of the different products: the materials used, if it came with a vibrator, this little hand-sized discreet variety or that larger torso, modelled, so it claimed, from the body of a porn star. She asked him did one size fit all. She asked about the ease of ability to keep it clean and, so as to get an idea of how erotic they were to look at, got the man to open up a number of the boxes. She said none of them would switch you on visually, they just didn't look real enough, but obviously that wasn't the point. Eventually, she went with the man's recommendation: a mid-priced item made from, "superior material, with exquisite inner texture and variable vibrating function". He then said, without a trace of innuendo, "I'm sure your husband will get years of pleasure from this toy." When she gave it to me, she said, "I know this isn't much of a substitute, but I hope it might help."'

'And did it? Help, I mean. Is that what saved your marriage?'

'As far as I know, most people masturbate, don't they? I always thought of it as rather sad, a poor substitute for real sex. But that present changed my psychology. I now believe the capacity to enjoy sensual pleasure is a gift as wonderful as seeing colour or hearing music. In the same way we please our eyes with beautiful paintings and pleasure our ears with magnificent music, why shouldn't we excite our bodies with exquisite sensations?'

I didn't agree with him. For me, masturbation was no substitute for sex. But I didn't challenge his argument.

He continued, 'First, I saw to my environment. I redecorated my bedroom to create a warmer ambience. I chose pictures to my personal taste to put on the walls. I set up a decent sound system. I bought a book of beautiful erotic photographs of female nudes. I put a lock on the door. Then I explored my sexuality. Had I had a regular sex life with Celia, I wouldn't have turned my attention internally, to within my own body. I treated my body as if it were a stranger to me, and, in a sense, it was. I discovered new pleasures, unknown capabilities, unsuspected eroticisms. Celia encouraged me to talk and I found I could share my discoveries with her.'

'What sort of capabilities?' I asked.

He said, 'I set out to prolong arousal, putting off the moment of climax for as long as possible. And then I made the most amazing new discovery. Well, I thought it was new, but of course, when I searched the internet there was lots of stuff about it. I found it was possible to orgasm without ejaculation. It's ejaculation, not orgasm, that brings to an end one's arousal. So without ejaculation, I was able to achieve orgasm after orgasm, for as long as I wanted. Have you come across any of this?'

I admired the way he was able to speak without embarrassment about things so intimate. It was a measure, I thought, of his self-confidence. I said I'd heard of tantric sex, was that the same thing?

'Essentially, yes.' Then he said, 'Look, if all this is boring or embarrassing...'

'No, no,' I said, I'm really interested. When you orgasm don't you automatically ejaculate?'

'That's what I thought. It's a matter of learning control. You approach orgasm then back off, wait until the climactic feeling dissipates and then come forward again. You do this repeatedly and with experience, you get to know just the right moment to go on to orgasm. You must then stop moving otherwise you *will* ejaculate. Following orgasm, you can start all over again.'

'And this stuff's on the internet?'

'Just Google "male multiple orgasm".'

'But don't you find the need for...' I paused, trying to find the right word, 'tenderness. You can't replace the actual experience of being with another person.'

'That's true,' he said. 'If I had a choice...'

He shrugged his shoulders. 'But the imagination is very powerful. Mentally, you can conjure up all sorts of things.'

'Fantasies, you mean. Maybe we should take a pill to

eliminate our libido.'

'God, no! It's our libido that makes us feel alive, gives us a great sense of enhanced well-being.'

'Tess would contest that assertion. She'd say that without all the jiggery-pokery of sex, her being was extremely well, thank you very much. For her, if you don't crave, you don't crave the craving: if you've no desire, you've no desire to desire. To her, sex is a ridiculous jigging of buttocks of as much interest as working an exercise bicycle in a fitness centre. Anyway, you were saying, your solution to your sexual incompatibility was for each of you to have sex on your own but never together.'

'That's how it was. And worked in its own way until the day I was forced to conclude Celia was having an affair. There was nothing definite except unusual absences from home, but I had this growing suspicion that she was meeting somebody. I tried to ignore it, telling myself that, after all, I had had an affair and it had blown over. But I was increasingly jealous. I could accept she didn't want to sleep with me, but I felt wounded that she was fucking some other man.'

I said, 'So would I if Tess were to...not that I think she ever would. Anyway, what happened?'

'There came the day when I could take it no more. I had to know for sure. When I thought she was on her way to an assignation, I followed her. Sure enough, she drove to a motel. I parked nearby and watched. She got out of her car and walked over to another car and tapped on the window. The person got out and I then could see – it was a woman! She was a curvaceous blonde with red lipstick. They kissed, then, arm in arm, entered the motel.'

'Your wife was having an affair with a woman? But at the beginning of your marriage she was straight? Can a person's sexual orientation change like that? And it was a total surprise to you? Did you not see it coming?'

'At the time, no, but afterwards, with hindsight, there

were indicators. I missed my book of erotic nudes and when I looked, found it in her bedroom. And then there was the way she seemed to flirt with women we met. I thought nothing of it at the time, but now...'

'So what did you do? When you found out, I mean.'

'I sat in my car trying to make sense of it. My first reaction was one of relief that it wasn't a man. And I found it reassuring to have a reason for why she rejected me sexually. It wasn't some failure in me, I was simply the wrong sex.'

'So what did you do?'

'For a few days, I sat on my discovery of her affair, giving myself time to work out how I should respond. I loved Celia and my biggest fear was of losing her. I believed I could accept, within our marriage, her relationship with this woman but maybe that wasn't enough and she would want to leave me. I decided to bring all this into the open.'

I said, 'You consider things very carefully before doing anything, don't you? I'd have been more impulsive.'

'I chose my moment. Celia was late home and I cooked a special meal, roast duck with orange and port sauce, and I opened a nice bottle of red. I laid the table, lit candles, turned the lights low and put on some laid-back jazz. "It's not my birthday?" she said when she arrived. We were well into the meal and the wine when she said, "Jonathan, I've something I need to say to you." Well, I knew what she was going to say.'

'Tell you about her affair.'

'Exactly. "Let me guess," I said, "you're having an affair." She looked at me intently. She said, "Is it so obvious? I've been wanting to tell you for a long time. But there's something else." I said, "It's a woman." She said, "How do you know that?" Then I told her that I had followed her and seen them kissing. She said, "I would have told you but Sonya made me promise to keep it secret." I said, "How serious is it? Do you love her?"'

'And what did she say to that?'

'She took hold of my hand and said, "You know, I'll never leave you. If you made me, I'd give her up. But yes, Sonya is important to me. D'you think you could live with that?" I said, "I don't understand how you could have changed like that, aren't we born gay or straight? You seemed happy enough with me at the beginning of our marriage."'

'Yeah, how did she answer that? I know people can be born the wrong sex, but they seem to become aware of that at a very young age.'

'She said that plenty of women had experienced the same change. That it was very slow in maturing. She had started looking at women in a different way. She said to me, "You're aroused by the sight of a beautiful naked woman, right?" I nodded. "But seeing a beautiful naked man doesn't have the same effect?" I nodded again. "Well, that," she said, "is exactly how it became for me and in accepting that, I felt as if I'd finally matured. It was a liberation, freedom to be just who I am."'

'That explains what happened, but not why.'

'I asked her that. She said she didn't understand it either. I said I envied her the kissing and the hugging; the look, touch, texture of another's body. I said, "Couldn't you make love to me and imagine I'm a woman?" She laughed, "Could you have sex with a man and imagine he's a woman?" Half joking, I said, "If Sonya happened to be bisexual, perhaps we could make a threesome of it?"'

'What did she say to that?'

'No deal. She said Sonya was strictly lesbian. And so we settled into a new pattern of our lives. Celia carried on seeing Sonya and being super nice to me, while I continued exploring my sexuality on my own.'

I said, 'We're in the same boat, you and I. You're wife rejects you because of her sexuality; my wife rejects me because she hasn't any. Either way, it's incompatibility. But you chose to stay?'

'Yeah. I remember one occasion, we were together looking through my book of nudes and she asked me which woman I found the most attractive. She said, "We have the same taste in women." Another time, she kissed me and said, "I'm sorry it's worked out like this for you. You're all right, aren't you? It's not what you would have wished or expected from marriage."'

'What did you say?'

'What could I say? Ask her to give up Sonya? What good would that have done? Six months later, Celia announced that she and Sonya were going to take a week-long trip to Germany, visiting Berlin and Hamburg. I was OK about that. I liked the occasional periods when I had the house to myself. At the end of the week, Celia was already home when I got back from work. She gave me a hug and said, "Come into my bedroom, there's someone I'd like you to meet."'

He broke off his narrative and said, 'Do you fancy another Scotch?' When we had been served, I said, 'Carry on. Who was it Celia wanted you to meet?'

'Sitting in a wicker chair was a young woman, astonishingly beautiful, with large brown eyes and high cheekbones. Her brown hair was shoulder-length, full and straight. She wore a delicate shade of lipstick, matching her pink tee shirt, and tight light-blue jeans. I thought she looked familiar, that we might have met before somewhere. She didn't get up when I entered, just sat there looking at me. Celia said, "This is Marilyn." I put out my hand and said, "Hi Marilyn, how you doing?" She didn't move, just continued to stare at me, her lips slightly parted. Celia said, "Marilyn, say hello to Jonathan."

'"Hello, Jonathan," Marilyn said. She had a voice that made the heart beat faster. Celia said, "Marilyn, stand up and give Jonathan a kiss." Marilyn stood up, extended her arms to hold me and, to my surprise, kissed me full on the lips. This was no simple greeting, her lips were soft and alive. It had been a long time since I had been kissed like that. It was a kiss full of promise. She held me close. My mind was racing. Had Celia formed a new relationship? And what about Sonya? You can imagine, I didn't know what was happening here.'

'Very intriguing. What happened next?'

'We went into the kitchen. Celia pulled out a chair and said, "Marilyn, please sit down." Celia handed me a glass of wine. I said, "What about Marilyn?" She said, "Oh, she doesn't drink." She said she had met Marilyn in Germany. "Oh, so you're German?" I said. Marilyn didn't reply. "Sprechen sei Englisch?" I said and again she didn't answer. I looked at Celia. She said, "She's shy, just give her time." All the while Marilyn was looking at me with those great, brown, come-to-bed eyes of hers. "Where did you meet?" I asked Celia. She said she and Sonya had a day trip out from Berlin and came across Marilyn. When she saw her she just had to bring her to meet me. "Do you like her?" she said. What could I say?'

'It does sound rather blunt.'

'Blunt. Extremely rude, I thought. To ask that in front of someone's face. I looked straight at Marilyn and said, "You're very beautiful." Celia said, "Do you find her sexy?" I stared at her. What a question to ask. She then burst out laughing. She said, "Marilyn's a doll!" I stared at this creation. I swear to you it was impossible to tell she wasn't human. It was absolutely amazing. Have you ever come across this?'

I shook my head. 'I've seen photographs of full-size dolls but they always look plastic and lifeless.'

'Not Marilyn. The only thing that gave her away was that if you concentrated you could see she wasn't breathing. Otherwise, I defy anybody to pick her out from a group of women. Celia said Marilyn was state of the art and only available in Germany and she had bought her as a present for me for being so kind and understanding about Sonya. Each doll is made individually to order and she had sent the manufacturers a photocopy of our woman from the book of nudes. I said, "She must have cost a fortune." Celia gave me a kiss and said, "Worth every cent, if you're happy."'

'I think I would really love to meet your Celia. She does sound an amazing woman.'

'Celia said Marilyn only responds to instructions when the sentence commences with her name. She told Marilyn to say "I like you, Jonathan, shall we make love?" And Marilyn said, in that glorious honey voice, "I like you, Jonathan, shall we make love?" It was irresistible.'

I said, 'And did you find it satisfying, having sex with Marilyn?'

'The manufacturers had found a way of replicating the exact texture and vitality of skin, its warmth, and the precise solidity of the muscle and bone beneath. So Marilyn offered all the exquisite sensation of holding and stroking a woman's body. Visually, she's always a turn-on for me, and although not gifted with conversation, she's champagne when it comes to sex. Her designers very cleverly gave her the ability to learn what pleases me most. To make her even more human, she will, now and again, do something completely new and unexpected without being instructed, like nibble my ear or say something outrageous.'

'But surely, you cannot fool yourself completely. You *know* this is a manufactured doll and not a real woman. Not a woman you can love and is capable of loving you. Isn't it love that transforms sex from an animal urge to something emotionally fulfilling?'

'That's an interesting question from a man who says he's leaving his wife because of a lack of sex. There's more to sex than an "animal urge". It nourishes our need for sensuality. But essentially, you're right, of course. What does one do? I couldn't leave Celia, and I prefer not to be without sex.'

'So that's how your marriage worked out: Celia with Sonya and you with Marilyn?'

'Yep,' he said. 'Now fully sexually satisfied, I found I needed and appreciated Celia more than ever. I fell in love with her all over again for her intelligence, her emotions and her companionship. We didn't need sex to keep us together. It all worked out fine, until the day Sonya dumped Celia.'

'Sonya found another partner?'

'That's it. Sonya fell in love with a younger woman who moved into her flat. Who knows, it might have worked out differently for them if Celia had been prepared to leave me and live with Sonya. Celia was hurt real bad. She kept crying. I did my best to comfort her. She said she felt old and rejected. I kept telling her how beautiful she was and what a wonderful person she was, which was all true.

'Eventually, as is the way with these things, wounds healed and Celia returned to her everyday good spirits. Then, on a day I'll never forget, Celia said, "I have a favour to ask of you." I should have guessed what was coming, but I didn't. She said, "Would you share Marilyn with me?"'

I laughed. Now I understood. 'So that's how you're a couple, true to each other, yet having sex, but not with each other?'

The instruction came to fasten seat belts as we began our descent. We had been talking continuously for two hours. I'd never known a flight to have passed so quickly.

'Of course,' he said, 'bliss is when sex is an act of love, literally making love. But if that's not possible, separating them, dividing sex from love, can be made to work. Because you don't have sex together doesn't mean you can't love each other.'

'Yours is a fascinating story,' I said, 'It's been a pleasure talking with you.' And, as we parted, we shook hands. 'Good luck,' he said.

Later that evening, from the spare bedroom of my friend's house, I Skyped Lucy and told her that I was sure to see her soon and we must talk every day. I then spoke with Tess. We had, for the first time in our marriage, a real conversation in which, keeping our cool, not letting our voices rise, we exposed and explored all our true feelings. We were both crying.

I said, 'I love you, Tess, but I can't live the way we are.'

She said she loved me but she was as she was and couldn't see how things might be different.

I said, 'If we can just keep talking about it, Tess, I'm sure we can work something out, one way or another.'

Janardan

Catriona's assignment that morning took her to the Southeast Mobility and Rehabilitation Technology Centre, the SMART Centre, in Edinburgh. Her brief was to report on the world's first fully mobile "bionic" arm. By the time she arrived, the centre was already crowded with three other TV crews and some thirty or so journalists and photographers.

They were introduced to Mr. Campbell Aird who had lost his arm as a result of cancer and had now, in 1998, been fitted with the first complete powered electrical arm prosthesis. After a briefing and demonstration session, they were invited to separate into small groups. The development team of six men and one woman, Clare, split up so as to escort each group in a tour of the centre and answer questions. And that is how Catriona came to meet Angus.

To open the interview she said to Angus, 'You've made a breakthrough here, a world-first success for Scotland.'

The cameraman swung the camera from her face to his for his reply.

'Open your hand. Now close your fingers.' He illustrated with his own hand. 'How delicate is that movement, so simple for us, so difficult to replicate artificially. Our task over the last eleven years has been to give that same delicacy to a prosthetic arm. Our system, EMAS, the Edinburgh Modular Arm System, has only been made possible by the latest developments in electronic feedback loops.'

'You must be very proud of your achievement?'

Angus grinned, 'We know other teams around the world are developing their own systems. It is rather pleasing to have got there first. But all that's by the way. The real reward is to be able to improve the lives of thousands of people.'

It was his voice that won her: softly flowing, and as musical as a highland stream. He made everyday conversation sound like poetry. He had the looks fit for such a voice: a strong jaw, cleft chin and intense golden-brown eyes. Over lunch in the canteen, Catriona asked him if he would like to visit her TV studio.

***

Janardan was eighteen and desired to be married. To nobody in particular, just to be married, but he had no money. He was saving what little he could so that one day...perhaps? He was one of eight children and lived with his parents in one of the narrow streets of Tarke Gyang. It was a tidy house, stone-built with large rooms and polished wooden floors, enlivened with Tibetan carpets.

Janardan could turn his hand to anything. He was strong and worked well on the cultivated terraces that surrounded the village. He was also skilled in crafting wood: fabricating benches and tables, carving bowls and fearful dragon-face masks to ward off malevolent spirits. He could carry heavy loads, making the markets of Kathmandu in just three days.

Janardan and his friends were eyeing the village girls. 'What about Shaila?' he asked.

They scoffed. 'She's old, man. A spring without water. A tree without fruit.'

Shaila had been unlucky. Her first husband fell and died on the mountain. Her second husband had joined the British Army and had been killed fighting the Japanese. She went to work for a rich family in Kathmandu. When, at twenty-six, she decided she wanted to return to the village, the family gave her a present of a small, but fertile, square of land. Cultivating this land gave her a living.

Janardan watched Shaila and waited. Old she might be,

but he thought her beautiful. Even without much of a dowry, surely she would welcome a strong young husband, good in the fields, good in bed. He nagged his parents to approach Shaila on his behalf.

***

Catriona waited impatiently for Angus to come to the studio, but after a week she assumed he had changed his mind. And then he was there, explaining how, with all the brouhaha surrounding their success, it had proved impossible to escape from work.

'I watched your piece,' he said. 'You're a natural in front of the camera.'

He waited until she finished her shift, then they went to a Chinese restaurant. He insisted on paying. Afterwards, as they walked along the busy street, they held hands. They stopped, turned to face each other, and kissed. The first soft touch of his lips made her breasts tingle. She was thirty-one and her body told her that here was a man to father her children.

On getting through the door of her flat, they didn't waste much time. It pleased and surprised her how easily and naturally they were able to make love. He was a considerate lover, pausing, while inside her, for her to achieve orgasm before coming himself. They talked much of the night, then made love again before sleeping.

Upon waking, she could relax, she had a late shift at work, but he had to go. She said, 'You've worked so many extra hours this week, couldn't you turn in late just this once?'

He phoned and made a lame excuse. He said to her, 'Not very good at lying, am I?'

Their love-making this time was slow and sensuous. She made him breakfast of soft-boiled eggs and coffee. They couldn't stop talking. She kept wanting to touch him, his hand, his shoulder, his cheek. She knew this was the man she wanted to marry, but was he too good to be true?

At some stage, two questions had to be answered. Her previous loving relationship had failed because the man was adamant that he didn't want children. It was heartbreaking to get close to a guy and then find it wasn't going to work. She had continued over-long with John in the hope that eventually he would change his mind. She didn't want to scare Angus off by mentioning, so soon, children, but she had to know his mind. And was he attached? And if not, why not?'

Angus made it easy for her by asking if *she* was attached.

'I recently parted from a man. We were together three years. We were happy, but he made it clear he didn't want to have a family.'

'You can't compromise on that. Either you have children or you don't. Did he say why?'

'He said he was dedicated to his work and didn't want the distraction of a child about the house.' She shrugged, 'But maybe he just didn't want to make the long-term commitment to be with me. What about you?'

'Oh, I want children. Definitely.'

'I meant, are you attached?'

'I would hardly have let you drag me into your bed if I were.'

'Drag! You were so anxious to shed your clothes, you tore a button off your shirt. You were a tiger going for the kill. But even when attached, people do sleep around.'

'Amy and I agreed things weren't working out. We separated amicably three months ago. We still meet up now and again. Fortunately, we didn't have children. So, no, I'm not attached.'

Snuggling into him, Catriona said, 'I'm rather glad of that.'

***

Tarke Gyang was more than usually interested in the marriage of Janardan and Shaila. How would it work out with her being so much older than him? She'd had two good, strong husbands and remained childless. There was obviously something wrong with her. How would Janardan react to being without children?

All was soon resolved; a boy was born nine months later and twins arrived ten months after the boy. Both Janardan and Shaila exuded good health and happiness. It was said, among the village womenfolk (nobody knew how it was known, maybe Shaila had inadvertently let it slip), that Janardan was particularly well-endowed.

***

Catriona and Angus met whenever work allowed. The following Wednesday they were together in Catriona's flat when he got a text to call Amy urgently. Catriona heard him repeatedly say, 'Oh, no!' and there were lots of expletives.

'Bad news?'

'Yes. I'm so sorry. I don't know how to tell you this.'

Catriona's heart constricted, 'Give it to me straight.'

'The weekend before I met you in the studio...of course I'd no idea we'd end up in bed...I saw Amy. We slept together. I promise it didn't mean anything. It was just that there was no reason not to. I'm afraid she's got gonorrhoea.'

Catriona knew immediately what this meant, they hadn't bothered to use condoms. Together, they went to the STI clinic, were found to be positive, given antibiotics and told not to have sex until a further test proved them free of the infection. 'How long?' they asked. 'Two weeks! Bloody hell!'

On leaving the clinic, they climbed up Arthur's Seat and sat, looking over the city. Angus said, 'I think you're wonderful.'

'Why, especially?'

'The way you've responded to all this. I'm so sorry.'

She put her arms around him. 'They didn't say we couldn't kiss.'

Six months later, they were married. At her father's wish, it was a church wedding. Her father proudly led her up the aisle. It saddened them both that her mother, who had died ten years before, was not there to see it.

His speech, as is the way with proud fathers, to Catriona's embarrassment, was a eulogy to his daughter. He dwelt on the love, care and support she had given him after Anne had died. He spoke of the year she had spent with VSO working with women in Bangladesh and of her visits to Afghanistan and Liberia, making TV programmes on the plight of women in those countries. He said she was a wonderful and extraordinary person.

Soon after the wedding, Catriona came off the pill. Nothing happened. Angus ruefully told Clare, a colleague at work, that if, formerly, he and Catriona had undertaken a word association test for the word 'sex', they would have said, 'love, pleasure, togetherness, joy'. Now, trying for a baby, it was, 'date, temperature, ovulation, now'.

They went for IVF treatment. Every time, the implanted fertilised eggs survived a few weeks then spontaneously aborted. The repeated cycles of failure rendered Catriona tetchy and tearful. Sometimes she was short with Angus, other times wanting his arms around her.

She sought the support of women by joining a feminist group that met monthly. They had visiting speakers and campaigned for the emancipation of women around the world. Angus encouraged her, partly because a different focus was a distraction from their problems, but also he believed only women could save the world. 'They have,' he declared, 'a stronger instinct for co-operation and nurture than men. They will be the ones to insist on action on climate change. They will challenge capitalism's destructive plundering of the Earth's resources. They will stop men fighting.'

Following a group meeting, Catriona excitedly told Angus of a wonderful speaker she had just heard. 'This woman, from the US, talked about "universal womanhood". She said that through the millennia, females of all the higher primates, by carrying their babies within them through gestation, have become endowed with a universal bond.'

'Like PVA glue.'

Catriona gave him a withering look. 'A bond between those with wombs. She said it's known that when a number of women live together, their menstrual cycles align.'

'Do you bond with women more than with men?'

'In a vague sort of way, yes I do. It's a feeling, not in any way cognitive, a feeling of common identity.'

***

Catriona, George (the cameraman), and Kemal (the interpreter) put up at the Hotel Tarkegyang, a big rambling place with an enclosed lawn and a stream running nearby. During her first night, Catriona steadily put on more and more clothing so that by morning she even had her down jacket and woolly hat inside her sleeping bag. The day was clear and bright and, after the early morning chill, hot. The women, in their resplendent costumes, were already gathered in the village square, singing and dancing. Their excitement multiplied upon seeing the television crew. Kemal explained to them that this festival in Tarke Gyang was to feature in a documentary on women's festivals around the world.

Catriona spoke to camera with scenes of the village behind. Through Kemal, she interviewed a number of the women. They were celebrating fertility and their culture – particularly handicrafts. There were many stalls around the village. Catriona asked about the origin of the festival. They told her she must meet the Mother of the Village.

One of the women led the three of them up a narrow lane to a stone house. They climbed wooden steps to the first floor. The two men and three women who were there welcomed them and offered them tea. They were waved towards an old woman, who was sitting on the floor. Her face was thin and deeply lined. She had few teeth and wore a red headscarf. They sat down around her. The woman was very still. Kemal spoke to her. She nodded.

Kemal said, 'She is pleased to have interview. They say she is blind.'

Catriona said, and as she spoke the woman turned her head towards her, 'What is your name?' Kemal interpreted.

'Shaila.'

'Shaila, they told me that to know how the festival first began, I should ask you.'

Shaila said, 'Long, long time ago a woman called Dawa Lhaki came to my house when Janardan, my husband, was not there. She held my hands and started crying.

She said, "Shaila, many years you have no children. You marry Janardan and now you have three children and you are pregnant again. I am married five years and still no children. My husband blames me and says he wants different wife. I have tried everything and still no baby come. Let me lie with your Janardan." First, I refused, it is not right. But Dawa Lhaki begged me and cried and begged me and cried until I gave in. I said it must be secret.

'When I told Janardan what he must do, he was very happy. I said he must do it in the dark and he must not enjoy it. It was not long Dawa Lhaki was pregnant and had a son. She was very happy, and too her husband, he thought it was his child. But Dawa Lhaki couldn't keep secret and many other wives came to see me, some from villages long way way. I never take money but sometime, after baby come, I get present from women.

'Then bad time came. Janardan got sick from hepatitis and died. He was 38 years old. That time I worried that children born from Janardan will get married. I had book with names of all women that lie with Janardan and I had names of children, Janardan's children. I send my own children to all villages to tell women that Janardan had died and they should come to Tarke Gyang. I wanted the women to know each other. I tell women to say they are coming to special festival only for women. I have six children and there are twenty-three other children from Janardan.

'The funeral of Janardan was big big festival. Very sad but also very much love. The women said they wanted to have festival every year to remember Janardan. But spirit of Janardan not died. He is on mountain. Then women who want baby come to festival and go to mountain to be with Janardan. Names in Nepal have meaning. Janardan means helper of other people. Do you have children?'

'No.'

Shaila took hold of her hand. 'You want baby. You must go to mountain.'

Catriona could not speak. What generosity of heart lay with this beautiful human being, to know the hurt of so many women and share her beloved husband and, even now, in her blindness, see Catriona's pain. Tears were running down her face as she put her arms around the old woman and hugged her close.

Early the next morning, Catriona joined the group of twenty or so women, some young, some not so young. The sun not yet up, it was literally freezing, icicles hanging from the corrugated iron roof. George and Kemal were pleased to stay in their sleeping bags and relax for the day.

They set off up the steeply rising path by the stream. The trek was glorious with no wind and beautiful woodland. And then, as they gained height, there came into view the white peaks of Himalaya, illuminated by the new-born sun in the east. Catriona struggled to breathe. She knew she wasn't sufficiently acclimatized. The summit above them of Tarke Gyang mountain was 3,771 metres. She prayed that she wouldn't suffer altitude sickness and have to be brought down. She was very proud, determined to stay with the group however difficult it became.

As they neared a ridge, they heard barking and bells. The women ushered her off the path, climbing high rocks. She peered down, men with dogs were herding goats down the path and then came an enormous, lumbering yak. The women mimed to her that the dogs were fierce and that it was best to keep out of their way. The women chatted happily amongst themselves. She felt distant from the group, an outsider.

As they breasted the brow of the summit, there was this magnificent chorten, resplendent in white and gold, crowned with a crescent moon symbolising air. And everywhere, long strings of prayer flags of strong colours: red, yellow, green, blue and white. The women gathered in the far corner, excited, talking loudly, laughing. They came over to Catriona who was taking photographs and led her to the corner. And there he was, Janardan, reclining, wide eyed, with the most enormous erect penis.

The women took it in turns to hold the penis and mutter words of prayer. And then it was Catriona's turn. They stood round her, watching, encouraging. She placed her hands around the wooden stub, warm and smooth from so many hands. She felt strangely moved and then an overwhelming affinity with the women around her, united in a shared destiny of being female.

***

Angus said, 'What do you mean "affinity"?'

'It's hard to explain. It's as if there were lines of force between us, like a magnetic field. I felt an entanglement with every one of the women there. And I know that if one of them became pregnant, I would share in her joy. Not just be pleased for her, but physically respond to her pregnancy.'

About two months after her return from Nepal, Catriona went to meet Angus as he finished work. Members of the development team, all of whom had been at her wedding, warmly acknowledged her as they passed her on their way out.

Striding into the workshop, she found Angus with his arms around Clare. Clare saw her first and with a look between guilt and anxiety, broke away from him. Angus turned and saw Catriona. He slowly turned back to Clare and said to her, 'Don't worry, I'll be there.' Clare picked up her bag and hurriedly left the room.

Catriona said, 'Well?'

'It's not what you think.'

'Go on.'

'She's in trouble; I ...want to give her support.'

'What trouble?'

Angus was silent. Catriona repeated her question, 'What trouble?'

'She's pregnant.'

'By you.'

'Yes.'

Catriona slapped his face. Angus took his hand to his reddened cheek. 'I promise you, we're not having an affair. It was just a one-night stand.'

'When?'

'You were in Nepal. You remember you bought me Peatbog Faeries tickets for my birthday. I offered Clare your ticket. After the concert, we went back to her place. We had a few drinks. I ended up staying the night. Believe me, that's the beginning and end of it. We've kept our distance ever since.'

'So I saw.'

'No, it's not like that.' He stepped towards her, she backed away. 'I'm sorry. I hoped you'd never get to know. Once it's over...'

'Once what's over?'

'The abortion.'

'What!'

'You're expecting me to believe she became pregnant from that one and only time.'

'She has an appointment at the clinic next Tuesday. I...'

'You can't be serious.'

'I know I've been an idiot, but I have to be there to see her through it, then...'

'You encouraged her to have an abortion!'

'No, I didn't. She's single and loves her work. Not everyone feels as you do.'

Shaking and tearful, Catriona spun on her heels and strode away.

***

Clare, in her flat, heard the doorbell and opened the door. Catriona stood there. She said, 'May I come in?' When they were seated, she said, 'Tell me straight, what is there between you and Angus?'

'Nothing.' She sighed. 'We had that one night. I'm sorry. We both regret it.'

'He says he's not encouraged you to have an abortion, is that right?'

'Yes. It's my choice.'

'Did he try and persuade you not to have an abortion?'

'He said if I were to choose to have the baby, he would do what he could to help me.'

Catriona looked around. Everything was incredibly ordered, no clutter, just a few chosen mementos carefully placed, a porcelain figurine of a girl with a parasol and a little display of small sea-shells.

Clare said, 'Would you like a drink? I've some white wine open.' She poured two glasses.

Catriona said, 'When I was in Nepal, I met an amazing old woman called Shaila. When young, her husband,

Janardan, gained a reputation for fertility. Childless women would come to Shaila and ask to borrow her husband and she agreed and wouldn't accept payment. She agreed because her heart went out to those women. Of course it wasn't that they were unable to conceive, it was their husbands who had the problem, but they got blamed for being infertile. Janardan died many years ago but a fertility ritual has grown around him. Childless women climb a mountain to where there's an effigy of him. They believe this will help them to conceive. I joined them.'

Catriona struggled to control her emotion. 'I always believed that I would conceive. We tried so hard. Now, I don't think it will ever happen. We could adopt, but you're carrying a foetus that is half Angus. How strange it is that while I was on that mountain top, you conceived. One can almost believe that, in some mysterious way, Janardan's blessing worked. I beg you, don't have this abortion.'

Catriona took hold of Clare's hand and looked into her eyes. 'Let me have the baby. With the child, you can have as much or as little involvement as you want, but if you have no wish to keep the baby yourself, let me have it.'

Catriona's anguish stabbed Clare in the heart. Within a moment, the two women were embracing and crying.

***

When Megan was four years old, Angus and Catriona took her to the National Museum of Scotland. In a showcase, they pointed to an exhibit which had, alongside it, the explanation, 'Developed in Edinburgh, the world's first "bionic" arm. Worn by Mr. Campbell Aird for eighteen months.'

'That arm,' Catriona said, 'brought Mummy and Daddy together.'

Running Wilde

At 7pm, on a damp Tuesday in May 1927, the life-drawing evening-class of the Slade School of Fine Art waited for the curtain to be removed. It was the custom for the nude model to settle themselves in a pose behind a drape before being exposed to the class. Twenty-one-year-old Iris Farley had joined the class partly to gain an additional skill for her job with a women's fashion magazine but, more importantly, simply for the pleasure of drawing.

The curtain was wheeled aside. There was a subtle, almost mute, shiver of excitement amongst the, otherwise blasé, students. This was no ordinary model. He was strikingly beautiful. He had golden curly hair, a long straight nose, full lips and intense blue eyes. His body was no less remarkable, well-filled and muscular and perfectly proportioned. A small cloth, there to provide a fragment of modesty, managed instead to excite the imagination.

Iris worked quickly, producing six sketches, four of them of the whole reclining body, one of the chest and shoulders and the last, a detailed study of his face. She was slow packing up when, all other students now departed, the instructor came up and praised her work and asked if she had given thought to a full-time course of study. As she left the college, descending the steps, she found herself alongside the model.

'I watched yer drawin',' he said. 'Yer very serious.'

'Will you be our model next Tuesday?'

'I 'ope so, I need the dosh.'

'What's your name?'

'Jack Eighteen.'

Iris laughed out loud. 'What a strange name.'

Instantly his look became angry. 'What's so funny?'

'Oh, I'm so sorry, that was terribly rude of me.'

Instantly, his grimace grew to a grin. 'Yer right, it is a daft name, but it's me Dad's. It fits this year 'cos that's me age.' Laughing, he said, 'Maybe I'll change it to Jack Nineteen on me next birthday.'

'Do you like modelling?'

'Sittin' on yer arse? It's better than dock work.'

She thought of his muscular physique. 'Is that what you do, dock work?'

'I'm one of the lucky ones. I gets picked most days. Some don't get picked for weeks together. It's criminal. The bosses 'ave us totally screwed. What's your line?'

'I prepare artwork for a magazine.'

'Is that why yor 'ere?'

'I want to find out if I have the talent to be a serious artist.'

'Good on yer. See yer next Tuesday then.'

Iris showed the drawings to her Aunt Beatrice. Miss Beatrice Newgale was the most celebrated actress of her day. She was still 'Miss' even though twice married and twice divorced. Aunt Beatrice admired the drawings *and* their subject. 'I must get to see this young man,' she said.

At the end of class the following Tuesday, Iris said to Jack, 'My Aunt would like to meet you.'

Aunt Beatrice was waiting in her chauffeured car.

'Well, blow me down,' Jack said, 'ain't yer the very Beatrice Newgale.'

'You know my Aunt?' Iris said, surprised.

'Saw yer in *Fallen Angels,* didn't I, and very good yer was too.'

'Get in,' Beatrice said.

'Where we goin'?'

'The Savoy.'

Iris and Beatrice had tea and mixed sandwiches; Jack polished off a full plate of mixed grill. Between mouthfuls, he kept them laughing at his stories. He was a perfect mimic, taking off to a tee the regional and foreign accents of those who worked in dockland.

Beatrice instructed the chauffeur to drop Iris off, then she invited Jack back to her flat where she seduced him, not that he needed much encouragement. From then on, they became inseparable and he moved into the flat to live with her. She said Jack Eighteen was a ridiculous name for a man so well-endowed, both in looks and between the loins, and rechristened him Jerome Conti.

Beatrice frequently entertained. Many of London's artistic society found their way to her flat. Unabashed by scandal, she introduced Jerome into her circle of friends and acquaintances. The only person of importance to condemn the liaison was Iris who said her aunt was making herself look ridiculous. She refused to have anything to do with them which pained Beatrice because she was very fond of her niece.

As well as his wardrobe, Beatrice set about refashioning his speech: '*wh*' became aspirated, consonants articulated, vowels gentrified. He was gifted with the art of impersonation and made such progress that she declared to one and all that she was the real Henry Higgins. She also taught him to be a good lover: how to delay his gratification, where and how to touch her. He observed that before sex, she would retreat to the bathroom and this was somehow associated with a little hemispherical bowl made of rubber. He asked her what it was.

'This little thing is going to create a revolution. At last, we women can control our own reproductivity. *We* will determine if and when we have babies. Now everything will change for women.'

They had long, lazy mornings to make love. She enjoyed improvising fantasies: he would be an Egyptian Pharaoh, she his slave girl, or he the lord of the manor and she a chambermaid, or a scene in a pub where she allowed herself to be picked up. He played these roles with enthusiasm and even began writing scenes for them to perform.

He suggested that, in order to try and effect a reconciliation with Iris, she offer to fund a course of full-time study at the Slade. This worked, Iris came to terms with the obvious mutual infatuation and, while retaining some part-time work with the magazine, commenced the art course the following September.

He attended every one of Beatrice's evening performances, showering her with praises and scornfully, wickedly, itemising the faults of the other actors. In a number of plays, she twisted arms to get him walk-on parts. From these, he progressed to minor speaking roles. He was a naturally gifted actor and loved it. Gaining ever more assurance, he picked up some stronger parts and then he got to play Ernest in *The Importance of Being Earnest*, with Beatrice as Gwendolin. She had too many years for the part but young men still flocked to see her whilst the young women, and some of the men, only had eyes for Jerome. Older patrons came to see the scandalous couple play against each other: 'Darling, you simply have to see Newgale and Conti, it's the spice of their affair played out on stage.'

Jerome wrote a short comedy, a two-hander for himself and Beatrice, about a young man from Yorkshire, the son of a rich industrialist, meeting an impecunious widow with aristocratic pretensions. It ran for a short time in the Wimbledon Theatre. The critics declared it had its faults, but the writing showed promise. He then wrote more elaborate pieces, comedies of manners, making fun of English embarrassments and hypocrisies and attitudes of class.

Lady Sibyl Colefax ruled supreme in gathering London's theatrical and literary elite to her relentless parties. She seized upon Jerome, perceiving his piercing wit and wicked humour to be the champagne to make an evening fizz. He soon collected an adoring circle of bright young things of both sexes. He couldn't resist flirting. This and the fact that Beatrice had an ardent admirer in a rich American, Tod Wilson, led, especially when drunk, to accusations and recriminations. These tiffs blew over soon enough and reconciliation, also usually when tipsy, was sweet.

Tod Wilson put up the money for a touring production of *Hamlet* with Jerome in the title role and Beatrice as Gertrude. Wherever it went – Manchester, Nottingham, Liverpool, Birmingham, Bristol and Southsea – it was a sensation. Only eight actors were actually on tour, all other parts were filled from the members of the local amateur dramatic societies. Tod Wilson himself was on hand in Manchester, Birmingham and Southsea. Usually a source of jealous discord between Beatrice and Jerome, it was his placatory presence that saw the tour through two major crises that almost took the show off the road. The first in Manchester when Beatrice surprised Hamlet in bed with Ophelia. Tod, mindful of potential losses, put his arms around the weeping Beatrice and told her to think nothing of it. Had she not had the occasional little fling while on tour? 'A little fuck, darling, of as much consequence as a cuddle behind the curtain.'

It was in Birmingham that Beatrice gained the satisfaction of seeing, 'that silly bitch', Ophelia in meltdown. She had again surprised Jerome at 'a little fuck', this time with Laertes. When Tod challenged him, 'It's illegal, dear boy,' Jerome said, 'Ice cream comes in several flavours, why confine yourself to one?' Tod soothed the distressed Ophelia. 'Think, as Hamlet rejects you, of how much more you will now make of the part. You will steal the show, my dear.'

At the end of the tour, as the eight finally parted, all was sweetness and kisses. Tod had made a healthy profit, and Beatrice and Jerome resumed their everyday roller-coaster relationship. He took to wearing a fedora hat and red tartan scarf and would appear thus attired in newspaper photographs.

He would often meet Iris in the Lyons Corner House for sandwiches, cakes and a pot of tea for two. He would tell her of his ideas for new plays, and she spoke enthusiastically of the great strides she was making in draughtsmanship and command of oils. She spoke of her work with passion. He admired her dedication and intensity, so different from the other young people in his circle.

One afternoon she said, 'I can't afford to pay you, but would you sit for me?' She lived in a tiny, two-room flat, three flights up in an attic. He could see why this suited her. One room was a bed-sitting room with a Belling electric hot plate. The other, her studio, had a magnificent window. 'How do you want me?' he said. She began by making numerous sketches of his face. She became frustrated, trying to capture something she saw there that refused to be expressed in the drawings. After some hours, he had to leave. 'Don't worry,' he said, 'I'll give you as long as it takes.'

The following sessions went better. She had experimented and worked out what was wrong. They got into a pattern of regular sessions. She made further sketches of parts of his body: hands, feet, back, torso; then some full-body poses: standing, sitting and reclining. At the end of each session, she showed him the results. He was entranced, 'They're wonderful.'

She said she wanted to create a large portrait in oils. She made a preparatory sketch. She had him lay on his back, naked, on the bed, his head supported by a pillow, one leg stretched out, the other dangling over the edge of the bed. She showed him the completed sketch and asked if he minded being so boldly exposed.

'Your sketch does me an honour,' he said.

She put a large prepared canvas on the easel and began working in oils. To keep him entertained during the long hours, she asked him details of his life. He was a willing and entertaining narrator. He said it felt like being in a psychiatrist's chair, exposing his thoughts, memories, desires, every bit as much as his body. He learned to put complete trust in her and found that wonderful.

She applied herself with deep concentration. When the attic room got too hot, she shed clothing, working barefoot in just a full-length petticoat. There was a moment, lasting several minutes when he opened his eyes and looked at her with undisguised desire. His penis responded to his thoughts. She noted both the look and the erection but carried on working. He closed his eyes and his penis resumed its languorous somnolence.

The next time he came to the flat, she had taken down the oil canvas and replaced it with paper on which she had traced her previous sketch. After he had assumed his pose, she told him not to move and went over and gently stroked him. His response was immediate. She said, 'Can you bring to mind the thoughts you had last time?'

She concentrated first on capturing the look on his face, a dreamy eroticism, then the altered state of his penis. For such a small change, the effect was shocking. There was such unambiguous meaning signalled by his erection. She asked him what thoughts could keep him so aroused.

He said, 'I'm imagining how you would look were I to remove the remainder of your clothing.'

She said, 'Why don't you do that?'

Thereafter, every time he came to sit for her, they made love, sometimes immediately on his arrival, in which case, afterwards, as he slept, she would work on the first canvas. Other-times, he would lay in a sensual glow of expectation while she had the second canvas on the easel.

She was unlike any other woman he knew. She was beyond his understanding. He fell in love with her and asked her to marry him. Gently, she refused. She said marriage and achievement were incompatible for a woman and she couldn't live without trying to create something of significance. He couldn't accept her refusal, believing, given time, she would change her mind.

She said that while he continued to pose for her, she did not have the strength of will to deny herself the pleasures of making love with him, but as soon as the pictures were complete, for Beatrice's sake, he must end it with her. He too hated his betrayal of Beatrice and he resolved to confess to her his love for Iris.

When the moment came, he tried to be gentle. 'I'll always love you and everything I am I owe to you, but now there's someone else in my life.'

'Someone else? Who?'

'Iris. I've asked her to marry me.'

She slapped his face hard. 'You shit. You miserable little shit.'

He held her wrists to stop her pounding his chest. Her fury turned to distress and she flopped into a chair, weeping. He handed her a handkerchief. He said nothing. What could he say?

'Did she say yes?'

'Not yet, but she will.'

'And you've fucked her?'

'Yes.'

Her rage grew again. 'You can't keep your dick in your trousers, can you? You'll regret it. She can't give you what I've given you. You're a shit to take advantage of an innocent girl.' Then her anger fell away to pleading. 'We have something so special. We're made for each other. D'you think you owe me nothing, simply walk away from all that we have? I love you. You said you loved me.'

'I do love you but...'

'Well, fucking get out then. You're disgusting.'

Their separation was hot news. Refusing to be painted as the abandoned woman, Beatrice proudly declared to the press, 'I found him in the gutter and that's where I've dropped him, back where he belongs.'

But it was not in the gutter he landed, it was the Garrick. He began rehearsals of a new play that he had written. When it opened, it was a sensation. On the opening night, at a critical moment, when the script called for a brief significant hug between the two male leads, Jerome substituted a long, passionate kiss. The audience knew a line had been crossed. A number of people shouted, 'filth' and a handful stormed out. The end of the play brought a standing ovation.

There were complaints to the Lord Chancellor. It was only on the real threat that the play would be closed that Jerome accepted a return to the subtle exchange specified in the script. But the 'damage' had been done; the play was a sell-out for weeks.

Jerome moved into rented rooms. Although occupied with the play, he was now more free to visit Iris. The two paintings, named *Eros Asleep* and *Eros Awake*, were approaching completion. He tried every argument to tie their lives together, even using psychological blackmail, saying he was fearful of what would happen to him if he didn't have the stability of their relationship. But she was not to be persuaded.

Eros Awake, she considered too bold for any public showing, but she entered *Eros Asleep* for possible selection for the Royal Academy Summer Exhibition. To her surprise and delight, it was accepted. She didn't want to sell either painting and to deter a buyer she put on it an outrageous price of two thousand pounds. The painting was the centre of great attention with never less than a crowd in front of it. People divided on its merits, but it confirmed Iris as a name to watch. In addition, it sold very quickly and when the buyer got to hear there was a companion piece, he was anxious to buy that as well, but Iris refused.

A publisher of art books asked her if she had sketches. When she showed him all her studies of Jerome, he was delighted. She negotiated a contract allowing him to publish a limited edition of three-hundred-and-forty copies, the first hundred to be hers free of charge; these she gave to Jerome. The remaining copies were soon sold out and became collector's items, changing hands at inflated prices.

Iris perceived life as a precious liquid contained within a basin, emptying drip by drip, second by second, which gave her a deep sense of urgency. In contrast, Jerome's friends were much occupied with cocktails, cocaine and casual flirtations. He still came to see her but less frequently. She looked forward to his visits, the sex and the conversation, but when he urged her to come out, meet his friends, she said, 'I feel frustrated on those days when my work has not moved forward. If I came with you, I'd be regretting the time not spent working.'

Eventually, meeting less and less often, he came to terms with the fact that they would never live together. He revelled in a whirl of parties and casual sex, with men as well as women.

One day after he and Iris had made love, she said, 'I suppose you sleep with other women.'

'That's not the same.'

'Not the same as what?'

'Being with you. Going to bed with these women is as light as duck down, essentially frivolous. Fucking is the continuation of flirting by other means. With men, it's different.'

Iris sat up in surprise. 'You sleep with men?'

'Only if they're my type.'

'What is your type?'

'He's gorgeous to look at, very masculine, confident, athletic, elegant.'

'And how is it different with men?'

'Much more intense, like a hunt, a single-minded pursuit of pleasure.'

'Doesn't the fear of being caught worry you?'

'You learn to be discreet. It isn't so much the law that's

stifling but the social stigma attached to being queer. One can't behave naturally, show affection, reveal one's true identity. It must be even harder for those men only attracted to other men. At least my liaisons with women screen my other desires.'

'If you were forced to choose just one sex, which would it be?'

'The male form is more beautiful.'

'So you could fall in love with a man?'

'That would be a disaster. Anyway, this is all by the way, I love you. You're the only point of stability in my life. Without you, I don't know what would happen to me.'

***

George Slythe Street walked across Hyde Park to his dingy office in St James's Palace. He hung up his umbrella and bowler hat and settled down to read that day's offerings. Top of the pile was *Polite Society*.

He claimed, with some truth, that, at his age of sixty-five years, his knowledge of contemporary British drama was without equal. If asked his job he would say, 'Water taken from the River Thames is a mixture of the pure and the filth. When passed through a filtering process and suitably treated, it provides healthy drinking water for all of London's people. For the flow of new plays to Britain's theatres, I am that filtering process. Separating pure from putrid, I will see to it that audiences are offered healthy, unpolluted plays.'

He overstated his status: he made detailed reports on all new plays submitted to the office, but it was his boss, Lord Cromer, the Lord Chancellor, who made the decision to accept or reject a play.

That morning, he began to read *Polite Society*, a play in three acts by Jerome Conti. Oh yes, he thought to himself, I know this Mr. Conti who skates upon the thinnest of ice above the pool of licentiousness and moral depravity. We shall see if he breaks the surface.

An English country mansion, eight friends, five women and three men, arrive for a weekend party. In a flurry of bright banter and quick-fire comic conversation and a little cocaine, there are flirtations and hysterics. Flippancy rules and hypocrisy and suspicion are rife in a futile chase of sex. At the end of the weekend, an adulterous couple, an older woman and a young man, leave their spouses and run away together.

George Street called upon Miss Taylor to come into his office to take down his words in her elegant shorthand. '*Polite Society* is an amusing light comedy and the main part of it, though risky in a way, might well pass. The atmosphere is that of frivolous people who speak in a tiresome jargon, everything is "too divine", etc. There is a characteristic immoral twist at the end. Apart from this more serious question, there are a couple of trifles in the dialogue which I have marked: in act one, a sentence which suggests lesbianism and, in act two, "Byes" apparently means bed and the sentence, if so, is too frank. Apart from these minor alterations, I recommend the play be licensed.'

The next day, George read the response from his Lordship, 'This picture of a frivolous and degenerate set of people gives a wholly false impression of Society life and to my mind the time has come to put a stop to the harmful influence of such pictures on the stage. I am inclined to ban the play entirely but before a definite decision, I will seek the advice of the Advisory Board.'

George was invited to sit in as an observer at the meeting of the Board. Sir Douglas Dawson said the piece was scurrilous, giving the worst possible impression of Society, a play liable to foster class hatred. Mr. Higgins said that if the play were set in the poverty of the East End of London there would be no question of refusing it a licence. Lord Buckmaster agreed, 'No one has ever protested against plays disclosing brutalised behaviour on the part of the poor.' Sir Douglas renewed his objection, 'We have lost a generation of young men to the war. We are now faced with the unhappy situation of many women without any likelihood of gaining a husband. It is natural that men too young to have been killed in the trenches should become the focus of amatory attention. We do not need Mr. Conti to pick at a sore that is best left to heal.'

Lord Cromer agreed and ruled the licence should be refused.

On hearing the news, Jerome approached George Street who suggested that he request an interview with his Lordship. Lord Cromer obliged and invited George to stay for the meeting. Jerome set out to woo the elderly lord. He performed scenes in front of them, demonstrating the moral undertone of his writing. His Lordship was amused. 'What d'you think, George?' he said.

'The piece is light-hearted entertainment. Audiences will be incited not to revolution but to laughter.'

'All right, Mr. Conti, you have your licence.'

In spite of the critics finding it 'vulgar, disgusting, shocking, nauseating, vile, obscene and degenerate', the play ran in the Globe Theatre for 372 days. Jerome took the lead part for three months then withdrew to concentrate on writing.

Iris made repeated attempts to make a reconciliation with her aunt but Beatrice refused to see her. In 1936, she travelled to Paris and the French Mediterranean coast and her exposure to the new art she found there had a profound effect on her work, more experimental with bold colours. She was shocked by the outbreak of civil war in Spain and, when back in England, donated paintings for auction in support of the International Brigade.

Jerome's new play was altogether more serious. Leonard and Sylvia are on the verge of divorce. The problem, inferred but not made explicit, is Leonard's latent homosexuality. It's only the work they do together as organisers of opulent weddings that keeps them from separating. Leonard brings home Victor, a dashing young man. Leonard and Victor form a close friendship. Sylvia, too, is attracted to Victor and they begin an affair. Leonard discovers it and his intense jealousy is only assuaged when Victor makes it clear that he has equally strong feelings for him as well as his wife.

The play ends with the three dancing. Jerome named the play, *Serenade for Three.*

'Oh dear, oh dear,' George Street said to himself. He never liked to down a play, especially one written with such panache, but this glorification of licentiousness! A subtle hint of homosexuality might be entertained, but overt bisexuality! 'This will not do.'

Miss Taylor took down his dictation, 'The facetious wit and acute social observation cannot redeem the underlying absence of morality. The author refuses to take a stance, the audience being left up in the air at the play's conclusion. The impression generated is that in society today, anything goes.'

Lord Cromer consulted the Advisory Board. Sir Douglas Dawson spluttered his revulsion, 'Every character in this play glories in obscene behaviour. There is no serious purpose in the play except titillation. What better propaganda could our enemies wish for than this portrayal of our nation as morally degenerate?'

Jerome went to the press. The Evening Standard carried the headline, 'My very moral and banned play'. In the following article he was quoted as saying, 'The Lord Chamberlain has banned my really very moral play, *Serenade for Three.* It confirms my opinion that, in this country, the authorities do not encourage dramatists. I shall take the play to America where they are more enlightened and I am taken seriously, whereas in England people think I am out for salacious sensation.'

Tod Wilson took Jerome at his word, declared his faith

in the play and took it to New York. At the opening, the house was full and there was great excitement. But with the fall of the curtain after Act One, Jerome stormed off the stage in a blind rage. 'It's a serious comedy yet these oafs laugh all through the first act. I'm damned if I'm going on with the play.'

The director said, 'If you insist on writing such funny lines, how do you expect the audience not to laugh.' The play was a great success and Jerome had his name up in lights on Broadway and his photograph in the *New York Times*.

Soon after he returned to London, Hitler invaded France. Jerome went to see Iris in her garret. 'That's new,' he said, seeing the painting on the easel. In the bottom left corner was a sector of a circle in magenta. The colour suffused into the rest of the painting, becoming darker. Indistinct, abstract surfaces were highlighted as if caught in the light of the magenta glow.

'I'm trying to represent the idea of radiation,' she said.

'I like it,' he said. 'The colours are beautiful and it has such depth.'

'I hear you had success with *Serenade for Three*.' She had laughed when he had read the play to her, recognising, in the character of the woman, much of herself.

'Huge success. But I've not come to talk about that. I want to join up, but they won't have me. They say they want me in a unit producing propaganda films.'

'Are you surprised? You're far more useful keeping up morale.'

'But I want to see action, do my bit.'

'Why don't you ask them if you can get some first- hand experience, so you can write about it.' She put her arms around his neck. 'But for goodness sake, don't get yourself blown up.'

He worked for the Crown Film Unit and travelled in blacked-out trains to factories and coal mines and military installations.

On the evening of 10th May, 1941, Iris was working in her attic room when a bomb scored a direct hit. The basin that contained her life was shattered. She was thirty-five. Jerome wept. He felt that the safe harbour of his life had been destroyed. Beatrice was at the funeral and together they mourned. In her will, Iris left all but one of her unsold paintings to Beatrice. Those in the attic were destroyed but many others were stored in a warehouse. To Jerome, she left *Eros Awake* and the rights to the book of sketches. The remainder of her estate went to her parents.

Beatrice arranged a posthumous exhibition of the paintings. To the assembled crowd, Jerome delivered a powerful encomium. Unable to look at it without crying, he kept *Eros Awake* hidden in a cupboard.

In the years following the end of the war, Jerome ran wild. He lived in a haze of celebrity junkets, innumerable and unmemorable sexual encounters and extravagant drinking. He did have one longer-term relationship. He was invited to stay at the house of a new acquaintance, James. The weather being unusually hot and there being a secluded garden, Jerome took the opportunity to sunbathe naked. For James, the sight of him was a revelation. His sexuality had been harshly repressed at public school and the vision of Jerome's body brought an overwhelming desire to touch him. He hesitated, unsure of himself, nervous of being repulsed. But then he gave way to impulse, undressed and placed his hand on Jerome's chest. Jerome kissed him and they became lovers. There was no pretence of being in love. They were satisfied with an easy-going sexual friendship. Jerome remained promiscuous because he was without love. Who knows where it would have ended had it not been for the tour of *Much Ado About Nothing* in 1954, that took him to Leeds.

***

Frank Hooper hovered nervously at the entrance of the Wilde Hall until Stella arrived and pulled him inside. The hall was named after the Mayor of Leeds, John Wilde, who stumped up the funds to build it. The amateur dramatic society who rehearsed there called themselves, 'Running Wilde'. Stella was its oldest member.

Stella said to the company, 'This is Frank. During his National Service in the Army, he performed in a number of productions and now he's going to join us.'

Frank was uncomfortable. Stella had overstated the situation in two ways: his thespian involvement in the Army was confined to the technical (lighting and sound), and his intention with Running Wilde was to see what they were like before committing himself.

In both Cyprus and Germany, where Frank had served, the men had been encouraged to put on shows to relieve the boredom. The standard was high with actors and directors of ability, some of whom went on to professional engagements in the theatre once back in civvy street. Although Frank's involvement was only peripheral, he enjoyed the excitement of it all. It was the possibility of experiencing that fun once again that drew him to Running Wilde.

Frank sat down to watch them rehearse *Lady Windermere's Fan*. He was entranced by the young woman playing the part of Lady Windermere. Her name, he soon learned, was Debbie. She was nineteen, vivacious with blonde hair to her waist and a figure that attracted attention. She worked in Reynolds Department Store which had a reputation for employing glamorous female sales staff. They were famously known as 'Reynolds' Girls'. In no time at all, Frank was in love.

He took over the organisation of set construction and control of lighting and sound. Following lengthy rehearsals, *Lady Windermere's Fan* was taken to the Playhouse Theatre. There were four performances to full houses and all received rapturously. For Debbie and Frank, this otherwise wonderful experience was blemished by having to deal with Mickey.

Doorman, caretaker, general factotum to the Theatre, Mickey liked to give out he was the manager. He was married with two teenage boys and believed he possessed a certain charm with women. He had once had sex in a dressing room with one of the performers of a touring company. The memory, never far from his mind, prompted him to try his luck with any woman who crossed the threshold of the Theatre. Debbie, gorgeous and flirtatious, immediately caught his eye. He pushed himself upon her. She rejected him with such obvious disgust that his usually unassailable vanity was bruised. He told anyone who would listen that in spite of her hoity-toity airs and graces, she was just a common slut.

'You know what Mickey's saying about Debbie,' one of the cast said to Frank, 'she's as quick to drop her knickers as take a curtain call.' Frank found Mickey behind the stage and gave him a hefty kick in the shin. 'You slag off Debbie and you'll find my fist in your gob.'

Frank and Debbie started going out together. They went to the Odeon Cinema to see a comedy of theatre folk, *Curtain Up* with Robert Morley, Margaret Rutherford and Kay Kendall. Their enjoyment of the film was different to the rest of the audience's because it might have been Running Wilde they were watching on screen. It was in that happy communion that he proposed to her.

He had little to offer. His wage as assistant in a furniture store was meagre. He left school at fifteen without qualifications. He lived with his Mum and Dad. He did not have a motorbike. But, he was good-looking and he could dance – waltz, quickstep, cha-cha. Most of all, what Debbie perceived in him, and was attracted by, was the mixture of introversion and determination in his personality. He hung back in a crowd and was softly- spoken yet revealed a fierce pride and enquiring mind. He had a fascination with how things worked: constructing a radio from parts, reading books on astronomy, learning how to use a film projector.

Against her parents' advice, after some delay, she accepted him. They were married in Holy Trinity Roman Catholic Church and the reception was held in the back room of the Bricklayers Arms. The Johnston Trio, piano, bass and drums, played for dancing. Barry Johnston sang *Here is My Heart.* The men drank pints of best and the ladies, lager and lime. Most of them got at least tiddly. Frank and best man, Jim, got drunk. Everybody said it was a good do.

In spite of sessions of intense snogging, Debbie was still a virgin, her knowledge of sex gained from other girls who claimed they had 'gone all the way'. At least her understanding, albeit limited, was, by and large, correct. Frank, also a virgin, had been exposed to barrack-room jokes, fantasies and tales of exotic prostitutes, stories of women with extraordinary sexual appetites and the incontrovertible truths that stinging nettles on the cock will cure the clap and masturbation makes you blind.

Their marriage was consummated on the night of their wedding but neither of them could recall much of the process. Jim had provided Frank with a packet of Durex but these remained unused. On the day that Britain exploded its first atomic bomb, they moved into a small flat above the furniture shop that Frank worked in. They had a Belling electric ring for cooking and an Ascot gas heater for hot water. Their windows overlooked the High Street.

Over time, Debbie and Frank's marriage settled into routine: Sunday lunch with one or other of the parents, cinema with friends on Friday night, dances in the Lido on Saturday, sex on Tuesdays and Saturdays.

Over yet more time, the dancing became infrequent. Instead, Frank downed pints with his mates in the public bar, while Debbie chatted with her friends in the lounge. Sex on Tuesdays stopped. One by one, Debbie's friends had babies. Frank was adamant that, for now, they couldn't afford to have a family. On Saturdays, Debbie stopped going to the Lido and went round to her mother's instead. She was always in bed when Frank, with beery breath, arrived home. Sex was brief.

One thing they kept up together was involvement with Running Wilde. It was *Romeo and Juliet*, Debbie of course was Juliet. Flirtatious as she was, she encouraged men more than she intended. Frank became increasingly jealous and at rehearsal one evening, gave Romeo a black eye for wooing too passionately. Frank was asked to leave Running Wilde. He demanded of Debbie that she leave with him; she refused.

They increasingly found that little things irritated them about what the other did or said. Debbie resented the money Frank spent drinking. She went to stay with her parents. It was no grand breakup, few words were exchanged. It was a relief to them both. Neither of them could say if it were permanent, it was just an arrangement that worked for the moment.

Incongruously, soon after Debbie left, Frank stopped going out on a Saturday night. He joined the Public Library and began to read. Firstly novels of a lighter sort which he increasingly found to be shallow. Then authors that explored people in all their complexity: Hardy, Forster, Greene, Lawrence and Cronin. Living through the problems besetting the characters in the novels, he escaped his own. He joined an evening class to study electronics.

Living meagrely, he saved money. He asked Bob Drain, the owner of the furniture store, to lend him the cash to buy a television set. He then loaned it out on a rental basis. He learned how to repair radios and televisions. He worked in the furniture store during the day and on his television sideline in the evening. He found he could afford the repayments and increased the loan so as to buy a second television set.

Professional repertory companies on tour in Leeds would ask Stella to recommend members of Running Wilde to take minor parts. At the Playhouse Theatre, Debbie had been a serving wench, a harlot, a maid in waiting and a murder victim. She was delighted to be invited to perform the part of Margaret in *Much Ado about Nothing* especially when she heard that Jerome Conti was to play Benedick.

On Wednesday, the company arrived in Leeds to find they had been booked into the Commercial Hotel. It was a seedy-looking place with a seedy-looking manager called Browne. Jerome and his fellow actor, Ben Turner, took in the room they were to share: the narrow twin beds, cracked wash basin, single pendant light bulb in a battered shade, the door to the neighbouring room locked and, above it, the rectangle of what once was a window now boarded in with plywood. 'We'll stay one night and look for another place in the morning,' Jerome said.

Late that afternoon, in the theatre, the touring actors met the eleven recruits from Running Wilde to rehearse the bit parts. Debbie was thrilled to meet Jerome; he was, she thought, so gorgeous and charming and brilliant. There was a scene in the last act of the play when, alone on stage, they have a brief exchange of light word-play. The director wanted more from Debbie and suggested that, following the main rehearsal, she and Jerome work on it together. They found an empty dressing room.

Jerome said, 'If you don't mind me saying so, you speak the lines as if you do not understand the innuendo. When you say, "To have no man come over me!", yes, you do mean as if you were a stile, but you also mean, take me sexually. And when we speak of "bucklers" which are circular shields and "swords", these round and pointed things have other meanings, you understand.'

Debbie laughed, 'But that's so rude!'

When Debbie left, Mickey, who knew Jerome's reputation for seduction, said, 'You won't get anywhere with that one, frigid as an iceberg.'

Jerome said, 'Icebergs melt, eventually.'

'Not in the time you've got.'

'I've got 'till Saturday.'

'Bet you never make it.'

'A tenner I do.'

'You're on.'

***

Detective Sergeant Brewer of Leeds police loathed 'poofters'. He saw them everywhere, from those hiding in the cracks of society to those at the very top (aristocrats, politicians, judges) and those in between like theatre people. He especially hated theatre pansies because they celebrated their depravity. He knew where they did their dirty business: in cinemas, public toilets and private guest houses. They were deviants who corrupted Britain's youth. 'If I had my way,' he declared, 'I'd put them up against a wall and shoot the lot of them.'

He was not without official backing. The Home Secretary, Sir David Maxwell-Fyfe, had summoned magistrates and told them of a drive against male vice. The Government wanted action. It was time for a repeat of the Oscar Wilde trials of 1895 which had, for fifty years, so successfully deterred dissidents.

There was no one, in Detective Sergeant Brewer's eyes, more loathsome than Jerome Conti. On discovering that he was to perform at the Playhouse, he thought, I'll nail the bastard. He went to visit the Commercial Hotel. He knew Browne was into a number of shady deals but he chose to turn a blind eye in return for tip-offs concerning the hotel clientèle.

'Conti's sharing with another actor, Turner. I think they're going to move out tomorrow.' Browne told him.

But Jerome and Ben Turner didn't move out. Inertia

prevailed; they couldn't be bothered to pack up and find another hotel for the remaining three days. The travelling salesman who had the room next door booked out early Thursday morning. DS Brewer moved in. He was certain he would catch Conti and Turner in the act. He placed a decorator's step ladder alongside the adjoining door and drilled a peephole in the plywood boarding. He now prepared to take turns with PC Trotman to sit on the little platform of the ladder and spy on them. The nights proved to be useless: sounds were too indistinct and if there were shenanigans, they did it in the dark. The mornings were the best bet. But he was frustrated. On both Friday and Saturday, he had nothing to report. That only left Sunday morning before the actors booked out of the hotel.

The play drew capacity audiences. Debbie was thrilled by the whole experience, not least appearing on stage with Jerome Conti. After each performance, the cast made for a nearby pub and there Jerome wooed her. On Thursday night, as she left the pub to go home to her mum and dad, he kissed her goodnight. On Friday night, he ordered a taxi and, with many a kiss and cuddle, saw her back to her home.

Mickey goaded Jerome, 'Two days down, one to go, you're not going to make it, chum. That tenner's mine.'

'You just see. If you'll leave the stage door unlocked, I'll bring her back here sometime after the end of the performance tonight.'

The Saturday night show received rapturous applause, not least from Frank who had come to see Debbie perform. Frank immediately perceived Jerome's gifts as an actor and the remarkable way he inspired everybody on stage. He went to the stage door to congratulate Debbie. Mickey said, 'What do *you* want?'

'I've come to see Debbie.'

'Oh, so you want to see Debbie. You know your way up to the projection room. Go and wait there and I'll sent her up to you.'

On occasion, Frank had stood in for the resident projectionist. He looked down on the almost empty stage. A single spot was still on, illuminating a couch used in the final scene of the play.

Minutes passed. He grew tired of waiting and, on trying to leave, found the door locked. Was this one of Mickey's unpleasant pranks? To isolate the noise of the projector, the room was soundproofed, no good shouting then and the intercom from the stage was one-way only.

Three of Mickey's drinking mates tapped on the stage door. He held out his hand. 'If there's no performance, you'll get your money back.' They each slipped him a fiver. 'Now you know, lads, absolute quiet and no blabbing or I'll be in deep shit.'

Half-an-hour later, after drinking in the pub with the others, Jerome arrived back at the theatre with Debbie. They walked onto the stage. How strange it was, empty and silent, when, just a short time before, it had been so full and animated.

Jerome held her hands then sang out, 'Pray thee, sweet Mistress Margaret, deserve well at my hands by helping me to the speech of Beatrice.'

Debbie turned to face him. 'Will you then write me a sonnet in praise of my beauty?'

'In so high a style, Margaret...' As he spoke the words, he slid his hands up her legs, lifting her skirt, and grasped her bottom. 'That no man living shall come over it...' He pulled her close 'For in comely truth thou deservest *it*.'

They kissed. Then she walked to the couch and lay back upon it. 'To have no man come over me! Why should I always keep below stairs.'

He started removing her clothing. 'Thy wit is as quick...' then, kissing her breasts, 'as the greyhound's mouth; it catches.'

She put her hand to his genitals. 'And yours as blunt as a fencer's foil, which hit, but hurt not.'

He pulled off his trousers and pants and showed her his erection. 'A most manly wit, Margaret; it will not hurt a woman.'

Then, stroking her between the legs, 'And so, I pray thee, call Beatrice. I give thee the bucklers.'

She placed her hands around his penis. 'Give us swords; we have bucklers of our own.'

Now both naked, he took her place, lying back on the couch, and pulled her on top of him. 'If you use them, Margaret, you must put in the pikes with a vice; and they are dangerous weapons for maids.'

Debbie burst out laughing, 'Have no fear, I'll hold firm the buckler. How manfully can you thrust in the pike?'

'Shake your buckler, Margaret, my spike will hold firm.'

Debbie had never ridden a man. It was strange and exciting to be the one in control. She explored the new position slowly before becoming more confident. But then came the urgency, the tickling urge that had to be assuaged. She got into a stride, a regular rhythm. Breathing more heavily, she said, 'Are you all right?'

'Fine,' he said, 'keep going.'

She rode steadily for a long time but then felt herself losing control, taken over entirely by the impulse to keep moving. Her legs ached. She was hot, sweating and struggling for breath. Her eyes tightly shut, she cried out, 'I can't do it, I can't do it.'

Jerome said, 'It's all right, take a rest.'

She flopped down upon him, panting for breath. 'It's hopeless. Why can't I do it?'

He stroked her back. 'You will. It just takes time.'

'I think I'll give up. It's too much effort.'

'No, don't do that.'

She sat up and started moving again, and the urge returned. Again, everything became obliterated except the single overwhelming desire to climax. Rapidly jigging up and down, she felt as if her thigh muscles were going into spasm, she felt as if her heart would burst, but she couldn't stop now. She had to reach the top of the hill. She cried out as a mantra, 'Don't stop. Don't stop. Don't stop.' And then, 'I'm coming. I'm coming. I'm coming.'

It was with a great cry of pleasure, release, relief, exultation that she collapsed onto him, steeped in sweat.

Mickey's mates silently slipped away. They'd got their money's worth. Mickey congratulated himself. He had given Frank a poke in the eye *and* he was a fiver in pocket. He quietly unlocked the door to the projection room and made himself scarce.

Frank continued staring at the stage even after they had dressed and left it. He had seen it all through a spectrum of emotions: anger, then jealousy, feeling wounded and then vengeful. Most of all, he was left feeling inadequate.

***

DS Brewer wrote in his notebook, 'Sunday, 8th June, 1952. 10-36am, man X, about 25, dark hair, enters room. Conversation inaudible. 10-38am, Turner leaves room leaving Conti and X alone together.'

By 11.19am, Brewer had seen enough. Together with PC Trotman, he burst into the room next door and arrested Jerome Conti and Mr. X for 'gross indecency'. Mr. X gave his name as Frank Hooper.

At the police station, they were formally charged and released to appear in court for the committal proceedings. After three weeks, they both attended the magistrates' court. Jerome's solicitor reserved his defence and obtained his release on £50 bail. Frank, however, was held in custody pending the trial proper, to be held at the forthcoming Quarter Sessions. The case was taken up by the local press and then the nationals.

Homosexuality was in the news. The *Sunday Pictorial* ran a series of articles exposing this 'conspiracy of silence'.

'Most people know there are such things – "pansies" – mincing effeminate young men who call themselves queers. But these obvious freaks and rarities represent but the tip of an iceberg. The problem is much greater than people realise and now the time has come to tackle it.'

Debbie's mother said to her, 'I always thought there was something fishy about your Frank.' Jerome believed the hostile press would end his career. When the news broke he was in Liverpool with *Much Ado.* He was so paralysed by nerves that the prospect of going on stage seemed impossible. The leading lady said, 'You have been a silly bugger.' Then she grabbed him and led him firmly on to the stage.

To everybody's astonishment and indescribable relief, the audience gave him a standing ovation. They cheered, they applauded, they shouted. The message was quite clear, this was their chance to show that they didn't care tuppence what he had done in his private life...they loved him and respected him dearly.

Debbie went to visit Frank in the prison. In the crowded visiting room, they sat opposite each other at a table.

'You've come, then,' he said.

They had so much to say to each other, but impossible in that place. They looked at each other in silence. Debbie wanted to cry.

Jerome engaged a QC, Henry Montague.

'The charge is that you committed an act of gross indecency,' Montague told him. 'If found guilty, this could get you two years' imprisonment, but six months is usual these days. It's just as well you're not charged with 'buggery', that attracts a much harsher sentence. There was a recent case involving some academic mathematician found guilty of gross indecency who didn't receive a prison sentence at all but was required to undertake something called "organo-therapic treatment" to reduce his libido.'

'I'd prefer prison.' Jerome said.

When the day came for the case of *Regina v. Conti and Hooper*, the court was overflowing. Frank was quiet and shy, overawed by the attention. Jerome was calm, self-assured and smiling. When he saw Frank, he gave him the thumbs up sign. Frank saw Debbie and, when she saw he had seen her, she gave him a little wave. They pleaded not guilty. Prosecuting lawyer, Giles Stevens, immediately called DS Brewer to the stand.

Brewer read from his notebook. 'Sunday, 8th June, 1952. Ben Turner and Jerome Conti in their room in the Commercial Hotel, Leeds.

10.36am, young man X, tall with dark hair, enters room. Conversation – inaudible.

10.38am Turner leaves room. More conversation – inaudible.

10.41am, X sits on bed. More conversation – inaudible.

10.52am, Conti removes clothing exposing his penis.

10.59am, X removes clothing exposing his penis.

11.03am, Conti engages in masturbatory activity.

11.04am, X also engaging in masturbatory activity. Conversation – inaudible.

11.07am, Conti puts his hand on X's penis and manipulates it. This continues for 12 minutes.'

Brewer looked up. 'It was evident that an offence was taking place and in order to forestall a further offence, namely that of...' he paused for effect... 'sodomy, I, together with PC Trotman entered the room and arrested them both. When asked, X gave his name as Frank Cooper.'

Stevens said, 'You're quite certain you saw the two men having intimate contact of a sexual nature?'

'Yes, sir, quite certain.'

Montague rose to his formidable height. 'Detective Sergeant, please tell the court how it was you came to witness the events you describe.'

'From a room adjacent to that of the accused.'

'Through a *spy* hole?'

'A hole in the wall, yes.'

'A *spy* hole. And what led you to set up this *spy* post from this room?'

'I had information that Mr. Conti was sharing a room with Mr. Turner.'

'It is usual practice, is it not, for men, travelling salesmen, for instance, to share a room? Do you make it a regular practice to spy on guests in the Commercial Hotel?'

'If I believe, as I did in this case, that an illegal act is to take place, it is my duty to intervene.'

'And why did you believe such an act was about to take place?'

'Mr. Conti has a reputation...'

'Detective Sergeant, Leeds, I imagine, has its crop of robberies, arsons, violent disturbances and even murders, yet you choose to spend many hours on an investigation based on rumour and speculation. Do you have a specialist interest in sexual deviancy?'

'It is my duty to investigate crimes wherever they arise.'

'But you have a need to prioritise?'

The Judge, James Langdale, intervened, 'Mr. Montague, please clarify the relevance of this line of questioning. Is the Detective Sergeant's competence being disparaged?'

'My intent, Your Honour, is to demonstrate that the Detective Sergeant was of such a predetermined mind that it would not have occurred to him that there could be a conclusion to what he witnessed other than the one he was determined to find. With Your Honour's permission, I will pursue this line of questioning.'

'Proceed.'

'Detective Sergeant, you state that there was a lot of conversation between the accused that was inaudible to you. Did you not hear a single word?'

'They were speaking quietly.'

'Did it not occur to you that they might have been discussing something other than having sex together?'

'It was quite evident what they were up to. Their actions said it all.'

Montague had come to a decision that Frank's quiet, thoughtful demeanour would be an asset in the witness box. Frank had told him about Debbie and he wanted Frank to tell this to the court, but Frank was adamant; he didn't want Debbie to be mentioned.

Jerome said he welcomed an opportunity to inveigh against the injustice of the law relating to homosexuality.

'Mr. Conti,' Montague said, 'I hope you accept I have had a great deal of experience defending a wide variety of cases. Yours is not being contested on a level playing field. The inclination is against you. The Home Secretary has called upon the judiciary to play their part in rooting out homosexual behaviour. No judge looking to the Home Secretary for advancement can afford to appear sympathetic towards homosexuals. Of course the trial will be fair, Langdale will avoid any justification for a retrial but...' Montague shrugged. 'In this context, my strongest advice to you is not to enter the witness box. Your defence is that your behaviour was not homosexual. To suggest in any way that you condone homosexuality seriously undermines your case. If that is your intention, I am left with no choice but to withdraw as your lawyer.'

Jerome immediately backtracked. 'I see your argument, but surely there's advantage to be gained by my corroborating Frank's testimony. What if I stick simply to answering your questions?'

'It isn't my questions I'm worried about, it's Stevens'.'

'Don't worry, I'll play a straight bat.'

Frank was called to the witness box.

Montague said, 'Mr. Hooper, please tell the court why on being cautioned and in the days that followed, you offered no explanation as to why you went to Mr. Conti's room that morning.'

Frank spoke so quietly, Montague had to ask him to

speak up.

'Because it's embarrassing to speak of such things.'

'What things?'

'Sexual things.'

'You do understand that you are required to offer an explanation now?'

'Yes.'

'What is it, exactly, you are embarrassed about?'

'I am not able to satisfy my wife.'

'Sexually?'

'Yes, sexually.'

'And that was why you went to see Mr. Conti?'

'Yes, I went to seek his advice on how to prolong sex.'

'And was Mr. Conti helpful to you?'

'Yes. He was kind enough to demonstrate how a man can delay reaching a climax.'

'So your conversation was about how to become more sexually competent. And during the course of this consultation, it became necessary for him to demonstrate practically how to acquire certain techniques.'

'Yes, that's right.'

'So when Mr. Conti touched you, he was, in fact, showing you how to delay orgasm.'

'Yes.'

'Did you go to see Mr. Conti because he had propositioned you for sex?'

'No.'

'Did you go to see Mr. Conti to proposition *him* for sex.'

'No, of course not.'

'Did he, at any time, make sexual overtures to you?'

'No. His conduct was very regular.'

'By regular, you mean clinical, as if visiting a doctor?'

'Yes.'

'No further questions.'

Prosecutor Stevens said, 'Mr. Hooper, you say you went to seek Mr. Conti's advice on how to prolong sex. Why did you believe he could provide such advice?'

Frank glanced at Debbie who blushed. 'Because I think he's a person with a lot of experience.'

'Experience of sex, with both sexes.'

'With women. I read in the newspapers and magazines of his friendships with women.'

Did you have any contact with Mr. Conti prior to meeting him on the morning of 8th June?'

'No.'

'Why did you imagine that, with a person he had never met before, Mr. Conti would for one moment respond to such an extraordinary request?'

'I took my chance. Sometimes people do respond to pleas for help.'

Frank knew this was lame but it was the best he could think of.

Stevens pounced. 'None of this story of yours is credible. You claim you have a sexual dysfunction. Have you sought professional help from a clinician? No. Instead, you call upon a man who, you say, doesn't know you from Adam. You then would have us believe Mr. Conti, out of the kindness of his heart, gives you three quarters of an hour for *sexual therapy*!

'This is all nonsense, a story concocted between yourself and Mr. Conti. In fact, you had made a prior arrangement to visit him in his room that morning to engage in homosexual sex.'

'No, that's not right. Everything I've told you is the truth.'

Jerome took the witness stand. 'The first time I saw Frank Hooper was when he tapped on my door that morning. I asked him what he wanted. He said he loved his wife and that sexual incompatibility had led to problems in his marriage. He thought that if he were able to satisfy his wife sexually, they could overcome their difficulties.

'I had the knowledge to help Mr. Hooper in his distress.

My Sunday morning was free. It would have been ungenerous to have refused. If the driver of a car which has broken down appealed to you for help and you had the skill to repair it, would you walk away?'

Stevens said, 'In your so-called "therapy session" you found it necessary to take hold of Mr. Hooper's penis. Most normal men would shrink from such an act. Yet you did this with ease, if not pleasure, as one would expect from a homosexual.'

'If a patient approached a doctor with a complaint concerning his penis, the doctor would examine him which could well involve touching the man's penis.'

'But you exposed *your* penis. If a doctor were to do that to a patient, they might well face charges and be struck off the register.'

'In rehearsal, theatre directors often take to the stage to demonstrate how an action should be performed.'

'You change your metaphors with remarkable ease. We have mechanics and doctors and theatre directors. By profession, Mr. Conti, you create stories and this story is designed to obscure the truth. The truth is that driven by base carnal desires, you procured Mr. Hooper to come to your room to engage in homosexual sex and it was only the timely intervention of Detective Sergeant Brewer that prevented you from engaging in a more obscene offence.'

Jerome was roused. 'None of these allegations are true. But even if they were, what two people do together, with consent, in the privacy of their room is of no interest to the state. That which is obscene is a law which gives licence to bigoted, obsessive individuals to enter our private worlds and persecute innocents. It is obscene that Frank Hooper and I are in this courtroom. It is obscene to condemn a great natural gift of nature, a person's sexuality. The law on homosexuality is a repulsive sickness in our wonderful country. One day it will be repealed. One day, people of any sexual persuasion will be free to live their lives free from the fear of persecution. We may even live to see, one day, a priest join together two men in holy matrimony.'

There was a shout of 'never' and booing and clapping. Montague closed his eyes. Judge Langdale said, 'Mr. Conti, I have given you great licence to make your speech, but none of it is relevant to this case.' Turning to the jury, he said, 'You must not be influenced by your judgement of the suitability or not of the law. It is your task to apply the law as it stands.'

For the prosecution summing up, Stevens said, 'The evidence is not in dispute. Mr. Conti and Mr. Hooper engaged in sexual activity. The story they have put forward to excuse their actions is not credible and leaks like a rusty drainpipe. Can anybody believe Mr. Hooper did not have contact with Mr. Conti prior to arriving at his room? Why else would Mr. Hooper have known he would be admitted? And why else would Mr. Conti have received him? The homosexual activity they engaged in is illegal. They are guilty as charged of gross indecency.'

Montague said, 'Witnesses reporting an incident can contradict each other not because they differ in what they have witnessed but in their interpretation of what they have seen. A poisoned mind can find innocence itself proof of guilt. How rightly this is demonstrated in Shakespeare's Othello. Desdemona's very innocence becomes proof to Othello's poisoned mind that she is guilty of betraying him. Minds poisoned by bigotry and prejudice are blind to the truth. Frank Hooper and Jerome Conti are innocents. The one guileless and naive and the other involved by chance in a situation in which he becomes a victim of suspicion. Frank Hooper, suffering a dysfunction that causes him anguish and deep embarrassment, seeks help from where he believes, rightly, he may get a sympathetic and knowledgeable response. Jerome Conti, to his credit, knowing he can help, offers that help without any motive other than compassion. It is ironic that they find themselves in court today through no act of homosexuality but to save the heterosexual relationship of a man and his wife. Members of the jury, I call upon you to find them not guilty.'

Judge James Langdale addressed the jury. 'The law governing this case is the criminal Law Amendment Act of 1885. It states that:

"Any male person who, in public *or private*, commits, or is a party to the commission of, or procures, or attempts to procure the commission by any male person of, any act of gross indecency with another male person, shall be guilty of a misdemeanour, and being convicted thereof, shall be liable at the discretion of the Court to be imprisoned for any term not exceeding two years, with or without hard labour."

'The term "gross indecency" covers any male homosexual behaviour short of sodomy. Detective Sergeant Brewer's evidence is not contested. The defence asserts that the accused were solely engaged in a session of sexual therapy. Here you have two questions to consider: do you find this assertion compatible with Detective Sergeant Brewer's evidence? And if you do so find, was this session of sexual therapy devoid of homosexual behaviour?

'If your opinion is that, within reasonable doubt, the accused did not engage in homosexual behaviour, then you must find them not guilty. If on the other hand, your conclusion is that they did engage in homosexual behaviour, then you must find them guilty of gross indecency.'

The jury obviously had difficulty coming to a conclusion; it took them over four hours. The verdict was guilty. Judge Langdale sentenced Frank to one month's imprisonment. Having already spent three weeks in detention, he had one week to serve. Jerome, judged to be more culpable, received two months. He made good use of his time in prison, writing a pamphlet on the need for homosexual law reform.

Debbie was waiting for Frank at the prison gates. They

caught a bus to Golden Acre Park. They walked along one of the trails. They found it hard to talk. Then Debbie said, 'It was brave of you, what you said in court. Whereas I'm ashamed of myself.'

She turned to face him. 'I don't want secrets between us. I want to be honest with you. I need to tell you, I had sex with Jerome Conti.'

'Are you going to continue seeing him?'

'No, of course not. It was just that one night, the last night of the show.'

'I know, I saw you.'

'You saw me!'

'Mickey locked me in the projection room. Getting his revenge.'

'Oh Frank, that's sick. So that's why you went to Jerome on Sunday morning; you had seen me.'

'You didn't think I was queer, did you?'

'But why didn't you tell the court?'

'Why d'you think? I didn't want to broadcast to the world that you... And how would I have looked if I said I came to seek advice from a man because I'd seen him with my wife.'

'Do you think we could try again, Frank?'

'I'd do anything to have you back.'

Frank persuaded Bob Drain to set aside an area in the store to sell and loan out television sets. Debbie became their accountant. Their big break came on Tuesday 2nd June 1953 when all the world wanted to watch on television the coronation of Queen Elisabeth.

Jerome came out of prison a changed man. He sold Iris's painting *Eros Awake* for a huge sum and put the money into founding a campaigning organisation, 'The Right to be Gay'. Between shows and writing plays, he spent his days at the campaign office.

In May 1953, a tall, well-built man, wearing a Savile Row suit walked into the office and said, 'You need my help.'

Peter Conway was larger than life, confident, always laughing, generous, quick-witted. He was a successful lawyer and was offering free advice on how to reform the law relating to homosexuality. He also brought with him contacts with politicians of all parties. Jerome embraced him, figuratively and literally. Within a few short weeks, he had fallen in love. He had, at last, found a stable, monogamous relationship that was to last his lifetime.

In 1967, they rejoiced at the repeal of the hated 1885 Act which had created so much misery. Jerome died in 1983; he was 74. He was buried in East London Cemetery, not far from the docks where he worked as a lad. At his wish, he was placed alongside the grave of Iris Farley.

Resurrection

Alzheimer's!

'Yes, yes. Manifestation quite advanced. You should have come to see me earlier. I think you begin to notice your memory setting sail for oblivion.' Dr.Nuryan had a pictorial way with language, particularly the medical.

My name is Aiden Sillman and I was born and bred in Anoka County, Minnesota – Garrison Keiller country. Somehow I landed up in San Francisco, California, but I don't want to go into that now. Dr. Nuryan was recommended to me as a consultant specialising in problems of the geriatric.

'How long have I got?' I said.

'Your heart and lungs sing as sweet as a nightingale. You have to fashion a gymnasium for the neurones. Strengthen the muscles of the mind. Learn Urdu, play bridge, write a novel, take up the clarinet. Music. Yes, music massages the brain.'

'Thanks,' I said, 'I'd rather you'd find a cure.' The diagnosis did not come as a surprise, I was reluctant to have confirmed what I already suspected. 'But tell me,' I said, 'what can you do about my other problem? It's embarrassing in a man my age.'

'What are you talking about?'

'My libido. It's gross. At seventy, I'm as spiffy as I was when seventeen. I get aroused at the slightest provocation. Can't you give me something to quieten me down.'

'You are very fortunate. Make splendid use of your blessing.'

'It's not much fun on your own.'

***

Alzheimer's! I know all about alzheimer's. I regularly go to the nursing home to visit Janis. I wouldn't go there if Marianne hadn't made me promise. I still take flowers. Even if it means nothing to Janis, the good people working there appreciate them. She doesn't even find it strange that a man she doesn't recognise comes to visit her.

'Manifestation quite advanced.' Oh, mercy! I felt just as sorry for myself as I did when Marianne died. Back then, I sought oblivion in alcohol. Now, the last thing I wanted was to muddy my mind. Some people find solace in poetry or religious texts. I gain comfort from the writings of an ancient Chinese philosopher, Hoo Li Wei. His *Treatise on the Mind*, published bilingually in Mandarin and English, puts all human experience into long millennial perspective. Even one's grief at the death of your loved one of thirty-six years is soothed by his wisdom.

It isn't just Hoo's understanding and compassion for humanity that speaks to me. His bleak vision of human society chimes with my revulsion at the course of world events. Wars and torture, poverty and greed, democratically elected governments ousted by a ratings agency, God damn it, and everywhere the intrusion of governments and corporations into our everyday privacy. How sure we once were that a world at peace, a world that was free, a world of global justice, was but a generation ahead of us. We were so naïve, Hoo had the truth of it.

But this chapter I was reading, was taking a different tack. The trouble with Hoo is his elliptical style of writing. You have to work at it in a poetical sort of way. I couldn't make any sense of it. I telephoned my friend Gracie who lives in the Mission District.

'How are you?' she said, on greeting me at her place.

'I'm losing my mind.' I said.

'Stop taking those drugs,' She said.

Gracie was born in China and arrived in the States many years ago. She and Marianne were great buddies. She has her hair drawn tightly back from her face and her skin is as soft and unwrinkled as a woman half her age. Now and again she insists on taking me to buy new clothes. 'We can't let you looking shabby can we?' she says.

She teaches Mandarin at the University. I showed her the problem chapter.

Speak softly as if to a baby.
Speak slowly, the Mantra, many time.
Make asleep but not asleep.
Say 'sing' and he will sing.
Say 'dance' and he will dance.
Say 'tell me your heart'
and he will tell you his heart.

And then came some instructions, including: use sparingly and only for good purpose. Pass on the mystery only to those you can trust.

'It seems to me,' Gracie said, after studying the text, 'that he is describing hypnosis.'

***

'George,' I said to my old friend, as we played our daily game of backgammon, 'I want to hypnotise you.'

I spoke the Mantra many times, slow and soft as if to a baby. It took a little practice but hey, it worked.

'Undo your shirt, George,' I said. 'Now do it up. How do you feel, George?'

'I've got backache.'

I tried something more daring. 'What do you dream of at night, George?'

'My mother.'

'What do you think of me, George?'

'You'd be quite a nice guy if you weren't so mean with your money.'

When George was out of hypnosis, he said, 'What did I say?'

'You said I was a mean bastard.'

'Well, so you are. The next beers are on you.'

***

I haven't told you yet, I am in love. She has blue eyes that light up when she speaks. She takes an interest in everything I say; I can't think why. She has small even white teeth and when she smiles, when she smiles, it is with her whole face. She has a petite, lithesome body, Oh, she's so beautiful. And her beauty isn't just confined to her looks. She's wonderfully intelligent and empathetic. She shines from the inside. She's unlike any woman I've ever met. Her name is Julietta. She's twenty-three years old and she lives with Benedict in the apartment next to mine. That Benedict is a very lucky man.

When I get spiffy, and I get spiffy most nights, I think of Julietta. Julietta kissing me. Julietta stroking me. Julietta...I don't need to go into details, you get the drift.

You probably think me reprehensible, an old man having lascivious thoughts about a young woman, but I am not one to confuse lust and love. In my life, I have been in love but twice, the first was Marianne and now, Julietta. Whatever my feelings, my behaviour is impeccable. For Julietta and Benedict, I'm a lonely, elderly gentleman on whom they should keep a neighbourly eye. They check they've seen me every few days, and now and again, they invite me to eat with them.

On these occasions, I try hard not to let my gaze fall uniquely upon Julietta. I make myself turn to Benedict. He's Julietta's age, more introvert than she is, gentle with a fresh face; attractive, I would have thought, to women. They are in love. They touch each other, lightly, every now and again. A person who's not been touched for eleven years notices these things. At one of our get-together dinners, I took photographs of them both: together (with Benedict's arm around Julietta's shoulders) and separately (Benedict looking seriously at the camera and Julietta laughing). At the end of these evenings, little signs tell me it is time to take my leave. I guess they want to make love.

It was Benedict's birthday, a weekday. There was to be a party at the weekend but would I like to join them that evening to help them celebrate on the actual day. I took round a bottle of red and a framed print of a Chinese master. We'd had a bit to drink when I entertained them with the story of the hypnotising of George. Benedict was fascinated, wanted to know every detail. Would I hypnotise him? I demurred, 'I'm a dilettante, a complete novice. Why don't you seek out a professional who actually knows what they're doing?' He persisted. He said he trusted me. Eventually, I gave in, agreeing to meet the following Tuesday evening when Julietta would be at work. By then, I hoped, Benedict would have forgotten the whole damn thing.

Friday, Josh phoned. 'Dad,' he said, 'Tamara and I and Kate would like to come over and see you tomorrow. We'll bring a take-away.' Before they could even enter the apartment, Kate had thrown her arms around my neck. There used to be a time when Grandpop would swing her round and round but now she was taller than me. Soon, she'd be swinging me round and round.

Over dinner, Josh became serious. 'Dad, we've something to tell you. I've got a placement in Lima.'

'That's great. Congratulations.'

'Tamara's coming out there with me.'

'What about Kate?'

'Kate too. She'll be at the International School.'

'So you're all going? How long?'

'Two years minimum. Dad, we want you to come with us. Come and live with us.'

Tamara said, 'As it is, we don't like you living here all on your own. We want you to be with us.'

I took hold of Tamara's hand. 'You're very kind, but I don't think so.'

Josh said, 'But what keeps you here. You know you're becoming more and more forgetful and you've always said you never see enough of Kate.'

'There's nothing wrong with me. Besides, it's sunny here. Isn't Lima always in a blanket of cloud?'

'I knew you'd be obstinate.'

Tamara said, 'We know it would be a big wrench for you but promise us you'll think about it. Maybe come out a bit later on when we're settled in.'

I didn't need to think about it. It's a no-brainer when you're going to lose your mind. No-brainer, that's good, just about sums it up.

***

Tuesday evening, Benedict was at my door.

'This is not a good idea,' I said.

'Nonsense. You're too risk averse,' he laughed.

So I repeated the Mantra over and over, soft and slow. Benedict was a natural, went off like a baby at the breast.

'Benedict,' I said, 'what do you think of me?'

'You're a good man but unhappy.'

'Benedict, do you love Julietta?'

'Yes, I love Julietta very much. But...'

'But what, Benedict?'

'We have problems.'

'Problems, what problems, Benedict?' He was silent. 'What problems do you and Julietta have?' Again he was silent. 'Benedict, do you trust me.'

'Yes.'

'Is there a secret you would like to tell me about?'

'He made Mummy cry.'

'Who made Mummy cry.'

'Daddy did.'

This was getting too hot for me, I was way out of my depth. When Benedict was awake he asked me what he had said. 'You told me I was an unhappy man,' I said.

Benedict laughed, 'Is that all? You know something, I feel happier for the experience. Like...Oh, I don't know. Just happier.'

'I think you should try a real hypnotist,' I said.

***

I went to the airport to wave goodbye to Josh and Tamara and Kate. There were tears. 'Don't worry,' I lied, 'I'll come and visit.' Over the next months, Benedict badgered me for another hypnosis. I read more books, delving into psychology. Nightly, I was visited by visions of Julietta. I bought a bottle of her perfume to spray on my pillow. Once, we all went swimming. Julietta in a bikini! I wore my loosest swimming trunks and hoped nobody would notice.

***

'Gracie,' I said, over the phone, 'I have another problem.'

'I told you, you mustn't keep taking those drugs.'

'No, no, it's Hoo again, chapter eighteen. Can I come and see you?'

She served me tea from an exquisite porcelain teapot and little macaroons on a delicate plate.

'Are you looking after yourself?' she said. 'Why don't you stay for dinner? I'm making prawn stir-fry with rice noodles.'

After dinner, I showed her the text:

Behind a bamboo screen, you can see yet not be seen.
The Mantra of Tei-shung is the key to unlock the temple of the mind.
Air comes into a room, air goes out of a room, nothing can be changed.
See with another's eyes. Hear with another's ears.
Walk in another's steps.

There followed a set of instructions which involved swallowing a preparation of tamarind root dissolved in an infusion of fresh juniper leaves, then sharpening the mind 'as to the blade of an axe', then repeating the Tei-shung Mantra and finally, concentrating the mind on the chosen person. It said the trance would last for up to an hour.

'What do you make of it?' I said.

'It seems to me,' she said, 'like an attempt at telepathy.'

I telephoned Mr. Chung's Emporium. 'We have tamarind root. We have juniper leaves dried, but for fresh, I need to ask around.'

***

Benedict had been so easily hypnotised that I tried the procedure using him as my subject. Nothing happened, except trying it gave me a headache.

'It doesn't work,' I said to Gracie.

She laughed. 'You didn't think it really would, did you?'

'Hoo Li Wei hasn't let me down before.'

'Telepathy! It's all mystical nonsense.'

'I'm as ardent a rationalist as you,' I said, 'but there are things out there of which we know nothing.'

'I know, I know, "more things in heaven and earth, Horatio...".' Gracie studied the text again, this time pouring over the Mandarin. 'You know, the text doesn't exactly use the words tamarind and juniper. There are descriptions of plants here, the translator has made a best guess of what they might be.'

Two weeks later, Gracie phoned, 'You'd better come round.' She showed me a page of writing in Chinese characters. 'It's a copy of a page of Hoo Li Wei's original manuscript faxed to me from an archive library in Beijing.'

It may have only been a faxed copy, but I held the page with reverence. Across all those centuries, a direct link to this most extraordinary human being. I felt as if I too had become a disciple.

Gracie explained, 'As with the English of Chaucer and Shakespeare, Mandarin has evolved over the centuries. Your copy of Hoo Li Wei has first been transcribed into modern Mandarin and then translated into English. There are errors in both the transcription and the translation. This original contains a detailed description of a shrub from which to take the root, and a tree to obtain the leaves. These have been taken to be tamarind and juniper but Hoo doesn't use those words. I have written out the descriptions for you.'

'You've gone to a lot of trouble considering you think this is all a load of hooey, if you'll excuse the pun.'

'I like the way you venerate our Chinese culture.'

I took the description to Mr. Chung. His dark Emporium is a wonder, with red wooden Chinese dragons and jars of strange, shrunken shapes. 'I don't know,' he said, 'but I have friend in Shanghai, maybe he know.'

Mr. Chung phoned. 'Very difficult. Very rare plant. Very expensive.'

I bought enough for three attempts.

'George,' I said, 'come and sit opposite me.'

I sharpened my mind like the blade of an axe. I murmured the Mantra. I stared into George's eyes. I swallowed the potion.

George gazed back at me. Nothing happened. And then, slowly, like a projection coming into focus, I began to make out an image. What I saw was myself. I put my hand on my head and the vision did likewise as if in a mirror. I became aware of backache, George's backache, and of letting lose a very gentle fart, George's fart. It was like having a vivid dream while, at the same time, being aware that I was dreaming.

'George,' I said, 'go out for a walk for an hour then come back.'

It was incredible. I sat on the chair inside my apartment but knew the heat outside, the bright sunlight, the wind on his face, the taxi hoot as he crossed the road, the dull ache in his back. *Behind a bamboo screen, you can see yet not be seen.* I experienced the aroma from the hamburger stall, his temptation. I tried to stop him, he eats far too much crap food. *Nothing can be changed.* I knew his pleasure: the soft bap and the grease and the burger and the onions. I felt the gas in his gullet and heard, through his ears, the audible belch.

After fifty minutes, the phenomena faded. I lay flat out on the floor, utterly drained. When he returned, George said, 'I need to sit down, my back aches. But I had a great hamburger, scrumptious onions.'

'Yes, George,' I said, 'I know.'

***

Now that I knew it worked, what to do with my second potion? I thought hard about it. A number of ideas came to mind. What decided me was that I really wanted to know what was in store for me. What it was actually going to be like rather than what I imagined.

Just before I was about to leave my apartment, Josh rang me.

'How are you, Dad?' he said.

'Fine. I'm fine.'

'What are you going to do today?'

'I'm going to the home to see your Aunt Janis.'

'Dad,' he said, 'do you know what day it is today?'

'Nope.'

'It's Kate's birthday.'

'Ahh heck! How could I have forgotten my special girl's birthday? Put her on, put her on.'

'Hi, Grandpop.'

'Hi, my sweetie pie. Happy birthday.'

How could I have forgotten her birthday?

I took in a bunch of freesias, Marianne's favourite. She loved their scent.

Patricia, the young Filipina nurse, pretty but overweight, led Janis in to see me. 'Shall I put those in a vase?' Patricia said.

I sat down opposite Janis. I concentrated my mind as sharp as a sword. How much longer would I be able to do that? Mumbling the Tei-shung Mantra, I took the infusion of root and leaf and concentrated my gaze on Janis's face.

What was I expecting? Fog. Like driving along in a mist, peering through the windscreen. Objects, now rendered unfamiliar, looming up, disconcertingly, out of the murk. I expected her to be confused.

It wasn't like that at all. As with George, I saw myself as I appeared through Janis's eyes. Everything was perfectly clear, in focus, in colour. Nothing wrong with her vision. Patricia came back with the vase of flowers, 'Aren't they lovely, Janis? Don't they smell nice?' Patricia's presence and voice was as familiar as the wallpaper, the scent of the freesias soothing.

'Mr. Sillman,' Patricia said, 'would you like to wait while Janis has her lunch.' I'd forgotten that midday was not a good time to visit.

I experienced Janis walking into the dining room. Through her eyes, I saw the other residents seated at tables. I heard her conversations. I experienced the taste of her food. Everything was clear. What was lacking was thought. It was like watching a film in which short clips of random events have been spliced together in no discernible order. We don't realise that in the second by second sequence of our lives, our brains are working furiously to create order. Using memory, the mind links one snapshot experience with the next to form a continuous pattern. Janis had all the experiences: the smell of freesias, seeing the faces of the other residents, the hard plastic of the dining chair, the noise of knives and forks, the taste of roast chicken; but she had no thinking that could unify these experiences. She lacked comprehension.

This didn't mean that she lacked responses. On this occasion, she was contented. I knew that if hungry or frightened, she would be distressed. If tickled, she would laugh. Her experience of the world was as a baby.

After lunch, she joined me and I was inside her head as we walked the garden. She wasn't unhappy, but I was dismayed at the chaos of her mind. She wasn't distressed by having to rely on others to care for her, but the thought of having to suffer that repelled me. I was relieved to be coming down from the effect and withdrawing from her, away from her vulnerability, back to the security of my own mind, being in control, making sense, having meaningfulness.

***

I understood immediately the implications of my discovery. In medicine, doctors would no longer have to guess at the location and intensity of poorly described pain, they'd be able to feel it for themselves. In sport, we'd be able to experience jumping from an aeroplane, or extreme skiing, or running a marathon. Clinical psychologists would enter the brains of psychopaths. Teachers would better understand learning difficulties.

On the other hand, what discovery has not been used as an instrument of evil? Which individual could be trusted not to abuse the powers my discovery conferred. Corporations would even further invade our privacy.

Governments would seek out activists and protesters. The military would explore its potential for brainwashing. Human society is throwing itself towards the cliff edge, should I be giving it a helping push?

I had enough for one more shot. I brooded on what to do with it. It didn't have to be the last one. I could obtain more of the ingredients, analyse the active compounds, set up a factory. But...but for me the end was clear, I was going to lose my mind. For me, it was soon to be all over.

One last shot. What to do with it? Faust! Oh Faust! How I now understood you.

***

A simple meal they had prepared together, solicitous of my comfort and good appetite. Fine wine, teasing conversation, I made them laugh. And then...And then, those little signals. The nods, the smiles. 'I'm ready for bed,' I said.

Two minutes and I was back in my own apartment. I sat on the carpet, I sharpened my mind like the blade of an axe. I murmured the Tei-shung Mantra. I swallowed the potion, the last potion. And in front of me, I had the photograph of Benedict.

There was no certainty it would work. With both George and Janis, they were directly in front of me. But even the faintest of chances was beyond refusal. Through Benedict, I had the possibility of experiencing making love to Julietta, not in my dreams but in the flesh.

A mist clearing, then I was there, peering at Benedict's face in the bathroom mirror. Feeling the whizz of electric toothbrush on his teeth. The flavour of his toothpaste, different from my own. Pissing into the toilet bowl. Switching off the bathroom light. Julietta, naked, on her back, putting down the book she was reading. Smiling as she welcomed him. I sucked her lips as they kissed. I felt her body under his hands. I breathed in her sweet odour through his nostrils. I was in paroxysms of desire, my heart beating into my chest, my senses aflame.

Then I discovered, to my intense dismay, Benedict, despite Julietta's best endeavours, remained limp. So that was 'the problem' to which he had referred.

***

Gracie phoned, 'Did it work?'

'Nope,' I lied.

'Just as well,' she said.

I had a dream that I was in a maze of corridors. I was desperate for a piss but had to run from something menacing that was after me. The need to urinate became stronger and stronger but I couldn't stop because 'the thing' would get me. I woke up and knew I needed to get to the bathroom, but I didn't know where I was. Everything was dark, I didn't know where to look for a light switch. Then, after about a minute, I realised I was in my own bedroom. How did I not know I was in my bedroom? The dream was horrible but that minute of disorientation was worse.

I went to the hospital for more tests. Then on to Dr. Nuryan. 'The tentacles of forgetfulness are enclosing the brain,' he said. How brutal can you get?

'Can't you give me something that'll knock me off for good?' I said.

He was genuinely aghast. 'Good God! There's years of life in you yet.'

'That's what I'm afraid of.'

***

Josh called me on Skype. 'We're all settled in. Big house. Plenty of room.'

Tamara said, 'We've engaged Gabriela to help run things

here.'

Kate said, 'International School's great – folks from all over. But now it's the August break. Grandpop, why don't you come and join us?'

I said, 'What do you do with a dead tree when it's no longer giving shade?'

***

'Gracie,' I said, 'I need your help with this final chapter.'

> *The snow must melt on the mountain for the stream to trickle and flow.*
> *The stream must run into the field for the rice to ripen and grow.*
> *The rice must be cooked and eaten for the child to become a man.*
> *The man must transform the body to complete what he once began.*

There followed the words of a 'Mantra of Transformation' and the instructions: The mind must become as the tip of a sword. Take the fresh ripe berries of the blue-flowered tree. Place the hands in benediction. The Universe of the mind and the Universe beyond the mind shall unite and become whole again.

Gracie said, 'Quite different, isn't it, from the previous prescription which said nothing can be changed. This is all about one thing disappearing for a new thing to emerge.'

'What do you know of the "blue-flowered tree"?'

'There's hundreds of varieties of blue-flowered trees in China,' she said. 'I could find out if the original text is any more specific.'

A week later, Gracie came back to me. 'The flowers aren't, as specified in the transcription, blue but purple and yellow. The tree is only found in the mountainous region of Gansu Province. Also, you will be interested in this: in the archive in Beijing, there's an addition to Hoo's manuscript not published in *The Treatise*. I have a fax here. It was written by a student of Hoo Li Wei soon after the Master died. He says that Hoo instructed him that upon his death, *The Treatise* should be destroyed. He says that he could not bear to carry out the Masters wishes but rather he will hide the manuscript where it will not be found for a thousand years.'

I thought, better he had followed the instructions of the Master. Even after a millennium, mankind was no more benign.

'It says here that Hoo pressed his hands upon the student's head in an act of benediction and he felt the Master's wisdom flood into his mind. And, at that moment, Hoo died.'

So, I thought, Hoo found a method for transmigration.

***

I soon ascertained that the berries, when fresh and ripe as specified in Hoo's instructions, are highly toxic but, when dried, are used medicinally by Chinese herbalists. They ripen in September. My trip to the remote mountains of Gansu is a story in itself, but I won't be bothered with that now. Suffice to say, I found the tree with its ripe berries and gathered a handful. I was worried about them drying out. How to smuggle them back? I feared Security and Immigration and The Food and Drugs Administration and Customs and every Airline Official. I hid them between slices of bread and butter. They confiscated my toothpaste but weren't bothered by my sandwiches.

***

'Good trip?' Benedict said, full of admiration for my adventurousness.

'Great,' I said, 'I've learned an ancient Chinese method of hypnotism.'

Benedict took the bait, he'd never stopped asking me for another session. I acted reluctant, then gave in. 'What about tomorrow?' I said, conscious of the berries drying out.

***

I have put everything about my life in order. I wrote some letters, then tore them up. Benedict is seated in front of me, he went out like an old man in a hammock. 'Repeat after me,' I say, 'I am not responsible for Daddy hurting Mummy.'

I am placing the photograph of Julietta on the floor in front of me. I am bringing to mind my bedtime reveries of Julietta. It has the desired effect. I am sharpening my mind to the point of a sword. I am swallowing twenty ripe berries of the tree of purple and yellow flowers. I am opening Benedict's zipper. I am placing my hands firmly around his limp flesh. I am repeating the Mantra of Transformation...

***

You will want to know if it worked. Well, I will not be here to tell you. For that, you'll have to ask Benedict.

Or Julietta.

DARK RIVER,
DARK MOUNTAIN

by the same author

STREET OF THE SMALL NIGHT MARKET
FROG IN A COCONUT SHELL
A PAIR OF JESUS-BOOTS
THE LOSS OF THE NIGHT WIND
A SNAKE IN THE OLD HUT

SYLVIA SHERRY

DARK RIVER, DARK MOUNTAIN

JONATHAN CAPE
THIRTY BEDFORD SQUARE LONDON

FIRST PUBLISHED 1975

JONATHAN CAPE LTD, 30 BEDFORD SQUARE, LONDON WC1

ISBN 0 224 01069 7

SET IN 11 PT. BASKERVILLE, 1½ PT. LEADED

PRINTED AND BOUND IN GREAT BRITAIN
BY RICHARD CLAY (THE CHAUCER PRESS) LTD,
BUNGAY, SUFFOLK

For Janet Carter

DARK RIVER, DARK MOUNTAIN

I

It was chance – or maybe it was fate – that brought that small paragraph in the newspaper to my attention, a paper I was just glancing through to while away the time on the top of the bus. I was home, visiting my old mother in Newcastle after a long spell abroad. It was a summer's evening, the sun slanting down on the dark fronts of that northern city's streets, gritty air blowing in through the window, a chattering crowd of schoolchildren crammed into the seats around me.

POT-HOLERS TO ATTEMPT 'TOMB'

> Early next week, weather conditions being suitable, a group of pot-holers is to open up the cave in Wenningborough Hill, on the west of the Pennines, which has long been known locally as "The Frenchwoman's Tomb". It is said that during the last war a woman, believed to be French, became wedged in a spiral-shaped cleft in this cave-pitted mountain and died there. Rescuers found it impossible to get the body out and the entrance was sealed with stones and a burial service held. The pot-holers hope to prove the truth (or otherwise) of the legend and to explore what has generally been regarded as an inaccessible passage in the chain of Wenningborough caves.

The lurching bus and the sunny evening disappeared and I was on Wenningborough again, early morning mists shifting away across that wild stretch of the Pennines, a curlew wailing towards Wenningborough Peak, the silent and muddied group of men in various attitudes of weary resignation, like carved figures on that moorland of "mosses" and "forces" where the wind could make a weird music through the outcrops and caves. I was fifteen again, urgent and shivering with intensity and distress as I got ready to go down into the cleft. And then I was edging down, feet first into the darkness; the lights and the faces above were cut off as I rounded the first spiral; there was a sense of cold suffocation as I rounded the second. That was where she was. I said her name. I knew she was unconscious but I said her name. Painfully, I stretched my hand down, unseeing, groping towards her. I could recall, vividly, the limp feel of her fingers in mine. I could recall whimpering with shock as I realized she was dead. I could recall my desperate attempts to get further down to her, to get down and put a rope round her. And I could recall the despair when I was hauled out again, knowing I had left her to her lonely, foreign grave.

I stood up, shuffling a surprised and indignant teenager off the seat as I made hurriedly for the bus stairs. I had to get into the air and walk that nightmare away.

But it was not a nightmare but a ghost that pursued me through the streets of the city, the ghost of Marthe drawing me back through time, re-creating not the horror but a past phase of existence that I had deliberately shut away and that now demanded recognition. There was no question I must be there if they were going to disturb that tomb. By eight o'clock, in the soft light of a summer's evening, I was driving through the empty dales, my mind soothed by the bare undulations of moorland and the lonely cropping sheep and the eternal detachment of the hills. It took me back to my first discovery of the comforting isolation of the Pennines.

As I rounded a bend, Wenningborough, the dark mountain, was suddenly above me, its high mass, outlined against a brilliant western sky, throwing a deep shadow over its eastern side and across the valley. It startled me almost as the sudden appearance of an old enemy would have startled me, and the car swerved for a moment in response. I drove on, and the mountain on my left fell slowly behind the hills and then rose slowly again against a darkening sky, its head withdrawn in mist.

A few moments later I was on the steep descent into the village. I could see the roofs of its houses below me and the steeple of the church pressed against the side of the mountain. I stopped the car and pulled down the window.

I considered how much I had changed, how far I had travelled, since the day I first arrived there in September 1939, a sullen, bewildered boy. So much had happened to me since then. I had encountered so many more foreign and often hostile communities, and risked death in more dangerous environments, compared with the petty life of an obscure village in this old, calm country. The boy I had been then, inexperienced and vulnerable, had disappeared without trace, I thought, and I felt a bitter satisfaction as I went over in my mind the people I'd known here when I was always at a disadvantage, always an ignorant stranger to their life and ways.

I was surprised now by the lighted streets of the village. I had remembered only the darkness of wartime. And the local pub, the Fox, where I'd hoped to get a room, was transformed into a rather smartly turned out private house. And it was disturbing also to find I was causing an obstruction in that once-deserted street, and that a series of cars hooted warningly as they skirted me.

But the biggest shock of all was the sight of the old house, Higham House, the Major's residence in my time, denuded now of its protective shrubbery, standing starkly behind a car park, a sign saying it was the Wenning Hotel. The mainstay of life there as I had known it had gone. What had happened to the Major? Where was the elaborately clipped tree in the shape of a peacock that stood proudly on the edge of the lawn? Where were the high walls and the impressive ironwork gates?

The entrance hall – I remembered being in it once, the day I was employed by the Major – was now the bar. It had seemed to me as a boy a vast, high-ceilinged, darkly impressive place that smelt of wax polish and was insistent about its own dignity. Now it seemed much smaller. It was certainly less well kept, and its former owners could never have envisaged the small bar at the foot of the staircase with the fairy lights round it and the scattering of tables and chairs. One or two tables were occupied by stolid countrymen with beers before them to whom I was obviously an object of phlegmatic interest. But a woman standing at the bar drinking a whisky gave me a more comprehensive look. I felt she was in some way placing me – I couldn't tell how. I had an impression of stoutness in a rather out-of-date tweed suit, of a pleasantly un-outstanding face.

In a few moments I was climbing the staircase, once lighted by a chandelier and with huge vases of flowers on each windowsill, now solemn under a red, glass-shaded light. The landlord had been there only five years, he told me.

"Not one of our best rooms, Mr North, but the phone's not stopped ringing all day. People from London. Newspaper people coming up to see the cave opened. It was the same two years back when some pot-holers were cut off by a flood. They come, you know, and it's merry hell for a couple of days and they're gone. It makes you wonder. This is it." He opened a door and gave a critical look round the room. "I think you'll be comfortable. I hope I haven't put my foot in it?"

I couldn't think what he meant.

"You're not a newspaper man as well?"

My room was a corner one. From one window I looked out over the village, across the roof of Churchgates Cottage to the church. The clouds broke and moonlight flooded the scene, picking out, above and beyond the village, the flat head of Wenningborough, standing out boldly now against the night sky as I'd seen it so often in the past. It brought to me a sharp sensation of pain and I closed the curtain quickly over it and turned to the other window that looked west over the main road. There was a regular passage of cars on it. In my day it had been a quiet village street, electrified only occasionally by a rumbling army convoy, with a few familiar vehicles – a pony and trap resurrected during the petrol restrictions, the vicar's old Ford, the butcher's van, the local bus. And beyond the road the fields sloped to the flat water meadows of the Wenning, the dark river, meandering there among trees and beneath the railway bridge, a slow-moving, salmon-pooled river, glossy in the moonlight. I opened the window. There was a pause in the traffic and the night was as calm and silent, the air as quiet and clear, as I had known them in those wartime days. I looked down over the river, thinking of Marthe. "They were only games, Marthe," I thought, "games made up by anonymous men at the top with busy minds and the need to occupy them. War games. And we all joined in. And they killed you."

I had to pass through the bar on the way to the dining-room. There were strangers there now in eccentric clothes, their luggage and equipment piled on the chairs. They were busy people doing a job, and they awarded me only a moment's dismissive glance. But the eyes of that woman, calm, thoughtful, reflective eyes, held mine. She stood at the bar, obviously at ease, enjoying the talk, at home in the atmosphere, listening to the landlord's account of his wartime experiences which involved shipping horses to Poland. She had an air of confidence, an air of knowing, an ability to join completely in the talk of the war and at the same time to watch me as I walked through, with a thoughtful air. She would have been, I reflected, at home in an officers' mess during the war, an officer herself. And yet I knew, somewhere, I'd seen her before and it wasn't in those circumstances. For the first time since my arrival, my protective anonymity was shaken.

After dinner I went to look at the village, walking slowly along the main street that ran parallel with the river. There had been a pill-box, I remembered, but it had gone, and instead there were two new bungalows.

I made straight for Churchgates Cottage, loitering for a few seconds to look again at its abundant garden, its windows that had been hung with red curtains. Miss Gwynne had always been fond of red. Lucky colour, she would say. But I did not risk knocking at the door. Surely by this time Emily Gwynne must be dead? Not many of us live on into our eighties, after all. And there was no point in disturbing the new tenants with my old memories.

Yet I had no recollection of leaving that cottage for the last time. I'd been ill, of course, in a state of shock. But as I passed the gate, a memory gripped me painfully – my meeting there with Marthe when we tried so unsuccessfully to understand each other. I could almost see now that flushed and angry face, the grey eyes flashing, the brown hair tossed back from her shoulders, and her voice saying intensely, "You English! You do not know how to fight! You do not know how to hate! You have no emotions. How do you fight a war with no emotions?" If I could only have communicated my emotions to her then.

Next to the cottage the pavement ended in a short flight of stone steps that led to the churchyard gateway. The black shadow of the church fell across the graves. I made my way among the old tombstones. I recalled the exact site of the old Gwynne family tomb. No new names had been added to the stone. I hesitated, and feet shifted on the gravel path behind me.

"Looking for a particular grave?"

The familiar, sharp, military tones startled me into uprightness. I was even trembling, his voice brought back so much. Against the light he was just a squat shape, and so much smaller than I remembered. So much smaller than I was! I almost laughed at the incongruity of that. But straight away the familiar antagonism between us asserted itself and so did my old suspicion of him. Had he deliberately followed me there? He'd never been given to walking in the churchyard.

"The Gwynnes'," I said.

He grunted as though someone had punched him.

"This is the old grave," he said. "The brother and sister are up beside the wall."

I thanked him and started to walk towards the dry-stone wall that made a pretence of keeping the bulk of the dark mountain out of the village.

"Did you know them?"

"A long time ago."

I didn't stop: I went on to where the two plain white stones stood side by side before two neatly mown grassy mounds. Emily Gwynne: Richard Mortimer Gwynne of Wenning and the Federated Malay States. All that was left of them. I never knew he was called Richard Mortimer. I'd known him as Bunny.

When I turned round, the Major had gone.

2

The approaching rhythm of a train through a deep silence troubled my mind, and the insistence of its whistle brought me awake. I heard it clearly then, loud and near at hand as it slowed in passing through the station behind and above the hotel. I got up and lit a cigarette as the past began to come back to me, clear in every impression even after that long stretch of years. I remembered the trains that had wound at a comfortable rate among the Yorkshire dales, trailing plumes of white smoke and always visible, raised on high viaducts, moving with the smoothness and certainty of ships at sea through the tops of trees and above houses. During that hot early summer, that desperate summer of 1940, it was one of those trains that brought Marthe into my life, just as one of them had earlier transported me not only from one environment to another but from one state of mind to another, and could never return me. Just as they had carried, since September 1939, bewildered evacuees over the surface of the country to mysterious destinations.

It was the day after the Germans began to move into Poland and bomb Warsaw. Saturday, September 2nd, 1939. I stood at the open window of a train in the station of my home town, looking down at my mother on the platform. She said in a thin voice, "Now mind you keep that pound note in your *inside* pocket, our Colin," and the train jerked and began to pull out of the station leaving her crying and waving goodbye. We moved slowly along the backs and ends of the streets of terraced houses where I had lived – backs and ends that I had never seen before. There was a last glimpse of the yellow dome of the local cinema, a hand shaking a duster from a window, a man in shirt-sleeves and braces sitting out on the back stairs with his newspaper and looking up casually as the train slid past. Somehow it was the sight of that man that forced into my mind the realization of my despair and loneliness, for I felt I knew that man – I knew everything about him and how he lived, because that was how *I* lived – and he had no notion that I was on that train being carried away from our shared existence. I stared and blinked hard to keep back the tears as the hoardings – 'Ah Bisto!', 'The *North Mail*: Your paper', 'Lifebuoy Soap' – moved slowly across the window into my past. "It's not fair," I thought. "It isn't. It's not *fair*!"

I wasn't one of the official evacuees who filled the train. I was fourteen and a half, been left school for six months and working as an assistant engraver making identity discs. There was a real rush on for them just then. I was a reluctant private evacuee because my mother, a widow, had worked out that if she could get me a job as an agricultural labourer she might save me from the bombs, call-up into the forces and almost certain death – from all the glory and heroics, in fact, that me and my pals had been contemplating all summer. And we just *happened* to have distant relatives on the other side of the country who would help. We were both quietly stubborn people, my mother and me, and there'd been a stormy few weeks before she'd got me on that train. My grandmother, called in to adjudicate, had sat back helplessly with her hands folded in her lap and shaken her head.

"Well, Jane, he's like you. Once he gets his teeth into a thing he worries it like a whippet. Your dad was the same," and she waited for the outcome.

But my mother had won because she had the trump card. She begged me not to break her heart by putting myself in danger and leaving her alone in the world. I had to give in. Dad had been dead only two years and I could still remember her grief.

Well, I thought, there were two good things anyway – the war hadn't started yet and it might never start, and if it did I would join the Air Force the minute I was eighteen – earlier if I could get away with it – and shoot the enemy out of the skies. That I mightn't have the educational qualifications for this or that *I* might be the one to be shot out of the skies never entered my head.

The sun blazed through the window and the train thundered in its regular and monotonous and inevitable way towards my destination through an unfamiliar landscape of vast, empty fields and hills that suggested a new, dangerously unconfined way of life.

In the late afternoon I was left at Wenning Station with a dozen or so pale-faced and fretful women and children. It was hot; the station roof was castellated; there was a bed of flowers with the name "Wenning" picked out in the middle in white stones; there was an irritable exchange between the station-master and the billeting officer; there was a cloying scent of animals and manure and hay; there was a vast silence surrounding us that seemed to flow from the strangely-shaped mountain that loomed blue in the distance; and there was myself standing stiffly and deliberately apart, a small island of loneliness and hate and some fear, because it had begun to dawn on me that being sent away like this might not be as bad as not being claimed by somebody or having got myself to the wrong place.

But I was singled out by a small woman, as small and bright as a bird.

"You'll be Colin North," she said.

"Yes."

"I'm Emily Gwynne. We're some kind of relatives, aren't we? Though I'm not quite sure how." Her hand in mine was small and smooth, like warm ivory, and the bird-like impression was somewhat contradicted by the eyes, deep-set under thick, greying brows, and the halo of untidy white hair.

She took the carrier bag that contained my packet of sandwiches and bottle of Tizer (untouched), and I carried my suitcase with my gas-mask bumping in its cardboard box on my hip. We passed the blank side of a big house. "That's Higham House," she told me. "That's the Major's. You'll be working for him. Be careful here – not that we've a lot of traffic coming through" – that was where the road narrowed and the pavement disappeared. Then the village was in front of us. The houses and cottages seemed to me to be pressed up against the side of that mountain I'd seen from the station, and gazing up at it I nearly ran into Miss Gwynne.

Churchgates Cottage, the strange house that was to be my new home, was the final straw. Nothing about it reminded me remotely of my own home. It confirmed by its absolute strangeness the severance with my old life. When I was alone in the sloping-roofed bedroom with its tiny windows that looked out over the fields and river, I put my case down, my gas-mask on the bed, and looked round at the wardrobe, the dressing-table, the floral jug and bowl on the washstand where I was to wash before supper, and

I laid my head down on the eiderdown and wept. Nobody knew of my weakness. I wept alone and then I washed my face and sleeked my hair with water – Tapolene, my dad called it. I looked at myself carefully, in the mirror, a weedy-looking boy, narrow-faced, with a mop of very dark hair, given to immobility of feature and the habit of standing with my feet slightly apart and my hands clasped behind my back, in the manner of an earnest bank manager. You couldn't tell I'd been crying. In my new flannel trousers, open-necked shirt and tweed sports-jacket I looked, I decided, extremely smart, and I was, I knew, extremely lonely. It weighed on me very heavily that I was come to live with 'posh' people. I could tell the Gwynnes were that – by the way she spoke and acted, by the look and feel of the house. They would have all kinds of 'posh' ways of doing things, and I was sure to get in a mess over them.

The house was very quiet. I opened a door downstairs and a blast of hot air came out at me from a room with a roaring fire in the grate and in front of it, lying on the mat like a huge sofa, a man in roomy pyjamas of a floral pattern reading a book.

He looked round and we regarded one another, a bit surprised on both sides, for a few seconds. Then, "Ha!" he said. "You'll be Colin. Come in, come in," and he stood up and put on a brocade dressing-gown.

"Yes, *do* go in." Miss Gwynne was behind me carrying a tray. "I expect you're hungry. I hope the heat won't bother you."

I shook hands with her brother and she made tea from the black kettle on the hob, and we had supper – a bacon-and-egg tart, and sausage rolls and cake. My fears were all justified. They went in for tray-cloths and starched napkins and unnecessary pieces of cutlery and thin china cups and saucers. My heart sank as I looked from all this to her small upright body and kindly smile and to Mr Gwynne with his smooth, bronzed face, his long, white, fine hair, his small, white goatee beard and very red lips. Not just posh but peculiar as well. Talk about the luck of the Norths! We listened to the chimes of Big Ben on the wireless and then to the nine o'clock news in a tense, devotional silence.

"We'll be at war in two weeks," said Mr Gwynne, and took a sip of brandy.

"Two weeks," murmured Miss Gwynne, shaking her head.

My mouth felt dry.

"I don't think there'll be a war," I said stoutly. It was about the first thing I had said since I arrived. I only said it because I was determined there *couldn't* be a war.

"I think, you know," said Miss Gwynne gently, "my brother is right. He generally is."

But I was not convinced. He was an old man living in the depths of the country. I was from the town – I knew what people had been saying there. There wouldn't be a war.

Next morning, Sunday, September 3rd, when Miss Gwynne got back from church, her brother switched on the wireless and we heard Chamberlain tell us in a reedy voice that we were at war with Germany.

"That's it," said Mr Gwynne, "that's it," as though it was entirely due to his organization.

"That's it," echoed Miss Gwynne and they exchanged a long, serious look.

I went out into the back garden and sat on the seat under the apple tree and thought. That *was* it. I was stuck here.

3

I was kept waiting outside the kitchen door of Higham House next morning by the servant who answered my knock. Couldn't be the Major I wanted, she told me in a contemptuous way. It must be John Dale. A young girl sat at a table shelling peas. I remember her looking up at me with a curious stare that humiliated me even more. It was my first experience of class distinctions in a solid, workaday form. Until then I had come up against the petty authority of school and civil servant and had often been angered but never ashamed. After all, my father had been first sales in the gentlemen's outfitting department of the Co-op. It was a position that brought us prestige if not a lot of money, and it was remembered with pride in my family. I loitered in the yard, burning with anger.

Then John Dale came tramping along dressed in an assortment of clothes with an old felt hat on his head. A thin, black and white collie followed him, and he said, "Stay, girl, stay, Mavis," to her and she sat down and looked up at him steadily. Then he looked at me for a few seconds, with a kind of comic dismay. It was my suit, I imagine. Quite unthinking, I had put on my usual office clothes – what had once been my best navy suit, a white shirt and brown city shoes. As a recruit to farming, I must have looked ludicrous. And then, I think, he saw the dislike and resentment in my face.

Suddenly he smiled, clapped a hand on my shoulder and said, "Now then, feller, how you gettin' on? Feelin' a bit lost? Nay, don't upset yourself. We'll not put you in field with bull on your first day. We'll leave that till tomorrow."

I suppose I smiled a little because he added, "Come on then, feller. Meet the Major. And don't let him put the wind up you."

He took me through the back entrance, along a passage and through a green baize door into the hall, where we stood waiting just inside, in a polished silence, until from the dining-room came a very small man, round of head and round of body, brushing toast crumbs from his waistcoat.

"Good morning, John," he said briskly, and waited.

"This is the new lad, sir," said John Dale deferentially.

The Major turned his protuberant blue eyes on me. They stared hard and straight. He was a man of unimpressive appearance, bulky features and inert expression, yet he was disconcerting. He spoke very little, but he kept his shoulders squared, and his eyes fixed on your face unless they moved like lizards under the thick, hooded lids, and he had a round stubborn head and a round stubborn nose and round stubborn hands.

"Miss Gwynne's relative. Fourteen years six months," he commented, quite objectively and surprising me by his knowledge. "Doesn't look strong. Will he do, John?"

"I think he might, sir."

"Lick him into shape, then."

And he dismissed us, standing there quite still while we left, getting entangled with each other in the doorway in a way that annoyed me because it was undignified.

We walked some distance past the railway station to the group of buildings that had once been the centre of the home farm and went into what I came to know as the shant, where three or four farm-workers waited for John Dale and the day's instructions. Uncouth men they looked to me then.

"By God," said one – Albert, he was called – "tek's all sorts. City-slickers now, eh?"

Fortunately, then, I couldn't altogether understand the dialect, and I didn't understand their humour. But later I began to fathom the nickname 'city-slicker' or 'c.s.' that they used for me, and references to my top hat and tails.

"That's enough of that." John Dale dismissed them to their work and turned to me. "Puzzle where to start you off. Hast done any farming afore? Ah well, likely the shippon'll be best if we can find you something to put on."

Later, in a pair of wellingtons two sizes too big and one of his old jackets that draped me like a collapsed bell-tent, I started to muck out a shippon for the first time, appalled by the dirt and smell.

John Dale stood watching me quizzically. He wasn't to know it, but I was burning up inside. I was in a world of strangers – not a soul I could really talk to, everybody to be approached across a distance; I'd been told what would happen and what I should do; I'd been laughed at for an ignorance I couldn't help and I'd been made to do undignified things. And I'd got, as my grandmother would say, "my dander up". When I suddenly slipped and sat down in the cow dirt, that was it.

I propped my shovel carefully against the shippon wall, took off the coat he'd lent me and handed it to him.

"I'll bring the wellingtons round when I've changed into my shoes," I said, and began to walk out.

"Here – hold on, feller. Where's off to?"

I faced him. "I don't have to work here. I don't have to work anywhere. And I'm not going to."

"Hold on, feller." He came up to me, looking down over his long nose. He was a perceptive man, was John Dale, the first friend I made there.

"Now then, as I've heard it, the idea is that you work here so you won't be called up into His Majesty's Forces. And, looking at you now, feller, I can see that could happen at any time."

I wasn't sure if he was making fun of me or not.

"Now you might find it hard to believe, but the Major'll pay you fifteen bob a week for work of this sort. And putting the matter on a purely economic basis – can your mother afford to pay the Gwynnes all your board and lodging?"

I frowned. It hadn't occurred to me that my mother was having to keep me out of her small pension.

"And putting it another way, have you got the cash for your fare home – if that's what you have in mind?"

"I've got a pound," I said stubbornly.

"Well, 'tis better than a kick in the pants, I suppose ..."

But I was beginning to see his point. I hadn't thought about wages or board and lodgings – I'd only wanted to get out.

"Look, feller, why don't you give the job a try? Say for a week or so. It's not all mucking out shippons – we've got horses, and there's even one old tractor that we can sometimes get started. Happen there's somat you'll like doing. And after all, feller, when you get to be a wage-earner, like, you have to look all round a question before you go haring off at a tangent. Bear in mind, that when a feller gets to a certain point in life he's got to start thinking like a grown man and not like a kid."

I rose to his challenge. I was a man all right. I looked him firmly in the eyes.

"I'll give it a try – for a month," I said.

"We're more than grateful, feller. More than grateful."

As I walked home that night, weary after a day's physical work in the open air, I was sustained by the thought that I was now a wage-earner – independent, a person of means; and straight after tea I brought the subject up with Miss Gwynne. What was I to pay for board and lodgings?

"Well, Colin, I told your mother I didn't want anything for your keep so long as she saw to your clothes, you know. But she insists on paying five shillings a week."

I was, in my new status as independent wage-earner, annoyed that such negotiations had gone on behind my back. I was no longer a child.

"I'm getting fifteen bob a week – I'll pay ten bob, and Mam can have her five bob back."

I was satisfied. I wouldn't owe the Gwynnes anything. And I could save quite a bit myself – maybe for that return home.

4

My strongest recollection of that time is a sense of isolation. At home I'd been gregarious, always one of a crowd. Now I was alone, not simply lonely but always carrying about with me the sense of an invisible barrier that separated me from intimate contact with the people around me, a barrier made up of strange customs, strange ways of thinking, strange ways of talking. I became a more silent, more withdrawn person, accustoming myself to this inner sense of isolation, becoming used to observing and to drawing my own conclusions without feeling the need to communicate them.

I suppose I developed then the independence of spirit and the urge to go out alone and explore new places that determined my future life. I didn't see it in that way then, I only felt I was alone even when I was working with the other farmhands, even when I shared the Gwynnes' hot parlour during the winter evenings. John Dale was the only one whose humour and sympathy could break through that barrier for me.

The Gwynnes can never have realized that the silent boy who sat at their table at meal-times or huddled over a book by the fire or listened with them nightly to the nine o'clock news was privately observing them and attempting to come to grips with them as a new phenomenon, to

grasp the fact that they had lived nearly all
the Far East, where Bunny Gwynne had ma
mine and Miss Gwynne had travelled for mil
jungle in a bullock-cart and set up a school in th
tains, and that they had chosen to retire to the
they'd been born in. I was disconcerted by their
references to strange-sounding places and customs, an
Mr Gwynne not being able to stand the cold after all
years in the tropics. The slightest drop in temperatu
brought on his bronchitis. He never left the house excep
to visit the outside lavatory and then he put on an extra waistcoat and his overcoat, and sometimes took one of the stone hot-water bottles clutched against his chest. His time was spent reading, looking over their collection of tropical butterflies, coins, photographs, Chinese pottery and strange pictures of weird gods.

Sometimes, working in the fields, I would feel the most poignant homesickness when brief recollections of my past life would come back to me: unimportant details like the battered iron mug at the lion-head fountain in the park from which I'd drunk an iron-tasting water between games of football, the river with its swing bridge shuddering out to let the colliers steam down-river to the sea, the 1,500 steps up to the top of Grey's Monument in Grainger Street that we raced up – it was an adventure and seemed to me to take sheer courage to go on climbing when you felt your legs were coming out of their sockets, but then there was the view of the whole city's skyline in front of you, the thin murmur of the crowds below and everybody looking such midgets down there.

I would turn from these memories to my isolation, an isolation that was the more frustrating because it seemed unnecessary. For after all that disruption of my life, ot razing our cities, German sold- Channel to invade us. The blackout , the trenches dug in the garden for ns, all seemed pointless. Some ships rman U-boat got into the naval base October and destroyed the *Royal Oak*. y way, a Bore War.

vell go back home," I said hopefully to

mpulsive," said her brother. "Don't under- rmans. They're coming. They're coming."

ey're coming," murmured Miss Gwynne. She often nded a gentle confirmatory approval of her brother's remarks.

I wrote to my mother putting forward the same idea.

"There's no point in being over-hasty," she wrote back. "The country air'll be doing you good. And everybody you knew around here has gone away anyway."

So I accepted my loneliness and deliberately cultivated it. I looked for ways of being alone, for activities that would reinforce my sense of individual achievement in the face of my isolation. I bought a secondhand bike for a pound – my first grown-up bike, a racing model with low, curved handle-bars entwined with impressive brake cables, and three-speed gears as well.

"Now you've got a real bargain there, feller," said John Dale. "A real bargain. Cheap at half the price and your money back."

I was never sure whether John Dale was laughing at me or not.

I began to get about the countryside, exploring in my free time and untroubled by having to rely on the local bus that chuntered through the village three or four times a day. Whatever was strange, remote and outside my normal experience attracted me like a magnet, as did the lonely and the isolated. My sympathy went out, my imagination was stirred by these reflections of my own condition in the world around me. And it was this that led to my first brush with death.

5

Whenever I paused in my work, my gaze would be drawn to the mountain and my imagination saw it as a submarine breaking above the waves, or a headless sphinx, or the head of a whale lying flat against the sky. I made plans to climb it and absorbed in these one day I was deaf to the talk around me until I heard Albert's raucous laughter and his friend Len's comment:

"Crackers on old Humpty-back is that lad."

"Who's old Humpty-back?"

"*Who's* old Humpty-back? *Yon*'s old Humpty-back. Yon mountain, you daft gaupie."

"When Humpty-back's got his cap on, happen we'll have rain afore evening," said Len.

"Aye, and when old Humpty's got a smile on tha'll not need a coat i' the morning."

"Aye, and when Major's got his eye on you, you'd best get on with the work," commented John Dale. The Major was strutting along the edge of the field.

"Most important man i' this village," said Albert solemnly picking up his hay-rake.

The Major always kept at a distance, giving instructions through John Dale, instructions that often brought a frown to John Dale's face, and as I got to know more about farming I understood why John Dale often ignored these instructions. Once, seeing that I observed this, he said,

"Ah well, the Major's new to all this." That surprised me because the Major seemed a landowner born and bred. "No, no. He bought Higham House a year back. Foreigner he is."

Never in my presence – because I was a foreigner as well – did anyone openly criticize the Major for his ignorance, but I was often aware of the muted cynicism with which he was regarded by his farmworkers.

"He's on the Gestapo Black List," John Dale said with his usual half-smile.

"What's that?"

"List of people who'll be shot when the – *if* the Germans invade. Very important man is the Major."

"How does he know he's on the list?"

"Beats me, feller, but he says he is. Tell you something. He says there's a White List as well. Now I wonder who's on that?"

"Happen that'll be thee and me!" chortled Albert, but for some reason that didn't please John Dale and we worked in silence till my gaze was caught again by the mountain.

"How high is it?"

"He's off again!" Len said.

"That mountain," said Albert, "is evil. You keep off it. 'Tis all right as far as High Meadows, but 'tis devil's country after that."

"That mountain," John Dale corrected him, "is one of nature's miracles. But it's dangerous. Look, feller, have you ever seen a maggotty cheese?"

I couldn't recall that I had.

"Well, you can imagine what a maggotty cheese looks like?"

"Full of maggots?"

Albert chuckled. "Like tha head!"

"Full of holes and tunnels, feller, that the maggots have eat out. Now that mountain's like a maggotty cheese – all holes and passages inside. Pot-holes and caves. Only it's water that made them tunnels, streams digging away at the rocks to find their way down to the valley and join that there River Wenning."

"Can you get into the caves?" I asked, excited.

"Oh aye," said Albert, "you can drop down a pot-hole in the dark and not be seen again."

"You can get lost in them caves," said Len.

"My old uncle used to say," said Albert, "that when the great flood came, the flood waters came up from these here pot-holes and then drained back into them. And that means they've got a direct link with the devil!"

John Dale did not refute this, but his eyes twinkled over his long nose.

"You're having me on."

Albert looked fierce. "I'm telling you, lad, there could be monsters in them caves!"

I half hoped he was right just for the sake of excitement, but John Dale said to me that evening as we were bringing the cows in for milking,

"About Wenningborough, feller."

"Wenningborough?"

"Yon mountain – the dark mountain. All them old tales mean nothing, but that mountain's dangerous. There's a cave in there big enough to hold York Minster. Now there's fellers make a hobby of going into them places, but that's their business. Those pot-holes are death-traps for man and beast. So you watch it. We lost a sheep last year down Witches' Pot. And she was in lamb. The Major was fair put out."

Witches' Pot! The name settled it. I was going up that mountain – I was going into those caves!

I set off on my bike the next weekend under a sky heavy with rain. The lushness of the valley ended at High Meadows, and after that I followed a steep track between rough stone walls over bare moorland. When the track gave out I stood, out of breath, in a fine drizzle, on Wenningborough Edge, the flat shoulder of mountain before the final ascent to the peak. There is nothing like the deep silence of Wenningborough Edge. Behind me the valley was spread out, still sunny; before and above me the mountain's head was concealed in mist, and around me was an empty, bird-haunted land, bare moorland, yellow with patches of dried bracken and purple with sweeps of heather lapping the white outcrops of limestone.

After all I'd been told I wasn't conscious of any sense of evil or danger, but only of a deep sense of peace.

To my left a track led past a group of trees to a farmhouse. That was Fourstones Farm – empty now – and the trees guarded the entrace to Witches' Pot.

I propped my bike against the wall and ran over the uneven ground, stumbling and leaping, and in a few moments I was clinging to one of those trees and looking down the steep slope into Witches' Pot, a dark opening in the ground with a stream falling into it. From below came a breath of colder, danker air, the distant splashing of water. It was the entrance to the unknown, to miles of galleries and waterways inside the mountain. I was going to explore them no matter what warnings I'd been given.

I had equipped myself, in my ignorance, with a rope and a torch and a piece of chalk. I thought this last was a rather cunning idea. I could leave marks on the rocks as I explored and so find my way back. I fastened the rope to one of the trees, took a last look down the pot, and swung out into space. And swing is what I literally did. The rope began to twist and I was spun round, clinging desperately to it with my hands only. It took a great effort to get my feet braced against the rock wall and stop the spinning, and the experience left me trembling and sweating. But I wouldn't give up. Keeping my feet against the rock, I began to climb down, clumsily.

Looking back now I can see all the risks I was taking – the rope might not have reached to the bottom, my torch might have dropped from my pocket and smashed on the rocks beneath, the knots I'd used might have slipped. At the time, these possibilities didn't occur to me, and after climbing down thirty feet I reached the bottom, let the rope go and switched on my torch. It revealed a low tunnel stretching into darkness. The stream ran clear over the rocky floor. Splashing into the icy water, I started along it. My head bumped on projections of rock, I slipped and stumbled on wet stones, I plunged unwittingly into a pool up to my waist, I crept along narrow shelves of rock when the stream became too deep to wade through, and I came at last to a low, round cavern filled with a deep pool and with only a narrow, rocky track round it. I sat down shining my torch around, listening to the heavy, awesome silence of the inside of the mountain.

And then my torch flickered and went out.

I couldn't believe it at first and pressed the switch on and off, but it did no good. Darkness pressed heavily on my spirit. The chill of the caves began to seep into my bones – and so did fear. For the first time I regretted my urge to explore.

I moved cautiously about, my hands sliding over the walls of the cave trying to find the passage I'd come along, afraid of slipping back into the pool. The prospect of a slow, blind crawl along that passage to safety was like a promise of heaven compared with the possibility of remaining in the caves. And then I realized I'd lost all sense of direction. I didn't know where the passage was, and I could easily make a mistake and follow another passage further into the mountain. I squatted in the darkness, frozen in panic.

6

I know now that I was in that cave without light and without sound for no more than three hours. It seemed like a year to me. I tried to keep calm and I kept on speaking aloud to myself in that blackest of black nights. At least my voice was a presence. I told myself that even though I might not survive I had to move along the cave. I put down my useless torch and I crawled thirty paces, the water soaking through my trousers, and that was comforting in a way because of the feeling that there was more than rock surrounding me. There was a sediment in the water like soil and I hoped that meant that the surface wasn't far and that I'd come out somewhere. I forced myself to creep on for another fifty paces, but the rock became dry and I couldn't recognize the feel of the cave. Thirty and fifty – that was eighty paces and I was exhausted. I wanted to stop and rest and sleep – anything to forget where I was.

But I'd promised myself I'd go only that distance and then go back, so I turned like a crab and paced out eighty movements back, slower and slower, just pushing myself on. I should have been back then to the point where I'd left the torch, but when I groped around it wasn't there. I went on for another fourteen shuffles before the torch hit my face as I slumped on the ground. I went to sleep then with the torch held to my chest.

If luck had not been with me that day I might now be a small, white skeleton lying on some ledge thirty or so feet below ground, a tribute to man's indomitable and foolish sense of curiosity. But I was saved from becoming such a sacrifice.

Through the silence I heard a scratching noise. It came nearer, taking on the sound of scrabbling and scuffling and then of thudding. I had a sense of something approaching out of the blackness, and Albert's stories of prehistoric monsters troubled me. I was convinced I would die anyway – either from starvation or at the hands of whatever was approaching.

Then I saw a dim light that came nearer and suddenly showed me a thin, dark figure stooping, the light on its head throwing into view the rocky floor of another passage and a pair of very human legs ending in stout boots. And behind it came a similar figure and then another, and as they all crouched down on boulders at the opposite side of the cavern, the lamps on their helmets brought back to me the low roof and the smooth water, and ultimately revealed to *them* my crouching figure.

Terrified that they might not see me, that they might turn and go and leave me there, I shouted – it came out as a croak.

"Aye, lad. Happen you need help," came the response.

The pot-holers didn't stop then to tell me how stupid I'd been. They helped me round the pool to yet another passage and urged me on along it to another pot which they'd already laddered for their exit. Above me I could see daylight and that gave me the last spurt of energy that took me up the swaying ladder and I lay cold and exhausted in the long grasses of Wenningborough Edge.

In the flagstoned kitchen of Fourstones Farm they

brewed me hot tea and told me not to try that again. But they offered to show me how it should be done if I hadn't had enough. They were enthusiasts, and they made me one.

Next day I borrowed a large-scale map of the area from Miss Gwynne and pored over it for hours. In time I got to know every footpath, the site of every known pot and cave on the mountain. It was the exploration of a new country and I was completely absorbed.

Quite often I would meet John Dale on Wenningborough Edge. He had business there because the land was part of Higham House farm. When we met we would both be rather guarded about what we were doing. I always said I was fell-walking.

"I can see that," said John. "I tell thee, feller, you're wearing away parts of this mountain. I can see your legs getting definitely shorter each time you've been up here."

January and February 1940 were bitter months when the moorlands were wastes of hard-packed snow swept by blizzards. It was a new experience for me to face nature in this form while I helped John Dale dig out buried sheep and carry them to safety, and broke the ice on the water trough in a morning so that the cattle could drink, and tried to find my way about a land whose familiar landmarks had disappeared under snow.

But spring came and Wenningborough shook the snow from its head, the countryside was loud with the noise of streams, and the Wenning swelled over its banks, flooding the water meadows. Spring brought new hope – I began to look forward to getting back to the caves, and the war didn't seem to be a threat any longer. If we heard disturbing news about Russia or Germany, it was about places with strange names that didn't mean a lot to us. We felt comfortably certain that the government was dealing with the matter. Albert said the war would be finished that summer, and when he was asked who would win he said, nobody – there would just be an agreement.

"An agreement?" said John Dale. "What sort of agreement?"

"An agreement to stop fighting – what else?"

John Dale looked at him humorously.

"I tell you, Albert, it'll take more than an agreement to stop the Germans. They're not as daft as you take 'em for. The war hasn't started yet."

"The daft gaupie," Albert muttered when John left. "Thinks he knows it all and he knows nowt. I'll bet any man five bob this war'll be over come the end of summer."

Len said afterwards that Hitler's spies had heard Albert say this and to prove him wrong Hitler invaded Norway in April 1940. The Bore War was over. On Whit Friday morning we heard that Holland and Belgium had been attacked, and less than a week later the Dutch capitulated and then Brussels fell. We began to realize that we might yet have to defend our own country from invasion. There was a sudden flurry and a reawakening of committees and a looking into plans that had been shelved and forgotten. Stocks were added to the first aid post. We had air-raid practices when the wardens went about blowing whistles and the W.V.S. attended to the "wounded" – generally the girl guides and boy scouts. The half dozen new Home Guards (to begin with they were called the Local Defence Volunteers) drilled on the water meadows and tramped through the village for Sunday church parades. It was all a bit like a comic opera when you saw it against the emptiness and silence of the north-western fields and skies, and it was all played out against a backdrop of growing threats from Europe.

"We'll be on our own in a month," Bunny Gwynne prophesied, sipping brandy and stroking his beard.

How did he know that?

"In a month," his sister murmured.

I could almost hear the tramp of jack-boots on the road.

He licked some brandy from his red lips. "Hang on to that thought, Colin."

"Hang on," murmured Miss Gwynne.

On May 27th the news began to come through that we were evacuating our troops from Dunkirk. It was the day after that Marthe arrived.

7

I was with John Dale driving a herd of sheep and lambs from one meadow to another, and we had to take them through the village. As we reached the lane from the station a car shot out hastily to get ahead of the flock and its noise made the sheep halt and turn and mill about. John's old dog, Mavis, went racing round them in response to his whistles, and I waved a stick in the rear. And then I saw the girl appear at the corner of the lane and put down her suitcase to rest awhile. In the hot afternoon her face was flushed, and her hair hung stickily over her forehead. For a few moments she stood watching us, as though she had seen nothing like that before, then she picked up the case again and began to walk awkwardly towards the village. I wanted to help her to carry the heavy case. I had lived in the village long enough to recognize a stranger, and I knew how she felt for I had once been in the same position. She stopped again, putting down the case and looking round in bewilderment. A natural reserve and a shamed consciousness of my working clothes prevented me from helping her, but as he drew level with her John Dale called,

"Canst manage yon great heavy case, miss?"

The girl looked at him for a moment, almost as though she was thinking what to say.

"I am looking for Miss Robson's house." She had a strong foreign accent.

"You'll be her niece, happen?'

Again the same hesitation, and this time a slight toss of the head.

"Where is the house, please?"

"Round by the left ..."

I looked at her with even greater interest. The arrival of Miss Robson's niece had been awaited with great interest by the village. Miss Robson lived round the corner from Miss Gwynne and was one of the aristocracy of the village, having been the sister of some past colonel. She was lame now with arthritis and couldn't get around much and everyone was saying that it would be a good thing for her niece to be with her even though she *was* French. There were stories that this niece had escaped from France under very dangerous circumstances. But there was a definite shadow over her because her mother had married a Frenchman. Such things were not done in the village.

Along the narrow pavement, moving clumsily and unevenly, came four stout figures in slacks with snouted rubber masks over their faces and swaying between them a stretcher with a prone figure covered in blankets. As they came nearer, it was plain that the prone figure had its head swathed in bandages. The foreign girl gave a cry and pushed her way through the sheep, across the road to the group.

"Let me help – I can nurse. Let me help ..."

The prone figure sat up.

"Here – keep tha hands off me, wench!"

The foreign girl started back, the stretcher was set down, the bearers pulled off their gas-masks revealing Wenning's stretcher party of Mrs Simpson, Mrs Todd, Miss Cragg and Miss Furness. Joe, the A.R.P. warden, came round the corner escorting a batch of "walking wounded" – half a dozen of the older evacuees sporting a variety of bandages. The sheep turned restively back on themselves, Mavis started into movement. The foreign girl looked round in something like panic.

"Here, what's doing? What's holding up exercise?" demanded Joe.

"This – person ..."

"Seems to think it's real ..."

"S'not real, luv ... Just a practice ..."

"There was nowt said about strange wenches when I were asked to do this." Albert, the stretcher case, threw off the blankets indignantly and stood up.

"Here, Albert, I thought you were on spreading muck today," said John Dale.

"Major gie me time off for this ..."

"Major said nowt to me about it ..."

"Happen he didn't to you, but he did to me."

"Come on, Albert, lie down again or we'll never get finished and get a cup of tea ..."

The foreign girl pushed her way back in confusion as a tussle began round the stretcher. John Dale whistled to Mavis and shouted, "Here, lass! Here now!" but he was watching the foreign girl. I went over to her.

"Let me give you a hand ..."

She turned on me fiercely, her face flushed. "I can carry it!" she snapped. And then, seeing that I, a boy, honestly meant only to help her, her eyes brightened with tears. "Thank you. You are kind," she added, "but I can carry this."

As she disappeared round the corner, John Dale winked

at me. "Now then, feller, what dost think of that? Yon's a wench worth looking twice at. And you were quick off mark."

He shouted to Mavis and we got the sheep rounding the corner.

"She's a stranger here. I know what it feels like," I called to him over the jogging grey backs of the sheep.

"Aye. But you're not a stranger now, feller. You're a – a local stranger, eh? Eh, feller?" He gave a shout of laughter. "Ah, but Colin, she's another damned foreigner an' all. And we've got enough of them."

We had the sheep safely in the field. John Dale closed the gate and leant on it, Mavis lying panting at his feet. His pale blue eyes looked them over carefully.

"The French are our allies."

"Allies? Oh aye. Makes you think though. This war's like dry rot. Whole timber's rotten before you know it, and down it comes."

"The French will hold out."

I was shaken by John Dale suddenly doubting their reliability.

"Must be some plan behind it all," he went on reflectively. "The army couldn't be dropping back like this without something up our sleeves. Must have something."

But the tone of his voice was not reassuring.

"You've been to France, haven't you?" I asked.

He turned abruptly away from the fields. "Oh aye. Thereabouts. Who gave you that piece of information?"

"Len."

"Got a mouth like a barn door. We'd best be getting back, feller."

We walked in silence for a while and I reflected that John Dale must not like people to know things about him.

It hadn't struck me before that he was secretive because he'd always seemed open. And his home – it was like him, neat, orderly, everything there, nothing hidden away. Maybe it was a love story that had an unhappy ending, I reflected. He wouldn't want to talk about that.

"Allies maybe," he said suddenly, "but they're still foreigners and milling over here by the hundreds. There was another trainload through day afore yesterday, and the W.V.S. out feeding them."

They were people of German extraction being rounded up and shipped to the Isle of Man for internment. I suppose a lot of them had lived in England a long time, and a lot more were refugees from Hitler. The train had had to wait at our station till it could go on to Liverpool, and the vicar had called out the W.V.S. to supply tea and biscuits. I'd gone up there – curious like most of the village. It really upset me to see so many lost and bewildered faces and the hard disapproving look of those ladies dispensing tea to "foreigners". I sympathized. I was a foreigner myself.

"Some of them have been here for years," I protested.

"Ah well, you're probably right, feller." He gave me an amused grin. "All for underdog, aren't you, Colin?"

"Somebody has to be."

"Aye well. There'll always be somebody to stand up for them. But think on this – some of them being rounded up could be spies for Hitler."

"But some Englishmen could be spies for Germany – like the fifth column in Holland and Belgium and Norway. The ones that helped the Germans. They're worse aren't they?"

"Worse or not, they can all be hanged for treachery now if they're caught."

The threat of invasion had brought on a spy-fever that affected us even in the depths of the country. Anything out of the ordinary roused suspicions now, and at dusk and dawn the wardens crept along the hedgerows, disturbing the wild life in their watch for enemy parachutists.

I even got suspicious myself sometimes – about all the foreign mail Mr Gwynne received and the foreign stations he listened to on the wireless late at night. Things like that made you wonder.

"But what makes a spy, John? What makes an Englishman spy against his own country?"

"Generally, I reckon, feller, because he thinks he's i' the right."

"But how could *anybody* ...!"

"I'll tell you something, feller. Yon mountain, Wenningborough. To me the top of that mountain's good for nothing and it's dangerous. To pot-holers, it's a paradise."

I looked at him quickly.

"Do you get my meaning? Same mountain, two different ways of looking at it – and both right."

Yes, I got his meaning, but it didn't help. It only made everything more confusing. If a man was acting from conviction, could you condemn him?

"The Major said all traitors should be shot without trial," I suggested. "And Mr Gwynne said in times of national emergency we have no concern with the finer points of conscience."

"I'll tell you somat, feller, you're getting to be a very deep thinker, and it's very exhausting to watch." He looked down at me, his eyes glinting with laughter. "If you're going into this question you'd best speak to vicar next – and he'll tell you something entirely different!"

Back at the farm we went straight to the shant, the old

stone barn untidy with farm clutter. It was here we had our baggin, as lunch was called. The shant was empty.

"Happen we're first off today." John Dale swung a heavily-booted leg over a box and poured out some tea. He took a gulp and sat ruminatively gazing at the hay-rakes stacked in the corner. "Next wet day, feller, thu'd best go over yon and mend them as needs it. And mower best be got out and oiled."

"Right," I said. Watching him, I thought what a strange fellow John Dale was – what a mixture. For a start, he was ugly. He was one of the ugliest men I knew – I mean, there's a difference between being just plain or ordinary and being downright ugly. John Dale's ugliness stood out, but it wasn't a nasty ugliness, it was funny ugliness. He had a sense of humour, and his face was funny to look at as well. He had a narrow forehead, and his eyes were small and set close together, and he had a great big nose, a long nose that started narrow between his eyes and gradually grew and expanded down his long face. He reminded me of an elephant, except that he hadn't big ears. And his mouth was like an elephant's – unobtrusive until it broadened into a grin under his nose.

I began to eat a meat-and-potato pie from my basket. It was a good pie and I was hungry. For a few moments we sat in an amiable silence. The shant was musty-smelling; a strong shaft of midday sun fell from the window above; through the open door I could see a tangle of bicycles in the empty farmyard; tall trees nodded above the roof of the barn opposite, and a slight breeze skirmished among the dust and stray strands of hay on the floor of the shant. In moments like that you could almost forget there was a war on.

A black figure on a bicycle rode into that square of

sunlight and stopped, slowly dismounting and leaning the bicycle against the wall, and a gaggle of voices followed it. P.C. Burton. He shouted something to the others outside and then, "In shant, is he?"

"Aye, Bill. Come in!" John Dale replied, slowly turning his pale-blue eyes towards the door. "What's up now? New regulations for us?"

When the constable arrived there was always a lot of joking, though recently he'd brought some sobering news with him at times. But suddenly I noticed that John Dale's fingers grasping his mug of tea were clenched so tight the knuckles were white, and looking quickly at his face I thought I saw a wariness in his eyes.

Constable Burton came in with his helmet in his hand, sweeping his handkerchief over his face and followed by the men, who immediately straddled the forms and boxes and began to eat. A mug of tea was handed to the constable. He was stout and cheerful and well-liked in the village. He came originally from Merseyside.

"How do, Bill?" said John Dale.

"How's things?" said Bill, and took a noisy drink of tea. "Thirsty weather."

"Here," said Len, "didst see yon niece of Miss Robson's? Made a bee-line for Albert, she did. Didn't she?"

"Girls always goes for Albert."

"Aye, he's a right lady-killer is our Albert ..."

"The French girl? She's arrived then?" said Bill.

"She'll stir things up a bit hereabouts."

John Dale's voice cut firmly into the joking.

"What's to do, Bill?"

"Present for yer." Bill unrolled some papers he was carrying and handed a poster to John. "Thought I wouldn't trouble the Major about it."

"He's away off anyway," said John.
"Off again?"
"Aye. Another of his secret missions." The Major was always visiting important headquarters – secret visits that everybody knew about.
Bill grunted and looked thoughtful.
We gathered round John Dale, reading the poster over his shoulder. It produced a long silence:

> Farmers: In the event of an invasion, unless military action in the immediate neighbourhood makes it impossible, farmers and farm-workers must go on ploughing, sowing, cultivating, hoeing and harvesting as though no invasion were occurring.

Old Albert looked at Bill with suspicious eyes. " 'Oo sent this out, then?" he asked.
"Government. Who else?"
"Looks bad, don't it?" said Len. "Is Jerry comin' over, then?"
"We have to be prepared. That's all," said Bill. I think he felt suddenly a certain hostility in the atmosphere – I felt it myself. Like me, he was a local stranger and sensitive to unspoken emotions directed at him. He finished his tea and stood up with dignity. "I'll be getting on, then. Let the Major see it, John, and put it up somewhere, will you?"
There was silence after Bill had left. We went on eating and drinking while a bee buzzed lazily. The gnawing fear, like tooth-ache, that had come and gone all through the early spring of 1940 was back. Were the Germans going to invade? What would we do if they did? I looked round at the men. Their faces gave nothing of their thoughts away. Then old Albert looked up under his thick white brows

that descended and concealed his eyes whenever he laughed.

"Happen there's somat queer about this," he said.

"Aye?"

"Aye. What I want to know is – 'oo wrote that thing?"

"He told you – Government."

"Well, Government's a queer lot."

"Aye, 'oo d'they think they're ordering about?" asked Len. "'Oo's going to stand in t'fields hoeing and cultivating and so on with Jerry firing guns over your head? Lookin' after beasts is one thing. Risking your life to cultivate crops for Jerry to reap's another!"

"And 'oo", asked Albert, "is the fathead telling people to sow afore they cultivate?"

They agreed, nodding gravely.

"And why be there no mention of shepherds?"

"Aye, and stockmen?"

"Bit ignorant, that is."

"Or mebbe not," said Len. "Mebbe it's deliberately trying to put us about, confuse us."

"You mean," said John, "it's the work of a spy?"

"A spy in Government," said Albert.

"It's happened afore," said Len. "Look at what happened in Norway."

I didn't say anything and neither did John Dale. We were the only ones who didn't join in – it never occurred to them that not everybody knew about farms the way they did. They thought what they did was the most important thing in the world and everybody should know about it. If you didn't you were daft, a gaupie. Or even a spy.

"The Government", said Albert, "be better employed looking into those lights up on Wenningborough Edge."

He spoke with a due amount of authority and we all waited for an explanation.

"We've seen them when we've been on duty up at the Home Guard post. Two nights we've seen them. I've told Bill Burton about them but he thinks we're seeing things."

"They could be anything," said John Dale. "A few lights in a field – could be anything."

"Could be spies, signalling – and you'd best come on duty some night and see for theesel'. You're not much around with Home Guard these day, John."

"Come on now, Albert, with you up there, there's nowt for anybody else to do."

"You can laugh all you like. There's been other things seen as well."

"What?"

"Parachutists."

"Parachutists?"

"Well, there was one. I saw him come down."

For some reason, the others didn't laugh at this. John Dale looked at them over his humorous nose.

"Did you report this?"

"Report? Aye. We told the policeman. Only gets you laughed at, like."

"I saw him come down – swinging down there like a monkey – I *did*!" insisted Albert. "So did Len. Then we saw a hell of a lot of other things – like a vehicle of some kind going slowly over the cart track there wi' no lights. Aye. But people don't believe us."

"Well, it's likely, isn't it?" said John. "It's likely Germans 'ud drop spies out on Wenningborough Edge? They'd be lost up there – wander round in the dark and drop down a pot-hole. Helluva lot to spy on in this part, isn't there?"

They made no response. They sulked ostentatiously over their meal.

"Ah well," said John. "This won't get the work done..." But after the others had left, and we were standing together in the farmyard he said to me,

"Think you could get up to the post tonight, feller? Albert and Len's on 'first house'. Maybe you can pick up something. They'll talk more afore you. They tek no more notice of you than a fly on a wall."

"Think they've really seen something?" I said, ignoring the jibe.

"It'll stand lookin' into."

8

As far as I was concerned, a request like that from John Dale was the same as an order, and at about half past six I was wheeling my bike out of Churchgates Cottage. I cycled up the south slope of Wenningborough, pushing the bike through the soft darkness when the road got steep, to the shooters' hut on the edge of the moorland where the Home Guard were on duty every night now that the emergency was on. The hut was just a dark shape against the sky. The limestone outcrops loomed up whitely all around. On the road stood the old Austin from the farm – the one that had only the driver's seat left in it – that took the 'first house' up there for Home Guard duty.

Half a dozen faces looked up at me suspiciously from mugs of tea. The hut was thick with cigarette smoke.

"John Dale hasn't been about for long enough," they told me.

"No, 'im and the Major both – they've give us up."

"We haven't had a parade or a drill since."

"Forgotten army, that's us."

But they didn't object to me being there. After a bit, they offered me a mug of tea and went on discussing motor-bikes. I was very quiet and just listened. People used to think in those days that I was quiet but that was quite wrong. In my own mind and to myself I was always talking. I think this was because I was never too certain of myself. But I could listen to others. I liked to watch faces; the extraordinary way faces move – mouths opening, eyebrows raising, lips going up and the lines of the mouth going down in glumness.

The door was flung open, someone fumbled with the blackout curtain, and Albert appeared full of excitement.

"They're there again – over yon way. The lights."

We all looked at him.

"What *you* doing 'ere, lad? Oo's not in Home Guard," Albert objected.

"Same place are they, Albert?"

"We'd best take a look."

Outside, it was so dark we could see nothing, but Albert told us we must look over to the north, down into Reed Valley.

We stared down in silence while the wind tugged at the grasses round our feet and the men breathed heavily and earnestly.

"There, there!" hissed Albert.

"Where?"

"Nothing there, man!"

"Nothing down there, anyway."

"The old Hall's down there."

We considered this. The old Hall was a deserted mansion on the hillside.

"Look, Albert," said Len, "there's no lights tonight whatever you've seen other nights."

"What about", asked someone, "the man with the black face?"

Albert shook his head. "Haven't seen him again."

"Who's the man with the black face?" I asked.

I felt that this was another mystery that worried them

but it was so dreadful that they were doubtful about speaking of it to anyone outside their group.

"Was only Albert thought he saw a feller on the fells night or so ago with his face all blackened."

"I *did* see him."

"No law against that," I said.

They regarded this comment with resentment.

"Aye, and no law for it neither."

"And why should he black his face?"

I asked about the parachutist but all Albert would say was that he had seen him come down on to Wenningborough Edge and then the vehicle coming along the track. And he would stand up in a court of law about that.

"There's something going on. This man with a black face – he could be signalling enemy planes."

But in the silence there was no sound of planes. Behind us, to the south over Manchester, we could see the beams of searchlights sweeping the skies, and the noise of ack-ack like a distant celestial typewriter.

"Better put it in the book," said Albert, and we went back into the hut, and in the report book was recorded: "Ack-ack to south at 9.30 p.m.," but after a long discussion they decided not to report the lights.

"If it were back end of year it could be the Morgans ploughing late."

"But it ent back end."

"And 'tis a bit late for bringing cows in for milking."

"Aye, and Morgans have marked cows with white paint to see 'em in dark."

They decided to brew another pot of tea. I slipped out into the blackness of Wenningborough Edge and found my bike. I didn't think any of them had seen anything – or nothing that couldn't be explained as country folk going about their affairs. It was the spy-fever again and things were likely to be imagined or misinterpreted under that influence. Besides, I knew very well that sometimes, especially late on a Saturday night, Albert and Len were likely to be not too sober when they went up to the shooters' hut. And Wenningborough at night was a place not exactly haunted but conscious of its long history. I believe such places have their own spirit, and people like Albert and Len could be sensitive to it. And why would Germany drop parachutists or employ spies in this remote part of the country? The convoys that trundled through the village now were all moving south-east, down to where the Germans were expected to invade, away from this quiet rural area with no military targets to be seized. All the Home Guard here could find to guard was Devil's Bridge and the local power-station.

Half an hour later I swept silently on my bicycle along the empty village street that was now bright with moonlight, and straight past a figure walking towards the Village Institute Hall. I startled whoever it was, and I heard her give a little cry as I passed. I braked sharply. It was the French girl.

"Sorry," I said. "Didn't mean to frighten you."

"Oh – it is the boy with the sheep."

"Yes." I hesitated, shyly, then I said, "I'm Colin North – I'm staying at Churchgates Cottage here."

"I am Marthe Durand," she said formally. "I am the niece of Miss Robson."

"Yes, I know – I mean I know you're her niece. We were expecting you to come soon ..."

"So – everybody talks about it?" She laughed rather ruefully. "I thought it would be so. But you were kind to me today."

"Well, I know what it's like being a stranger here."
"You are a stranger also? Yes. You do not speak like these other people."
"I've been here a while though, so they call me a local stranger."
She laughed when I explained it to her.
"Maybe they will call me a local stranger?"
"It takes time."
"And we have not very much of that, eh? This is the postbox?"
"Yes. Collection tomorrow morning."
"But there is no way of getting a stamp? My aunt did not have one."
"I've got one." I always carried a few in my wallet for letters home. "Just a local letter is it?"
"It is to go to Morecambe. This is not far?"
I was surprised she knew people at Morecambe.
"Know many people hereabouts?"
She dropped her letter into the box. "No. I have no friends here. I have my aunt, and I have one friend in London. That is all. My parents and my dog and my cousins and – they are all in France. And I may perhaps not see them again."
Her voice was sharp with emotion and she turned away and began to hurry along the street.
"Hi!" I called to her. "I'm sorry ... I didn't mean ..."
She didn't look back. "It is all right – it is all r-i-g-h-t..." and her hand waved at me. That was all.
Well, I thought resentfully, she wasn't the only one. I suddenly missed sharply the city and my friends and the busy streets and the danger. The last train north went by, a dark shadow through the tree tops beyond me. I wished I was on it. I hadn't wished that for a long time.

I put my bike away in the garden shed and went in through the back door of Churchgates Cottage. I realized it had become home to me. I knew its smells and the routine of the house, and the feel of its furniture and the atmosphere of its rooms. And my real home – it seemed to have dwindled and faded.

Miss Gwynne and her brother turned towards me as I came in. They had accepted me as part of their life, as I'd accepted them as part of mine.

"Did you go far, Colin?" asked Miss Gwynne.

I shook my head.

"I saw Miss Robson's niece outside. Her name's Marthe."

"What was she doing out at this time of night?"

"Posting a letter."

"I expect she was writing home," said Miss Gwynne comfortably.

"No. It was to Morecambe."

"Morecambe? Who does she know in Morecambe?"

9

But homesickness was still with me next morning, and it sent me up to Wenningborough Edge again with ropes and tackle to take my mind off things; and I know the exact date of that. It was May 29, 1940. It is still marked there on my map of the area. It was the day of my discovery.

I left my bike by the wall where the road ended and started walking over the grass towards the big outcrop of limestone where a few bushes crouched low from pockets of soil. I sat for a moment's rest on a boulder on that wind-restless moor, gazing down over the panorama of the Wenning Valley, a landscape that arranged itself gracefully into flowing ridges, flashing arcs of water, clusters of trees, with grey-stone villages raised on small hills, each with a spire pointing heavenwards. My eye began that day to appreciate the meaning that lay beneath this, to reconcile me with the loss of the city. I knew that I was sitting on top of about 1,600 million years of the earth's history, and my own history would be an infinitesimal addition to it.

A curlew swooped overhead and far down over the valley. It was such a clear day that I could see right across to the pale sands and the hint of blue sea. John Dale went there every Saturday night, to Morecambe – where

Marthe Durand sent her letter – to see a friend. He took me with him once, though that flat mud stretch and distant sea did not impress me after the sands and headlands of the north-east coast! But we all went to a café and had fish-and-chips. And then I wandered along looking at the amusements while John and his friend had a drink. It was a good day. But that was months ago and now John said you couldn't get near the beach because it was a defence area and there were barriers of barbed wire and soldiers on guard.

A formation of fighters, high and transparent, like tiny creatures in a pond, flashed across the sky. It was a strange time to be living.

I'd been sitting on the outcrop of rock, my legs dangling, when suddenly I was aware of a cold draught of air about my ankles, and the grasses at my feet stirred though there was no breeze. At first it didn't seem to me so unusual, and then I thought, That's funny. I jumped down and got on my hands and knees, trying to trace the source of the air. A cold breeze was coming from under the rock I'd been sitting on. In a frenzy, I tore up handfuls of turf and bracken and flung them behind me. In a few moments I'd cleared the entrance to a narrow opening underneath the rock.

Flat on my stomach, I crawled under the overhanging rock for about six yards, and then my lamp showed me for the first time – the first time anyone human had seen them – the pale-brown walls, the smooth sandy floor of *my* cave. I will not forget how I stood upright in it and felt its atmosphere about me and heard the deep-throated murmur of a stream running somewhere out of sight.

The sandy cave gave way to a short, steep passage that led to a cavern with a high roof, not a large cavern but large enough, with a deep stream flowing through it, and across the stream another wide, sandy area scattered with boulders. The roof there sloped down to the floor, but there was an opening, a narrow cleft in the rock-face behind a curtain of limestone, and when I dropped a stone down I could hear it rattle and rattle and then it seemed to fall silently until finally it landed with a distant thud far below. The stream entered from a low-roofed passage that could be followed back, but at the other side of the cavern the roof sloped right down to the surface of the water and the stream disappeared beneath it.

It was very important to me that my cave should lead somewhere, that either by following the stream or by venturing through that narrow cleft a way through to another section should be found. Recalling the information I had of the area, I felt certain that beneath the cave must lie the longer stretch of the Lower Wenningborough series of caverns, but I could not venture on that exploration alone. I was not so foolhardy as to attempt it.

I scrambled out again on to the emptiness of Wenningborough Edge. My hat, I remember thinking, I've discovered a new cave! My very own cave! And I began to dance around. I must have looked the nearest thing to a lunatic – a thin, solemn-faced lad wildly throwing himself about the empty hillside in a fine and penetrating rain. I was brought to an abrupt stop by a voice calling from further down the Edge.

"Feller! Hi, feller!"

John Dale was running towards me, his raincoat flapping out round him like wings.

"Hi, feller!" he exclaimed breathlessly as he reached me. "Feller! Thank God you were about. It's my dog Mavis – she's fell down that damn Witches' Pot and poor beast I can hear her yelp but I cannot get at her. Will you get down to farm and get help? Tell Albert and Len to come up here wi' ropes and ladders fast afore dark – aye and they'd best bring some lanterns ..."

I remember I listened to him in some puzzlement. What was he demanding all this for, when he was speaking to an experienced pot-holer? Then I realized that I'd never told anyone on the farm about my pot-holing in case they made fun of me. But I had my ropes coiled on my shoulder now, and my rope ladder and helmet in my hand. John Dale saw them suddenly.

"Here, but – you've got ropes and ... what you up to, feller? Here – bring them over here and let me get down."

"You'd never get down there and back up," I said. "I've been down Witches' Pot. There's a ledge about twenty-five feet down. I reckon Mavis'll be on that."

We ran over to Witches' Pot and he stood beside me while I weighed things up.

"Getting down to her's not difficult," I said to him. "But getting hold of her and getting her back won't be easy. One thing, she knows me well enough not to snap, so what we need is a sling to tie her in."

"A sling?" He looked round desperately. "Where the hell do we find a sling ...?"

"Your coat'll do. Now I'll take it with me and tie her in it and fasten the whole thing to a rope. When I shout to you, you start pulling her up. Now do it slowly and listen out for me in case I tell you to stop. We don't want her going into a spin and knocking against the rock wall. I'll be coming up the ladder at the same time and guiding her. So listen to what I tell you."

We were both crouching together on the edge of the Pot

and our eyes met and we both suddenly realized that for the first time I was giving orders to John Dale, and he was the inadequate one. I felt embarrassed. And I think he felt a bit put out.

"Aye, well. Right," he said, and then we both tried to forget that our positions had been reversed.

I got the ladder fastened to the tree that I normally used, and rigged up my own life-line from the same spot. Then I fastened the rope for Mavis on to a rock near by.

"Now mind", I said, "you pull her up by that. Don't let her drop, and do it slowly."

I tied his coat into a bundle and slung it on my back. I fixed the light on my helmet, and I swung myself on to the ladder.

"Here, feller – are you sure you'll be all right? Are you sure it's safe?" His face, peering down at me, was fretted with concern.

"Don't worry," I said. I tried to sound confident, which I wasn't really. I could get down there right enough, but could I persuade Mavis to let me get her in the sling? I got over the edge and started down.

There wasn't much space on that ledge, the water made an awful noise and soaked us both, and she was terrified. So I sat down beside her and talked to her and stroked her quite a while. Then when she was calmer I got the coat round her. I suppose she smelt John on it and she didn't struggle much. The journey back up was difficult. I had to hold my ladder with one hand and steady Mavis with the other. I had to go very slowly, otherwise we'd both have started swinging, and the strain on my arms and legs was tough. Halfway up I had to shout to John to stop pulling so I could rest, and I began to wonder if I'd the strength to make it. When we got to the top I just rolled on to the ground and lay there panting under the dripping trees.

When I had my breath back I sat up. "By," I said, "I'm glad that's over."

John Dale was crouched beside me, his arms round Mavis who was licking his face.

"Feller – you all right? Can you get up, lad?"

"Why not?"

"I'll tell you, feller, you did that like a hero. Never seen anything like it. You'll be useful to yourself with that talent."

"I've been down a lot of pots now, since I told you I'd climb the mountain."

"Well, I'm – I'm speechless! Never thought you had it in you. And I won't forget it. Anything you want, feller, any time – you ask me. And where did you come from? You come out of the earth like a ghost. You get about these fells like a good 'un. And you certainly got yourself in a mess down there. I'll tell you, feller, you want to be careful. Them caves – they're not good places. You wouldn't catch me down one. Death traps they are, for animals and men."

I'd never seen John Dale in such a state of emotion.

"Mind you, feller, I've every cause to be thankful to you and your pot-holing, and so's Mavis here, haven't you, old girl?"

It was when John said things like that, and when I saw his devotion to his old dog, that I felt especially his friend. And his admiration of my abilities – well that meant a lot to me.

I stood up. Below us was Reed River, the tributary of the Wenning, and on its far bank the old Hall, quiet among its trees.

"There's people down there!" I exclaimed.

"Aye. I've been watching them. Here –" He handed me his binoculars. I could see clearly a couple of men, one in uniform, and a Jeep in the drive of the old Hall.

"I wonder if they're the ones with lights the Home Guard saw ..."

John Dale glanced at me. "Find out any more about that?"

"I don't really know that they saw lights. But they did say they'd seen a man with his face blackened.

"A blackened face? They're dreaming!"

"Albert's certain he saw a parachutist coming down as well, you remember."

"Listening to too many rumours," he said quickly. "Right daft one is our Albert. Who'd want to drop parachutists up here?"

"But who *are* they down there?"

With a word to Mavis, John Dale turned away from the Edge towards the footpath. We began walking together to the road.

"Place seems to have been taken over by the Government. There's a notice outside saying Ministry of Defence and prohibiting access. All been done on the quiet. Nobody knows what's going on these days."

"What do you think it is?"

"Maybe a Government department moved up – or an army headquarters or something."

"Funny place for a headquarters, isn't it?"

"I tell you, feller, it's a damn funny place. Unless ..." he didn't finish that, though I waited for him to. "Ah well. Saturday night. I'm off to Morecambe for me fish-and-chips and a pint."

"That foreign girl," I said, "Miss Robson's niece ..."

"Marthe Durand?"

"Yes, well, she must have a friend in Morecambe. At least she was posting a letter to Morecambe yesterday."

"Might have been her aunt's letter."

I hadn't thought of that. "Probably was," I said. "She told me she only had one friend in England and she lived in London."

"That's so? Well, that's a fair distance, isn't it?"

Before we reached the road a clap of thunder sounded out over the sea and the rain slanted down heavily.

"Look, lad, you're soaked already and you'll catch yer death. We'd best get you home quick. Did you come on your bike?"

"I left it on the road."

"Well, I've got the Austin there so ... but wait a bit." He hesitated. "All this trouble with Mavis, I clean forgot. I meant to check the barn at Fourstones was locked up. We've got a bit of gear there still. You go on and get your bike stowed in the car and I'll not be a minute."

He went swiftly away into the rain, and I ran to the car at the end of the track, the old Austin from the farm that had no passenger seats in it. I got my bike into the back and sat on the floor, shivering. He wasn't long though, and I crouched on the jolting floor with Mavis as we drove back to the village. I was tired and my head was full of the cave and I wasn't thinking about anything else, except that at the back of my mind was the idea there was something I should take note of.

I think I was becoming imbued with the country habit of minding my neighbour's business, or maybe being infected by the growing atmosphere of doubt and suspicion.

"After all, she couldn't have a friend in Morecambe, could she?" I said.

"Who's that?"

"Marthe Durand."

He laughed. "Rare old nosy parker you're becoming, feller."

Once he said as he shifted gears, "I think the world of that old dog. That old Mavis, eh girl?"

And another time he said, "Looks like you've got this mountain taped, eh, feller? Might have something to put to you about that."

And as we reached the village, "How old are you now, feller?"

"Fifteen. Soon be sixteen." And already I'd discovered a cave and done a rescue! I sat basking in the glory of my success.

We reached the village, and suddenly John Dale slowed down and asked, "Now then. What's to do here?"

10

The village was full of soldiers. Two of them were digging up the signpost at the road junction and another two were heaving at the old milestone that could hardly be read it was so worn. By the Village Institute a lorry was parked and its driver leaned against its bonnet smoking a cigarette. A soldier on a ladder was painting out the "Wenning" above Wenning Post Office and Shop, and Mr Dobson, the owner, was watching with a kind of furious bewilderment on his face while an officer beside him tried to calm him down.

John Dale parked next to the lorry, and we both got out of the car. I was stiff and already beginning to shiver in my wet clothes, but I couldn't miss what was happening. Len and Albert were watching and we went over to them.

"And how's strangers hereabouts to know where the hell they've got to?" asked Albert.

"They won't," said the lorry driver. "That's the whole idea, yer plummy. Unless somebody tells them."

His strange dialect and manners made us all feel antagonistic, and Albert and Len sensed that here was a townsman trying to come it over the country folk.

"Nobody hereabout's likely to tell a stranger where he is ..."

"More likely to tell him where to go!" There was a ripple of laughter at John Dale's remark. He had saved village face by his wit. He stood looking humorously at the driver over his long nose. Mavis crouched at his feet. Then he pulled out a packet of cigarettes and offered the soldier one.

"Stationed at Lancaster?" he asked casually.

The soldier bent his head to light the cigarette at the match John Dale had struck.

"For my sins I am," he grunted.

"Not such a bad place. Thought you might be at the old Hall, up the Reed Valley. It's been taken over."

"Oh yes," said the soldier. "The army's moved in," but he didn't know what for.

"And when", asked John Dale, "is Jerry expected?"

The driver shrugged. "Pretty soon, way things are going, mate."

The signposts were piled into the lorry and Mr Gwynne appeared at the window of Churchgates Cottage with a gun in his hand. He looked, with his brown face and white hair and beard, very military and impressive.

"Who's the general?" asked the soldier with a wink.

"General Nuisance," retorted Len.

"He's a very important gentleman," put in Albert aggressively. "Lived all his life abroad ..."

"Daft to come back, then, wasn't he?" said the soldier. "Well. Looks as if we're off," and he climbed into the driver's seat.

"If the army's taken over old Reed Hall they've kept very quiet about it," said John Dale reflectively.

"What'll they want it for? Training?" I asked.

"Not enough land. And it's not research neither. Must be a headquarters. Maybe for the north-west. But they've got a headquarters in Manchester – doesn't make sense ..."

The lorry drove off and the villagers stood about talking in the quiet street. We had a sense of deprivation, a loss of identity, at the removal of signposts and place-names, and in the renewed quiet a sense of apprehension, of waiting for the enemy to arrive.

John Dale had turned to read the various notices on the Village Institute notice-board. "In Case of Invasion", "Blackout Regulations", "Emergency Powers Act", "Whist Drive and Dance in Aid of the Red Cross" and "Any lady interested in knitting socks for the merchant navy ...". Some kid had drawn a little match-stick man in chalk in a corner and printed beside it, Arrived. Absent-mindedly, John Dale took a bit of chalk out of his pocket and put a big cross through the match-stick man.

"John," I said impulsively, urged on by a fear I'd had in mind for some weeks, "if the Germans come – what will you do?"

In my own mind I'd seen three possibilities. I could fight them and die, I could go off and find my mother, or I could do as I was told – knuckle under. I was acutely conscious that it might seem easiest to do the latter, and I was afraid that I might do that, that I might prove a coward after all.

As soon as I'd asked the question, I regretted it. It seemed to me to reveal my fears.

"Would you kill yourself? Some people say they would kill themselves."

He gave me a long, straight look, a strange glint in his pale-blue eyes. "No sense in that. I'd have my duty to do, after all." Suddenly he laughed, shortly. "Aye. I'd have my duty to do. But the Major there – that's another story. Of course, he's a damned sight more important than me and you, if we can believe all he says. Tells me he's got cyanide put away to take if he's captured. They would torture him, you see, to give up his secrets." I thought I detected a mocking note in John Dale's voice, but I looked at him and he was perfectly serious. "What secrets do you suppose *they* would be, Colin?"

"Well," I said doubtfully, "you can't tell. But he knows who Hitler's supporters are."

The Major was an enemy of Germany, an outspoken one, and he frequently published articles in the local paper commenting on the progress of the war and attacking Germany bitterly. They were rousing articles that said, "We are paying for this war, we the people, and we will see it won. Let no one stand in our way!" I remember one of the Major's articles that said, "The followers of Hitler are among us, spreading the evil of his mind. They are here, in our own area. I know them. I will seek them out." That increased uneasiness in the village and everybody became suspicious of everybody else.

"Mebbe," said John, but not as though he believed it. "And how long you going stand around here, feller? Till you get pneumonia? I'm off to have a clean up and go down to Morecambe. Be seeing you ... And, feller," he added, pausing for a moment, "I won't forget what you done for Mavis."

The old Austin roared off in the dusk. I went into Churchgates Cottage by the back door to get rid of my wet clothes in the kitchen. I could have a rub down there to warm me up again and my dressing-gown was kept hanging behind the door so that I could change into it straight away.

"That you, Colin?"

Miss Gwynne came along the passage.

"Is the blackout up?" she asked anxiously putting her head round the door. "Oh good. When you're ready come in and have some hot tea."

In the parlour – and for once I was glad of the heat – I drank tea and ate a hot sausage sandwich and watched while Mr Gwynne cleaned and polished a curving sword that had always hung on the wall and that he said was from Malaya. On the floor beside him was his hunting gun that had also been on the wall. It was a bizarre sight in that comfortable parlour. He was getting prepared, he told me, for invasion. He would go down fighting if any Germans came in his direction. That hunting gun, he said, had shot two tigers in Malaya – man-eaters. One of them had picked up a Chinese shop-keeper on the road out of Kuala Lumpur and the poor fellow was never seen again. The whole street had watched it happen. Not a thing they could do. They could see his face looking at them and yelling as he was carried off. Had to kill the brute. Trouble was he had "no blasted ammo" for the gun now.

I wasn't listening really, except to wonder why he was always coming out with those pointless stories. That day I'd discovered a cave and I'd done my first rescue. I was elated. I spread my map on the table and carefully marked the position of my cave and put the name beside it – "North's Discovery" – and in the margin I wrote: "Found by Colin North at four p.m. on Saturday, May 29th, 1940." I looked at it with an enormous sense of satisfaction. In my mind I was already back in the cave, going over it, wondering how I should begin to explore it. It would have to be upstream through the passage, I decided. I couldn't risk that narrow cleft without help and no one would dare swim underwater with the stream as you couldn't know whether there would be a chance to re-surface.

This was my first claim to fame. It was to go on to maps of the area, ultimately, and it was to have its own renown and history – a tragic one that I had no inkling of then. I know that since then a great deal has been said, especially in the newspapers, about the sinister atmosphere and reputation of North's Discovery, and it has been compared with Henne Morte, but it never had such an atmosphere. The evil that came to it was brought by man.

Miss Gwynne's quiet, calm voice broke in on my thoughts.

"We had a meeting tonight," she said. Well, they were always having meetings, I thought. What was special about this one? I yawned, suddenly overcome with weariness.

"Think I'll go to bed," I said.

"They won't be ringing the church bells any more," she added. There was a note of urgency in her voice I'd never heard before.

"Why not?"

"They're only to be rung to give warning of an invasion."

The familiar cold feeling crept over me.

"Wish I'd kept some damned ammo," said Mr Gwynne gruffly.

"We're to have a talk – next week," Miss Gwynne's voice went on, quite calm, with just that hint of unease. "Someone is coming to give us advice about what we do if the Germans invade. I've got posters to put up in the villages all through the valley."

I folded up my map.

"I'll help you put them out," I said.

"No, no, Colin. You've enough to do on the farm. And Marthe Durand – you know, Miss Robson's niece – such a nice girl – she said she would help. And I wondered – would you lend her your bike, Colin? Would you mind?"

"It's a man's bike," I objected.

"She'll be wearing slacks." Miss Gwynne hesitated. Then she sighed. Her smooth, pale brow wrinkled. "I suppose she could go by bus, but she can't get to outlying places that way."

"She can have the bike," I said. After all, it was work of national importance.

"That's good of you, Colin. I wonder – could she borrow your map as well? She doesn't know the area ..."

"I could borrow one of John Dale's – he's got a lot. Saw them in his cottage." I couldn't lend mine – it had North's Discovery marked on it.

"Are you sure?" She sounded puzzled, and I thought to myself it was a bit odd. After all, he knew the area like the back of his hand.

"I'll ask him tomorrow."

I went up to bed early – I was dog-tired – creeping up the dark stairs with an unlighted candle so that I could pull the blackout curtains before I lit it. The street outside was filled with a pale glow from a moon that was mostly hidden by clouds. In the field opposite was the pill-box that had recently been built, though, as Miss Gwynne pointed out, they'd built it wrongly and anyone firing a gun from it would hit the church. I was closing the curtains when I saw something move in the shadows by the Village Institute just along the street. There was somebody standing there. I watched, just full of idle curiosity, and whoever it was moved from the shadows. She was just opposite my window. I was fairly sure it was Marthe Durand.

For a moment she paused beside the notice-board of the Institute, then she walked on again towards the corner, all alone.

11

There was a definite gloom over the village the next day, a definite increase in the sense of suspicion and vulnerability that the removing of the signposts had brought about.

"They even dug up them white stones old Bob Parker had laid out at station to show the name," said Len. "That's sacrilege. I told Bob that. Sacrilege."

"Aye, 'tis bad enough," said Albert. "They're not doing all this for nothing. Something's coming. But what I'd like to know is – 'oo were them soldiers what did it?"

"'Oo were them soldiers? They were soldiers."

"Aye, but 'oo's? They could be Germans – sowing disruption already. That driver had a right queer way of talking."

This was an entirely novel idea and it silenced all of us. Albert was pleased at the result. "Did anybody ask for his identification? No! We just let 'em cart away what they wanted. How do we know that that parachutist I saw coming down didn't organize all that?"

But Albert bringing in his parachutist didn't help the argument. We were all more than a little doubtful about that parachutist. There was an idea about that Albert wasn't quite right in the head on that subject.

John Dale was full of beans. Just as if he'd got some good

news. Dashing all over the place, he was. He came suddenly into the shant where we were having our midday meal, standing in the doorway against the light like a big black shadow.

"Now then, how long will you all be sitting in here on your backsides? Like a mothers' meeting you are."

The men looked up at him, disgruntled.

"Give over, John. We'm entitled to our baggin."

John Dale wiped a hand across his face and relaxed, leaning against the wall. "Aye well, maybe."

"Hast had thee dinner?"

"I ate in fields – Major's back."

"That'll be trouble."

"He wants that old beech at far end of lawn took down. Says it's dangerous."

"That old beech?" Albert expressed the utmost disbelief. "He's off his rocker!"

"Anyway, Len, you come and give a hand when you're ready. And, Albert, take Big Horse down to smithy. She's thrown a shoe. Rest on you can start whitewashing shippons. Best get that done while weather lasts. And when you've finished, Colin, get over to shed. There's a fair bit of rubbish to be got rid on, and the fire'll have to be out afore dark."

John Dale left and the men exchanged glances.

"Do hisself an injury," said Albert, his mouth full of bread and cheese.

"In too much of a bloody hurry."

"Well, there's a war on," I objected.

"Oh aye. Telling everybody their business. *You* wouldn't notice, of course. Never has a cross word for you ..."

John Dale was waiting in the shed, among the piles of old wooden crates, bits of sacking and empty bags.

"This lot – get rid of it, and there's a pile of hedge-clippings in yard. Mind you don't set fire to theeself."

"How's Mavis?"

"Fine, feller, just fine!"

"John," I said, "can I borrow one of your maps?"

"One of my maps? What for?"

"For Marthe Durand."

"Yon foreign wench? What's she want a map for?"

I explained about the notices and collecting information. It was a while before he replied, then he said,

"Well, these days I'm not that happy about handing maps out to foreigners."

"But the French ..."

"I know, I know. Our allies. We hope. All right, feller. Come along to my place tonight after work."

I went to get Connie yoked up, "t'owd 'un" as she was called, the old brown-and-grey pony that had been born in Canada and had served in the First World War. When I went to her stable she nuzzled her old nose against my jacket, and I gave her sugar and yoked her up.

We carted the rubbish out to the field above the road, and I sprinkled it with oil from the tractor and got a good blaze going. Connie didn't like the fire and smoke and indicated she wanted to go, so I unyoked her and she ambled away. The flames shot twenty feet into the air and the acrid smoke billowed across the grass. I kept it under control with a long pike. I had some potatoes from the store in my pockets. When the flames died a bit, I would roast them. The burning timber fell with a crash, the flames leaped higher and the breeze trailed the smoke right across the field and over my face and I coughed and spluttered.

Then through my smarting eyes I saw a strange figure in the smoke, moving towards me, a tall man with a big hump on his back and a long, thin pole over his shoulder.

12

I stood quite still. I was sure it was a paratrooper dropped by the Germans, but as he cleared the smoke I saw it was a British soldier – at least he wore British uniform – and he was carrying a knapsack radio from which came bleeping noises and a tall, fishpole aerial.

"Hello, kid," he said. I didn't answer. I wanted to be sure he was British. I gripped the pike firmly.

"You deaf, then?"

"No."

"Don't act like you were, then. You live here?"

I nodded.

"You've got a bloody big blaze going, haven't you? Have you ever thought it could be dangerous?"

"It's under control. And you're trespassing."

"I am? That's a joke. Listen, kid, anybody you know around here is a radio ham?"

"A what?"

"A radio ham. Got his own transmitting equipment – you know."

"The Government took them all in."

"But somebody mightn't have handed his in, eh? What about it?"

"Wouldn't be any of your business, anyway."

"Now look, kid, you get cheeky and I'll do you."

He paused, looking round the field and towards the farm.

"We've been picking up signals from a strange station. Could be innocent, could be not. Now then?"

"You mean a spy?"

"Maybe."

"You from the set-up at the old Hall?"

"Never mind that ..."

"Well, there's no transmitter here – not that I know of."

He hesitated, looking round the farm again.

"Keep your eyes open, then, eh?"

"All right. I will."

He turned to go and I saw an army Jeep parked on the road below.

"Hi – mister!" I shouted. "What do I do if I see anything suspicious?"

"Tell the local bobby!"

I watched him walk down to the Jeep, and the Jeep moved off along the road.

He was certainly a British soldier, not a German in disguise. So he must have been picking up signals from near the village. But who would be using a transmitter there? And could it be a spy? In that small village? I thought about Albert's man with the blackened face, the mysterious lights, the parachutist. Maybe there *was* something in it. Maybe something *was* going on. As the fire died down and the ashes glowed red, the potatoes I put in were baked. I raked one out and sat on my haunches eating it. A bird was singing high up above me and the cattle stood in the water-meadows like great blocks of granite. It didn't seem possible that there could be a war and that there might be enemy agents already at work in Wenning.

And who could they be? Nobody I knew – and I knew most people. Maybe I should have a word with John Dale and see what he thought.

I looked up from the fire and saw Marthe walking along the footpath at the end of the field by the plantation. She walked slowly, thoughtfully, and her shoulders drooped. I hesitated for a while, then, taking courage, I stood up and shouted, "Hi! Hello!" I couldn't bring myself to use her name – but she heard, turned, saw me, then walked slowly across.

She stood looking down at me, a sad, quizzical smile on her face. She had a narrow, beautiful face with high cheekbones.

"It is not hot enough for you, Colin? You need fire also?"

She made me feel a lot younger and a lot more foolish than herself. I squatted there, glaring into the fire, the remains of the potato in my hand suddenly losing all savour.

She didn't seem to notice my reaction, though. She stood there looking towards the river and then at the train, the 5.05 south, as it trundled over the viaduct.

"Nearly time to pack up work," I said, and began to rake out the fire. There were still two potatoes left, nicely done. I hesitated over them, then raked them out. *She* wouldn't eat potatoes with me. "I am worried for France," she said suddenly. "The news is very bad."

I couldn't think what to say. I knew that she felt lonely and afraid, as I had done.

And then she said fiercely, "If I could only go south I would offer my services to de Gaulle. Today I try to join your W.V.S., isn't it? After a long time they say I can be attached to first aid, but I will have no uniform. Also I can be a helper at the school. What is a helper, I wonder?"

Then she looked down at me and laughed, and knelt beside me.

"Those potatoes you have cooked?"

"Want one?"

We sat eating in a friendly silence.

"Not bad, are they?" I asked.

"Very good." And then, "Colin, what do you do with yourself here? When not working?"

"Well, there's the pictures in Lancaster ... " I felt myself blushing. Maybe she would think I was going to ask her to come with me. Maybe I would at that!

"Nothing else?"

"There's the dances and whist drives. And there's a sort of concert at Christmas, the church ... "

The smoke swirled round us, enclosing us in a small private world. She attracted me strongly even though I'd only spoken to her a couple of times. Like Wenningborough, she was remote and strange and beautiful, and like me she was displaced and lonely.

"What I like doing best ... "

"What is that?"

"Exploring the caves in the mountain – that mountain."

"There are caves there?" She glanced round at Wenningborough.

"Lots." I shuffled a bit closer. "You know what? I've discovered a cave – a new cave. Nobody's seen it before..." The sense of intimacy between us encouraged this confidence. "And I haven't told anybody yet ... "

We were so close the cuff of her sleeve brushed my hand. Her coat was made of an unusual smooth green cloth. I looked up at her face. But she wasn't looking at me. She was looking at the fire with a slight frown of concentration.

I'd never known anybody before who wasn't English, except for a Chinese who had a laundry in the street next to us at home and that was different – he spoke hardly any English.

"Colin – would you take me sometime – up there? And would you show me this countryside?"

"I'd like to – but you'll need a bike."

"I think that will be all right."

"Well I don't know about that. Bikes aren't easily come by these days ... "

"There is one in my aunt's shed. Maybe it is not good. Maybe you would look at it for me."

"It'll be a pleasure. Anyway, Miss Gwynne said you wanted to borrow my bike to give out leaflets about the meeting. Do you want it for tomorrow?"

"Tomorrow – yes, tomorrow might do. But can you tell me, Colin, where is this Cramforth?"

"Cramforth? Nowhere round here as far as I know. There's a Carnforth."

"Carnforth, is it?" She took a letter out of her pocket and glanced quickly at it. It seemed to be a kind of list. "Yes, maybe it is Carnforth. There is a railway station there?"

"That's right. It's not far. Road's a bit winding but on a bike ... "

"I could get there?"

"Course. Want to catch a train, or something?"

"No. I am just interested in places."

"Well, I'll borrow a map for you – I'll bring it over with the bike. How about tonight?"

"Yes. All right."

I wanted to put out a gentle hand and touch her face and yet I didn't dare in case our intimacy was suddenly lost. She seemed quite unaware of my feelings, more interested in what I was saying than who was saying it. The moment had gone and my courage had failed me.

"How d'you get over here – from France – Paris, I mean?" I stumbled over the unfamiliar ideas.

"How do you think? By train and boat." The bitterness returned, and with it abruptness. "It was all legal. I was questioned – interrogated. They make sure of me."

"I didn't mean that!"

She stared.

"I didn't mean ... well ... "

"I sailed from Le Havre. There were minefields and German planes ... we landed in England in the early morning and it was all – how is it? Misty? And I did not know where I was. And England seemed very cold and dark. But safe. Somebody gave me a cup of tea. How I hate tea!"

I think that was the most astounding thing anybody had ever said to me. Hate tea? But what did she drink? Before I put that question a long convoy of tanks and lorries passed slowly along the road below us, and the soldiers shouted and waved – at her. She watched them with a slight smile. Then she turned to me.

"They are Canadians, eh? I think that is the Canadian uniform, and those voices ... They would come from Glasgow, I suppose. Going south."

I could have told her that some convoys and lorries did come this way from Glasgow, but I didn't.

"And where do they go to? Poor young men, to their deaths some of them – maybe most of them."

I chose that moment to put my foot in it. "We don't talk about troop movements. It's best not to. You never know who's listening."

She turned to me sharply, a small frown between her eyebrows.

"Well, you have to be careful ... "

She suddenly flared at me. "What are you accusing me of? Do you know what it is to have your country overrun by Germans? Do you know what it is to have left your parents in that country? No! You know nothing!"

She had stood up. Now she turned and began to walk swiftly and angrily away. She passed John Dale who was coming towards me and he nodded and grinned rather foolishly and said, "How do?" And she didn't even look at him.

When he reached me he was grinning broadly.

"What hast been up to, feller, to make that wench angry? I shall have to watch you!"

"Oh – shut up!" I retorted, raking at the fire.

"Aye well. You'll have to learn to be careful with wenches, feller. Now where's t'owld horse? Has she been settled down? And why hast not got that fire damped down?"

He walked back with me to the farm.

"Major's straightway had an accident, and we're all set by the ears. Aye. He got in way of that tree we were felling. I told him to stand on t'other side. Very stubborn man is our Major." There was a note of cynicism in his voice and eyes as he spoke. "I pulled him out of way, but he caught it on his leg. He'll be laid up a day or two. Funny feller, the Major.

He realized I was not saying anything.

"What's up wi' you, feller? That wench upset you?"

Well, she had. And I was brooding over what she'd said, but I couldn't tell him that. Quickly I told him about the soldier with the transmitter.

"He said he was picking up signals in this village? Must have been kidding yer, feller."

"There could be a spy here like anywhere else."

"A spy here? And what would he spy on here? We've a prisoner-of-war camp and some army down in Lancaster. That'd occupy a lot of his time."

"All the same ... "

"You know, feller," he said in disgust, "it makes you wonder how the hell we'll beat Jerry with soldiers wasting their time and equipment like that. They should all be down in south-east where invasion'll come."

We'd reached the farm and stopped at the farmyard.

"Now you wanted a map, didn't you? Hang on half a second and we'll walk round to my place ... "

But a voice, loud and deep and commanding, suddenly shouted, "Hi! Dale!"

It was the Major, sitting in his car with someone else at the wheel. His face glared at us through the open window.

"Hi! Dale!"

"Thought we were shot of him for a bit," muttered John. Then, "Coming, sir!" he called. He took a key from his pocket and handed it to me. "Look, feller, there's the key to my place. If I don't catch up with you, the maps is on the bookshelves to the left of the fireplace. Just leave key on mantelpiece."

John Dale lived alone in a tiny lodge at the gate of the Major's estate. It was a funny little place, very elaborate, like a Swiss chalet outside, and inside very plain and masculine. All his books and maps were together in the bookcases on either side of the fireplace. He had two or three maps of our area, and I wondered if it mattered which I took. He hadn't said anything. The first I pulled out was a very large scale map, and on it a number of places were marked with black circles in ink. There was one circle right over the Major's farm, and that seemed very odd. Thoughtfully, I folded it up and replaced it, and as I pulled out another, smaller-scale map, a booklet dropped on to the floor and a long strip photograph fell open like a pack of cards and hung dangling, one end caught among the books. I began quickly to re-fold the photographs until I saw they formed a panoramic view of the north-west coastline near us. It was fascinating. I could recognize lots of towns and villages, and I could pick out the hills in the background, especially Wenningborough. Thoughtfully, I re-folded it and put it back, then I stooped down and picked up the booklet. It had fallen open, face downward, and the front cover had printed on it "The Countryman's Diary, 1939". But as I turned it over to shut it, I saw pages of diagrams and print. One title caught my eye: "Improvised Bombs: For outdoor booby traps you must aim to kill by splinters not by blast. A cocoa tin filled with gelignite fitted inside a biscuit tin is easily assembled. Auxiunit packing is O.K. for gelignite ... "

I was aware that somebody was behind me and I swung round. John Dale was standing in the doorway watching me, and for a few seconds I felt a hard, cold hatred emanating from him. I was suddenly afraid. I didn't speak – I couldn't. He came swiftly towards me, menacingly, I thought, and I shrank back, the booklet dropping from my hand. But he simply took one of the maps from the shelf.

"Come on, feller. What you up to? I said left-hand side."

"I just couldn't find a small-scale map," I stammered.

"Well, it doesn't matter with wenches. They generally try to read maps upside down."

It was his old joking way, but I felt his voice was hard

underneath and there was no humour in his eyes, only a cold calculation. I felt it on my back as I walked away, leaving him standing there with Mavis beside him and that booklet still on the carpet behind him.

It was difficult for me to accept the suspicions that were in my mind. He'd been a good friend to me. But surely they pointed one way – the maps, the photograph, the booklet? "How could anybody be a spy?" I'd asked him once. Because they thought they were right, he'd said. Could it be as simple as that?

13

I got back to Churchgates Cottage, washed and changed and went into the parlour for my tea, my mind still on John Dale. I wasn't sure about John any longer – I wasn't sure what his friendship meant, what strains it would bear. If my suspicions about him were right, he'd been taking me for a fool all this time.

Miss Gwynne was sitting in the parlour with her hat on, a notebook on her knee and a parcel wrapped in brown paper at her feet. All this, combined with a worried frown on her face, indicated that something disturbing had happened, but I was so preoccupied with my own thoughts I hardly noticed and sat down at the table to eat without a word.

After a while Miss Gwynne asked, "Did you take your bike to Marthe?"

She couldn't have said a worse thing.

"Not yet."

She hesitated, then added gently, "I think you should, Colin. I'm sure that meeting is important and the posters must go out."

"Well Marthe Durand's not *that* interested," I burst out.

"Oh, I'm sure she is, Colin. What makes you think … ?"

"All right, all right. I'll go after tea."

There was another pause.

"I'm sure she'll take good care of it."

I said nothing and her brother said nothing. He looked like an expensive brocade eiderdown propped up in a chair. Then Miss Gwynne said,

"Colin, would you bring in the tea-tray that's on the kitchen table?"

It struck me, as I went out, that there was something funny going on. She wouldn't usually have asked me to bring anything from the kitchen – she was always independent – and I saw another look pass between them. Well, I suppose I would have thought nothing of it, but the door of the parlour didn't quite latch behind me, so that I heard her say quietly,

"Bunny, I think Colin should be told."

I never could get over that ridiculous nickname. I wondered whether he'd ever looked like a rabbit.

"Well, I don't know, Emily. It is, after all, confidential, isn't it?"

"But I've told *you*, and *you* aren't supposed to know. And Colin's all right. We can trust him."

Bunny Gwynne cleared his throat.

"Emily, it would be a mistake," he said firmly.

I heard no more than that, but when I went back to the parlour I realized there was a strained atmosphere, and I felt I'd interrupted some important conversation. I began to be suspicious of them again – of their foreign mail and the phone calls Bunny Gwynne made to someone he called his stockbroker. I thought I'd do a bit of testing out and I told them about the soldier looking for a transmitter and asked if they knew anyone in the village who had one.

"The Major had," said Bunny Gwynne, munching a scone, his lips all glossy with the butter.

"He *said* he used to have, Bunny," said Miss Gwynne.

"I don't think he had one here. And he would have had a licence for it and have handed it in when the war started."

"Never know what *he's* up to," said Bunny Gwynne. "Anyway, must be signals from all sorts of places going out these days. Surprised at the army wasting time like that. During the last war, I had a bit of experience in that direction myself, and I tracked down a fellow in London sending information out by pigeon."

"What happened to him?" I asked.

"Shot him probably. Ate the pigeons, I expect. Dangerous game, spying."

He went on munching and she went on looking at him anxiously. What was the point of that story, I wondered? To put me off the scent? What were they up to? What was it Bunny Gwynne didn't want me to know about?

When I went out after tea to take my bike to Marthe, it was almost dark. By the telephone-box outside the post office I stopped. Someone was standing there and I though I knew who it was.

"I was just coming to see you," I said.

"Oh – Colin! I am so pleased – Colin, I have to phone my friend in London and I do not know how – can you help me?"

She seemed to have forgotten our quarrel. I had a torch with me that gave the regulation pin-point of light. I got through to the operator, gave the number and waited till the phone rang. A very crisp female voice said,

"Agnes Dove."

"Hold on please." I gave Marthe the phone and squeezed out of the box.

Marthe was only a dark shape in the booth, because there was no light inside, but as she moved restively I saw the moonlight gleam on her hair and then on her profile, pale against the pane of glass. She was older than me, about five years. I told myself that wasn't much. What was five years? I wanted very much to be her friend, her boy-friend if she'd let me, only she had that sudden temper that would send you right back into yourself. I didn't know how to play it with Marthe.

I leant against the booth, pressing my hand against the glass where I could see her face dimly outlined. The glass was cold and smooth, but I felt I was close to her that way. She'd turned to me when she was in trouble, hadn't she? *That* was something.

Gradually I became aware of her voice raised in anger or distress. I thought she was protesting at something. Then she burst open the door of the booth and said rather hysterically, "Colin, I have no more money – I must have more money ... "

I fished out some shillings and pence and handed them to her without speaking and without taking my eyes off her. The door closed behind her. I heard the money fall into the box. Then she started to talk again.

I didn't want her to think I was listening in. In fact, I didn't want to hear her conversation – honestly. So I walked a bit down the street.

I stood in the darkness looking up at the clouded sky, thinking. Thinking that the Germans might come, that my mother was a long way away. Thinking about John Dale and those photographs and the booklet, about the possible secret radio.

It occurred to me then that all this must be second time round for Marthe – she must have gone through all the fear and anxious days in France, all the heart-ache of leaving her family. And worse than me. After all, she didn't know what might happen to them.

I heard a noise behind and turned. Marthe was leaving the telephone-box, but instead of coming towards me, she was fairly stotting off along the road to Miss Robson's.

"Hi – hang on!" I shouted, and she turned. She seemed in a bit of a daze – as if she'd forgotten all about me.

"Colin – oh, I am sorry. I was thinking ... " She stopped suddenly and gave a sob and then a shiver.

"Marthe – what's the matter? What's wrong?" I put my hand on her arm and to my surprise she put her head on my shoulder and burst into tears.

I was absolutely overcome. I patted her shoulder and made encouraging noises.

"Please – I am sorry," she said, after a while. She dried her eyes.

"Anything I can do?"

"Have you ever regretted something very much? Something that seemed so fine once and then twisted into something – evil?" she sighed. "But never mind. I will do what has to be done. Colin – why were you touching the glass in the telephone-box like that when I was phoning?"

I stammered out that I didn't know I had been – just nothing else to do ... and I offered to see her home. "I'll not stay ... " I said.

"No, please. You must come in. You must show me how to ride your bike and show me on the map where I go to." She seemed quite frantic. "Please, do not think I am not grateful. Colin – whatever happens in the future, do not think that!"

A couple of hours later I was walking home through the dark village. I wasn't thinking about John Dale or the Gwynnes or spies or invasion. I was thinking about the trips we were going to make together, Marthe and me.

Especially to Carnforth. She had some kind of thing about Carnforth ...

The Gwynnes were both in bed and the fire was banked down and the oil lamp turned low in the parlour. It was very quiet. I whistled silently under my breath. I was going to light my candle at the fire when I saw that the bundle Miss Gwynne had had at her feet was on the table and opened. There were lots of leaflets inside. The black type of the top one came out at me ...

> What do I do ...
>
> if I hear news that Germans are trying
> to land or have landed?

I stopped whistling. The familiar cold feeling was there again.

> I remember that this is the moment to act
> like a soldier. I do *not* panic. I *stay put*. Our chaps will deal with them.

'Our chaps'? That was the forces and the Home Guard. And John Dale was in the Home Guard. Could he be trusted to deal with the invaders?

> Do not give the German anything. Do not
> tell him anything. Hide your food and
> bicycles ... Hide your maps. See that
> the enemy gets no petrol. If you have a
> car or a motor-bicycle immobilize it.

They were official leaflets issued by the Ministry of Information. I thought things must be very serious for the Government to put them out.

My hand was shaking slightly as I lit my candle and

turned out the lamp. I shivered in spite of the heat. I knew what panic could do, turning thousands of refugees on to the roads to be machine-gunned by enemy planes. I'd seen newsreels of air-raids in the Spanish Civil War and refugees shuffling through the high passes of the Pyrenees. I thought of my mother, alone and miles away. How could I get to her if the Germans invaded? I went quietly upstairs.

The wardrobe in my room, when it felt so inclined, had an uncanny habit of opening of its own accord, slowly and with a sad groan. It did that now and, startled, I twisted round. I was looking at a stranger. A lean, dark boy, almost a man, with straight shoulders and a tanned face who looked at me firmly and watchfully. It was me! In the mirror on the inside of the door. I suddenly realized I'd grown taller and older in the last months. I was no longer stooping and earnest and rather worried.

Well, I'd have to do something. Churchill said we all had to help. I'd do my bit by making sure if the Germans came here the secret agent they were counting on wouldn't be around to help. If it was John Dale – and I thought it was – well, even *he* would have to be got out of the way. I didn't know how I'd do it. But I *would* do it. I would make up my own list of suspects, my own Black List. And it would be a good idea to consider that Albert's man with the black face and his parachutist weren't things he'd dreamt up. Maybe more enemy agents had already been dropped.

14

The Germans, Albert declared, were devils. And if there were local folks in this area prepared to help them – *they* were devils an' all!

It was finishing time and we were all collected in the yard.

"Now then," objected Len, "tha can't say that. Our Liz's daughter married one on 'em – Hans, he was called, and I never met a nicer feller."

"Oh aye."

"I never met a nicer feller. Well, you met him, Albert. They come over here for a holiday 1938 – was he a decent feller?"

Albert had to grant that he was a decent fellow.

"Aye well, that's right," said Albert. "And as I mind it, he was less inclined to Hitler than John Dale was. Real old Hitler-lover was John in them days."

"That's enough of that talk." It was John, who had come upon us unexpectedly. "No man says that of me."

There was an uneasy silence.

"Ah, but, John, I were just recalling them arguments you had with that feller Hans – you thought Hitler was doing all right in them days."

"That was two years back. We've learnt different since."

We all felt the threat in his voice and nobody spoke.

Albert went on fiddling with his bike and Len shuffled his feet.

I didn't look at John Dale but I knew he was watching me.

"You've got an impressionable youngster here," said John. "Don't want ideas put into his head."

"Nobody's putting ideas in my head," I protested.

"There'd be plenty of room for en," commented Albert. "Anyways, they've picked up three of Mosley's lot at Morecambe, so police must have their suspicions."

"Dirty Nazis."

"Best behind bars."

"They could do a lot of damage at Morecambe," pronounced Albert, "flashing lights out to enemy submarines."

John Dale gave a loud, cynical laugh.

"Well," went on Albert after a disapproving silence, "there's fifth columnists all over and we can't be too careful. That's my belief."

"Like the men with blackened faces."

"Aye, like them. Them as nobody's proved to me don't exist. And *you* can be careful," he turned to me, "getting off with yon foreign wench. Oh aye, I saw yer together in phone-box last night. I saw yer. Look at his face!" yelped Albert, and they all grinned. "Aye, he writes her letters in some foreign tongue – and wench left one in phone-box. Here!"

He snatched a paper from his pocket and waved it about gleefully.

"I've written no letters."

"You haven't? Then who sent it to en? She left it in phone-box — look, you writ that, didn't you?"

I took it from him. It was a plain sheet of white paper

with some writing on it, done in block capitals but unreadable because it was obviously in code.

"How do you know it's hers?" I asked.

"It was in phone-box after she come out. I went in straight after to phone our Jane and paper were there. *And* I saw the two on you walking off together!"

"I'll give it to her," I said.

"Ah-ha!" cried Len. "That's an excuse for seeing wench again!"

"Now then," broke in John Dale, "hast got mowers ready? We'll start hay-making soon."

"Start hay?" The men were doubtful about that. It was a bit early in their opinion.

"Your opinion's not wanted," snapped John. And really that was that.

"Trouble with that feller, he can't bear to see us sat down for two minutes. He's got ants."

John didn't hear them for he'd already walked towards the house. Albert slowly followed, mounting his bike and wobbling over the cobbles of the yard and then through the gate, and then Len's motor-bike burst into a roar and he disappeared through the gate leaving a trail of smoke and noise.

I followed on foot. I hadn't so far to go. But at the gate John Dale stopped me.

"Now then, feller," he said, "don't let that lot worry you. If they're not teasing you, it'll be somebody else."

"I'm not worried." I spoke sharply and nervously. I wasn't sure what to do about John Dale. He fell into step beside me.

"Anyway, yon wench's too old for you."

"Is she?"

"Meks all the difference."

"Not to me."

"Sounds like tha's set on her."

"I'm not!"

There was no friendship between us now, only suspicion. I think we both knew it. He was looking guardedly at me and I was looking guardedly at him.

"If you must know, I was helping her to put a phone-call through to her friend in London last night."

"Oh aye. I remember she had a friend." He was very thoughtful. "And where does this bit of paper come into into it?"

"I'll ask Marthe tonight if it's hers."

"I don't want to interfere, feller, but do you mind if I have a look at that paper?"

"I'll see Marthe about it first," I said, stubbornly.

"Strikes me it could be important. Maybe the Major should have it."

"After I've seen Marthe."

"Suit yourself," he snapped, and walked away. I felt I'd won that round. No doubt he wanted that paper. It was obviously a message in code. It could be his. And what about his support for the Nazis that Len was talking about? It all tied up.

"Feller!" He was beside me again. I twisted round. "Feller. I've got something to say to you – something important."

"Go on, then."

"Not now. Can you meet me tonight, about six, outside the Fox?"

"The Fox?"

"That's it. And if you can keep quiet about it, I'd be obliged to you."

He was off before I could say anything. Was it a trap, I

wondered? But how could it be? The Fox was a public-enough place. What was he up to? Would he try to recruit *me* as an agent? Or was he fishing for information? I folded the piece of paper carefully and put it in my shirt pocket. *That* wasn't going out of my hands.

When I got home, neither Miss Gwynne nor her brother was in the parlour, which was the most unusual thing that had happened yet!

Suddenly impressed by the silence of the house, I went out into the kitchen to see if Mr Gwynne was there. And I saw them both through the kitchen window. They did not see me. They were standing under one of the apple trees, almost concealed from view, and they were burying something! As I watched, Miss Gwynne began shovelling earth into the hole and Mr Gwynne began to walk back to the house. I went quickly back to the parlour and sat down. I was so tense I jumped nervously when he came in.

"Ah, Colin!" he said, and went quickly across to his chair by the fire. "Cold evening."

He'd been out in the garden without an overcoat – an act of sheer madness for Bunny Gwynne! Now what were those two up to? I pretended not to notice anything. I was getting good at pretending.

I'd never been in the Fox before, and now I was there I stood nervous and sullen behind John Dale. I didn't trust him any more. I had to be on my guard.

I could now see from the inside what I had formerly only glimpsed from the window – the bar with the barrel at one end and a row of glasses behind, the long wooden table at right angles with a wooden settle behind it, a bare, wooden floor, a picture of sheep and a shepherd on the wall, and an ordinary electric light with a white globe on it. A working-man's bar without frills. A place to be with men. A country bar.

Ernie, the owner, was stout and had a pronounced limp and was a veteran of the First World War. He stood behind the bar in shirt-sleeves, leaning with one hand on the bar and the other clutching the shelf behind him, sideways on to the world.

When he saw me he said,

"Hookin' the fish, John?"

"Aye, we've a bit of business to talk over, Ernie. Thought you'd be quiet about now."

"Keep an eye on things while I'm down cellar." And Ernie descended.

He left John Dale with a pint before him and a glass of cider before me. John sat for a few moments looking thoughtfully into his beer. Then he took a long drink.

"Ah, I needed that. Now then, feller, you mind when you saved old Mavis I said I would have something to put to you? Are you interested?"

"I might be. Depends what it is."

"Well now, whether you are interested or not, feller, I must have your word that not a mention of this conversation gets beyond these four walls."

I was very suspicious of all this. I was sure it was a ruse on his part to cover himself. I kept thinking of his maps and photographs and his attempts to get that paper from me.

"If I don't know what it's about, how can I make a promise like that?"

We looked each other firmly in the eyes.

"You always could be an awkward bloke." He took another drink of beer. "Still, I don't think you'll object to keeping it a secret when I tell you. The Major wasn't keen on me approaching you, but considering the way things is going and everything that's happened, he came round to my way of thinking."

"The Major?"

"Not so fast, feller. No names, no pack drill. Now you know the Germans are going to invade any time. And between you and me and the gatepost, I don't know what'll stop them. So the Government have set up secret units – auxiliary units – all over the country to delay the invasion as much as possible. Aye, and to make sure there's sabotage after the invasion's completed. What you might call trying to win the defeat." He grinned at me. "What do you think?"

I was thinking a lot.

"That book in your house ... the photographs ... "

"So you *did* see them? Thought that's why you were walking two yards round me. What did you think? That I was a spy?"

"And the secret radio ... ?" I countered.

He took another drink, looking thoughtful. "Aye well, that's being gone into. But look here, feller, answer a straight question. Are you interested?"

"You bet."

"Understand – if the Germans occupy the country, you'll have to take to the hills as part of the resistance ... "

"The man with a blackened face!" I exclaimed – everything was dropping into place!

"Look, feller, you're not taking this seriously. And we haven't all night."

I looked at him then with what was curiosity and doubt rather than excitement. It did not seem to me credible that a serious adult like John Dale could be suggesting a secret organization that sounded childish and fictional.

"Do you understand what I'm saying?" John Dale asked sharply. "This is not a game, feller." It was almost as though he read my thoughts. "It's pretty certain the Germans will invade this summer. By then we could be living in the hills. Now look – it's no game. And it's top secret." He hesitated again, almost as though he was doubting the wisdom of speaking to me. His great, powerful, ugly face came nearer.

"See here, Colin, it's a great thing you've been chosen. It's because we know you're good at getting around the hills, and because a boy of your age, with a bicycle, can carry messages and not be taken too much notice of. But it's not a game, Colin." He finished his beer. "That map you saw shows the other auxiunits in the north-west. That's secret information, and you should never have seen it. You'll keep your mouth shut! I'd best make one thing clear. We all mean to keep the auxiunit secret, and we'll have our own ways of dealing with blabber-mouths." He paused thoughtfully as Ernie appeared from the cellar. "That's a fact, isn't it, Ernie."

And there was something about Ernie's jovial wink, the gesture of his hands as though he were wringing the neck of a chicken, that frightened me. He said, thoughtfully, "We could fake a fatal accident up on Wenningborough."

"All right, Ernie. No need to scare the lad too much."

"You don't need worry about me." My voice was gruff, and I cleared my throat.

"Happen you'll be all right, then, feller."

He lowered his voice so that even Ernie couldn't hear – and he didn't try!

"Couple of more things. What you saw in my house – you mustn't mention to anybody, not even other unit members."

I nodded. And I knew what was coming next. The paper Albert found in the phone-box. He would want it. It must belong to the unit. And if it didn't, then there *was* a German agent in the village. But not Marthe. It couldn't be Marthe. If Marthe was an agent and the unit got to know – wouldn't those determined men kill her?

"That piece of paper ... "

"I haven't got it on me," I said quickly – too quickly.

He relaxed.

"That's all right, feller. Thing is, that's the route, in code, for an escape plan through Liverpool to Dublin – if any of us need to get out. I don't know which damn fool left it about. But if I can rely on you to burn it and say no more ... "

I gave him my word. I was relieved – almost reassured. But not quite. Not quite. There was too much urgency in his voice.

"You'll get a message from me soon, feller. Be ready for it."

The street outside was like a dream world. The light hurt my eyes after the gloom of the Fox. Normal village life seemed like a shadow-play acted by puppets. The real life of the village was a secret one.

15

I'd promised to see Marthe that evening and fix up the old bike, otherwise, the way I felt, I'd have gone up to Wenningborough to explore North's Discovery and calm my mind.

It was a mild evening: the longer period of half-light already had a suggestion of summer in it. Marthe sat on the lawn and watched while I mended a puncture and tested the brakes. Miss Robson stood beside us, leaning on her sticks and talking about the people in the village and about newcomers to the village, mostly because for some reason Marthe wanted to know about newcomers and how long it was before the village accepted them. I didn't really listen. As I worked on the bike my thoughts were busy with the auxiunit and what it would be like to be part of it. At that time I was still thinking rather in terms of adventure. The real meaning of what was involved hadn't begun to get through to me. One thing I was relieved about and that was the explanation of the man with the blackened face and probably the lights that Albert had seen. It didn't mean spies, it must mean the unit. That only left the parachutist. Albert's parachutist. Well, Albert was Albert, and anything might look like a parachutist on a dark night out on Wenningborough – a trace of mist, a low-lying cloud, a hint of moonlight. But I wasn't completely convinced. Just as I wasn't completely convinced about that piece of paper John Dale said was the plan of their escape route. Yet I should have been convinced …

It was something Miss Robson said that brought my thoughts back – something about the Gwynnes being newcomers in a way.

"But they used to live here – they were born here, weren't they?" I asked.

"No. I don't think so. Their parents and grandparents lived and died here, but Emily and her brother were born in London and I remember they came here once or twice for holidays. That's all."

"So you didn't see them after that till they came back from the Far East?"

"No. They were quite strangers when they returned. But they soon settled in … "

"But how do you know they really are the Gwynnes?" I demanded.

"What an extraordinary thing to say! And about your own relatives! Who else would they be?" She looked at me as if I were in the last stages of insanity. But if no one really knew them – well, they might be just pretending to be the Gwynnes, and how did we know they'd been in the Far East all those years and not somewhere else? Maybe Germany?

Miss Robson hobbled away into the house. I think she was disgusted. Marthe and I sat on the lawn, rather uncomfortable, and she idly spun the wheel of the bike that lay beside her.

"It is a good bike I think?" she said, trying to make ordinary conversation.

"It'll do."

I was very tense. I had something to ask her, and I was afraid of the answer.

"This yours, Marthe?" I laid the paper before her. She didn't pick it up. She just sat, saying nothing and looking down at it.

"It was found in the telephone-box that night – after you phoned."

She shrugged. "It is not mine. It is some child's writing, isn't it? It does not mean anything."

Her voice sounded flat, uninterested, but I thought she seemed wary.

"Well, it was Albert at the farm who found it … "

"And he was spying on us? And saying unpleasant things about me, eh?" She was suddenly very angry, her eyes flashing.

"Yes, but Marthe … "

"And you listen to him – and you believe him, and let him make jokes … "

"Now listen, Marthe," I began, angrily, "you listen to me. I don't allow … " but I saw she *wasn't* listening, wasn't even looking at me.

A car had pulled up at the gate. A woman got out and saw us and raised her hand in salute. Then she leaned back into the car and brought out a brief-case and an attaché case.

"Is this your friend, Marthe?" asked Miss Robson, calling from the door. "I thought she was coming later in the week?"

I looked at Marthe, and for a moment I saw a look of sullen dislike on her face. But it went swiftly and she walked across the garden to open the gate. For a few moments the two women stood together talking, then they came towards me.

"Aunt, this is my friend, Agnes Dove. Agnes, this is Colin North."

I felt instantly antagonistic towards Agnes Dove. She wasn't especially smart or pretty. She was a bit older than Marthe, plain, her hair done in the tight roll round the head that was fashionable then, and with a kind of green felt, Robin Hood hat on top. She wore a green tweed suit and lisle stockings that were wrinkled round the ankles. She took no notice of me. But I knew straight away she would come between me and Marthe.

I picked up the paper that still lay on the grass.

"How are you settling down, Marthe?" she asked. She had a deep, mannish voice. I had an almost irresistible urge to mimic her, which I fought down for Marthe's sake.

That frown had appeared on Marthe's face, and the distant look in her eyes that I was coming to know.

"I'd better be going," I said.

"No – Colin. You stay for supper. Can he?" she asked her aunt.

"Yes, of course," said Miss Robson, but she didn't sound all that friendly.

I had my head down – gauche. I didn't stay where I wasn't wanted. "I've got things to do," I said bluntly.

I started to wheel the bike to the garden shed, but suddenly Marthe darted ahead of me, got *my* bike out of the shed and brought it to me. We stood there, the bikes between us. She looked anxiously into my face.

"Colin – I am sorry – I am afraid the trip we planned for tomorrow ... "

"That's all right. Plenty of time." I was bitterly disappointed, but I wouldn't let her know it. "Be seeing you ... "

I didn't look back till I got to the gate and turned to

shut it behind me. Marthe was standing there still, holding the bike and watching me, and Agnes Dove was also watching me – and Marthe – with keen interest.

I spent a restless night dreaming I was being chased over Wenningborough by Ernie and the Major and trying to dodge German troops, and Agnes Dove for some reason was watching the whole show with an interested smile. I was pleased when first light wakened me. The quiet of my bedroom was very peaceful. I tried to sort out my thoughts a bit. I had to get to the bottom of things or I *would* go mad. I'd cleared John Dale and the Major. That left the Gwynnes.

I got up and went out into the back garden and began to dig under the apple tree, quietly so as not to disturb the Gwynnes. About a foot down the spade touched metal. I unearthed a square, tin box. A biscuit tin. I was afraid to open it – it might be a bomb. But there was only one way to find out. I could feel the perspiration on my forehead as I prised off the lid. Inside there were some official looking documents – things to do with banks and shares, I thought, and several bundles of pound notes. I put the whole lot back quickly. I still didn't know what they were up to.

16

The news was getting worse all the time. We were waiting to hear that France had fallen, and we were afraid of what the future would bring. And so there was a big turn-out for the lecture on invasion. People came from miles around in the hope of hearing something that'd give them courage and hope. Maybe they expected to be told that invasion wouldn't happen even though Churchill had been reported as saying that it was possible that Liverpool might be captured by paratroopers.

The lecturer was the most illustrious stranger we'd had to talk to us, and therefore an object of curiosity in his own right. He was a retired Scottish colonel and entirely incomprehensible most of the time because of his dialect. The Major, who told us all afterwards that he had known the colonel as his junior in India (which might have been true), led him on to the platform in the schoolroom, limping still as a result of his last accident, and introduced him. I looked round the packed room at the intent faces, and I wondered who among those people were members of the auxiunit, and I wondered whether the colonel knew about the auxiunits or whether their existence was kept secret except to a few people high up. I saw John Dale and stared at him, hoping he might look and maybe give me the hint, the message he'd promised. But he didn't. I couldn't see

Marthe but Miss Gwynne was in the front row, small and upright, as though she hadn't buried anything in a biscuit tin in the back garden.

The colonel stood there with the old black stove that heated the room in winter in front of him and a picture of the Child Jesus kneeling in a flowery meadow with a halo round his head on the wall behind him, and a large cardboard Easter egg the infants had made in the corner.

So far as we could understand him, he explained that invasion, if it came, would start in the south-east and might not reach us for some months. He gave the impression that our part of the world was of the greatest insignificance, would be ignored until the last minute, and could offer little resistance. It would be a matter of doing what little we could to make things uncomfortable for the invaders.

It seemed to us that he recommended such things as strapping mattresses to the roofs of cars as protection against machine-gunning from the air, trip wires across roads to bring destruction to enemy motor-cycles, the use of long steel rods thrust into their tracks to disable tanks, and the flinging of a grenade or any other explosive into a car's open window by a man passing on a bicycle.

Crushed into the tiny infants' desks, the local farmers heard him out with an air of confident disbelief. I think they felt that he'd got the invasion plans all wrong, and in any case they would see first what Jerry got up to and then set him to rights as they did with most strangers.

In the middle of the talk, the door behind us squeaked open and we turned round to see who was the late-comer. In the doorway was the soldier with the radio on his back, as startled as we were to see him there, and the Major half rose from his chair, but John Dale, being nearest, quickly got up and went outside with him.

At question time the questions were rather perfunctory, especially since the answers could not be understood. Then Joe, the Air-Raid Warden, stood up and began insisting on the strategic nature of our area, and how we planned to hold it against all-comers. He kept on repeating 'against all-comers' and local loyalty supported him in a number of murmurs and hear-hears, in spite of what the ex-colonel might say. But what brought a hush to the proceedings was old Albert getting up and asking how the colonel could explain these 'fellers with blackened faces as were seen hereabouts at night'. The colonel was startled and most of us rather embarrassed. Old Albert was letting us down, but he kept going on about them – 'up in High Meadow' he'd seen them and 'under Devil's Bridge once' and round by the Hall. They didn't answer challenges and they disappeared real fast. Now who were they? Were they these here fifth columnists? And if he couldn't tell us, wasn't the ex-army bigwig just the feller who should be able to tell us insignificant folk in the north-west what was going on in their own territory? When other members of the Home Guard piped up to confirm what Albert was saying, P.C. Burton began to look interested, and the Major quickly stood up, closed the meeting and told the W.V.S. ladies to bring in the tea and biscuits.

The platform party collected round them people like Miss Gwynne and the local farmers, but a noisy group round Albert went on talking about 'these here men with blackened faces'.

I felt a bit sorry for Albert making a fool of himself when I knew what it was he had seen, but he didn't mention the parachutist.

John Dale hadn't reappeared and the Major limped out

of the hall also. I went over to Miss Robson to ask about Marthe, but she said very coldly that Marthe was entertaining her friend from London. I could see Miss Robson hadn't got over my remark about the Gwynnes. There wasn't much point in hanging about.

I had to squeeze past the soldier, the Major and John Dale all standing in the entrance porch in a huddle.

I didn't speak to them, but John Dale followed me outside.

"Feller," he said. "Got a minute?"

I stood still – waiting.

"Feller – the shant, tonight, ten o'clock."

He said it quietly and then he went back to the Major. I kept my face expressionless and walked on down the street.

17

At ten o'clock I was waiting in the moonlight beside the shant for John Dale. I was shivering slightly, not from cold but from nervousness. The farmyard was stark black and white, and far off among the trees I could see the dark outline of Higham House.

John Dale emerged from the shadows. I mean he 'emerged'. I didn't see or hear him coming – he was suddenly just there beside me. That was my first experience of the auxiunit's special skills.

"Ready then, feller?" he asked quietly.

"I'm ready".

"Remember, feller, in the darkness keep below the skyline, stick to shadows and move slowly. If you move slowly in shadow, you won't be seen. Now come on."

We didn't go far – only to the cellar beneath the old farmhouse. The house was used for storage and as long as I'd been there the door into the cellar had never been opened. There was a conviction among the farmhands that the cellar was unsafe and that a body was rotting inside. At least, that's what they told me. I don't say I believed them, but I'd never been tempted to explore. Now John Dale pushed open the door which moved silently on well-oiled hinges. We were in a curtained-off entrance. When the door was closed again, we went through the blackout curtain into the cellar. I don't know what I expected – masks, I think, and secret passwords. Instead, by the light of an oil lamp standing on a trestle table, half a dozen men were engaged in various occupations. And, furthermore, I recognized them. Mr Williams, the local builder, who was a very taciturn man, was sitting on a big wooden crate cleaning a rifle. Ernie from the Fox, who gave me a wink and his fearful chicken-neck twisting routine, was sitting at the table. Willie Morgan, who had a badly-kept small-holding on Far Fell and was known to be a poacher, was standing beside him watching him twiddle with the knobs of a small wireless transmitter. Mr Miles, who was a teacher at the grammar school, a Methodist preacher and an amateur magician and fire-eater, and who had such a light of wild enthusiasm in his eyes at times that he worried me (I'd seen him at concerts in the village and he could disguise himself so swiftly and completely it was disconcerting), was handing round mugs of tea. The Major sat alone at the head of the table, bent over a map. They all wore Home Guard uniform and, among wisps of cigarette smoke, the lamp flung their bulky shadows across newly whitewashed walls. I felt small and insignificant among these men who were so obviously a close-knit group.

The Major looked up and regarded me with his unmoving stare. After a moment he nodded. "Sit down."

I followed John Dale and sat down on a box by the table. Mr Miles sympathetically thrust a mug of tea into my hand. It was scalding hot.

"Now then, John, does this boy know what the set-up is?"

"He does."

"Yes, but properly – does he know everything involved?

He can't opt out later by saying he didn't know this or that."

"Well, sir, I've told the feller we're secret and we'll be living as insurgent groups in the hills if the Germans come. He knows it'll be dangerous. Don't you, feller?"

I nodded.

"He looks too young to me – still, now you've introduced him – what kind of shot is he?"

"Not bad. Given the practice he's had. He'll soon be up to standard." John Dale put a reassuring hand on my shoulder, and I sullenly and deliberately drank some tea. The Major, in all the time I'd known him, had never addressed me directly, but always as 'he' through another person, as though I were some kind of idiot. I knew he hardly ever communicated with anybody except through John Dale, but I heard him direct orders occasionally to the other farm-workers – never to me. I began to resent it strongly. I suppose, thinking back, and odd though it must seem given the difference in our ages and position, the Major and I were mutually antagonistic – an instinctive response that I don't think either of us understood.

"Right," said the Major. "He'll have to sign the Official Secrets Act. Does he know what that means?"

"Means they'll shoot me if I break it," I blurted out, angrily.

The Major turned his protuberant eyes upon me, thoughtfully. I returned his stare, cheekily, I suppose.

"See to it, John," said the Major, "and give him the equipment."

He sat watching while I signed the form and while Mr Miles produced a uniform – the smallest they had, which yet fitted me rather as a barrage balloon might have done – and a pair of rubber-soled boots. Before me on the table was laid a rubber truncheon, a revolver, a Fairburn Commando dagger (which I still have) and .22 rifle. Finally they added a badge which indicated that I was now one of the 202 Battalion of the Home Guard.

I suppose my face showed some of the mounting consternation I was feeling. I was in the middle of a very serious organization.

"Cheer up, lad," said Mr Miles sympathetically, "there's worse to come."

"Aye, feller," said John Dale, "all these crates here ... "

But the Major interrupted quickly.

"What part do you see him playing?"

"Well, sir," said John Dale, "he's got his bike, and he knows the area, especially the fells, very well – he could act as messenger and scout. And he's a good pot-holer, so getting over obstacles and into places should be child's play to him."

The Major grunted, clearly indicating his doubts. For the first time, he spoke to me directly.

"You belong, for purposes of enemy interrogation, to the 202 Battalion Home Guard. Officially, there is no such Battalion and if captured by the Germans you are likely to be treated as a spy. Never forget that."

I glanced round. The other men were all listening intently. They hadn't moved from their places. They didn't even look at the Major, but they didn't miss a word. It seemed so strange to me. I'd never heard him spoken of with any respect, but now he was here, the leader, they gave him a great deal of respect.

"Your first aim must be to become as skilled as you can in the arts of self-defence and sabotage. If you are a weak link, you could betray all of us. When you are on patrol or exercises, you will wear dark trousers and pullover, and probably blacken your face. You will have to find some means of leaving and entering your home without discovery." He paused, his eyes still on my face. "Now this armament must look pretty fierce to you at present, but after a few training sessions, you'll know how to use it. The truncheon and dagger will enable you to kill the enemy silently at close quarters. This rifle – it has high-velocity bullets – can kill a man a mile away. We've grenades here," he waved his hand towards the casks, "time pencils, detonators and plastic explosive. If the enemy occupy this country, we are ready to sabotage them."

That shadowy scene of which I was now part, that group of quiet, tense men surrounded by lethal equipment and inspired by deep, unexpressed patriotism, has now to me the quality of an old photograph, crystallizing a past phase of existence. At the time, I felt only pride and some anxiety at being part of it, as well as a sense of disbelief that it was happening at all. There was relief as well, that came to me as I reflected that the transmitter the soldier had been looking for must be the auxiunit's and that Albert's men with blackened faces had nothing to do with a spy ring but were part of *our* defences against the enemy. I was smiling slightly, I think, in a kind of euphoria which was not allowed to last long.

"And the revolvers", said the local builder, "are for the collaborators."

"Collaborators?" My newly found sense of security wavered. "You *know* there are collaborators?"

"There are always collaborators," said the Major.

They all looked thoughtful. I saw that they weren't thinking what I was thinking.

"Well, John," said the Major briskly, "get him put through his paces. He'll take part in the exercise in a fortnight's time. Let's see if he's up to *that*!"

The drill was that at the end of a meeting we left individually at timed intervals. John Dale was always last and was responsible for seeing that the place was locked up. That night I had to leave with him, because I wasn't used to getting about invisibly like the others.

He was just going to put the oil lamp out when he paused, turning round to me, the lamp-light casting a yellow glow over his face.

"Feller, I meant to ask you. Did you burn that piece of paper Albert found?"

"I've still got it. Got it here." I fished it out of my shirt pocket.

"Well, now you're one of us, you'd better let me have that and we'll destroy it. It might fall into the hands of somebody who could break the code."

"Maybe you'd better tell me what it says again, though," I said. "I mean, I should know the route, shouldn't I?"

He held the paper over the glass shade of the lamp and it began to turn brown and shrivel.

"No, no, feller. It's not necessary yet. If we're invaded, everybody will be given that route to memorize." The paper flared up and he dropped it on the stone floor and ground it into black ash, thoughtfully. "That's the safest way," he murmured. "That's the safest way."

18

The clouds over Wenningborough were a threatening navy blue, but it had been fine when we left the village and below us the valley still smiled in the rays of the sun.

"This country," said Marthe, "it is – what is it I want to say? It changes so quickly. It is moody, isn't it?"

Like Marthe, I thought. Beautiful, but moody. We were sitting in the long grass and bracken on Wenningborough Edge, our bikes beside us. Restlessly she twisted a strand of grass between her fingers, while she looked around.

"Does it not frighten you, that mountain?"

Frighten me? Well, yes, it had frightened me, several times. That was part of the fascination.

"It frightens me. It is forbidding, I think. It seem to threaten."

"It's different when the sun's out." I tried to sound reassuring. I studied her face anxiously. I'd taken her to Carnforth the day before and I'd explained different ways of finding out where you were even without signposts. I mean, certain pubs were in certain villages; you couldn't miss the A6; and there were still parish histories in the churches that gave names and described places, and there were tombstones. Well, if you were beat, the gratings over drains still had the local council's names on them. Marthe thought it was all very clever, and she had a look at Carnforth station – crackers about stations, that girl! Agnes

Dove had gone and I was pleased about that, but I thought Marthe wasn't well. She looked pale and strained.

"You worried about France, Marthe?" I asked. "I mean – the news isn't so good, is it?"

She looked at me and I saw her eyes were bright with tears.

"Please do not talk about it!"

I tentatively put my hand on hers and she let it stay. Her hand was cold under mine and I felt she was trembling. We were living through tragic times and on the edge of destruction. She was already an exile, and in a few weeks we could both be dead, or prisoners, or I could be hiding up in the hills with the auxiunit. We could neither of us be certain we had any future. I think it was the first time I appreciated this, and that death wasn't necessarily glory.

"Anyway," I said in my usual thoughtless way, trying to be cheerful, "you were lucky to get out."

And characteristically she turned on me, snatching her hand away. "Lucky! You call it lucky! I leave my parents in Paris – That is lucky?"

"But I suppose your parents – I mean, they wanted you to come – they'll be relieved you're safe ... "

"Oh, yes. Like your mother. She want you to escape. My parents also. But it is not easy. Not in any way." She made a desperate gesture with her hands. "I do not think I will see my parents again. And France is a parent and you English do not understand that!"

I was going to protest at her ignorance of the British, but she added, quietly, "It means you are always – vulnerable, if you have people on the other side." There was such pain in her voice – pain I was just beginning to understand.

"But after the war – you'll go back?"

"After the war? What is that? What will there be then? After the war – that could be when the Germans have conquered *your* country." Her voice ran on without pause. "Have you ever thought how difficult it is for the people who send us away to safety and stay at home themselves? Do you not think that is the greatest courage?" she asked, and her words went right home.

"You'll see France again," I said in a voice that was uncontrollably gruff with emotion. "You'll see it. We'll win this war. We're not as unprepared as all that – and we don't give in." Almost I told her about the auxiunit. Almost. I didn't though, and afterwards I went hot and cold when I thought how near I was to giving away that secret on a surge of emotion.

"I think you are very kind," she said. "You try to make me happier, eh? And I will try to be happier. Who lives there?" She pointed towards Fourstones.

"Nobody. It's empty. It's Fourstones Farmhouse."

"That is Fourstones? Can we go and see it?"

"If you want to. Nothing much to see, mind, but I want to show you something else first."

"What?"

"It's my secret – something I discovered myself. My cave."

"Oh – caves! Yes, that is an English boy. France is falling, England will be next and you speak of caves – caves!"

I stood up. "All right," I said. I was deeply hurt. "It doesn't matter. We'll go back."

She took my hand quickly. "Sorry – I am sorry, Colin. Forgive me. You must forgive me. You must understand. I am not always so – so … " She fumbled for the word.

"Bloody-minded?" I suggested with a grin.

"What is that?" she asked startled.

"Never mind – forget it. It's not very polite."

She laughed then, and her face was changed entirely. She was moody, all right.

I just *had* to show her North's Discovery. I couldn't have left the place without doing that. But she wouldn't go inside.

"I could not, Colin. It would make me feel – in prison. I would die in there. I am sorry, Colin. I do not mean it is not exciting, but – I could not go in."

I turned away.

"Ah, Colin, I am sorry. I disappoint you. But I cannot help this. It is what I feel – inside. It is a fear. Look – we will go to that place Fourstones before we go back?"

From the front door of the farmhouse we looked down into Reed Valley and the old Hall on the opposite fell. Marthe regarded it silently. I took her into the farmhouse and showed her how the pot-holers brewed tea there. She listened politely, but she wasn't happy.

"It is very depressing. What happened to the owners?"

"I expect they went to another farm. Come on. It's going to rain."

I could see the mist coming down from the mountain's head, but I couldn't get her away. She had to walk round the old barn. You couldn't see inside – the door was padlocked and the windows boarded up. She was too inquisitive and I started to walk back towards the bikes. For the first time I noticed that the track from the road to the farm was rutted as though it had been recently used by a heavy vehicle. But that wasn't possible. I don't know why – I suddenly thought of Albert and his parachutist.

"I am sorry, Colin. I am too curious, ah?" she came breathlessly after me.

"The rain'll be on us soon," I said gruffly.

"You are angry?" I didn't say anything. I don't know why but I had a suspicion growing that she was using me for her own purposes and that there was no true friendship between us. It couldn't be so – what purpose could she have? But the doubt was there and depressed me. "Colin, tomorrow you come to my aunt's house for tea. I will show you photographs of my France and my home. Is that agreed?"

Well, that made a difference, and we swept on together ahead of the rain at a dizzy speed into the valley, shouting as we went. We swept on to the main road and then on again and down the steep hill into the village that lay crushed up against the mountainside. Then we stopped to get our breath back. We could see the mist groping towards us down the fellside and in advance of it the rain began to fall softly over us. Marthe turned up her face to it.

"Ah, that is so cool!" she exclaimed.

I think it was the last time I saw Marthe really happy. And I wasn't able to share that happiness with her, for I was thinking that for the next few weeks I wouldn't see much of her. I would be too busy training with the auxi-unit. And I couldn't explain that to her. I would have to lie and prevaricate and she would get angry ...

Suddenly she turned to me. "Colin, you remember that piece of paper – with writing on – that was in the phone-box?"

"What about it?"

"Have you got it?"

"I gave it to John Dale," I said, thoughtlessly.

"John Dale? That *farmer*?" Her grey eyes were wide and questioning.

"He's a good friend of mine."

"But why give it to *him*?"

I couldn't tell her why! "Well – he thought – he thought it shouldn't be just left lying about because it might be something private … "

She stared at me, a look I couldn't understand on her face. "So – *he* has it!"

"No, he hasn't. He burnt it."

She got back on her bike and began to ride into the village. I followed, mystified. And as we went there were more people than usual about in the gardens and on the pavements and at the shop, talking. But we took no notice and we both pulled up at Miss Robson's gate.

"That was all right, wasn't it?" I exclaimed, and then we both noticed Miss Robson, hobbling on her sticks up the garden path towards us, her face full of pity.

"Marthe, my dear Marthe – there's bad news, such bad news … "

"It is France!"

"Yes – France has fallen. It's just been on the news … "

Marthe didn't say anything out loud, but spoke to herself in a kind of mumble, "Now it has all ended and now it will all begin, and it will be so much more difficult."

I didn't understand her, and that's the truth.

"Marthe, we'll beat them yet," I said.

She shook her head and wheeled her bike down the garden path. I pedalled slowly round to Churchgates Cottage. I didn't think there would be any tea at Miss Robson's the next evening.

Miss Gwynne and her brother were sitting in the hot parlour having a cup of tea and a biscuit.

"Have you heard, Colin?"

"Miss Robson told me."

"Poor Marthe ... Well, now we're alone." She stuck out her chin in an unconscious movement of defiance and poured me some tea.

"They'll be over here in no time," said her brother. And that evening Churchill warned us on the wireless, "The whole fury and might of the enemy must now be turned on us."

The auxiunits were going to be necessary, I thought, and I began to look forward with anxious anticipation to my future as a resistance fighter.

19

During the next two weeks, by regular nightly application, I became – theoretically – a trained killer, a trained saboteur, a trained resistance fighter. I could get out of Churchgates Cottage at any hour without being observed, I learned to move at night and in daylight without being seen, I knew how to kill a man silently, how to make a Molotov cocktail or blow up a bridge. I was shown how the unit had mined bridges and certain main roads in the area which would be blown up if the enemy came. I mastered the series of signals and dead-letter boxes our auxiunit made use of to communicate with one another secretly. It became my duty, when an operation or a meeting was planned, to put out the signals for members, which involved leaving a coded message in the builder's "letter-box" – an empty baked-bean tin in a ditch beside Mr Miles' cottage – and in a thicket of broom on the common within sight of Far Fell smallholding.

It was a very exhausting time for me but not for the other auxiunit members, for they took turns each night in training me. And whatever training I did at night, I had to be out on the farm next day. Miss Gwynne began to think I was "outgrowing my strength" and she thought I should be off to see the doctor for a tonic.

In spite of the tiredness and in spite of feeling that I was still a beginner in things the others did so well, I began to have a sense of real pride that I was part of the auxiunit, part of a secret network in the village, one of a band of men who were really skilled and really dedicated to the defence of the country. Albert and Len seemed to me, like the other Home Guards, to be innocents in the ways of the world.

Gradually, as I worked with them, I got to know the members of the unit better and to appreciate their individual skills. You couldn't beat Willie Morgan as a shot, and Jimmy Miles was very clever at thinking up ambushes, but John Dale was really deadly when it came to striking a victim and killing him silently. Mind you, as I say, all this was theoretical. But it was still impressive. And they all had their individual grumbles. Jimmy Miles confided to me one evening that he was worried about the ammunition store being in the farmyard. He thought it might be discovered and anyway it was dangerous there – suppose it caught fire? Willie Morgan thought the letter-box system was useless. Why couldn't we just go and knock on each other's doors? I remember Ernie, the night he was explaining the intricacies of the transmitter to me, grumbling that the one he'd been issued never seemed to work, and if a message ever had to go out he'd probably have to use a carrier pigeon. At the time, I remember, that remark of his sowed another seed of suspicion in my mind. If that transmitter had never worked well, could it have been the one giving out the signals that soldier picked up? But I hadn't the time or the energy just then to think it out.

At the end of one week I know I was going about with red-rimmed eyes that were feverish through lack of sleep, but I was getting an impression also – and at the time I thought I was mistaken and it was due to exhaustion – that the members of the auxiunit were edgy and anxious, and I felt that there was a kind of compulsion to go over plans time after time and examine weapons and ammunition with almost too much care. But what was concerning me most just then was the anticipation of the first exercise I was to go on with them the next Saturday night. It was John Dale who briefed me on it and the part I had to play, and he also seemed to be anxious. "Keep in mind, feller," he kept on saying, "it's your try-out and we cannot have anything going wrong."

It must have been eleven before the Gwynnes went to bed that night and I could get up and get dressed. I could move about in that old, creaky house without a sound. The floor was mainly linoleum-covered and was tacky to bare feet so I put my socks on straight away. I had my clothes ready, my boots tied together to sling round my neck, and there was plenty of soot in the chimney of the fireplace, that was only lighted on special occasions of sickness, to blacken my face and hands. I'd made sure earlier that the window slid open soundlessly, and in a few moments I had swung myself out on to the roof of the scullery and then climbed on to the rain barrel and so to the ground.

Now that the clouds had gone the back garden and the common beyond were bright as day, and even the churchyard to the right of me was white and black with moonlight and shadows. Remembering all my instructions, I kept to every bit of shadow that was available, and I moved slowly. If you move slowly enough in the darkness you will never be seen, I remembered.

The auxiunit was already in the cellar, sitting round the table, their faces blackened; their eyes glinted whitely. The figure at the head of the table put his hand out to the knife that lay beside him.

"Ah it's you. D'you know you're late, boy?" He consulted his wrist-watch. "Eight minutes. Twenty-three hundred hours we said. It's no good. These things must be taken seriously. Not a game we're playing. Eight minutes could be vital – life or death."

They all looked at me. Nobody spoke.

"Sit down, then, boy. Sit down. Don't waste more time." I sat down on a box of grenades.

I looked at John Dale's blackened face as he sat back in the shadows, watching the Major. Only his eyes were visible, shining in the lamp-light. I turned away from him, and watched the Major as he talked, a small man sitting stout and round at the head of the table. Like a fat jack-in-the-box just popped up there. But a jack-in-the-box with protuberant blue eyes that stared hard and straight at you, and yet had a sly look because the lids were thick and hooded.

"Got that, Colin?" he shot at me, sensing my mind was not on what he was saying.

I nodded. "Aye."

I couldn't understand what he was fussing about. The exercise that night was clear and straightforward. We'd discussed and planned it at length. But he always had to make a meal of everything.

20

To the north-west of the village, across the Wenning, and high up on the fells opposite Wenningborough, the army had taken over an old barn as a store. It was well guarded and surrounded with barbed wire. Our unit had to get in through the defences unobserved – and out again! Well, we'd done our preparations carefully. John Dale had been over the area, and he had plotted our route through plantations and ditches so that we could avoid the open and the moonlight. And Willie Morgan had reconnoitred the wire barrier and found one spot where there was space to wriggle underneath. I, as the smallest and skinniest, had been chosen to do the wriggling, plant a thunderflash at the entrance to the barn to show we'd been there, and then get out quick.

We travelled slowly, silently and in shadow. I could hear my heart beating with excitement but I felt the utmost confidence in being with these well-disciplined men. That was until, as I was squatting behind a wall with Mr Miles and the builder, waiting for a signal to go on and join the others ahead, I heard Mr Miles murmur, "Nothing gone wrong up to now, Ted. Think we'll be lucky this time?", and the builder reply, "Plenty of time yet."

What did they mean, I wondered? Did things usually go wrong?

Well, the route from the barbed-wire fence to the barn

was the safest, but it was the longest and most difficult. The patrol covered me from behind a wall while I squirmed through the fence. As I was getting under the wire, I heard footsteps and froze. The guard was patrolling that stretch, and believe me he stopped with his boots just in front of my nose! If he'd looked down, in spite of the shadow, he would have seen me. But he looked upwards and over the fields. Then he turned and walked on. I waited till he rounded the corner, then I squirmed out, slithered across the grass, planted the thunderflash, lit it, and squirmed back to the perimeter.

We were halfway across the next field when the thunderflash went off. Thunderflash did I say? It made the loudest bang and gave the brightest flash I'd ever seen. We all froze in our tracks, turning in amazement. That thunderflash must have been full of real explosive! In the moonlight we could see a black smoky hole with flames licking about it where the door had been, and in a few seconds there was another explosion inside the barn, followed by a string of smaller explosions. The place began to burn like tinder.

"What in the name of God!"

"Is there anybody inside that place?"

We could see men running from the barn and, forgetting our role as resistance fighters, we started back. But the Major stopped us. We mustn't show ourselves. We all felt he was carrying things a bit far, but what could we do? We retreated with him further along the fell. In a few moments the fire engine's bell came out of the distance, and one or two people from outlying farms came running. We lay in the grass watching.

"The village will have been wakened," said the Major. "We can't go back yet."

"What did you use, Colin?" asked John.

"A thunderflash," I said shakily. "The Major gave it to me out of the box ... "

"I told you to *get* one, boy," the Major said sternly.

"Well, yes, but you were there ... "

"Must have been faulted," said the Major.

"Must have been full of dynamite," said John.

"That's hardly possible," said the Major.

Something else exploded in the barn with a great roar and flames leapt higher against the night sky.

"My God!" murmured Mr Miles.

"Told you so, didn't I?" muttered the builder. "There's something fishy going on ... "

We were a chastened party when we eventually left the scene of destruction and approached the village, but we were stopped again by the sound of church bells ringing out a wild peal of alarm over the water-meadows. We sank back into the shadows of a hedgerow, listening.

"That's the invasion warning, sir," hissed John Dale.

I got the strongest impression that the Major was as shocked as the rest of us. It was a moment before he could control his voice and send Willie Morgan on ahead to see what was going on. The bells clanged on, insistent and nerve-shattering, and then suddenly stopped. The silence that followed was almost as unnerving. And through it suddenly we heard Albert's voice very clearly and then the village policeman's. Willie came creeping back.

"They've got road blocks set up," he reported. "The Home Guard's out and there's a couple of army Jeeps. We'll not get into the village easily."

"Any sign of Germans?" demanded the Major.

"Didn't see any."

"It's not the Germans," retorted the builder, "it's the

carry-on we started up that's got them out."

"I don't think so," said the Major tightly. "Church bells would not be rung if the official codeword had not been sent out nationally. No. Something's up."

We crouched again in silence. I was trembling uncontrollably. I clenched my teeth to stop them chattering. All the confidence and skill of the patrol seemed to have disappeared.

I thought of Marthe and how terrified she must be then.

"We can't sit here all night, sir," said John Dale deferentially.

"No, Dale, and we can't dash into an enemy ambush," snapped the Major. "Now we'll disperse singly. At intervals. Each of you must find his way home individually. Get the black off your faces and then mingle with the village crowd – whatever's happening, be part of it. If the enemy *is* arriving, I'll send out messages for re-assembly outside the village later on. That will mean we take to the hills."

"Aye, but the ammunition's all down in the village. I *said* that wasn't the place to keep it," interrupted Mr Miles.

The Major ignored this. "As to tonight's disaster – that thunderflash must have been faulted. No, it was faulted. You ought to have checked, Colin. In future, always check everything, understand? There'll be an inquiry into this. Bound to be. It's known we were to make an attack. I'll have to put in a report. But I'll protect you as much as I can."

"But … " I began to protest.

"Don't worry. I can pull a few strings, you know. You won't be in trouble."

"Did you know they kept ammunition up there in the

barn, sir?" asked John quietly. "Maybe *that* should have been checked."

"The object of our exercise was to get through their defences. We did it. Maybe they'll tighten security in future."

"Not over what'll be left of that store! And if the Germans *have* landed, there'll be no inquiry," said John Dale.

As my time came to return to the village he whispered, "Got your route worked out, feller?" I thought I had, and I set off towards the village wondering what I would find when I got there.

Everybody seemed to be out in the streets but I managed to reach the cottage and climb in without being seen. I won't forget my relief when I reached my own room. I hastily scrubbed off my camouflage, put on my pyjamas and pulled my dressing-gown on. The house was quiet, but the door of Miss Gwynne's bedroom was open and a candle burnt there on the table. I went in. She wasn't there. I picked up the candle to light my way downstairs, and it was then I noticed the notebook open on the table and a page of Miss Gwynne's neat, regular handwriting:

> Vehicles:
> One Austin car, Higham House Farm.
> One Ford, Vicarage.
> One lorry, J. Williams.
> One tractor, Higham House Farm.
> One motor-bike, Joe Martin ...

I turned the pages hastily. On the front cover was written "Invasion Book", and inside were lists of food supplies and their locations, lists of weapons available, and one entry which stopped me dead – "Site for mass grave: west side of church."

The creaking of the stairs startled me. I turned to the door. It was Miss Gwynne in a blue dressing-gown with her hair down her back in a long plait.

"Colin! Thank heavens! Where have you been?"

I stared at her. "I went outside ... "

"Well, it's all over – all a mistake! Oh dear! I don't want to go through that again. Come downstairs, I've made some tea."

In the parlour, where the fire was stoked up and the oil lamp burning, Mr Gwynne in his brocade dressing-gown had laid his kris and his gun on the floor at his side and was drinking his tea.

"Ah, Colin!" he said.

In spite of the heat I sat there shivering. It was reaction, partly, and partly it was shock at what I'd discovered. I couldn't sort things out. I just sat staring from one to the other.

"So," said Mr Gwynne. "A false alarm! What did you see out there?"

"Me? Oh – well it was all confused."

Miss Gwynne gave me a curious glance as she handed me some tea.

"It seems that the Home Guard thought they saw parachutists landing on Wenningborough Edge and then there was that explosion across the river – so they sent out an invasion alarm. Oh dear! We're all going to look silly tomorrow."

I drank the tea quickly. I wanted to get away from them – to think things out.

"I'm going to bed," I said.

Miss Gwynne watched me as I left the room. For the first time I felt really uneasy in that house.

From my bedroom window, as the light increased, I saw

the bizarre sight of a tractor slewed across the road at one end of the village and a huge tree at the other and a still figure on guard at each end. The street was silent now and empty apart from this, and the daylight showed a country-side as peaceful and undisturbed as ever. Before finally I went to bed, I saw the first bus on its way to Lancaster stopped by Len at the barricade. I had been at that window a long time, but my numbed brain had refused to consider any of the mysterious and disastrous events of that night.

21

As soon as my eyes opened that morning I remembered the fiasco of the night before, and I felt as miserable as it was possible to. How could it have happened – and on my first exercise with the unit – my try-out? What would they do? Would they stop me being a member? But how could they when I knew so much? I remembered Ernie wringing a chicken's neck and dread really did overtake me. I knew those men were in earnest. But John Dale wouldn't let it happen – he was my friend. From being the most exciting thing that had happened to me, the auxiunit was becoming a nightmare.

I sat on the edge of the bed, my head in my hands, and thought. What *had* gone wrong? That thunderflash couldn't have been full of explosive unless it had been deliberately tampered with. And only a member of the unit could have done that. I wondered if the others were coming to that conclusion. But would they still conclude it was me that did it since I was the new member? Then I remembered the nervousness before we went out and Mr Miles murmuring "Nothing gone wrong up to now". Maybe things had been going wrong for some time, so that would mean somebody was sabotaging that outfit before I joined. But who? Their faces passed through my mind, one by one. Could I believe any of them would be a traitor? It didn't seem possible.

It wasn't until I was washing in the cold water from the jug that the other events came back to me. Albert's parachutists again – and that book in Miss Gwynne's room. Could it mean that the Gwynnes were secret agents and other spies were already being dropped in the area? And somebody was sabotaging the unit! Somebody outside the unit who'd got a key to the farmhouse cellar? Miss Gwynne? Or did Bunny Gwynne prowl the village at night? Was he what he pretended to be, with his kris and his tiger-shooting gun and his need for that hot room? Or was all that just a cover for espionage? And how did I go on living with them and hiding my suspicions? How did I find out whether I was right? Should I take John Dale into my confidence? Should I sit up at night waiting to see whether Bunny Gwynne went out – or follow Miss Gwynne when she went off on village business? It wasn't easy to manage that sort of thing in a small community.

I don't think the Gwynnes noticed that I was a bit strained in my manner towards them at breakfast, though I saw her give me a questioning look once or twice. When they weren't noticing, I searched their faces for signs of treachery – surely such things must show? But her face was just as smooth and untroubled and he ate his toast and marmalade and drank his tea without a wrinkle on his brow.

At church we were a sleepy, yawning congregation to whom the vicar delivered his short, sharp, intellectual sermon on the value of community spirit. I was only half listening. I was trying to recall how I'd got that thunderflash, because if someone had specially primed it, that same somebody had deliberately handed it to me. Was it the Major? In the excitement of starting on the exercise I wasn't particularly noticing. I was more concerned to make sure I had it, didn't lose it, and managed to put it in position properly. I was sure the Major had given it to me. But he was putting the blame on me. And he was there – a great block of authority that I couldn't budge.

In the churchyard afterwards, John Dale was under attack immediately from Albert and Len, and the three of them stood among the old gravestones and the wild rose-bushes arguing and haranguing one another. Len and Albert, on duty, claimed they'd seen two parachutists coming down on Wenningborough Edge. This time they'd both seen them and so they'd sent out the alarm and put up roadblocks. John Dale, they said, should have been there – so should the Major. But no, in an emergency there was nobody to be found. And on top of this there was that fire at the old barn and the army had sealed it off. Now somat was going on.

But no parachutists had been discovered, no remains of parachutes, no trace of an escape. It had put Albert and Len in a very uncertain position. They were being looked on as a bit gone in the head, and they were insisting somebody else should take responsibility for what they saw on patrols.

There was a general sense of bewilderment among the villagers as they watched this. From being an invasion alarm in the night, the whole thing seemed to be turning into a colossal mishap that would probably get itself into the papers and make all of us in the village look the greatest fools.

John Dale didn't have much to say. He listened to the others, but there was no humour in his face. He looked very serious, and at times his gaze travelled up towards the Dark Mountain and there was an expression on his face I didn't understand and didn't altogether like.

I thought I might have seen Marthe at church – I hadn't seen her for days – but she wasn't there. And seeing Miss Robson hobbling along the path with Miss Gwynne didn't encourage me to ask questions of her, but as I caught up with them at the gate of Churchgates Cottage I heard her saying she thought Marthe had been out all night – all night! That was a joke, I thought. Nearly everybody in the village had been!

To get away from everything, I went up to Wenningborough Edge, but I was too tired to pot-hole. I lay down on the turf and was asleep before I knew it, and when I woke I was dazed by the blue sky above me and the rustle of the grass and the distant cry of a sheep. I sat up, and saw to my surprise that Marthe was lying close beside me, staring away towards Fourstones Farm. I looked in that direction and there was John Dale walking round the place, trying doors and examining the ground.

"What's up?" I asked, and Marthe said, "Quiet – and keep down or he will see us."

"It's only John Dale."

"What is he doing here?"

"Well, he's got every right. Fourstones is part of the estate and so he's responsible for it. And I expect he's seeing if there's any kind of evidence about what happened last night. You know the Home Guard thought they saw parachutists up here?"

"I know. I heard about it." She looked at me. "You are very tired, eh? You did not hear me coming."

"I was tired all right. Feel better now. Are you all right, Marthe?" I asked. "I mean – have you got over ... I mean, about your parents ... "

"I do not want to talk about it," she said brusquely.

"Your aunt says you were out all night."

"She is a fool. She thinks she can watch over me."

"Well, I suppose she feels responsible – like Miss Gwynne does for me. I don't let it get me down."

But something *was* wrong – with both of us. We sat there without much to say to each other.

Looking over the empty expanse of the mountains and the valley beneath I had a sudden idea, one that could account for everything strange that was happening.

"Have you ever thought", I said abruptly, "that this area wouldn't be a bad place to start an invasion."

She turned on me quite fiercely. "Don't say that! It is stupid!"

"It's not stupid."

I stood up.

"Where are you going?"

"Have a word with John Dale about my idea."

"No!" she pulled at my arm. "No – you must not!"

"Come on! He's a very sensible fellow."

"No! There is a law against it!"

"Against what?"

"Spreading rumours, frightening people."

"Don't be daft. I'm going to have a word with John Dale."

I knew Marthe was angry. But I couldn't stop. It was too important. I ran over the rough ground towards Fourstones. John Dale had parked the old Austin on the track there. I couldn't see a sign of him. Then I saw that the door of the barn was open. It was dark inside, but it seemed to me there was a vehicle in there. As I went in, from the sunlight into the darkness, my shadow fell across John Dale who was stooping beside the vehicle. He jumped with fright, and petrol spilled across the floor.

"Damn!" he exclaimed, then saw it was me. "Now then,

feller, what's the idea of creeping up like that? This stuff's on ration."

"I didn't know there was a truck in here."

"You weren't supposed to. Look, feller, Major keeps this old Aggie here, ready for use, in case the Huns come. The auxiunit'll need transport. I came to top the tank up ... "

I stood watching him. It seemed to me the old truck was being filled for the first time – at least he had two very big petrol cans there.

"I'm sorry. I didn't know."

"And how would you? You know now. But you know to keep your mouth shut."

He twisted the petrol cap on. "Now, then. Want a lift back?"

"Well – well, yes, but can we take Marthe?"

"Got that wench with you?"

But I hadn't. Marthe hadn't come with me, and she was nowhere to be seen.

"Well she *was* there."

"And watching what I was up to, like as not?"

"Well – " suddenly I realized that I might be putting Marthe in danger. The auxiunit was in earnest after all. "Well, she saw you, but not filling up the truck."

He shut the barn doors and locked them. We walked to the car. "Get in, feller," he said, "since yon wench seems to have deserted you."

I didn't tell him about my theory and I didn't mention last night's fiasco, the time wasn't right. He didn't speak, and neither did I. On the way to the village, we saw Marthe on her bike ahead of us.

"Let's give her a lift, John," I begged.

"All right. If *you* want to." He stopped the car abruptly.

"Want a lift, wench?" He shouted to her.

Marthe shook her head. I must have been mistaken, but I thought I saw fear in her eyes. I *must* have been mistaken. He pushed the first gear in viciously and we went back at a hair-raising pace.

22

As soon as I got to Churchgates Cottage, I went to my room and studied my map of the Wenningborough area and then looked at it in relation to the rest of the country. I was pretty certain I was on to something.

If parachutists were being dropped, the organization receiving them was very efficient, I reflected. No traces had yet been found, and no one had seen any strangers wandering about. If they were being picked up by some vehicle, it had to be almost immediately they dropped, and from Wenningborough Edge there was only one road down and that went through the village. Surely somebody must have noticed something.

I thought of all the empty places on Wenningborough's slopes and summit, I thought of the stretches of smooth meadowland and pasture, I thought of the main railway lines and roads running south from Glasgow that carried men and ammunition, I thought of the Midland towns close at hand with their major industries. It seemed to me possible that Germany might plan to drop men into the North-East and North-West at the same time as her troops were crossing the Channel. If it were carefully planned, with spies coming in first to prepare the ground, paratroops could be dropped in great numbers, planes could land packed with equipment, and there would be very little in our area to stop them – in no time at all they could assemble and move south. All our preparations, all our road-blocks and sign-removing – how could that stop an enemy that came dropping from the skies with a sound organization of agents already built up that had everything planned – the area mapped, routes marked, power stations, railway stations, telephone exchanges all ready to be taken over? And didn't Miss Gwynne's Invasion Book fit in there? That would be useful to the enemy. As I thought about it, the idea grew and with it a feeling of desperation. Suppose the necessary acts of sabotage were carried out quickly and efficiently, dropping-zones marked out, fields lit for planes to land in. The whole thing would be a surprise attack, entirely unexpected. What could Albert and the other Home Guards do against that?

I had an instant and sickening vision of the chaos that might result from an attack that came unexpectedly from the slopes of Wenningborough and not, duly heralded, from the south. I saw the lorries full of troops churning down the hillside in the light of dawn, the scream of brakes as they swung into the village, the running feet of soldiers, the deadly rattle of machine-guns. I could imagine the villagers listening and watching in horror as the troops descended on them, and then panicking and scattering over the fields.

I could hear the Gwynnes talking in the parlour below and I felt caught and helpless.

23

At the auxiunit's next secret meeting, the Major announced that the Germans would invade us on August 31st. "Their attack will be concentrated along a line from Ramsgate to the Isle of Wight." He looked round at us with his protuberant eyes and an air of having arranged it all himself.

"August 31st," said Ernie, in a slow drawl. "Is that official?"

"As near as we can gather."

"Sounds a firm date, sir," said John Dale. "Didn't think they'd let us know in advance."

There was a stir of embarrassment and a stifled laugh.

"Of course they haven't, Dale. But our agents in Europe report a massing of German troops at strategic points on the coast of France and the assembling of ships. An intercepted dispatch clearly indicates August 31st as invasion day, and what is more there will be heavy air raids as part of the softening-up process. Middlesbrough, Liverpool, London – hundreds will be killed in one night – all done with a purpose and that purpose is to lower morale, to create chaos, in advance of their invading forces. We have to be prepared."

He allowed a short, impressive pause. We waited for the rest.

"In ten days there will be a full army exercise in this area simulating invasion conditions and we, as the local auxiunit, will take part. The army will put in a force as the invaders and we will act as we would in the event of an invasion, that is, as resistance fighters. We do not need to report our plans and we won't know the invaders' plans. We will know only the date of the attack."

The men exchanged glances. I guessed what was in their minds. It was in the Major's as well for he added tersely, "Nothing must go wrong this time." I sensed that behind his military bearing he was very anxious. And he had need to be if we had enemy agents working against us. "Everything must be checked and re-checked."

"Aye, happen things always are," said John Dale. "Doesn't always seem to help. And what about this transmitter? Should be replaced with one that'll work."

"That will be attended to." We gathered round the map the Major spread out and watched his stubby finger trace the Wenning valley. "The exercises will be concentrated in this area. The invading forces will come from the south – that's all we know. But they'll have to use the main roads. Now, as you know, we've got all the bridges and strategic stretches of road in our area mined. But the explosives must be removed *before* the exercise and thunderflashes substituted. We want to make use of our plans, but we don't want to do any damage!"

A slow smile appeared on John Dale's face. It wasn't there long, but a humorous glint remained in his eyes. And yet, I thought, it wouldn't be funny if the explosives weren't removed.

"As for you, North, I've cleared you with the authorities over that thunderflash business, but you're to be reprimanded."

Well, a boy of my age didn't leap up and protest at that, but anger rose in my throat. Then I saw John Dale wink solemnly at me, and I swallowed my anger. At least somebody was on my side. The Major was very firm that we should change our hideout. It was useless in the village, he said. Look at what happened the night of the last exercise – if the Germans *had* invaded we'd have been cut off from our supplies.

"I've been saying that all along," said Mr Miles, but the Major ignored him.

"The question is, where do we move to? I want suggestions."

"There's plenty of hiding places up on Wenningborough." My voice came out rather more high-pitched and breathless than usual.

"The caves?" The Major brushed this aside. "Too obvious."

"Not the main caves," I said. "There's a lot more than that."

He ignored that. "Any suggestions?"

"Maybe Colin has an idea. I think we should listen to him," said Mr Miles, and Ernie nodded.

The Major frowned. "Very well," he snapped.

I hadn't anything very clear in mind, except that I knew dozens of caves that might have been used as hideouts.

"But is there one that would fit our requirements? Isolated, unknown, accessible – preferably dry – and safe?"

"That's a point, feller," said John. "After all, the cavers in this place are always hopping in and out of them places like rabbits. Suppose, after the invasion, one of them turned collaborator?"

It seemed obvious that the Major and John Dale were against the cave idea, and I hadn't convinced the others. It was this sense of failure that inspired me to blurt out,

"There's one I know – and I'm the only one knows about it." This wasn't quite true, but I couldn't see Marthe giving us away. "I discovered it. I'm still exploring it. And I bet nobody could find it!"

They had no idea of the sacrifice I was proposing for my country, for the cave was mine entirely, my find and my secret. But it was agreed I show it to them.

Then the Major brusquely dismissed it and me.

The fact that we'd been given a definite date for the invasion worried me, and when the others had gone and John Dale and I were left in the hideout, I said, "John, do you think this exercise'll go all right?"

"Why shouldn't it, feller?"

"Well, a lot of things have gone wrong – it looks as if somebody's trying to sabotage the unit."

"Don't listen to the other blokes, feller. They get depressed, you know."

"But John, look – something's happening." I'd got started now and couldn't stop. "Ernie's transmitter – he says it's never worked, so that soldier must have been picking up signals from another transmitter in the village – a secret one."

He looked at me sharply. "Could be."

"Well and there's the parachutists Albert and Len keep seeing. They've seen them at intervals of about a fortnight. I think they *did* see them. I think they're spies being dropped in preparation for invasion – and I think part of the invasion will start *here*."

I waited breathlessly for his reaction.

"How d'you work that one out, feller?" he asked slowly.

I explained my theory to him. "You see, John, if the Germans have a good, organized group of agents working here, everything will be ready when their troops arrive. I think more agents will be dropped. I think the next lot will be in a fortnight."

"About the time of this big army exercise?"

I nodded. At least he wasn't making fun of me.

"And who's the bloke behind all this?"

"I don't know. I've got some suspicions."

"Who d'you have in mind, feller?"

"Well – the Major." I was reluctant to cast suspicion yet on the Gwynnes – they'd been good to me. "He's a stranger here – he came suddenly at the beginning of the war. I know the last auxiunit exercise was a fiasco, but if parachutists were dropped that night *we* took the interest away from them, didn't we? The Major could have planned that."

John Dale regarded me solemnly.

"You could be right, feller, except for one thing."

"What's that?"

"He's on the Gestapo Black List."

"We've only his word for that."

I had a feeling that I hadn't convinced him and I suppose I threw in the Gwynnes because of that – it was a matter of personal esteem. I told him about the buried box and the Invasion Book. I got the impression then that that did interest him.

"Invasion Book? You sure about that? That would bear keeping in mind, feller, a thing like that. Though mind you, I can't see how the Gwynnes are involved in anything. They don't get about much, do they? – and *he* doesn't get about at all. Don't know when I last saw Mr Gwynne. Sometimes think he must have died on us secretly."

He wasn't taking me seriously. And yet I was very serious.

"All right," I said. "I'm wrong. Forget it. I'll solve the mystery myself."

"No, no, feller. I'm not saying you're wrong. Just seems damned funny, that's all. You mentioned all this to anybody?"

I shook my head.

"Not even that girl of yours?"

"Marthe? No – why should I?"

"Well don't. Not to anybody. I'll think about it, feller, and let you know – all right? And don't worry. It might never happen!"

I felt a bit happier after I'd told him. I felt I wasn't alone in trying to unmask the secret agent. I was sure he would help.

Anyway, I was full of pride and excitement when I showed the auxiunit my cave and pointed out its advantages. We could set up camp in the first cavern, and there was room for the stores there, and from outside we had a view of the whole valley which meant we could observe the approach of any enemy. And at the same time North's Discovery could be reached by several paths, and one which led up the south side of the mountain went through fields and copses which gave ideal protection.

"Well," John Dale said slowly after they'd all looked it over, "it's going to be a bit of a do getting the stuff up here and into the cave. Happen we don't want to disappoint the feller here, but there's the woods by Devil's Bridge – a bit nearer civilization. We could dig something out there."

But the Major'd made up his mind, I knew. When he finally said we *would* move into the cave, John gave a cough and put his hand on my shoulder, and muttered, "Well, that's that, feller."

When they had scrambled out again, I stood for a moment alone in North's Discovery and listened to the sound of the river through it, and felt its cold air about me, and flashed my torch over its walls. Well, I'd given it to them. It wasn't mine any longer. The Major was already taking it over and would probably change it from the way Nature had made it. But it was still my discovery. Nothing could alter that.

No hint came to me then of what was to be the history of North's Discovery, no suggestion of tragedy.

The Major started giving orders straight away. Cave entrance to be enlarged by means of small explosive charges, wooden door to be fitted, entrance camouflaged. Miles in charge of that. Have to be done in daylight – in three days. Ammo and stores to be transferred – two or three trips up in cars – one night should settle that. John Dale to be in charge. Stores to be placed on dry area across stream – and bedding, etc. to be put in dry place, Willie Morgan and himself to deal with the mined bridges and roads ... "I've done a recce. It's safe enough. Now, any questions?"

I walked away towards Wenningborough Edge, too angry to speak. John Dale followed me and put his hand on my shoulder.

"Now, feller, don't take on. 'Tain't worth it."

"But he's a fool – putting stores on the far side of the river. He doesn't know caves. *I* don't know that cave yet. I don't know what that stream will do after heavy rain or when the snows melt! He's doing the wrong thing again!"

"Nay, now, Major has a fair idea of things. And he generally manages to get through. You're tekin' it all too seriously, feller."

"But it *is* serious!"

"Not really. Not in the long run."

He said that in a queer way I couldn't understand.

"Have you thought any more about what I told you?" I asked. "About the secret agent?"

"Just leave it to me, feller. I'm thinking about it."

The next week was a busy one, and the whole unit was in a state of worried anticipation – so much so that I think we almost forgot the threat of the real invasion in getting ready for the mock one.

The exercise was to take place in daylight and we planned, to make the whole thing more realistic, that the unit would withdraw to the new hideout at the end, which is what we would do if a real invasion were successful. We'd been instructed that the members of the auxiunit would place themselves at certain strategic viewpoints in the valley, and that I would be up on Wenningborough Edge with a transmitter to have a general view of events and keep in touch with the Major.

The army did not know, I'm sure, that the unit had mined (but only with thunderflashes!) every road and bridge through the valley. They did not know that our hideout up on Wenningborough offered an unparalleled view of the valley, the hills and the sky; they did not know how skilled we were at travelling about that area, how quickly we could disappear into it, what a network of signals we had prepared.

The night before the exercise, I was in my room getting my equipment ready. I was just about finished when Miss Gwynne called upstairs that Marthe wanted me. She was sitting in the parlour looking paler and more distraught than ever before.

"I'll make some tea," said Miss Gwynne when she saw me. "You'll have a cup, Marthe?"

"Please, I wish to speak to Colin – alone."

We all looked dumbfounded.

"We can talk – outside," said Marthe, and made for the door.

I caught up with her at the garden gate.

"What's the matter, Marthe?" I asked.

She didn't look at me. She stood there with her hands gripping the gate.

"Colin, I wanted to tell you something – I have to tell somebody, because I am afraid ... "

"Well, come on then ... "

"Now I don't know. I think I should not tell. But I am so frightened!" Her voice had dropped to a whisper. I grabbed her shoulders and twisted her round to me. To my distress I saw tears were streaming down her face.

"What's all this? What's happened?"

"Colin – I have suspicions. About something. And if I am right, it could be very dangerous – for me, and maybe for you also."

I took her by the shoulders.

"What is it, Marthe? Have you seen something? Is it the parachutists?"

She pulled away from me, staring at me.

"Oh no! No!"

"But, Marthe, I suspect something's going on. I think there's an enemy agent working here. And if there is, he has to be found – and shot!"

"Oh no!" She moved back from me, shuddering. "I cannot tell you. Now I know I cannot. But if anything happens to me, Colin, I want you to have this – my parents' address. Please – try to contact them, please!"

I took the scrap of paper and pushed it into my pocket but I was mystified by her reaction and full of my own suspicions. I wasn't able to give her the support she wanted. I know that now.

"Marthe," I said. "Don't worry. I'm on to things. I promise you, there's nothing to worry about – only tell me ... "

"Oh you are such a fool. You English – you do not know how to fight! How do you fight a war with no emotions?"

She turned and ran off along the street.

I watched her go with that helpless feeling I so often got over Marthe. We never seemed to understand each other. I'd been trying to help her and she thought I was being unfeeling.

I went back to my room and looked at my equipment. Marthe must have seen or heard something. Why couldn't she tell me? It might have helped. I decided I wouldn't wait for the dawn when I was supposed to be up on Wenningborough Edge. I would go now – or as soon as the Gwynnes were in bed. I would go there and watch. It had occurred to me that the date the Major had given for the invasion could be a hoax – or another mistake! Maybe it would start tonight. And whatever happened, I would be up there where I could see and hear what was going on.

24

It was about midnight when I pushed my bike up the final slope to Wenningborough Edge. It had been hard going because of all the equipment I was carrying, and the night was overcast and dark. I took up a position near the hide-out, my rifle beside me loaded with the issue of dummy bullets, binoculars slung round my neck, the wireless on the ground at my other side. I wrapped myself in the blanket I'd brought with me and waited close to the entrance of North's Discovery.

Through the dark hours on Wenningborough, filled with the sound of wind movement through grass, the sleepy twittering of birds, the sad cry of a sheep, I dozed and watched. I saw nothing unusual, and I heard nothing unusual. There were no lights, no parachutists.

Towards dawn I woke again with a start. Through the grey suggestion of light I could see High Meadows beneath me, flat and featureless down the smooth steep slope of the mountain, and to my right the dark mass of Fourstones and the trees round Witches' Pot with a sliver of moon above them. I stood up, stiffly, and began to stamp up and down, slapping my arms round my body to restore the circulation. The tip of my nose was numb with cold. The eastern sky spread with pale gold, outlining the mountain's head. The light increased and the sky turned grey-blue, and the mountain began to make its way out of darkness.

Then I saw the plane, a tiny shape coming from behind the mountain and flashing silver as it caught the dawn light. Its drone was like the distant hum of a bee. I dropped flat on the grass and watched as it moved overhead and then fell lower over High Meadows, circling. A small light flashed skywards from the Meadows and the plane circled again, falling and falling and growing larger till it was almost opposite me and I could see the pilot and felt I could reach out and grasp it like a toy plane. Then it zoomed up and away again behind Wenningborough Peak, and a small puff of cloud was left hovering over High Meadows.

It was a parachutist, coming down like a monkey as Albert had said.

I gripped the binoculars tightly, focussing them on the parachutist – a young man clutching a small case.

If I was right – and it looked as if I was – here was another spy being dropped into the area and somebody, the master spy, should be waiting on High Meadows to help him.

But the next moment, I was wondering whether I wasn't quite wrong. Maybe he was just part of the army's invasion exercise. They might have dropped a parachutist to liven things up. I'd better be careful and not do anything to mess up *this* exercise.

It was 6 a.m. and the auxiunit would be in position down on the road. I got on to the radio with our code word. The Major's crackly voice told me to stay put and keep off the air as much as possible. No parachutists were planned for this exercise and I must be mistaken about seeing one. That was all.

But down there on High Meadows, the parachutist was rolling up his parachute. I could see him clearly through the binoculars. And then another figure dashed out towards him from behind a wall. *That* must be the main agent – the master spy! But I couldn't see his face. It wasn't the Major. It wasn't either of the Gwynnes. It was a slight, young figure in trousers and jacket.

Suddenly, at almost the same moment, the parachutist dropped to the ground and I heard the sharp crack of a rifle shot from the direction of Fourstones Farm. The agent swung round towards the farm and I saw the face clearly. It was Marthe!

My hands trembled so much the binoculars were useless, but as I watched the rifle cracked again, the wounded man staggered up and he and Marthe began to run towards the wall. There was another shot, but the two fugitives had disappeared. I forced my hands to be steady and directed the binoculars towards Fourstones and the man with the gun. I think I already knew I would see John Dale there. He started running towards the path that led down to High Meadows and in a second he was out of sight.

I ignored the Major's orders to stay at my post; I even left the wireless there beside North's Discovery. I took my rifle and started down after John. And I ran!

I couldn't believe Marthe was the secret agent I'd been looking for. Even though I couldn't think of any good reason why she should be there to meet that parachutist, I couldn't believe she was treacherous. And yet I recalled her distress the night before, her relationship with that mysterious woman, Agnes Dove, that paper with the message in code – had it belonged to Marthe after all? Had John Dale suspected all this before me? I panted as

I ran, the blood pounding in my ears. If John Dale reached them first he would kill them both. I was convinced of it. I knew the auxiunit members, and I realized John had been waiting and watching as I'd been and *he* wouldn't have equipped himself with dummy bullets.

High Meadows was flat and empty except for John Dale striding along by the hedgerow.

"Did you see them, feller?" he shouted to me.

"Yes ... "

He came up to me. "Who were they?" I asked. "Did you see who they were?"

"You were right, feller. A German parachutist and somebody to pick him up. I winged one of them – they must be hereabouts still."

There was something wild about John Dale. I'd never seen him like that before. He would search till he found them. And I had to save Marthe. I had to give her a chance to clear herself.

"What's that?" I exclaimed, pointing towards the railway line that ran along the far edge of the Meadows.

He twisted round.

"Can't see anything."

"Yes – I saw somebody. Dashing across the line. It's them! Come on!"

"Hang on, feller," he said, stopping me. "I'll handle this. You get back to your post on the Edge." And he ran off towards the railway line, his rifle at the ready.

I watched him go off on the false trail. It was the first time I hadn't been straight with John Dale.

I looked round desperately. Where was Marthe? There was no sign of her. Then I saw her, climbing over the stone wall that enclosed High Meadows.

"Marthe! Get down! Keep below the skyline!"

She dropped to the ground and I ran across to her. We crouched against the wall. She was very white and strained.

"Marthe, what are you up to? What are you doing?"

"You must help, Colin – please help! I can explain, later. But that man – he shot at us ... "

"You're helping a German spy ... "

"It is not like that. Colin, he is hurt – his leg. You must help me. Help me hide him. Please!"

John Dale appeared high on the railway line and then disappeared over the other side.

"Before *he* comes back!"

What was it made me, a devout patriot, forget my country and help the enemy? I couldn't leave Marthe to the mercy of John Dale – whatever she'd done.

"Can he walk at all?"

"If we help."

"Come on."

The parachutist was a long, skinny chap lying under the wall, his eyes closed, beads of sweat on his brow. One of his trouser legs was wet with blood. She shook him and he opened his eyes, saw me, and burst into a torrent of French. He didn't seem to speak much English at all. I couldn't see what had been expected of him in England. His clothes were obviously foreign, certainly not suitable for the country, and he had a case with him which, as we discovered, was full of brand new pound notes.

"What – he's not a *spy*!" I exclaimed.

"He is."

"But – he stands out like a sore thumb. How long did they think he would last?"

Between us we began to help him up to Wenningborough Edge. I knew the best ways – the ways that couldn't be observed, but still it was a slow journey and I was sure we would be seen. And I was sure as well the Major would be trying to contact me and I wouldn't be there.

I went ahead of them at last, and got the hideout opened. The cold air of North's Discovery came out to me, like a lost promise of greater things. When I turned round, the parachutist was leaning on an outcrop of limestone and Marthe was standing staring down over the valley.

"My God! They are Germans!" she exclaimed.

Through my binoculars I saw the first army lorries and Jeeps appear on the road, miles below, and several motor-bikes driving on ahead.

"It is invasion!"

Almost as she spoke we saw a flash of light beside one of the Jeeps as it crossed a bridge over the Wenning. A moment afterwards, there was a sharp report. The Jeep keeled over on its side. I felt a sudden, sharp doubt. Through my glasses I could see a large amount of distracted activity. I summoned the Major on the radio hastily. "We got them – we got them, sir!"

"We got *one*." His voice was remote, unemotional. "We saw it. Keep off the air as much as possible."

Considerably deflated – and angry – I took up my glasses again, but they were snatched from me, and Marthe strained them on the convoy.

"They have swastikas! They are German!"

"No they're not!" I snatched the glasses back. Further down the column, a lorry turned to the left on a subsidiary road. They were hoping to take the back road and avoid the busted bridge. A mile further on they would have to go under the main railway bridge to the south. We had that mined also.

"It is invasion?" she demanded again. "What is to happen to me!"

"It's not an invasion," I retorted, with a good deal of satisfaction. "It's just an exercise. Army manœuvres."

She stared at me, her hair blowing across her face, her eyes incredulous. Then she dropped face downwards into the grass. I thought she had fainted, but she rolled on to her back, gazing up at the sky.

"Thank God," she murmured.

"Look, Marthe," I said sternly, "I don't know what you're up to. I won't let John Dale get you, but you'll have to have a good story or I'll turn you over to the police."

She looked up at me, her eyes very large and a strange expression on her face.

"I have a good story, as you call it," she said.

"Well? This man's a spy and you're helping him ... "

"Yes, I am helping him. I will help him to escape. To Ireland. He will not be spying. I promise you."

"I can't believe that!"

She sobbed in desperation, then grasped my arm.

"Colin, listen. I came over here – I *got here* only by telling the Germans I would spy for them. All the time I meant to work for the British, but the Germans would not know this. I would be a double agent. Before I left Germany I was told I must come here and stay with my aunt. I had to contact the main German agent in this area – I was told how to do this. And I did. I get instructions from him."

"Who is he?" I asked.

Marthe looked at me, in a rather curious way, I thought.

"How could I know? The master spy is never known to anyone. It would not be safe for him. No, I know him only by his code name, Piper, and he sends all instructions in code by letter. The contact address is in Morecambe. All I have to do is meet new agents when they parachute in, drive them to Carnforth and put them on the train for Liverpool. They are met there by someone else ... But then the British wanted me to hand over these agents to them and I would not! These men do not want to spy. They were forced to come here to save their wives and families in France from harm. And I am to hand them over to be shot?" Her eyes blazed angrily. "All I promise the British is to find out who the master spy here is, who Piper is. The others I help to escape!"

I was stunned. I'd got so near the truth, but I'd never thought Marthe was involved.

"Have you a wireless transmitter?" I asked.

"No. I never contact Germany. Piper does that." She paused. "So – what will you do now? If you give me to the police I will never find out who Piper is. Already I think I know who he is, but ... " She stopped speaking, staring down with fear in her eyes towards Fourstones. "That man – that man ... "

"Get down!" I pushed her to the ground and crouched beside her. Near Witches' Pot John Dale was walking with heavy persistence towards Fourstones Farm. There was something menacing about that slightly stooping figure, that long nose, not humorous now, the rifle held in those capable hands. He was still searching. He must have realized I'd lied to him. He must have concluded they were still on the mountainside. He wouldn't give up.

"Get *him* into the cave," I told Marthe. "Hurry up. And keep down or you'll be seen."

She slithered away through the grass and I lay there watching. John Dale was methodically moving round Fourstones, appearing and disappearing as he searched.

I crawled to the entrance of North's Discovery. Just inside, Marthe and the parachutist waited. We kept a torch to the left of the entrance and I switched it on and then lit the lamp that stood ready always.

"Come on." I led them through the stream, their feet sliding and slipping, unfamiliar with the rocky floor.

Marthe hesitated, looking suspiciously at the equipment there.

"This place – somebody comes here?"

"Nobody will come for several hours."

"How can you be certain?"

"Look, Marthe, you've got to take my word for it – just for once! Stay here till I come back and fetch you and then we'll work out a way of getting you both to safety." The difficulties that problem would bring were just beginning to dawn on me.

"We can get away easily," Marthe said. "That is all arranged. If that man, that John Dale, will go away ... "

"I'll make sure he does."

I left them in the cave, huddled in blankets from the stores. The lamp cast black shadows on to the rocks, on the swift stream and on Marthe. There was apprehension in her eyes. She looked vulnerable and beautiful. It was the last time I saw her.

I went back with a troubled mind to my post on Wenningborough Edge. The radio was crackling irritably and I answered hastily. It was the Major. Naturally he wanted to know where the hell I'd been. As my excuses faltered, I could hear the growing note in his voice of curious interest. It was the note I dreaded. The sharp questions ceased. He told me brusquely that the exercise so far as the first part was concerned was over. I was to get down to the bridge at once.

I hoped that his mind would be diverted by other events from the problem of what I had been up to, but I doubted it.

I couldn't see John Dale anywhere.

25

As I went quickly down to where my bike was hidden, I remember getting a shock as our vicar stepped out on the path before me. He was a tall, bald-headed man, benevolent, bespectacled, and notable always for his good black clothes and highly polished, round-toed shoes. It was no surprise that he should be there, of course. But I was taken aback at being seen. I had dropped some of my caution and not taken the hidden trail down the mountainside.

"Ah. Colin. Beautiful morning."

He was so stereotyped, so much the accepted picture of a country vicar, that he blended into the landscape almost to the point of camouflage. I had to stop, emergency or not, and exchange a few civilities that were as nondescript and unobjectionable as his sermons.

"You're heavily laden." He was looking at my equipment with great curiosity which he didn't like to satisfy by direct questions. "I didn't know you were a marksman."

"I'm not very good."

"Do be careful. I know the sport's popular but guns make me nervous. The army's really going at it along the valley there. Lorries and tanks and motor cycles – and explosions. Quite an invasion. Very realistic."

I felt a nervous qualm then. How realistic was it? For

the first time I became aware of an acrid smell of smoke drifting up from the valley.

"I'm off to visit the Tuckers on Far Fell. I thought the walk would do me more good than the old cycle."

I ran the rest of the way to my bike, and pedalled furiously to the meeting place at the bridge. There was no one there, but I stopped dead for a few moments, staring. There was a hole in the road, part of the parapet of the bridge had gone and a Jeep was lodged in the gap. The Major's voice came from behind the hedge. "Hurry up, boy." I joined him, dragging my bike with me. They were all with the Major, crouched in the grass. I heard a number of sharp explosions, and the smell of smoke became stronger.

"Has it gone all right?" I asked.

"Gone too well," said Willie Morgan lugubriously. "We've blown up half the British army!"

"What?"

"Somebody must have switched the thunderflashes again ... "

The Major interrupted, red-faced and agitated. "The bridge has been demolished, the secondary road cratered and two lorries put out of action. Fortunately, so far as we can see, there are no casualties." He wiped his brow with a handkerchief. "Now look, boy, have you been playing around again?"

"I have not!"

"You knew the places we'd mined – did you replace the thunderflashes with dynamite again?"

"I did not!"

"Don't raise your voice! Where's Dale?"

"Last I saw of him was on Wenningborough Edge."

The Major did some hasty calculations. "Before we

report on this officially I want an investigation. I want to find the culprit. Now, we're going to the hideout straight away. And you boy, you find Dale and bring him there."

Dismayed I watched them creep away through the ditch. Marthe would be discovered. I had to get to the cave before them!

I couldn't waste time looking for John Dale. I started up through the fields, since the unit would be on the road and I had to by-pass them. I thought I could just do it if I moved fast enough. I'd left my bike in the ditch, but I was still carrying heavy equipment and was pretty well exhausted by the time I stumbled on to High Meadows. I was crossing them towards the final steep slope up to Wenningborough Edge when a hand gripped my shoulder and I was swung round. It was John Dale, his face gleaming with sweat, his eyes wild above that long nose. I shrank back from the stooping, shambling figure.

"Now then, feller, you told me a lie."

"I didn't, John!"

"Well, I haven't found those two. Have you seen them again? One of them's wounded. I winged him."

"I haven't seen them, and I've been all the way down to the bridge and back. And the unit's on it's way up, so if they're on the mountain they'll be found."

I tried to get away, but he held me firmly.

"Hold on, feller. What's the hurry?"

I had an uneasy conviction that his concern to capture Marthe and the parachutist amounted to a mania.

"Major's orders. Things have gone wrong. We've got to get up to the hideout at once!"

"Damn the Major!"

I twisted free and went on – fast, anxious to get to the cave. Maybe it wouldn't be so bad, even if the unit got there first. If they found her with the parachutist and she played it right, if she said he was her special friend – well, maybe they'd wink and laugh and let them go. But it meant the hideout was blown, and the unit blown. And they were determined men ...

I heard the scrape of boots on rock behind me and glanced back. John Dale was following. I climbed faster, gasping for air, my shoulders aching with the weight of the equipment. But I was too late. The hideout entrance was open.

When I got into the cave the men were across the stream. I could see their bent shapes in the lamplight as they moved boxes, checked stocks of ammunition. The Major sat on a box, hunched like a great toad, making a list of everything. The scene had a weird and strange air about it, for they were comparatively silent. It had the mutely incongruous air of a nightmare. But there was no sign of Marthe or the parachutist!

I sat down on a boulder, my knees trembling, sweating in the cold air after that race up the mountain. Where was Marthe? She couldn't be hiding in the cave. The two of them must have retreated along the tunnel. It was the only place. But if they went too far they could get lost. If only the unit would go and let me search for them!

"Come along, boy. Help out with the checking here," snapped the Major. I looked wearily at him. He was a very worried man, I could see.

John Dale arrived and stood still in the entrance, a dark, bulky shape.

"Where have you been, Dale?" demanded the Major. "I haven't seen anything of you on this exercise. Do you know what's happened?"

He began to tell John about the damage, about the

switch of ammo. He didn't say it aloud, but he must have been thinking as we all were – who was the traitor among us? I stood up. If the checking had to be done, let's get it done fast, I thought. They'd never seen anybody count things as fast as I counted them that day.

We checked the stores. A considerable quantity of dynamite was missing. That pointed to a traitor within the group. The Major looked stern. He insisted there was another explanation. Someone had issued the wrong stores. Someone ignorant of what he was doing. Well, this time, he wasn't blaming me. I told him that.

The unit didn't argue. They looked at one another with suspicion. They snapped at each other irritably. I didn't care. I just wanted them to go so that I could search for Marthe.

They went at last, their boots scraping on the rocky floor, their black shapes outlined one by one against the sky as they went into the open. Nobody took much notice of me. Not even John Dale. All he said was, "Coming, feller?" and went off to continue his own search. Nobody saw that I stayed behind in the cave – the cave that was mine no longer. It was the Major's cave, his personality had changed it.

I hurried to the entrance of the tunnel, splashing through the stream and shouting, "Marthe! Marthe!" My voice echoed back to me, the torch I carried lit up one section after another. There was no response to my calls. No sense of anyone waiting there in the passage the stream ran through. No sign of blood from that man's wounded leg. Fear grew in my mind. How far had they gone? Which way had they gone? I started back to the entrance cave. I would need ropes and another torch and some markers to plot my way through.

And it was then I heard it – a faint cry from somewhere in the darkness. I thought at first I was mistaken, but a groan followed. I went quickly round the curtain of limestone to where the narrow cleft in the rock was. I called down it. There was that faint, answering moan. I shone the torch down into the shaft. I could see nothing. Whoever was down there had gone beyond the first bend and was out of sight. Cold sweat prickled on my body as I realized this. If it was Marthe, or the parachutist, inexperienced in caving and pot-holing, who'd thought they could hide there – they were stuck. And they wouldn't have any idea of how to get loose. I shouted and shouted to them to answer me. But there was no reply. I got a rope and sent it snaking down the tunnel, but there was no reassuring grasp on it. I started then down from the Edge to get help.

And that was nearly the end of it for me. I remember vividly when I came from the cave to get help that the day had changed. There was a grey sky and grey mist creeping over the land. The sun was stuck into the greyness like a bright red counter and the trees formed themselves into long defensive lines that loomed across the fields.

All that day, that long day, they tried to rescue whoever it was in that cleft. And I was sure it was Marthe. I told them it was Marthe. I told a rambling story about her being there with me and running in to hide when the others came up. I helped to rope up men who found they could barely squeeze round the first bend. I went down myself, insisting on trying it head first, which they were all against because it was dangerous. It was then I realized that the air down there in that confined space was becoming foul. I began to despair. Another group of pot-holers was trying to find a way through from below to the cleft's exit, which must lie there somewhere. I knew that exploration was pretty well hopeless. As night came on, I knew from the faces around me that they had no hope of getting her out alive. It was then I insisted on trying again. It was then I was able to reach down and touch her hand. It was then I knew she was dead.

I didn't listen much then or afterwards to the various theories about the cave and Marthe's presence in it. I know the auxiunit stores there caused a lot of speculation. I remember the unit reappearing, watching, trying to help, but saying nothing. I remember that I saw Agnes Dove at one point – she must have come to see Marthe that day. I remember seeing, on my wild dash for help, that John Dale was still hunting along High Meadows, and that later he was standing among the rescuers outside the cave and he said to me, "Who's down there, feller? That wench of yours?" and when I nodded he said, "Nobody else, feller?" and then stalked away across Wenningborough Edge, a tall, dark, restless shadow.

There was a lot of talk. There was an investigation – several in fact, by the police, by some army top brass. I think the auxiunit disintegrated. I don't know. I was in a state of shock and exhaustion by the time they closed the cave finally and held the burial service over it. I sat most of the time in Bunny Gwynne's hot parlour, opposite him, gazing into the fire, while he watched me sympathetically and Miss Gwynne tried to get me to eat something. My mother came at last and tearfully took me away from the village. We left from the same castellated little station, and I did not even look at it as it slid away from me into the past.

26

I made the final stage of my pilgrimage before dawn next morning, driving as far as the shooters' hut that still stood on Wenningborough Edge and parking the car there. Eerily I was accompanied on that journey by the spirit of my younger self cycling up there in the darkness that morning so many years ago. I switched off the headlights and stood for awhile to let my eyes become accustomed to the darkness, then I began to walk slowly over that once familiar ground, now the graveyard where a love that died very young was buried. I moved again among whitely looming outcrops of stone, the rustle of grasses, the never-sleeping breeze. Since I was last there I'd tracked through swamp and jungle and over dried plain, I'd known the atmosphere of quiet tedium in old Spanish cities lost in a vast continent and the hostility of primitive native villages miles up one of the longest and most sinister of rivers, but I had never experienced the intensity of emotion I felt then.

When the sky began to lighten I was standing by the pile of rocks that sealed the mouth of North's Discovery. Below me the valley was spread exactly as it had been except that a sprinkling of lights marked each settlement that had then been unlighted.

I shivered now, as I'd shivered then, and I turned again, as I'd done then, towards the rustling, panting noise on the path behind me. It was a moment of indescribable shock when I saw a stooped figure, battling its way towards me.

I must have been as great a shock to that climber, but to me his figure was merged with Marthe's stumbling towards me, and I stepped backwards, away from the past that had come too vividly.

"Hello! Didn't expect to find anybody up here yet."

It wasn't Marthe's voice, but the flat, clipped speech of the Major. I could feel him preparing to justify his being there, preparing to find out what I was up to.

"Neither did I."

"Yes. Well, I'm a keen fell-walker, you know. Often up here in the dawn." His hard-drawn breath did not suggest the active man. He stood beside me, panting.

"Come for the show, I suppose."

"No. For the dawn."

He peered at me, trying to make out who I was, and I knew I stood obscured and mysterious in the half-light.

"Don't I know you?"

I did not reply. I felt full of a recalled hatred of him and his war games. He had no right to be there, beside her grave.

"They'll be here soon. The cavers. Opening up the old cave here, you know ... "

"North's Discovery."

"North's Discovery?" There was a note of incredulity in his voice. "Why d'you call it that? Who are you?"

"Are you waiting for the cavers?" I asked.

"Well," he said. "Yes. I am. I have an interest you see. A long-standing interest."

He sat down suddenly on the heap of rocks over the cave entrance, a fat, toad-like shape, his round head thrust forward, looking over the valley. He had taken possession again. He always would. He would always be first there, scheming to be the one who got most out of everything.

"Saw you in the churchyard last night, didn't I? Looking for the Gwynnes' grave." He did not notice my silence. He never had.

"Of course, it's my belief there's nobody in there. Couldn't have been. It all depended on some boy's story, you know. And he was a romancer. Still, he managed to persuade everybody he was right. Made them all look fools. And fools again, it seems."

"But they heard her voice."

"*Her* voice?" He looked at me again, suspicious. "What do you know about it? Who are you? Reporter?"

"I travel – you might say a part-time explorer," I said.

"Hm? Done a bit of exploring myself in the past. When I was with the army ... You mentioned the name North. There was a boy here ... "

"Colin North. That's me."

I enjoyed his consternation for a few moments.

"Now I recognize you – even with the beard. Never forget a face. Excellent memory." He was recovering fast. "Well. Come back for the show, eh? Let me give you a warning. These reporters'll be out for a story, so you watch them. There are things that can't be talked about. Official Secrets. Remember."

"Did you ever track down who it was sabotaging the unit?"

Again he was nonplussed, but he recovered.

"Oh, I had my suspicions. Wasn't the time to bring them out. Bad for morale."

"So the traitor is still alive?"

"That's strong talk ... " Suddenly he said, "You can't

be the North that did that trek across South America – I read about it," he finished lamely.

Having accepted my word for it he became abruptly sycophantic, questioning me about my experiences, comparing them, but very humbly, with his own. I liked his antagonism better.

"What happened to the unit?" I broke in.

"Well, naturally ... "

"I mean, the members – where are they now?"

"What? Well now Miles, he was called up. Died in Italy. Ernie's dead. Willie Morgan's still at Far Fell. The builder fellow – what was his name? – retired and went to live with a daughter in Birmingham. John Dale – he bought a farm on the fell opposite."

But our attention was suddenly caught by the activity near the shooters' hut. A van had stopped and a group of men were lifting out a lot of equipment.

"That's them. Pot-holers," said the Major.

By the time they started towards us cars were being parked thick and fast on that narrow road, and some were run on to the grass of Wenningborough Edge. A horde of people – hundreds, it seemed – straggled purposefully over the ground towards us, approaching like locusts.

I stepped back in distaste, away from the crowd round the group of pot-holers. They should not be there when the grave was being disturbed. Photographers were already taking photographs; someone had brought a transistor radio and the latest news about the opening of the tomb was being given. The Major was in the thick of it, talking to one of the pot-holers.

They went to it solemnly, carefully removing stone by stone the barrier at the cave mouth. I thought I remembered, among the men there, one or two faces – cheerful, but intense faces, now older, that I'd followed down pot-holes and through flooded tunnels. But I couldn't be sure, and I didn't especially want to know. Seeing their gear and the way they handled it, I recognized again the skill I'd once had, and had not used for so long. The mists curled away. A fine morning settled on to Wenningborough.

Why, I wondered, had I come? I didn't want her grave disturbed. I could remember Marthe without that. Was it my sense of guilt, that I'd been part of that tragedy? That I'd been responsible, entirely unwittingly, for her death? Was it atonement? No. I knew what it was. It was a desire to solve that years-old mystery; to find if I could that traitor who had been among us and had never been discovered. To finish Marthe's job for her. If it were possible now.

I searched the crowd for a face I knew. Surely someone else from the unit would be there? Surely the traitor himself? Or was he among the dead? Ernie? Mr Miles? Or was it the Major, who suddenly appeared again at my elbow with the urgent warning, sycophantically repeated, that I shouldn't talk to the press. Of course, if the news got about who I was ... there would be no holding them. No, I decided. It wasn't the Major. It couldn't be. I recalled his devastated state that day of the last exercise. But that devastation might not have been the result of the auxi-unit's catastrophic activities down in the valley.

A murmur spread through the crowd, a sigh like a wave breaking on a shore. North's Discovery was open again. The pot-holers were going inside. I moved away still further, walking slowly towards Fourstones, now a complete ruin. I couldn't stay and watch her remains being brought out.

"I hope you'll excuse me." I'd been joined by a tall man in good, dark clothes and a dog-collar, a shining bald head and shining round-toed boots. It was the vicar.

"I hope you'll excuse me." There was still the old-world courtesy, the unhurried manner of a man protected from years of change by a small community. "But I thought I recognized you. Weren't you here as a boy – during the war?"

I said I was. Working on a farm.

"Of course. And your name was Colin North. You were involved in that tragedy up there. You must be feeling very badly."

I wasn't in any mood for talking, and so *he* talked, lightly of unimportant things. It went over my head, until I heard him say,

"Lots of spies about then, you know. All kinds of spies! I was one myself – would you believe that? Yes, I was recruited secretly. By the Government, of course. So was the Invasion Committee. Did you ever hear about that? Emily Gwynne was on it and me and somebody else. We had to make up an Invasion Book listing the facilities of the area. Emily Gwynne did most of that. Active little body."

Yes, I remembered, she had been that.

"That would be about the time you were recruited for that unit. My job was, in the event of invasion, to send in reports of enemy activity – anything at all in the area. I suppose it seemed quite all right in those days. I don't think I could agree to such a thing now, you know.

"Oh yes," nodded the vicar. "I was reporting on the army exercises that day, you know, and I saw the parachutist land. I saw you helping him. And I saw him leave that cave. If only I'd known the young lady was still in there."

"He was a fair young man with a limp – the parachutist," I said. "Did you follow him?"

"No, no. Wasn't part of my job, you know. Only to report." He looked back at the cave. "I'd better go back. I feel I ought to be there … I held the burial service."

27

She was waiting for me at the ruins of Fourstones, the stocky middle-aged woman from the hotel, sitting on the wall smoking a cigarette. I remembered her now – Agnes Dove, Marthe's friend from London.

"Rotten, isn't it?" she said. "Pretty unhealthy sort of show." She waved her hand towards the crowd round the cave. "Of course, I can understand you being here, Mr North. I suppose you took her into the cave in the first place? It was *your find*, wasn't it?"

I wondered how she knew that, but I did not show my surprise.

"I know a great deal about you. I know all about your recent explorations. I keep up to date."

"Why should you keep up to date? What have my actions to do with you?" I was beginning to feel very angry. It didn't seem to worry her.

"She was deceiving us, wasn't she? Marthe?"

"Us?"

She smiled. "Of course, you wouldn't know. I'm tying up a few loose ends from the war, Mr North. Things I couldn't finish off then. I like to follow my cases to the end. Funny how many of them find a solution years afterwards."

"Marthe," I said the name aloud. It was a measure of my anguish.

"She was working for us. For M.I.5. I was what was known as her case-officer. I interrogated her when she came to us from France, and then I continued to guide her. She was an interesting person. But too temperamental and troublesome for the job."

"She was moody." I remembered her so clearly. I remembered her moods so vividly. "She told me she was a double agent."

"Thought she might have. That was the trouble, of course. She would always have talked."

"Except about one thing – the main enemy agent in this area," I said. "She didn't tell me who he was."

"But she knew?"

I nodded.

She looked towards the cave. "Pity," she murmured. "We never caught him out. And it's too late to do much now."

"She wanted to get that parachutist away. I suppose *you* wanted her to hand him over to you?"

"She managed to get herself taken on by Kliemann, a very important spy-master in France, and he sent her across here. Of course, she came over to us immediately. That was her plan. The double-cross. But Marthe had principles, you know. Strange principles, but principles. She received instructions from the German agent working in this area, though she never met him. Her job was to receive new agents as they were dropped and we wanted her to hand them over to us – but she wouldn't. She wouldn't betray them. She was enthusiastic, but ultimately unsatisfactory. She didn't co-operate. You know, each time there was a parachute drop she gave us the wrong date. She never meant us to get them. I wonder what happened to that last one."

I wondered what had happened in the cave in those moments when they realized they would be trapped. I had hidden them there with the best of intentions but Fate twisted in my hand. Had Marthe sent the parachutist off to safety and stayed herself with the same good intentions? To cover his retreat? Or was it blind panic, another twist of fate that sent one to safety and left the other there to die? Yes, Marthe had been moody and temperamental, but she'd also been true to her principles and unselfish. And that had brought her to her death.

"She wanted to get the parachutist to Dublin," I said. "I wonder whether he made it?"

"Dublin?" If she was surprised her face showed nothing. "That's interesting. Her code name was Match-stick Man, you know. Chose it herself. Can't think why."

Suddenly, and out of my past, I remembered that drawing on the notice-board of the village institute: Match-stick Man – Arrived. Had that been her message to the main agent? I remembered John Dale drawing a cross through it.

"I knew there was a route to Liverpool," she went on. "She told us about it. It started here," her hand tapped the wall of Fourstones. "In the barn. A truck was kept ready. She drove the spies to Carnforth and put them on a train. She wouldn't give us the Liverpool information, though. Yes, she was temperamental."

Memories began to stir again. I remembered the paper Albert found in the phone-box, the paper John Dale burnt, the paper *he* said gave the auxiunit escape route and *Marthe* said gave the spies' route to Liverpool. And I remembered that day on Wenningborough Edge when Marthe and I watched John Dale pouring petrol into a truck in the barn at Fourstones Farm. And Marthe watching him. And me telling him Marthe had seen him. I had a sick feeling I must have betrayed her. To him. To Dale. *She* knew why the truck was kept there – she used it to get the parachutists away. And she must have known then who the man was who was filling it up with petrol in preparation for the next journey – Piper, the master spy. And he must have known then that his cover was gone, that Marthe knew who he was. That was why he'd pursued her so desperately the morning of the army exercise. That was why she tried to escape from him into that cleft in the cave. Sabotaging the auxiunit must have been just a sideline – an amusing sideline – to Dale's other work, I thought ironically.

Agnes Dove startled me by speaking again. I'd almost forgotten she was there.

"Well, the trail's almost cold now. Where do we start, I wonder?"

I thought I knew. But it was *my* business. To settle privately.

"Best let the dead past stay dead," I said, and stood up. "I can't take any more of this."

Her eyes opened wide. She was a very shrewd woman and she suspected I was concealing something.

I left her and went to my car. As I opened the door I heard another murmur from the crowd, another sigh of the wave on the shore. I looked back. They were bringing a stretcher out of North's Discovery, a stretcher with a blanket over it. Already, I thought. Could they have got her out already when we had tried so long in vain?

28

The Major had said Dale lived now up on the fells, very high and isolated, opposite Wenningborough. The road climbed through smooth steep country that was bare of tree or bush and that was ordered only by those low, dry-stone walls that past generations of men had built there to divide the wilderness.

His farmhouse stood alone, a low, small building with a shippon attached and a couple of outhouses. It crouched on the fellside looking across to the Dark Mountain. It was silent and apparently deserted, but when I drew up in the yard behind the house a dog barked, and then a tall, stooping figure came from the shadowy door of the shippon with a hay-fork in his hand. And I saw again that face now much more seamed, more weatherbeaten with its small, close-set eyes and humorous nose.

"It has to be you, feller," he said. "I knew you would come."

It threw me off balance. It was just as though twenty years had not passed since our last meeting, and no suspicions could ever come between us.

"Come in, then, feller. Or should it be Mr North, now? With that beard? That what you've been doing all this time? Growing that?"

In the farm kitchen he settled into a wooden chair by

the table with the ease of long custom. He faced the window that looked towards Wenningborough, the light in his face, as though he had nothing to hide.

"Well," he said, "I can see you're as talkative as ever, feller."

I couldn't accuse him. Even when I remembered him hunting Marthe over the mountain side to kill her and protect himself. What vengeance could I bring now after all that time? And that hunter was only part of him. The other part was the man I'd known and liked and trusted.

"Do you have no regrets, John?" I asked suddenly.

His face changed. I saw the wildness in his eyes, the cunning as he glanced at me.

"So you guessed, did you, feller? That's a pity."

We sat in silence, a clock ticking loudly on the wall. He gazed across at the mountain.

"That's a pity," he repeated.

"But why?" I asked. "Why?"

"I told you why twenty years back, feller. Two different ways of looking at the same thing. My way – well, it was different from the rest on you. And it didn't work out for me. That's all."

He stood up, moving across to the fire. I was tense then. I felt I was no match for him in cunning.

"I don't know," I said, "what can be done about it all now ..."

"I know, feller." He turned with a rifle in his hands, pointing at me. "I hate to do this. But I've sat here many an evening gazing across there and thinking about this happening. So I was prepared. There's a gully nearby – it's deep enough. I could well see a feller losing his footing there and taking a tumble. A fatal tumble. Believe me, feller, I don't enjoy doing this. We was always good friends. But you shouldn't have come back ... "

There was a sharp rap on the window behind me. He turned sharply in that direction, his attention slackening. I leapt on him, the gun fell to the floor and so did he, heavily, his head striking an old wooden chest. He tried once to get up, his face twisted in pain, his hand stretched out to me. I did not go to him. Then he fell back.

I was shaking. I hadn't meant it to come to this, either. It did no good. To me or Marthe.

Agnes Dove pushed open the door and came in. She looked from John Dale to me.

"I thought it was worth following you," she said. "So that's the file closed."

I went past her and out on to the fellside and stood for a long time looking at the Dark Mountain.